OTHER BOOKS
BY L. W. HARRIS
(aka John H. McKoy)

Paying to Play in Hong Kong

Son of the Maya

MORE BOOKS FROM THE SAGER GROUP

*The Swamp: Deceit and Corruption in the CIA
An Elizabeth Petrov Thriller (Book 1)*
by Jeff Grant

Chains of Nobility: Brotherhood of the Mamluks (Book 1-3)
by Brad Graft

*Meeting Mozart: A Novel Drawn from the Secret
Diaries of Lorenzo Da Ponte*
by Howard Jay Smith

*Death Came Swiftly: A Novel About the Tay Bridge
Disaster of 1879* by Bill Abrams

A Boy and His Dog in Hell: And Other Stories
by Mike Sager

Miss Havilland: A Novel
by Gay Daly

The Orphan's Daughter: A Novel
by Jan Cherubin

Lifeboat No. 8: Surviving the Titanic
by Elizabeth Kaye

Hunting Marlon Brando: A True Story by Mike Sager

See our entire library at TheSagerGroup.net

A Novel

REUNION IN PARADISE

L. W. HARRIS

Published in the United States of America.

Cover and Interior Designed by Siori Kitajima, PatternBased.com

Cataloging-in-Publication data for this book is available from the Library of Congress

ISBN-13:
eBook: 978-1-950154-94-4
Paperback: 978-1-950154-95-1

Published by The Sager Group LLC
(TheSagerGroup.net)

REUNION IN PARADISE

A Novel

L. W. HARRIS

THE SAGER GROUP

Artifex Te Adiuva

CONTENTS

This book is dedicated to Helen, John and Paul McKoy whose memory I cherish daily; and to my amazing wife and life partner, Andrea Gay. It's also dedicated to Mildred Sikkema and the Thompson/Blankenfeld family, who made Oahu a second home for us.

I'd like to acknowledge the help and support of wonderful professionals who have helped bring this project to fruition: Charlotte Sheehy, Charlotte Gusay, Jenefer Shute, and Mike Sager.

PROLOGUE
June 2029

Mark and Sonya Morton had tickets to game two of the Washington Wizards and Toronto Raptors NBA Finals in downtown Washington, DC. Like many upper middle income professional couples, they left their upscale sedan in its garage and opted for Uber, Lyft, or Metro's subway for trips into town. This night, they decided to take the Metro to ensure they could get to the arena early enough to catch the charity clash between congressional Republicans and Democrats before the NBA feature. Throughout their marriage, sporting and entertainment events enveloped them in a zone that seemed to block out all personal or professional worries or tensions—a chance to recharge their batteries. So, they agreed to meet after work at an Asian restaurant in Union Station for a quick dinner before taking the Metro two stops to the arena.

Many of the other casually dressed diners in the ethnically mixed crowd were also transitioning from work to play: laughing, eating, and drinking into "playoff" spirit. Those who had them, removed jackets, sweaters, and ties and were undeterred by the hot and sticky DC June evening.

Soon, they joined the Mortons, as they descended the stairs to the subway.

After the Red Line left Judiciary Square Station and headed for Gallery Place, the train came to an abrupt halt. The lights suddenly cut out and the loudspeaker system fizzled.

Sonya grabbed her husband's arm. "What's happening, Mark?" she whispered.

"I'm here with you baby. I have no clue what's going on. But, this is why ridership continues to slip. Poor maintenance." Mark checked the illuminated face on his watch. Seven p.m. "Let's just be calm. We have plenty of time before tipoff."

The lights flickered momentarily, but the sound system didn't come back for another fifteen minutes. However, in the dark and crowded cars, with the heat rising, it felt as though three hours had elapsed. The mood of the fans was no longer festive; it was restive and tense.

"We apologize for the inconvenience, but please bear with us a few more minutes, and we should be moving shortly," promised the conductor.

As the minutes mounted and darkness prevailed save for cell phone lights, passengers became more vocal in their frustration and anger. Bodies leaned into one another, perspiring, and the dense air smelled of fear. Mark and Sonya's palms were clasped together in a sweaty bond.

"Mark, I'm feeling a bit claustrophobic," whispered Sonya.

"Here, lean against the door and sip some of this iced tea from the thermos."

Mark looked anxiously at his wife. "Better, babe?"

"A little, thanks," said Sonya.

After another quarter hour, a second muffled overhead voice notified the passengers that there had been a problem with one of the rails and a Metro employee would be coming through the train to guide people in offloading and walking safely through the tunnel to the Gallery Place station.

"Are you fuckin' kidding me? And they wonder why we drive or stay at home," was the rough exclamation from a burly b-ball fan next to Sonya and Mark.

Soon, a smartly uniformed Metro employee entered from the connecting car and calmly instructed passengers to follow her out one of the side doors.

"You OK to walk, sweetheart?" Mark asked Sonya.

"Thanks. Now, that we can move, I'm fine," she reassured him.

"You know, I'm less tense now that we are walking along the tracks and being guided to the station than I was back there in that dark rail car." Mark squeezed Sonya's hand.

"Me too," she said, with a shudder.

When at last they got to their arena seats, the charity game was winding down, but some familiar figures were still on the floor, among them former Speaker of the House Ryan Trane and the president's chief of staff, Ronald Barker.

A few minutes after the victorious Democrats vacated the floor and fans were thanked for supporting the charity, people saw the red, silver, black, and white warm-ups of the reigning champion Toronto Raptors enter the floor. Over the next three hours, Mark and Sonya enjoyed the spectacle of a close game, won by the hometown Wizards in the final seconds. They hugged, screamed, jumped up and down like teenagers, and, in their excitement, had totally forgotten the earlier Metro disruption.

As they headed for the Metro entrance after the game, they glanced at a huge monitor in the lobby and stopped, frozen.

CNN's banner headline said:

Group claims responsibility for Red Line malfunction. APOCALYPSE 2029 sent the networks a cryptic note in reference to this evening's attack:

"*Average citizens, even sports fans, must take responsibility for this government's irresponsible policies and actions. If the poor, the immigrant and the planet aren't safe, then neither will you be. We can get to all of you.*"

"What does that mean? Who are they, APOCALYPSE 2029?" asked Sonya, as they pushed toward the exit.

"Never heard of them," said Mark. "But let's call a Lyft."

"The trains are running," said Sonya. But she didn't resist when her husband pulled out his phone and ordered a cab.

In the taxi riding home, Mark said to Sonya in a low voice, "I may be overreacting, may be paranoid, but I bet this 'Apocalypse' group has something to do with Malcolm and Duke." Mark referred to two suspicious out-of-town radical activists who had been participating in his civic organization dedicated to DC Statehood.

"Sweetheart, aren't you elevating the importance of your encounter with them just a wee bit?" Sonya smiled and batted her long eyelashes. "There were no injuries or deaths reported, so this could just be some local hacker taking advantage of our Metro's woes."

"Think about it. NBA Finals in the nation's capital is likely to draw high-net-worth folks, major national politicians, foreign dignitaries, and plain old sports-nut folks. The political charity event increases the chances of drawing leaders. And, maintenance problems or not, given how bad the traffic and parking are around the arena, Metro is the most convenient way to get there from suburbs or from in town." He paused to think. "And, if you can derail a car, you can also blow up the system—so this is a warning shot. More to come, if whatever their demands are aren't met. Of course, there don't seem to be any specific demands yet . . . My love, this is not merely some local prankster. Bet on it."

They sat in silence the remainder of the journey home. Mark didn't want to further worry Sonya, but he reflected on an incident in which someone had locked him in his gym's steam room. He had immediately suspected the two radicals of trying to threaten him into allowing them to use civic organization resources. He also replayed meetings in which they had offered subtle hints of their access to more "sophisticated and weighty methods" of pressuring Congress than those discussed by Mark's colleagues. Too many familiar events for Mark to comfortably conclude that they were coincidental. He was quiet, but shaken.

The next morning, Mark called an FBI hotline but got no response. He then tried an old college classmate who worked for the bureau. His friend was polite, thanked Mark for the tip, but suggested that the District police and the bureau were on top of the investigation. Rather than satisfy his concern, the brush-off heightened Mark's anxiety.

Several days later, still unsettled by the subway incident, Mark took Sonya's advice to get a second family opinion and called his mother, the economist Mary Morton. He got her voicemail and left a very nonspecific message on her cell.

Later still, on a weekday evening, he saw his mother's number appear on his phone.

"Hello, Mom. How are you doing?"

"I'm fine, sweetie. And I apologize for not getting back to you earlier, but you know I'm from the generation that doesn't look at their phones every minute. In fact, I go days without having it on my person." Mary laughed.

"So, where are you? In New York?"

"No, we're in London for a couple of months."

"Well, say hello to Max for me. Mom, do you have a minute? I'd love to run something by you."

"Of course, dear. Max is out at a meeting, so I'm all ears."

Mark gave his mother a five-minute summary of the involvement of Malcolm Mohammed and Duke Wallace in his statehood project.

"Well," she said, "I think you would be smart to cut ties with them and to take a breather from the statehood thing.

I also agree that they seem to have viewed your project as useful for something else they may be planning. You would be able to assess better than I, but if you suspect that their real focus is something bigger and more pernicious than they revealed to you, you might notify the FBI." After she uttered those words, Mary realized Mark must have already figured this out for himself. What concerned her was that her son might have unwittingly involved himself with some very dangerous characters.

After a few moments, she said, "Mark. Are you there, did you hear me?"

"I'm here, and I heard. I've tried the FBI, to no avail. I'm just some community lawyer with a wild story, to them. I'm hesitant to push them further because they could start investigating our project, and you know how stuff gets mysteriously planted on groups that are out of favor with national policy. Especially with this crew in power now. No. I can't go back to them. Not yet, anyway."

Mary became even more uneasy at the notion of Mark flying solo and perhaps further alienating these shady types.

"Well, there is one very knowledgeable, politically savvy, well-connected, and trustworthy person you could contact," Mary offered cautiously.

"Who's that?" Mark asked, without thinking.

"Your father. You know he was quite a successful city councilman in Philadelphia before we moved to Washington," she said. Then, after thinking further, and with some hesitation she added, "And, I think he had some sort of security clearance during his later years, when he did all of his international work."

Mary knew enough about her divorced husband's career to know that his successes had not simply involved paper-pushing business activity. There had been plenty of dinners with Harry's business associates who, after several drinks, had told stories of Harry's heroics and ice-water-veined decisions in the face of danger. He'd been in life-threatening situations, she knew, involving unsavory elements in some of his international business negotiations. While his ability to block out emotions and make critical, cold-blooded decisions under extreme pressure had become a liability to their marriage, it clearly had been a business asset.

When she had accompanied him on a few Asian and African assignments, she knew he was being briefed and was in turn briefing "political officers" at US embassies. She was smart enough and observant enough to understand that large deals involving natural resources were rarely purely business propositions with certain regimes. Harry never said much about the nitty gritty of such deals; he didn't have to.

"Oh, right. The man in Hawaii with whom I haven't spoken for years. The man who's never visited his daughter-in-law . . ." Mark's tone was arctic.

"To be fair, Mark, you cut ties and said you didn't want him to be a part of your life. Remember?" Mary was loving, but firm.

"After the way he treated you, how could you stick up for him?" Mark asked, though he knew the answer.

"Son, you know that I long ago stopped blaming your father for our breakup. We both had lost connection. And he certainly never intended to hurt you."

"Well, I'd hate to be the recipient of his intended harm, then." Mark momentarily flashed back to the hurt and embarrassment he'd felt when he heard about his father's infidelity.

"OK, you don't have to ask him. But, no matter what you think of his actions after Hong Kong, he's one of the best resources I believe you have, from what you've described to me. He's been around the block a few times; I would trust his judgment on this kind of thing."

"All right, Mom. Let me think about it. Thanks. When are we going to see you again?" Mark wanted to end the call.

"We'll be back in a couple of months and will come down to DC. Love to Sonya. Bye, baby."

After Mary hung up, Mark sat back in his desk chair and thought about how happy and in control his mom seemed. A smile cracked his lips. Then he thought about her advice concerning his father. *I can't do it*, he thought, *no matter how smart and experienced he might be.*

At about one-thirty, Mark had been trying to sleep for half an hour. He turned in bed and looked at Sonya, who was also fidgeting.

"Why don't you just swallow your pride and call him? It's only eight thirty p.m. in Honolulu. You can't stay angry at him forever. Be real, sweetheart." Sonya turned away from Mark and tried to sleep.

"I keep reliving that time someone locked me in the sauna. And, now the awful claustrophobia in the Metro. And I keep remembering the fire in Malcolm's eyes when he described some of the stunts we should pull on congressional reps who opposed statehood. It's all scary, baby, and I just feel that it's somehow connected," Mark whispered as he sat up against the headboard. His neck ached and his stomach knotted with tension.

"Call your father, Mark. From what I've heard, he'll be able to give you some perspective. Even though you say he was secretive about some of his international activities, you know he was well connected and dealt with all kinds of business conflicts and negotiations. Maybe it's time to heal this breach." She pulled the blanket over her head. "Either that, or get some sleep!"

He got out of bed and padded into his study. Instinctively, Mark opened a drawer in a desk-side credenza that he hadn't opened for years and pulled out a framed shot of his father and mother walking in some garden at the National Arboretum in DC. An eight-year-old Mark was walking between them, arms extended as he held both their hands. "Happy days," he thought.

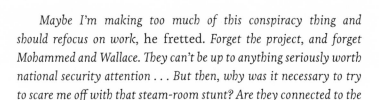

Maybe I'm making too much of this conspiracy thing and should refocus on work, he fretted. *Forget the project, and forget Mohammed and Wallace. They can't be up to anything seriously worth national security attention . . . But then, why was it necessary to try to scare me off with that steam-room stunt? Are they connected to the Metro incident? What if my gut is appropriately on alert?*

What the hell. Call him.

Mark finished the conversation with himself and picked up his cell, started to dial, and then decided to wait another day.

***

Harry Morton was finishing his twilight round, about to tee off the eighteenth tee at the challenging Ko'olao Golf Club in the middle of Oahu, when he heard the phone ring in his cart. He stepped away from the ball, waited for the ringing to go to voicemail, and then hit a perfect two hundred and ten–yard drive out toward a greenish-blue Pacific horizon, but landing in the middle of the fairway on a downslope not visible from the tee box. Harry smiled to his partner and friend, Paul Tanaka, former president of the University of Hawaii. Ten minutes later, as they were approaching the clubhouse, Harry finally listened to his voicemail. He nearly dropped the phone.

"Dad, this is Mark. There's obviously too much to say on the phone, but I would really like to talk to you," said the message.

"Paul, I'll meet you in the lounge. I need to make this call."

"No problem. I'll order two beers," said Tanaka.

It had been a call that Harry had long ago given up hope of receiving, a call that he had felt would tap intense guilt, sorrow, and sense of loss. With engineering precision, he had built layers of emotional protection around these feelings. So he tried to remain balanced when dialing back. Not too hopeful, not guilty, just pleasantly curious.

A little after midnight, Mark had read some mail and was heading back into the bedroom, when he heard his phone. His feet froze and his heart raced. He turned and was able to say "Hello" before the voicemail cut in.

"Mark, is that you?" His father's voice sounded the same as it had twenty-five years earlier, when they had last spoken.

"Dad, it's me. Thanks for calling back. I guess, in a way, I don't merit a return call . . ." Mark paused.

"Mark, you may have cut off communication, but you'll always be my son. Always. So, what's going on?" Harry hid neither his surprise nor his pleasure.

"Well, to be honest, I may be in a pickle and need some advice. Then, I'd like to figure out how we might catch up. Maybe meet on the West Coast, or something," Mark's voice betrayed his apprehension. The severity of the events that had descended on his successful, hectic, and happy life was beginning to affect him. Funny, he thought, that the voice on the other end of the phone offered a calm, reassuring comfort.

"Sure, I'd love that. As for the pickle, why don't you email me? Give me a chance to think about whatever the situation is, then I can call you back?" Harry moved from the entry lounge toward the bar/dining room.

"Perfect. I'll send you something, and I'll forward some dates when I could fly west." Mark exhaled in relief and sat for a while, with his head in his hands.

As Harry joined Paul in the bar, he filed the conversation with Mark in a compartment well below consciousness.

Mark headed back to bed.

"Well?" said Sonya, only partially awake.

"I got him. Tell you in the morning."

Over coffee with Sonya the next morning, Mark relayed the brief conversation with his father.

"You should fly to Oahu to meet him," she suggested. "You broke off the relationship, and now you are asking him for advice. You can easily afford the trip, and, from what I can tell, you can stand to be away from the office for a few days."

"How about you coming with me? It's time you met," Mark urged.

"Not this time. You two need to reconnect on your own terms first. Hopefully, this won't be your only trip to visit him," she said, smiling.

"Well, I'm going to send him a memo on the Malcolm-Duke issue this morning. To be honest, it is something I'd like to discuss in person. Let's see how he responds." Mark paused between sips of coffee and then grinned broadly.

"What's so amusing?" she asked.

"Well, here I am seeking advice on some gut-level hunch, flying out to Hawaii to talk to my father, whom I have never known as an adult, and I have no idea what he does these days. I vaguely remember Mom saying that after his international consulting he teaches. I think." Mark laughed.

"Well, if you do go, you had better do some basic research, my dear."

Meanwhile, on the drive back to his house, Harry decided to keep the Mark contact to himself. He was curious about the problem he was going to reveal but guarded about getting too excited about reconnecting. Best to see if he follows through on meeting. Practiced as he was at control, Harry's emotional scar tissue cracked ever so slightly. His blood seemed to warm perceptibly, and he couldn't prevent his mouth from curving up in a tentative smile.

MARK

CHAPTER 1

2028

Mark ascended the gradual ramp to Republic, a popular watering hole in downtown Takoma Park, Maryland. It was only about five p.m., so the coffee bar was sparsely populated. Mark chose a table surrounded by five deep leather chairs, ordered a glass of ice water and turned to face the two big-screen TVs at the rear of the room. After he caught the headlines, most of which were political news that he'd already seen on the barrage of hourly posts from blogs, Facebook, Instagram, and websites to which he subscribed, his attention shifted to the marketing challenges facing his biggest tech clients. He made a couple of notes on his tablet.

"You know you ain't bought shit," bellowed a handsome, muscular, ebony Black man standing over Mark's shoulder.

"David!" Mark jumped in his seat. "Did the staff see you come in? You know, this is a hip, but respectable, progressive spot in an Ethiopian part of town. I'm not sure they welcome brash affluent Nigerians."

The deep belly laugh almost shook the table next to Mark, as he stood and embraced one of his closest undergrad friends.

"Wow, you look relaxed and fit. Your last start-up must be doing well," said Mark.

"Well, I can still pay San Francisco rent for the office and the apartment. So I can't complain, maaan," said David Oweke, sinking into one of the chairs.

Before they could catch up, every other head in the open area in front of the bar had turned to the door. Mark didn't have to turn around to know that more of his old Harvard crew had arrived. A six-foot blond WASPy-looking figure and an even taller Chinese man stood side by side, blocking the late-afternoon light from the door on Laurel Avenue. The six-foot-four Asian-looking man wore an iconic midnight blue New York Yankees cap and the blond sported a blue and orange New York Mets cap. "Oh, my goodness," Mark exclaimed as Xi Yao and Herbert King approached, arms extended. Yao, a researcher with a top New Jersey pharmaceutical company, wore a checkered shirt and faded jeans, his standard office wear, while King was clad in a blue pinstriped suit—his daily Wall Street attire.

"Let's not sit on ceremony. How about a round of frosty Hoegaardens?" David said, standing to approach the service counter.

"Let's do a quick job, social, vacation catch-up so we can get into the important details of this Nationals game tomorrow. Getting with you guys is about the only time Megan asks no questions and displays no misgivings about my being away for a couple of days," said Herbert.

As they sucked the foam topping their beer mugs, the friends sat further back in their chairs and job-week tension slipped off of their necks, down their arms, and into the air around their table. Gone.

"It's hard to explain how relaxing it is to be with you knuckleheads." Mark raised his mug in a toast, but before he could form the words, Yao grinned and boomed, "Of course, the last one here is Rafael."

He stood up and hugged a five-foot-eight Rafael Marquez, special reporter for the *Boston Globe*. "I'll admit that it's embarrassing to get here late after David got his ass on a plane and flew all the way here from San Francisco before I could get down here from New England."

"Well, I'm glad we're all here, so that I don't have to endure repeated lectures about White privilege," said Herbert King, smiling.

"Wait a minute. Why not?" said Marquez, sipping the beer at his seat and staring intently at Herbert.

"Because, whatever White privilege I may have had prior to college has been eclipsed by the 'Harvard' privilege bestowed on all of us since graduation." Herbert's smile expanded to a gum-revealing grin.

"Fair enough, I suppose . . . for you Americans," burst out David.

"Oh, give it a break, David. You'll be a billionaire before anyone in our class," Yao exclaimed.

Mugs were raised around the table.

"Speaking of privilege, have any of you seen the condos and clothing retail that line U Street these days?" asked Xi, referring to the heart of an historic Black neighborhood and the social playground of Howard University students. "The architecture is modern Shanghai or Vancouver, the men's stores are like Milan, and the commercial streets are like San Francisco. What's happened to the old DC?"

Mark jumped in. "Like, I'm glad out-of-towners notice. It's like our generation of educated global citizens have made it, but the townies, the brothers, and homeless across the country are more marginalized than ever. And our success is generating alliances between left-out cats of color and rednecks, Salvadoreans, and Syrians, all sorts of crazy shit. Forget ISIS, man, we've still got serious home-grown terrorists right here in the US of A. That January 6, 2021, crowd has just grown."

"What's scary is that most 'professional' folks try to ignore how pervasive this working-class resentment and hopelessness is in cities," said the journalist.

"You'd think the last national election would tip folks off that the income and opportunity gap is a monster. And of course the Robert Spade administration and the alt-right clearly understand how to message political empathy to the newly left out," said Herbert. "It's like true believers don't care that this dude is a huckster, with as much real concern for rural Kentucky or north Florida as Vladimir Putin has. Folks on call-in talk shows are a trip."

"So, King. You woke, very smart New Yorkers listen to talk radio, do you?" Rafael mocked his buddy.

"Oh, I think the infamous power structure 'got woke,' and is well aware of the powder keg they sit on. After all, they captured the executive branch, the Senate, are packing the courts and have the economy booming. Soon, however, they'll have to deliver to the under- and unemployed, the new underclass now following them like lemmings. The jobs that are growing, we all know, don't go to Billy Bob, Keyshawn, or Humberto if they don't know jack about math, science, or technology," said Yao, the scientist.

"Spade is well on his way to another term, and if I close my eyes, he has all the tendencies of a West African dictator," said David Oweke.

Rafael Marquez added, "That means, of course more responsibility for those of us with education, skills, access, and power to reach back."

Mark tilted his head toward the ceiling as the overhead speakers played the Temptations' "Papa Was A Rolling Stone."

David leaned across the table. "Mark, are you with us? You look like you just cut out."

"Sorry, dude. That song sometimes gets me. It's like my dad's theme song. When he and Mom were married, he was

traveling all the time. Then he had an affair, they split, and he now lives in Hawaii."

"To be fair, amongst us chickens, you said you never wanted to see him after the split," David reminded him.

"That's true, but I guess I never thought he'd totally disappear," Mark confessed.

"I don't know the man, but it seems to me he made sure you got a great education and some bedrock values," said Herbert.

"I suppose. Anyway, let's order." Mark waved for the attendant.

They ordered and continued catching each other up on family, jobs, and the "crazy" political scene.

After a while, Mark said, "I need another brew, and I don't want to wait until tomorrow for the waiter. Anyone else need a drink?" Four hands raised.

"I'll go up with you," said David. As they approached the bar, David spoke softly. "Did you ever contact that kid from Hawaii whose proposal I sent you? I don't often pass you shit, but this dude is heavy. And . . ."

"My bad, for not keeping you in the loop. We've had a busy year. So, we're still looking at his game idea, but so far it looks like a winner. The characters are well thought out, the action is not overwhelming, the graphics will need work, but the overall concept could be perfect for today's environment. I like what I've seen and we'll make a decision soon," Mark replied. He knew that climate change worried the young global gaming market and demanded their attention.

"Good to hear. I was really impressed with him when he came up to me at Caltech. Although, I'm not sure how he's making it these days since his graduating class was several years ago. He was manning a booth with some of his ex-classmates. I got to admit, he looks like he's barely old enough to shave, but when he talks about his AI shit, he's amazing," said David.

"Yeah, I should have thanked you. So far, so good," said Mark.

They grabbed their beers and rejoined their mates.

CHAPTER 2

2028

A few weeks later, on a sunny Sunday morning, Mark looked out at his deep garden, its dry stream bed meandering through wisteria, Japanese red maple, pink and carmine crape myrtle, and cream-colored pear trees. A pebble path led to the back cedar fence, whose gate was guarded by two miniature stone pagodas. The two working residents of the household, Mark and Sonya, didn't spend as much time in their urban paradise as did their gardeners, but they often glimpsed or heard visiting gold-finches, wood thrushes, sparrows, blue jays, and cardinals.

The Mortons' ranch-style three bedroom home was in hilly Portal Estates, near where Mark had grown up in DC. Unlike many older Washingtonians, he never bothered to correct tourists' skewed image of his hometown as the Mall, Georgetown, U Street, and maybe the urban decay in the neighborhoods that produced DC's assiduously reported crime statistics.

Why commute from Northern Virginia or suburban Maryland, when I have all of this a half hour from the office? Mark often asked himself.

He never adjusted to the work-at-home established during the COVID 19 pandemic. So, on this Sunday, he drove to the office to get away from his mother and some of his wife's relatives who were in DC for the July 4 long weekend. He only needed a couple of hours to review some proposals he'd not had a chance to look at over the last several weeks.

He was forty and a recognized genius at spotting prospective high-value start-ups, primarily producers of software applications for young consumers. After five years as an investment banker in New York, he had been recruited by Walden & Rockefeller to come to DC. Partly due to the behind-the-scenes campaign of his mother, former Brookings economist Mary Morton, the firm had offered him the most lucrative package, and he had rewarded their confidence by spotting and nurturing three superstar companies in his first couple of years.

Arriving at his office, Mark settled behind his collapsible desktop workstation, opened his laptop and plugged in earbuds releasing Urban Knights and Brian Culbertson background playlists. As he always did, he glanced up at the black-and-white photos mounted on his wall above a four-shelf bookcase. To one side were pictures of his business heroes: Reginald Lewis, billionaire chairman of Beatrice Foods; Ken Chenault, long-time CEO and chairman of American Express; Bob Johnson, entertainment industry exec and co-founder, with his former wife Sheila, of BET; and commercial development magnate, Don Peebles. On the other side were shots of local political and civil-rights icons: Julius Hobson, Walter Fauntroy, Marion Barry and Dave Clarke. In the middle, were color photos of his mother on the steps of her long-time office at the Brookings Institution, and a shot of Sonya and himself at a Halloween costume party. She was wearing a frilly Mexican skirt, à la Linda Ronstadt, and he was dressed as a railroad porter, honoring labor leader A. Philip Randolph. Conspicuously absent was any photo of his father.

When Mark opened the new documents folder on his laptop, the first thing that caught his eye was a note from

David Oweke, reinforcing his support for the young game designer he had met at a lecture in Southern California. The proposal needed polish, but the concept struck Mark as brilliant, and he had already passed on the outline of Alaka'i Liu's game on climate change disasters to his review team. Given other priorities, he had not marked the proposal "urgent." He typed out a follow-up query to put the proposal back on the team's radar. Given his own quick assessment, Mark had been comfortable telling David that preliminary feedback was strong.

When the workweek began, Mark returned the proposal to the back of his mind as he focused on other business. He heard a pitch from a young fellow with a millennial sports app. Later in the day, he held a meeting with a stern, late twenty-something entrepreneur.

The presentation pitch was shown on a laptop computer that opened in front of Mark on his one-word audible command. It was yet another program designed to teach low-income kids how to love and master geometry. After five minutes, Mark could see that the references, images, and whole context for the app were those of a suburban, White, native English-speaking male child. He was polite but cut the pitch after fifteen minutes, suggesting that the Brainiac spend a couple of months in some low-income schools before redesigning his product.

A few minutes past six thirty p.m., Mark pulled into a parking space on Thirteenth Street NW, in the upper Shaw neighborhood of DC, and sauntered over to the Paul Public Charter School for a meeting.

As a board member for the advocacy group "New Columbia Now," Mark had been involved with the "Statehood Now" project for some time and had worked hard with this group of citizen activists to secure legislation granting DC full statehood status. He cared deeply about securing full, meaningful citizenship status for his hometown—but, recently, he had become increasingly concerned about some of the group's more radical interlopers.

His interest in statehood reflected his dissatisfaction with the declining power of people of color in his hometown. But, at the same time, he recognized that there were those associated with the movement who had been at it for a long time and who were so frustrated that they insisted this would be their last legitimate campaign for power. *If this current push in the Congress fails,* he thought, *then for these brothers, all bets for civil behavior are off.*

Mark recognized that, although he lived in the nation's capital and worked with some of the most talented and innovative young minds of his generation, he was living in at least two competing realities. Few of the millennial entrepreneurs with whom he worked during the day were focused on the impact their very comfortable lives in DC had on racial justice and poverty. Condos, upscale restaurants, bike lanes, and dog parks were part of the urban fabric in or near even the most downtrodden downtown neighborhoods. But economic hardship, overcrowding, and high crime had not been eliminated by the renaissance of the 2000s. The frustration and bitterness percolating in the progeny of older residents, families who prided themselves as "Native Washingtonians," generated anything but neighborly behavior. And few of his companions in the statehood movement could imagine, or indeed, care about the phenomenal changes potentially brought about by the brilliant innovations of clients he financed. Mark's perspective seemed unique.

"Glad you could get over to the hood tonight, my man," sneered Malcolm Mohammed, one of New Columbia Now's newest and most militant participants. Other than his bona fides as a national political organizer and proponent of dirty-tricks tactics, little was known about Mohammed's background. When he first appeared at the statehood meetings, he, and his sidekick, Duke Wallace, appeared to empathize with the group's frustration at not being taken seriously by Congress or the administration. But, after gaining some degree of group confidence, he began to suggest that more radical approaches were probably needed, pointing out that the current methods were going nowhere.

"Sorry to be a couple of minutes late, folks," Mark said, smiling at the ten volunteers.

Mohammed dominated the meeting from his seat near the front of the classroom. "So," he began, "let's quickly review our tactics for the reps from the most strategic racist jurisdictions."

The next fifteen minutes were devoted to reports from five committee members about potentially embarrassing data that staff had collected on legislators from Arizona, Idaho, Alabama, Florida, and Texas. Their research also included the health plans, doctors, schools, and shopping malls used by the families of these representatives. What's more, these committee members had begun to compile complete dossiers on the routines of every key congressional member in opposition to DC home rule. This data could be used for civil disobedience campaigns and for strategically harassing the families of Congress members to be targeted.

Soon, a soft voice with a West Indian accent interrupted.

"Could I just ask what our aim is here?"

"And you are?" asked Malcolm.

"My name is Jeremy So," responded a handsome brown-skinned man with Chinese-looking eyes and cheekbones.

"Well, maybe you are new to the group, new to DC, whatever. You might want to get caught up after the meeting," Malcolm said, dismissively.

"Actually, I've attended a few more meetings than you have and know you're trying to get the pending statehood legislation passed by a majority of the House. And I know why you want to go after key roadblocks," said Jeremy.

"OK, cool. You seem hip to what we're up to. So, what's the mystery?"

"Forgive me, but I still don't see what statehood buys us, given the types of problems DC faces," Jeremy went on.

"Well, maybe you need to study up more on how decisions get made up in here," responded a frosty Malcolm Mohammed. "Think about the budget, the legislative oversight, the use of DC as a playpen for conservative asshole projects . . . particularly those with a hard-on for guns. We get statehood and we get some small ability to be a player in the quid pro quo game up on the Hill."

"Sir, I'm aware of that potential. It seems to me, though, that the price of housing, the inaccessible mix of new jobs, the poor academic outcomes for our kids, and the pervasive crime in our neighborhoods aren't conditions that necessarily respond to statehood." Jeremy spoke quietly, but persuasively.

"Look here, my man, I'm not sure whose kids you think are 'our kids.' I mean you don't look like you from here, to me. But Black kids and adults need power to change shit. And power in this town is on the Hill," Malcolm boomed.

"Actually, both I and my kids are considered Black in this town. Even though I'm of mixed parentage from the Islands."

Before Malcolm could continue, Mark jumped in. "The brother's got a legitimate question."

"Oh, so now you got to defend the Chinese dude?" Malcolm fumed.

"I'm saying, I'd like to hear his argument, and I assumed yours was not the only valid point of view. MY MAN," Mark responded with emphasis, reasserting his leadership.

The tension passed quickly and, after the meeting's business was completed, the members stayed to chat and socialize over soda and pretzels. Even Malcolm joined in, evincing none of his earlier hostility. But Mark hadn't forgotten the cold, hard stare Malcolm had given him.

***

Malcolm and Duke had asked to meet with Mark, alone, a few weeks later.

"So, my man. Mark, are you finally fed up with these half-assed approaches to getting the mule's attention?" Malcolm Mohammed asked as they sat with Duke Wallace in the gym of an all but vacant DC public school building in Northwest Washington.

"It's clear that the usual lobbying, demonstrating, or otherwise pressuring Congress to give DC home rule is getting us nowhere. But, I'm afraid your Black Panther techniques won't get us anywhere but jail. And much as I care about home rule, I like my life as it is outside of prison. Thank you very much, my man," Mark shot back.

"This is you DC guys' thing, but I think Malcolm's new plan to put pressure in home districts and to multiply the reach and impact using virtual reality TV feeds can be big," interjected Duke.

"Remind me, what is your interest in this?" Mark turned quickly to face the blond.

"Like I said, this is you guys' thing. I'm only interested because I finally realized that the same game that's being run on urban Black and Brown communities is being run on poor Whites. Keeping the proletariat agitated, angry, and fighting amongst themselves for crumbs is universally one of the oldest strategies of the one-percenters," Duke said matter-of-factly.

"So, you're some sort of anarchist?" Mark continued to challenge.

"No, man. He's just a pragmatist," Malcolm said. "You don't see me runnin' 'round with lots of White boys, Mark. This dude's for real, despite his past electoral history."

"OK, OK," Mark sighed. "So, how do we get some response without going to prison?"

"All right. So, what is it about ISIS, Al-Qaida and the others that gets the attention of the West?" Malcolm asked.

"I thought we were talking no jail. They kill and behead innocent people." Mark stood up and paced the rickety gym floor under a basket.

"Hold on, man. They get attention because they appear to strike at people indiscriminately, and that makes folks feel vulnerable. If I catch a Metro in DC, if I get a Greyhound in Memphis, or stop at a toll booth in LA, I could be blown up, right? That's their key. Save for Pearl Harbor, Americans, European White adult Americans, never had to worry about indiscriminate violence. Not until Oklahoma City, Las Vegas, or the Twin Towers. That shit makes congressmen, Wall Streeters, CEOs, everybody nervous." Malcolm took a breath.

"And, the reaction to that vulnerability is to double down; it's not to negotiate. That's why it's not effective. We want to get even. It's a circular set of actions, none of it positive. If terrorism was so effective, how come these crazy White guys shooting up schools haven't caused significant reforms? Even attacking the Capitol in 2020 hasn't generated real reforms," Mark countered.

"Hold on. It's ineffective when the target is the general public. Suppose, however, the target is obviously the one-percenters and their lackeys in government? What if they knew they were targeted and were convinced their security force had left them and their families vulnerable?" Malcolm almost whispered.

"Possible. But how in the world could you make that sort of threat believable without breaking some law?"

"From what you've reported in some of your chitchat sessions, there are two congressmen and one senator who historically give no ground on home rule proposals." Duke picked up the thread.

"And suppose some of their kids' homerooms were destroyed during off hours?" asked Duke.

"Random act of property damage. Could be a disgruntled student or a prankster. And those three wouldn't necessarily feel targeted. Nor would they connect it to votes on home rule or statehood." Mark laughed dismissively, relieving tension.

"Absolutely, if that's all that happened. But if Monday morning each of those kids' transportation to school had a minor accident, and if each residence experienced a major water pipe leak or gas explosion while the houses were vacant over the following weekdays?"

"All illegal, reckless," Mark said.

Ignoring Mark's response, Duke said, "What if the media in each of their home districts reported landslides, flash floods, or fires in the neighborhoods of those fine elected representatives?"

"Mark, you're an educated dude. Ever hear of the 'War of the Worlds'?" asked Malcolm.

"Sure." Mark smiled for a moment, thinking of the 1938 radio hoax that created nationwide panic.

"Right. And you also know that the technology to create virtual reality scenarios is now leap years beyond what was possible early in the last century. Any video game genius can probably produce shit that would convince viewers that New York was now totally under water." Malcolm waited.

"So, the newscasts about destruction in the home districts would be fake?" Mark asked.

"Possibly," said Duke.

"Given the real events that could have occurred in DC, citizen anxiety would be high. Congress members would know that their homes could be reached, they would know they'd been singled out, they would feel incredibly vulnerable," Malcolm said.

"Maybe. But how does this get tied to statehood? And if it is seen as the objective of this campaign of terror, why wouldn't our group be suspect?" Mark was intrigued, but wary and skeptical. "Even if you could pull this whole thing off, why do you need our group?" he asked, hoping to get an unacceptable answer.

"Perfect. The right questions, my brotha," Malcolm said. He took a swig of bottled water, stood, stretched and looked around the empty gym. "A partnership makes sense because you all are a group of frustrated activists, unlikely to succeed in your mission. That's clear from the efforts of others like you over the last several decades. It seems to us you should be about ready to give up or go for the whole enchilada. If you're ready to step up, you have members all over the city, whom you have vetted. Troops.

"We have some technical and manpower resources and experience with a much more sophisticated PR strategy, if you will. A plan. Marry the two and you get what you have not been able to even sniff, and we soften up the resistance to us achieving our goals. It's simple, really." Malcolm finished and looked at Duke.

"The beauty is that there is no central organization. Your group may be the beneficiary, but all communications and demands, all planning, all operations are conducted by virtual groups with unaligned offshore bank accounts that are not traceable to any one source. Other than providing publicly available data on three members and listening to this fairy tale about some far-fetched *War of the Worlds* scenario, you're not involved. Nothing illegal for any of you." Malcolm leaned against the wall and pulled out a joint.

"Glad they legalized medical marijuana here," Mark said off-handedly.

He sat cross-legged on the floor and stared at the two men. Mark's mind was awash with reactions. Initially, each component of their plan approached the outside limits of credibility and acceptability, for him. Almost credible. As a whole, however, he thought the "plan" was over-the-top, nuts, crazy, unbelievable. Malcolm's delivery was quiet, reassuring, and confident. His tone and gestures approximated those of a freshman literature professor. But, Mark sensed that these two were not simply frustrated radicals who desired to jump-start respectable change, real progress toward statehood. They had bigger plans. Given their ability to captivate folks, to hold an audience, he felt they were dangerous. But, he wasn't sure to whom they posed a significant threat.

Malcolm watched Mark carefully for several minutes, then broke the silence.

"OK. I see your skepticism, so let's leave it for now. We have stuff to do elsewhere, So, let's talk in a few weeks," Malcolm suggested.

"Fine. But, to be honest with you, I don't see my view changing," said Mark.

They nodded and the radicals left the gym.

As they walked to their respective cars, Duke and Malcolm conferred.

"He's not in. Maybe we told him too much. He had a touch of that 'deer in the headlights' look," said Duke.

"It don't matter. I think we'll be able to do a national thing. We don't need the District to get what we want," Malcolm replied. Sensing Duke's concern, he added, "They don't know how to find us, even if they wanted to contact us. We found them and know how to reach them, remember? Besides, we told them a wild-ass tale, without relevant details. If they wanted to report us to someone, what authority would believe whatever they could present? By the time anybody can connect the dots, we're in the wind, baby. Relax."

When Mark returned home, Sonya was reading in the living room.

"Baby, you won't believe the shit I just heard," said Mark, as he came in, loosening his tie.

"Mark. Your language." She looked up.

"Sorry, but it was shit. These fools I've tried to collaborate with on a stronger statehood strategy have gone off the chain. They are into major property destruction and probably violence against families of Congress and the administration." He sank with a sigh into a deep maroon corduroy-covered armchair opposite his wife.

Sonya listened carefully to Mark's words and his tone. Although she had trained in finance at Stanford Business School, she had inherited political sensors from her father. He had been an effective moderate politician in Acapulco, before the cartels forced his family to flee, and he continued to master political practice and science as an adjunct professor at Berkeley. He'd met Sonya's mother in the East Bay, where she owned a left-wing bookstore. So politics was in Sonya's blood, and her ear for situational nuance was as acute as any on Capitol Hill.

"Well, you have been complaining about the lack of energy and imagination by the traditional DC advocates," she said, smiling.

"Yes, but I didn't call for the Klan, Branch Davidians or the Black Panthers. I'm going to step away from these dudes, as soon as possible. I'm also pretty confident that the others want to go slow and will avoid affiliation with Wallace and Mohammed," said Mark with conviction. "These guys are dangerous."

***

Mark couldn't focus on work. Worries over his last interactions with Malcolm and Duke kept interrupting his concentration. He finally told his long-time activist colleagues that he was dropping out of the statehood effort because of workload pressures. Unsolicited, many of them said that they were seriously concerned about the involvement of Malcolm and Duke. While he maintained that work was forcing him to step back, Mark concurred with their concerns. Leaving the meeting after announcing his resignation, he texted Malcolm to see if they could meet in the next couple of days. Within a couple of minutes, the message appeared on his phone.

How about Stan's at 15ᵗʰ and L Streets. downtown tonight at 6:15?

Mark knew the bar and felt that it might be too crowded to find privacy at that hour.

He thought for a minute, then typed, *How about the Hitching Post, front of Old Soldiers' Home, on Upshur St. NW? More private!*

See you then, came the pinged reply.

Malcolm was sitting by himself at a little table on the enclosed porch, when Mark entered the chicken-and-fries Caribbean joint.

"You look relaxed, brother. What can I buy you?" Malcolm said, not getting up from his seat.

"No, this is on me. My call," said Mark,.

When a ginger ale arrived for Mark, Malcolm asked, "You not a Muslim. How come you don't have a drink?"

"I'm headed for the gym afterward," Mark said matter-of-factly.

"Oh, one downtown on Connecticut Avenue, right?" Malcolm inquired nonchalantly.

"Right; how'd you know?" asked Mark.

"Saw you carrying your ratty-assed gym bag in there once," Malcolm smiled.

After Malcolm had had a few more sips of his Coke, Mark began. "I've thought about your and Duke's approach to the deal and still feel it's too far out there for us. My group seems to have lost focus and direction; they seem on the fence about a lot of things. But, they're not about to endorse any violence. Nonetheless, I'm personally dropping out of the project for a while."

"Change don't come cheap, my man. Got to be willing to put skin in the game." Malcolm smiled.

"Maybe. And I'm not at that point yet. I suppose that's what I found out," Mark admitted.

"Well, I can't say I'm surprised, 'cause to get what you want, power has to suffer. They ain't given nothing up for free. We know dat."

"I appreciate your input, man. No hard feelin's?" Mark asked.

"Hey, man, at least you honest with yourself. Better now than later. We cool," Malcolm said.

"So, what's next for you and your boy?" Mark tried to fill time until they finished their drinks.

"Who, Duke? We got a few things workin'. There's other places and other ways to get these mothafuckas to pay attention to the harm they doin'. Nah, we not done, not by a long shot." Malcolm was serious, but careful not to divulge any real information.

They finished their drinks, shook hands, and left grinning in mutual recognition, but not friendship.

Mark headed to the gym.

What Mark didn't know was where Malcolm headed next. Back down closer to the center of town, Malcolm found Duke at a table at Stan's bar.

Sliding behind another Coke, Malcolm said, "You was right. Dude backed out. He even backed out of his own project. Boy's too bourgeois at heart."

"No harm done. I think I have enough contacts, players, and money to put our plan into action. I've hooked up some old Navy buddies for the South Carolina action and some pissed-off Kentuckians for the Midwest stuff. If you can vouch for a few of the DC cats we've met and we can find a cyber genius, we're good." Duke drained a beer.

"Well, I have a feelin' that we need to scare old Markie a bit to make sure he keeps our connection to hisself. Least 'til we clear the country," said Malcolm.

"What you got in mind? Too severe might backfire on us," warned Duke.

"Nah. I thought about somethin' that'll just get his attention, but not really hurt, nor be traceable. I just sent a text to someone for assistance, while I was driving down here." Malcolm closed the subject.

CHAPTER 3

2028

On his way downtown, Mark called Sonya to tell her he'd pick up pizza on his way home from the gym, and also that he needed to talk to her to tell her the latest about the statehood project. He parked in his building's underground lot, checked his messages one more time, picked up his bag and headed for his sports club. Mark spent forty-five hard minutes on the StairMaster, rowing machine, bicycle, and weights before stripping in the locker room and heading for the sauna.

Wrapped in a towel, Mark lay down on the upper wooden slats in an all but deserted sauna. The one other occupant left after about five minutes, but Mark paid him no mind. Nor did he notice a burly Black man putting up a sign next to the window in the sauna's door, as he drifted off for ten more minutes. The tension that had lodged in his neck all day dissipated as the heat penetrated into his body. Drained and ready for a cold shower, Mark rose and pushed on the door leading to the shower stalls. It didn't budge. It didn't appear to be stuck, but locked somehow. Mark pushed gently at first and then he shoved more forcefully. The door didn't give. As he peered out of the double thick glass in the center of the wooden door, Mark saw no one in the showers. The stall curtains all seemed open. He rubbed moisture from the glass and peered at the wall opposite the steamer. On a mirror facing his potential coffin, Mark could see the reflection of the door. He saw that someone had stuck a sign on the outside of the door, next to the window. In adolescent handwriting, it read BROKEN.

Was there a malfunction of sort? Had there been a fire alarm? Was he accidently locked in the steam room? Lots of questions zipped around his brain, as he began to feel woozy from the extended exposure to heat.

He finally yelled, pounded on the glass and even kicked at the door with his flip-flops. Nothing roused attention or moved the door. Sweat pouring out of all his pores, head spinning, Mark began to panic. Then he began to have trouble catching his breath. He looked down at his arms and legs and saw that his light-brown complexion was turning red. He knew that he was rapidly dehydrating. In an effort to conserve energy, Mark sat back down on the slats. Then, he lay down and looked about his cedar prison for any object with which to break the glass part of the door. Nothing.

As his panic mounted, and his temperature soared, he grew dizzier, seeing black spots in his vision. Before long, he lost consciousness.

Mark opened his eyes to the sound of running water and the sight of the locker-room attendant standing over him with a worried expression. He explained that he had peeked through the door, removed some wooden wedges that had been shoved between the door and its frame, and pulled Mark out.

"Let me get you some water, man. You be awright," he said as he filled a cup with cold water.

After a couple of cups, and lying on a locker room bench for a few minutes, Mark revived enough to take a shower, leaning against the tile wall for support. He slowly dressed and drank a bottle of Gatorade that the attendant gave him.

"Lucky I came back in first, man," said the attendant.

"Back in, what do you mean?" Mark asked.

"Somebody set off a false alarm. Cleared the building. That's why nobody was down here. I git it. They must'a locked you in the steamer and put that sign sayin' 'Broken' on the door, then ran out before the emergency responders got here."

Even in his befuddled state, Mark immediately thought of Malcolm Mohammed. Could Malcolm actually have tried to kill him? Did he see him as such a threat to his radical plans?

"Good thing the fire department right down the street. I came in with them." The attendant simply shook his head. "You OK to get home, man?"

"Yeah. I'll be fine with a few more minutes' rest."

"Eat this energy bar before you leave."

"Thank you, man. Later."

Mark shuffled slowly out of the gym and to his car. He had regained enough presence of mind to remember to stop for a pizza on his way home. While waiting for the pizza, he texted an acquaintance he had at the Fourth District of the Metropolitan Police Department, asking him to expect a call on an "urgent matter" in the morning.

***

As he pulled into his driveway after his ordeal at the gym— still mentally reliving his near-death experience in the steam room—Mark remained physically and emotionally drained. He grabbed his gym bag, shuffled up to his front door, and inserted his key. His hand fell limp at his side, and he laughed.

"Damn," he said, as he trudged back to the car to retrieve the pizza.

"So, sweet thang, how was your day?" he asked as he slung his gym bag down in the front hall, shuffled to the kitchen, large pizza box in hand, and collapsed in a kitchen chair.

Giving him a kiss, Sonya said, "I know when you start like that, you have had a tough day and are only marginally interested in mine. Mine was fine, dear." She paused, pulled back and took a closer look at Mark. "Baby, you look exhausted! And your skin's flushed, and your hands are shaking . . ."

She took the pizza box from him, her face concerned. "Tell me what's going on."

"Well, you know that I pulled out of the statehood stuff because it's not going anywhere?"

"Right, it seemed like that's where you were headed, because of that shady pair—Mohammed and Wallace?"

"Yeah. So, their ideas got crazier and crazier. I don't know if they are philosophically radical, but the stuff they were suggesting was over the top, illegal, and just short of violent." He paused and took a deep breath.

"Anyway, somebody tried to suffocate me by locking the steam room door in the gym. I don't know if they wanted to kill me or just send a signal." Mark went on to describe the afternoon's incident, downplaying some of the details.

"Oh my god! Whether they meant to scare or kill you is not the point. You could have died." Sonya's usual stoicism was shaken. "Are you sure you're OK, Mark?"

"Yeah, I'm fine. Now, I'm sure it's a good idea to stay away from the statehood stuff for a while. Although, if I could prove today's incident was due to Duke or Malcolm . . ." Mark swallowed his speculation.

"Don't even think about it. Just leave it be. Stick to your decision," she insisted. She knew her husband well enough to recognize that his bravado was an attempt to mask his fear.

"But I don't like them thinking they bullied me away . . ." Mark complained, half-heartedly.

"Mark, before this afternoon, hadn't you concluded to drop out of the current movement?" Sonya reminded him. His ego might have suffered a bruise, but no way would she let him lose perspective and place himself in real harm's way.

"Yes . . ."

"And hadn't you concluded that the violent, radical approach would also fail?" she persisted.

"Yes, but . . ." Mark responded, feebly.

"Well, I think you need to get on the sideline for now. You're as tough as can be, but you're still human, my sweet. You're not yet a superhero," Sonya said with a smile, but also an air of finality.

"It's not just about statehood or about my safety. I think these guys have something bigger they're planning—some sort of major large-scale disruption involving cybersecurity. They have something in mind in which our little project was a minor piece. I just don't know enough of the details, but I have a very uneasy feeling." His frustration was building, overcoming his terror.

"OK then, why don't you call your buddy at MPD? At least report tonight's incident," she suggested.

"I've already texted him, but if this is all connected, this is beyond MPD. It's FBI territory," said Mark.

"To be honest . . . there's still a great deal of speculation in your story. And, what crime have they committed that you can point to?"

"Yeah, you're right. I might be getting ahead of myself. Still, just reporting it to MPD doesn't feel adequate," Mark said.

"I know you're frustrated. Why don't you bounce this off your mom? Run it by her? You always feel better after getting her input. I have no pride, baby," she said.

"Wow, this pepperoni is great, huh?" said Mark, taking a bite.

"OK. I'm dismissed on the issue, right?" laughed Sonya.

Later that evening, instead of calling his mother, Mark checked his phone contacts and punched another name.

"Rafael? This is Mark."

"Hey, buddy. How's it going down there?" cheerfully asked Mark's former college classmate.

"Everything is cool. What's going on with the *Globe*?" Mark stalled.

"Not too much. Basically, the same news you experience down there. What's up, dude?"

"So, you know that project I've been volunteering on?"

"You mean the home rule or statehood piece?"

Mark could sense Rafael's lack of interest, and suspected he was looking at an unrelated item on his screen. As quickly as he could, he filled him in on the recent events and his suspicions about Wallace and Mohammed.

"Wait. Isn't the Wallace cat a White supremacist and Mohammed like an old-school Black Muslim?" Rafael Marquez turned from his PC and focused on the phone conversation.

"On the surface, yeah," Mark said.

"So, there's no surprise that they want to make your strategy a lot more radical. But why would they need your group?" Before Mark could answer, Rafael responded to his own question. "Contacts. Like, you guys have congressional contacts. But I still don't get it. Plenty of DC groups have those contacts."

"Right. But the national groups don't have a network of workers on the ground here. Maybe they were hoping to pick up some 'foot soldiers.' Who knows their real motives?" Mark fished for a useful response. "Man, I'm sort of stuck. I have this nagging suspicion that I should not simply walk away. They are up to something."

"But you don't want to draw attention to the statehood project, 'cause it is not going to be this administration or the majority's favorite movement. Not to mention that these dudes may be ultra-dangerous. You don't need some 'guilt by association' problems," said Rafael.

"You got it," Mark sighed.

"I could sniff around, but I don't have the best radical contacts. And I sure as hell don't know the neo-Nazi crowd. Let me think on it, Mark. Got to run."

"Appreciate it, buddy," said Mark, as he sat back again.

"Hey, you got it. If you ever need contacts in Central or South America, I might be of real help. Can't promise anything useful on this one, though. Later, Mark." Rafael hung up.

MALCOLM & DUKE

CHAPTER 4

2027

To the casual observer, there was nothing unusual about the two men intensely engaged in conversation at a corner table of Declaration, a trendy bar/restaurant in Washington's gentrified U Street corridor. One was of African descent, coffee-colored skin, with a medium-sized Afro and full, but not bushy beard. The other was of fair-complexioned European stock, light brown hair covering his ears, and clean-shaven. Both were dressed casually in jeans and a light sweater. They arrived within five minutes of each other, and, after a friendly embrace, each surveyed the room to see that they were not recognized by any patron, ordered drinks, and settled into quiet, but passionate conversation.

"Listen, man, I want to see the destruction of this system as much as you guys," said Duke Wallace, in his slow Kentucky diction, "but I plan to live a full life on this here earth afterward. No suicide missions, Malcolm. Not for me."

"Look, Duke, folks got enough problems believin' you really left all that White supremacist shit behind. You're still seen as an allied Republican consultant, or operative. Ain't nobody expectin' you to convert to full-scale jihadist," whispered Malcolm Mohammed.

Their journey to this reunion had been a long and unlikely one. Barely a decade earlier, Duke had been excited about the election of a man he and his buddies thought would bring an empathetic perspective to the White House—a populist view of economic problems that placed the power of the most awesome position in the world behind finding jobs, training, and real opportunities for White poor and working-class people. Someone who would restore pride in, and respect for, Whites again in America.

Earlier, Duke had quit a well-paying finance job in a Michigan auto company, worked as a research assistant in the War College in DC, then did staff work for a North Carolina senator. He stayed only a half year before going home to organize in Kentucky and reunite with cronies who'd "stayed behind," dropped out and wallowed in their anger at everything they had seen as unjust to Whites like them. He had struggled and failed to convince them to do legitimate political organizing, but they had rejoiced and partied for months after the first autocratic populist of the twenty-first century won. Then after a centrist Democratic interlude with president George Borden between 2020 and 2024, another clever autocrat won the presidency: Robert Spade.

By inauguration, however, Duke had begun to question the sincerity of their candidate's commitment to populism and to the nonaffluent White folks he had seemed to understand so well during the campaign. Duke had not expected the president to publicly embrace an agenda of White supremacy, but he had expected full executive and legislative focus on the needs of neglected White workers. He had definitely expected the needs of Brown immigrants and Black welfare kings and queens to be last in line. And he sure didn't think gays would still be getting policy attention.

Duke had anticipated the conversion of campaign rhetoric into positive proposals for marginalized White workers, not standard conservative tax cuts. Beyond scapegoating of Borden programs, Mexicans and Muslims, he had expected targeted health care improvements, sustainable job growth, and relief on school loans. He began to fear that the president's self-promoting was an end in itself and not a brilliant means to install meaningful policies for poor Whites.

Increasingly disillusioned, he had decided to contact someone whose intellect he respected and whose views, while radically different than his, were honest. While playing football at Duke University, he had improbably befriended a teammate: the man who now called himself Malcolm Mohammed. Arguments, even fights, over Duke's role in electing the current president would have to be endured, but Malcolm's perspective might help Duke clarify how to best apply his own pragmatism, how best to help get a better shake for one of the country's most underserved groups. Of one thing he felt confident: Malcolm had served in the Army and thus had put country above domestic politics and ideology. So, he might also be struggling with how to resolve conflicting allegiances.

"Malcolm," he said, at their first meeting, "I ain't sittin' here because I all of a sudden love me some Black folk. You know we hooked up because I finally realized that these white-collared phony rednecks in power don't care about Appalachia any more than they do about Ferguson, Missouri. And since their silly-ass sons don't ever have to fight their wars, the best way to force change is to bring the revolution to their doorstep. Make it so if resources don't get spread, then nobody gits 'em. The divide-and-conquer strategy of theirs is so obvious when you sit back and watch it play out. I was such an idiot." Duke's agitation tightened every line in his face.

"I see why you're disenchanted with your golden president, but why should we trust or help you?" Malcolm spoke from behind the obscurity of his sunglasses. "After all, you admit that you're no friend of Black folk."

"Fair enough. Let me bring some resources to the table and then you judge for yourself if I'm committed to this fight," countered Duke.

"What sort of resources?" Malcolm's gaze fixed on the White man.

"You name the spot, and I'll provide proof of financial, material, and personnel resources," Duke responded with confidence.

Malcolm remembered well that this former college pal had once joined potentially hostile Black and Brown urban students as the sole White negotiator making the case to the university administration for more student say-so. Malcolm noted that he still spoke directly, truthfully, and without high or low affectation. He decided to listen to what he had to say.

Weeks later, sitting in the parking lot of The Arc in his beat-up faded red 2019 Camry, Malcolm Mohammed slouched a stiff arm away from the steering wheel and scanned the cars traveling in both directions along Mississippi Avenue, SE. The community center was in one of DC's remaining solid Black neighborhoods, offering housing to a full range of incomes. Dusk was descending over Southeast Washington as teenagers began arriving at the modern glass and steel multipurpose center for various after-school activities. Some carried instruments or folios of August Wilson plays, others held basketballs, and still others shouldered book bags of homework assignments to be completed at the campus library. No one noticed the bearded brother in a multicolored dashiki peering out of the well-worn Toyota sedan. Nor did anyone other than Malcolm notice a long-haired young White man of average height step out of a red District taxi at the entrance of the parking lot and head toward the front door of the center.

Malcolm allowed Duke Wallace to reach the door of the building and turn around to scan the parking lot before he pulled out of his space and stopped below the front steps.

"Quite a lush setting and fancy building hidden down here," said Duke, as he climbed into the front passenger seat of Malcolm's car.

"It's by no means hidden, and it's a well-established landmark to those who bother to learn the city," snipped Malcolm, as he turned off of Mississippi Avenue onto Southern Avenue, the border with Maryland's Prince George's County.

"This is the Hillcrest District on the right," said Malcolm as he drove north on Branch Avenue.

"I do know that at least one former mayor and numerous middle-class big shots lived there," said a relaxed Duke.

"A quick right on Pennsylvania Avenue SE, and a left onto Carpenter and we're almost there, on Thirty-Fifth Street," said Malcolm, as if narrating a TV scene.

As he parked, Malcolm waved to a neighbor taking out a leaf bag, opened the garage door and entered his single-story ranch house, the back of which overlooked a grove of poplar and maple trees in Pope Branch Park.

"Can I offer you a beer, Duke?"

"I thought Muslims didn't drink."

"I don't, but I got manners. And you ain't even one of them strict Protestants, so . . ."

"I would like that. Thank you."

Duke sat in a deep cherry wood frame chair whose seat was made of wildebeest hide. He looked about the living room, and one item immediately struck him as out of character with the design scheme: a plaque commemorating Malcolm as the top rifle sharpshooter in his Army unit. Duke decided not to bring up Mohammed's Ranger background at the moment. The walls were otherwise decorated with colorful Haitian crowd paintings and faded carved Idoma and Yoruba masks, and appointed with waist-high Shona sculptures.

"Where are the carvings from? They're stunning." Duke sipped his beer.

"The masks are from regions in Nigeria and the statues are mostly from Zimbabwe."

"Nice. Not what I expected."

"Were you looking for some hoods and crosses?" Malcolm stared.

"Now, that's low. You know I've left that shit behind me. People do grow, you know." He smiled.

"My bad. You right." Malcolm relaxed. "Thank you. So, let's talk about the strategy to make these pompous, double-dealing crackers, no offense, take notice."

"None taken. Here's how I think I can help." Duke moved up in his seat.

Despite his deep involvement stirring up resentment toward immigrants and Blacks in working-class White communities during the 2016 and 2024 national campaigns, Duke Wallace had always viewed his personal philosophy as one of pragmatism, not racism. Before the last campaign, he'd begun to question the efficacy of trusting federal officials to radically alter conditions for any group other than the rich and powerful. He empathized, however, with the view of newly impoverished Whites who didn't seem to be worth the political attention of Democrats and were becoming marginalized by powerful Republicans. Political and economic markets saw little profit in addressing the slipping status of his community. The community from which he, as a bright boy with college potential, had escaped. No one paid them attention until the primaries, when Sergio Sullivan and Robert Spade showed political empathy and refocused national attention on coal miners, steel millers, factory workers, and poorly educated Whites.

Duke was comfortable with the grassroots anger and xenophobia now outwardly expressed in the communities he'd help organize. But during the 2020 to 2024 Democratic interlude, Duke began to shift through future job options, as his confidence in the political winners began to wane. After several consultancies, he decided to try the political route again in 2028 and again worked the grass roots for the next populist, Robert Spade. But, his pragmatism morphed into renewed cynicism, and then into anger. Within a few weeks after the election, he sensed that he and his constituents, his "homeboys," had been used by the "populism" of the president's brilliant marketing. The former Tea Party stalwart evidenced little interest in expensive proposals to put the "rust belt" or Appalachia back to work, or to provide meaningful and accessible health care.

Duke knew that those he'd convinced to vote for the first time or to leave the Roosevelt, Carter, and Obama Democratic Party would take months, if not years, to realize what he now understood. But he doubted they'd be better off, save for in a few window-dressing towns where the president personally intervened to keep or restore a manufacturing presence.

Then, in the week between Christmas and New Year 2027, Duke got a late-night call from a cousin in Florence, Kentucky, near Cincinnati. The ringing cell phone wouldn't let him sleep.

"Hell is this?" Duke snapped.

"Dukie, sorry to wake you, but your daddy has died. Somethin' 'bout a mix-up with insurance at the hospital. But, he's gone."

"Bobby? Jesus, you said my daddy is gone?"

"Yeah. Come on over. It's a mess," answered Bobby Stabler.

Duke was by no means close to his father, who had left his mother when Duke was six years old, but the news still saddened him. His father's life had not been easy, and Duke knew he had stayed in touch with his mother and tried to provide for his tiny family. He had seen to it that Duke went to school and had supported the notion that his son could do better than his kin.

The funeral services were attended by about a dozen people who had known Johnson Wallace. Because his mother had died a few years earlier, Duke was the sole survivor. He was glad he didn't have to explain to too many family or friends why he had stayed away from home since college and was relieved that everyone was cordial. It only took him a few days to attend to his father's affairs; there were no real assets left, so the primary task was arranging for his burial. In a way, the trip "home" allowed Duke to put lingering, unclear emotions about his father to rest. He had been a "rolling stone" like in the Temptations' song, but he had tried to do the right thing by his son. So, Duke was at peace until he talked to Bobby about the details of his father's death.

It seemed that Johnson Wallace had started to apply for insurance under the Affordable Care Act, but had gotten inaccurate gossip about not being eligible due to a preexisting heart condition. By the time he checked with the government and understood that indeed he would qualify, he had begun listening to lots of campaign rhetoric suggesting that Spade would "fix" the current awful system. So Johnson Wallace delayed applying, assuming that the new coverage would somehow be better. Apparently, he had been at a bar in Cincinnati, drinking heavily, when he had a heart attack. An ambulance was called, but the attendants wasted time looking for Johnson's nonexistent insurance card. By the time he was taken to a public city hospital and officials again determined that he had no coverage, his admission was further delayed. Johnson Wallace died in a hall outside the emergency operating room.

Whether his father would have been cared for, operated on, and saved if he had had insurance, Duke could only speculate. But as he listened to the tale of his death, something deep in his psyche snapped. He didn't fully understand the debate about "Obamacare," but he sensed that his father would be alive had he gone ahead and signed up. The whole health care debate suddenly became personal. He suspected that the slogan "repeal and replace" of the 2016 campaign had left a lot of people, like his father, adrift without actual coverage. Were those he'd helped elect playing games with the people Duke had helped rally? He left Kentucky disturbed and angry about the change he'd helped bring about.

Now, sitting in Malcolm's living room, Duke said, "Malcolm, I know it sounds bizarre after the supposed 'far right' now controls the government, but I'm sick of the whole scene and thinking of getting out of politics totally." He paused, gauging Malcolm's reaction, then continued. "I have contacts on the ground equally sick of the sellout, I've got folks who financed the supposed populist and now see that it's about Spade, not the people. There's well-trained Navy guys not sure they trust this dude, who belittles and berates the military and Justice Department when it suits him. I'm tellin' you, a bunch of folks feel used. I can tap some, if we're serious about change."

"Hold up now. You won, man. You got the country feelin' it's just fine to hate niggahs, spics, rag heads. America's great again. You should be happy." Malcolm smiled sarcastically.

"You know my deal was not to put folks down. Yeah, we unleashed some nasty shit, and that I regret. I was, and am, all about helping those left behind, exurban and rural Whites who are getting fucked by all sides. You are smart enough to see that they don't even know it yet. What happens, Malcolm, when poor Whites realize that they've been shafted, yet again? You saw the January 6, 2021, fiasco."

"That's easy to see, my man. They'll feel like the brothas, Latinos, the Muslims, and everybody else who thought rushing to the polls was going to solve something," said Malcolm.

"So how come you're so relaxed about it?" Duke asked.

"Who says I'm relaxed? It's simply dawned on me that the only way to wake up these power elites of all colors is through real damage, real pain in their own backyards, at their own kitchen tables. Health care choice makes sense if you have income, education, and time to investigate and reflect on choices. Your kinfolk in Appalachia got that?"

"You know the answer. Hell, no," said Duke.

"Police is always right for them because that's who the police work for. Little Johnnie Blue-Eyes runs a red light in Scarsdale, drunk as a skunk, and he might get pulled over. But does he get dragged from the car, whooped over the head with a baton, and then shot in the back as he staggers away? No, he might get a lecture from the officer and a warning. But it's all in the family." Malcolm began to warm.

"That's not true for White toughs in Cincinnati or Memphis, or even LA," Duke protested, mildly.

"Duke, are you seriously going to tell me a White dude, clean cut, mindin' his business on a Dallas street is likely to get the same treatment from cops as some Black or Brown brotha with his music a bit too loud, or with his earphones big as cantaloupes, who looks at the cop the wrong way? You really think their odds of getting stopped are the same?"

Duke quickly retorted, "In case you haven't noticed, all White guys don't look preppy and Ivy League on the one hand, nor toothless with a cigarette hanging from their lips on the other."

Malcolm merely stared. "We in Iraq and Afghanistan with working-class dudes from Michigan, Wisconsin, and all over the south, puttin' it all on the line against stone killin' enemies. And these political thugs are clappin' their hands at

Russian interference in our elections. That's sho' nuff wrong. Is that making us 'great again'?" Malcolm balled his fists, at no one in particular.

Duke nodded his head in agreement.

"I didn't think so. My point is that those folks on Capitol Hill who your constituents voted for don't see authority as a threat to deport them or their relatives, to beat or shoot them with little provocation, or to emasculate their representation by redistricting. Most of the majority is cool with authority. It's there to protect their interests. So, as long as they comfortable, those White folks aren't going for redistribution of nothin'."

Malcolm stood and walked to the picture window looking out over the park.

"OK," said Duke. "Nor are they interested in training my folks, so they can benefit, should manufacturing be lured to their towns. If a plant comes back to the rust belt, the jobs will be more technical and digitized. That's obvious." He paused, then added, "You may choose not to believe me, but in the Marines, I saw every demographic; we got molded into a fighting force where each truly had the other's back. If you couldn't get there, you got weeded out in training. All the stuff about group culture, honor, commitment means something when your life depends on that other dude, man. What kills me is to see that commitment cheapened, taken for granted by this bunch of politicians."

"It's obvious to you and me, but a lot of the folks you organized don't see it yet." Malcolm turned back toward the room.

"And *that* callous truth is what pisses me off." Duke drained his beer.

Malcolm studied his old friend. He had a decision to make. Duke had matured into a strong leader committed to an allied cause. His White working-class and poor networks could provide valuable human resources for his scheme, but

Duke could have him arrested if he didn't buy all in. Malcolm hesitated, then went with his gut.

"Tell me about your time in Iraq," he asked Duke.

"It was Afghanistan. Why?"

"Humor me," Malcolm persisted.

"Not much to tell. Learned how to block out unpleasant thoughts about getting blown up during my next step. Learned how to contain and categorize my grief about a comrade being blown up, and how to hold back the rising stomach bile when looking at the decapitated corpse of some dude from whom I'd just bummed a fag. Learned how to shoot on the move, while seeking the next perpendicular object behind which to hide. Learned how to put trust in some motha just because of the uniform he wore. Learned that trust, courage, and reliability have no particular skin color," said Duke. "Not much, but I picked up a few things."

"So, for my part, I end up sort of where the Black Panthers were in the '70s and where jihadists are, in a way, today," said Malcolm.

"You mean, blow the motha up?" Duke chuckled.

"Not quite. But check this out. The NRA, who conservatives love so much, has made weapons so terribly accessible that many neighborhoods are as dangerous as where we served overseas. And the pols have stoked the anger of folks on all sides, and blamed all this tension on Muslims. But the US of A has basically not had to deal with political violence in a sustained way like the British, say with the IRA, or Europe generally now with home-grown jihadist attacks. These turkeys here are soft. Our national emotional coping skills are really unproven." Malcolm was flinging his arms for emphasis.

"So, what are you getting at?" Duke asked, cautiously.

"So, what happens if explosions begin to disrupt the home neighborhoods of the most racist and, let's say, insensitive members of Congress? What happens if their kids don't feel safe at school? What happens if the main industries, the big tax generators in their districts, experience constant electrical and communications failure? How will they cope with poisoned water supply, not in Flint, but in Michigan's tony suburbs—their families' towns? Or how about port towns getting flooded because of sea levels rising faster than anticipated? It's one thing for FEMA to be feeble in Puerto Rico, it's altogether different in the former Speaker's hometown, the majority leader's home, or any one of the president's country clubs." Malcolm's rhetoric was getting good to him.

"Chaos, fear, and maybe frustration." Duke nodded. "It can be mapped out, planned. But, how's that resolve our issue for poor Blacks or Whites?"

"Well, immediately, it doesn't. But if the high and mighty all of a sudden feel as vulnerable and helpless as your folks and my folks . . . And if they can't tell if the disruption is caused by 'radical Islamists,' disappointed skinheads, MS-13 from Central America, or who, then they suffer extreme anxiety, defensiveness, then despair. Finally, maybe, they gain a bit of empathy. Eventually, there's a need to fix certain 'national crises.' It's no longer 'their' issue, 'those undeserving poor.' The shit has hit the fan and it's splattering them, the privileged elites."

"With the most pissed-off White folks in Ohio, I wouldn't bet on empathy for folks they don't identify with," said Duke.

"And your point is? Look, it's about despair, fear, and vulnerability. The powerful are isolated from the impact of their policies. At best, they have to attend a few uncomfortable constituent meetings and issue vacuous promises. Those issues are intellectual constructs to them, not bread-and-butter or life-and-death realities. They are truly only concerned about their own portfolios or the well-being of their biggest corporate contributors. Look, the US didn't get into World War II, with the German atrocities throughout Europe and the Japanese gobbling up the Pacific, until Pearl Harbor got bombed. Then, all of a sudden, the evil around the world had to be stopped."

"I got it. I just don't see how in the hell you can plan, much less execute, disturbances sufficient to generate that sort of reaction, that kind of paranoia, and then force real collaboration."

"A step at a time, Duke. At step at a time." Malcolm collapsed deep into a chair.

Duke Wallace understood the depth of Malcolm's frustration and anger, and he saw the logic of his disruptive vision, but he thought the man was nuts. Disruption on the scale needed to cause real horror among the elites was unthinkable. The frown on his face communicated his utter skepticism.

Duke looked out the picture window for a minute and realized he really didn't know much about this ex-college buddy. He was hadn't kept track of what had happened to Malcolm Mohammed since college.

"So, hold up a sec. You never told me what happened to you, while I was eating dust in Afghanistan," said Duke.

"Well, you'll remember that, beyond football, I was into computers, but I also had a fascination with Africa. I had at least one Somali cousin that I'd met in Kenya and felt that I would dig finding a way to get stationed there. I thought about the foreign service, but didn't like the career lead time required to get one's preferred assignment. Then I thought about intelligence, but I didn't know if being tied to a computer, researching cables, holding boring meetings, and hanging out with Howard University–educated Africans would be cool.

"I don't know, but the idea of being an Army Ranger seemed, in a twisted way, to satisfy my need for action, learning about cultures, and chance to get to the continent.

I was young, man. Anyway, I had the smarts to learn the ops stuff, the brawn to handle the training, and the toughness to handle the racism. Bingo. I get in after the 2013 Al Shabaab raid in Somalia and the next year's rescue attempt in Yemen.

"After a few years of that shit, I decided that if I was going to die young, might as well be fightin' for my peeps back home. I ran into some crap with the VA in Florida when they wouldn't prescribe painkillers for some neck problems I'd developed. So I decided to look for a foothold up north in DC. Got a computer tech gig at the Library of Congress—OK pay, benefits, and time to do my 'community building,' attend conferences, do some writing and speaking. I knocked around with some other Black vets and grew increasingly pissed at the treatment they got, forcing brothas into unemployment, or dead-end jobs, drugs, and homelessness.

"I don't know when the light went on, but it became clear that the Congress I worked for was never going to get serious about nothin' involving poor people of color. Black president, or not. So, I started playing with ideas on how to use my combat training, my IT skills, and my network to make these mothas' lives miserable enough so they'd do something relevant and positive for folks. That's when I came up on Mark Morton and his pansy-assed DC statehood crowd. Well-meaning, but not about to change shit, no way, no how." Malcolm stopped and checked the time on his phone. Then he looked at Duke's face. "I know. You think I'm wasted on some ghetto drugs." Malcolm let out a raucous belly laugh.

"You know, I just came up here to get some advice on how to make up for the political hocus-pocus shit I helped pull over on my folks. I really only needed job counseling. I didn't expect to stumble on some far-out revolutionary bullshit." Duke drained his beer.

"You're reacting to scale rather than to strategy, my man. Dig it. Nine-eleven took down two towers and damaged one Pentagon structure, right? Timothy McVeigh and another dude pulled off the Oklahoma City federal building bombing, right?" Malcolm asked.

"Yes, and?"

"The hysteria those events caused still resonates today, right? Suppose you had a coordinated series of events targeting the worst of the political establishment assholes? But not just explosions. I'm talking about destruction that shows the lunacy of several of their dumb-ass policies, and simultaneously scares the shit out of them or their families, personally." Malcolm was back on a roll.

"Well, you'd get the mule's attention. But the resources, personnel, equipment, and stuff you'd need, not to mention the management, are impossible." Duke's skepticism turned to laughter.

"You see, you're showing that sort of limited thinking that I hope these fools will show. Look here. Suppose some of these destructive events are cyber creations? I mean, they only happen in supersonic 4-D video space, but they are simulcast over every f'ing media outlet, so that the events appear to be real? And suppose some of the catastrophe is real, in real time. But for a while, the public thinks it's all real. Not like in a f'ng 'reality show,' but stone cold-blooded real." Malcolm paused to take a breath.

"I don't follow you, Malcolm." Duke looked lost, and a little scared.

"Some events, like a tsunami that wipes out part of LA, are a movie. It's on every damn TV screen in America and reported widely on social media. But, the communications in LA are jammed, so that no one outside the area can verify whether what's on their screen is real time. A twenty-first-century version of that Orson Welles radio trick. 'War of the Worlds' never happened, but scared the bejesus out of half the fools in this country. By the way, did you check out the movie *Ready Player One*, came out in 2018? The technology is here, Jack, to tie your sense of reality up in knots, with or without virtual reality goggles.

"So imagine, at the same time, part of the president's enhanced and refortified Mexican border wall actually gets blown up, or new factory construction in a Midwest town implodes for real. A couple of private schools attended by kids of the congressional elite are blown up at five a.m., before anybody is in a classroom. Or the DC Metro is derailed during rush hour and some jihadist group claims responsibility. You don't need too many resources to create a paralyzing mix of fake and real disasters to throw this motha into turmoil." Malcolm sat back, pleased with his vision.

"OK . . . Even if you could generate this sort of mixed virtual and real disaster scenario, which I doubt, how's that force the powers that be to deal with the problems of our folks?" Duke asked, his skepticism returning.

"Man, you need to read more sci-fi. Ransom, that's how. Only, instead of demanding money, we demand specific legislation."

Duke bent over his knees in laughter. "Let me get this straight. We're goin' to leave notes instructing the president and the Congress to pass legislation on, let's say, decent health care, legitimate job training and placement, fair path to immigrant citizenship, or sane environmental auto policies, and they are goin' to run out and do it? That's your movie?"

"In a manner of speaking, yeah. That's it, brotha," Malcolm said, bowing at the waist.

"You are stone silly. That is science fiction." Duke got up and headed to the fridge for another beer.

"You think Osama bin Laden thought that a decade after 9/11, and years after his death, Al Qaida and offshoots like ISIS would still be causing havoc in the Middle East,

Europe, Africa, and South Asia? Who knows what sort of ripple effects this shit would have? Hell yes, if these mugs thought they were vulnerable physically, that their families were in danger, if they had no real idea where the threat was originating, and their National Security agencies were clueless, they would pass something quick and in a hurry."

"You really believe this, don't you?" asked Duke.

"Man. I don't have the critical details worked out. I know, however, that the technology exists to do what I'm suggesting. And I think there are enough pissed-off, crazy dudes who would love to see these mothas squirm. Shit, yeah. This is doable," Malcolm reaffirmed.

The men stared at each other.

"You came to me for advice on how to get some action for those crackers who you think are getting screwed. Well, what I'm suggesting would help a lot of needy folks and might just back 'the system' into doin' a few good things to save this motha. It's no crazier than a Black guy with a Muslim name running for the presidency, or a dumb-assed atheist, misogynistic, real-estate con man convincing Tea Partiers, Christian evangelists, and hillbillies that he's their righteous savior. Come on, man—you can't invent crazier shit than we've seen recently."

Both laughed.

"Malcolm . . . let me think on this. I don't know that I'm into this level of risk yet," Duke said, in a measured voice.

Duke realized that he did, in fact, know communications and explosives experts who could help pull the scheme off. The pool of those men angry enough at the country and/or greedy enough to help for a major paycheck was small. He suspected that he could probably find a small, safe group, but he worried about his ability to maintain distance and deniability. Cross that bridge when necessary, he thought. For now, he'd just listen—but he knew he was beginning to take Malcolm's idea seriously.

"Man, you once convinced people you say you care about to support a dude whose answer to a complicated immigration issue is to build a wall," Malcolm railed. "A man who thinks Frederick Douglass is out here today up and down Martin Luther King Avenue preachin' and shit. A man who told them that coal is coming back, big time. A man who convinced farmers he's their boy, as he loads tariffs on soybeans and pigs—the lifeblood of whole states. A man whose economic indicators suggest we're in boom times, until you look closely at who is booming. Duke, when those folks finally wake up and figure out that it's not the Mexicans, the Bloods, or the Muslims that's robbin' them, now that's what I call risk. We into some serious risk then."

"Let me think about it, man. There's the scheme; there's delivering the message convincingly; there's raising the money; then there's not getting detected; there's carrying out the plan; then, there's getting out of Dodge, having to go underground or needing to go abroad. It's a lot to think about." Duke shook his head. "It's a more complicated oath, with a less clear objective, than the one I took before Afghanistan. That was a clear enemy."

"How come they all hate us, then? Ain't nobody clappin' for us over there, that I can see," scoffed Malcolm.

Malcolm stood up, excused himself for a moment, walked into an interior bedroom and partially closed the door. Duke, not sure what just happened, sipped his beer and then stood to slowly walk around the living room to get a better look at Malcolm's painted art. The sunlight filtered by the light drapes added uneven depth and greater ferocity to some of the colorfully painted masks framing the bedroom door. As he moved past the door, Duke noticed through the opening that Malcolm was bent over a prayer rug in the middle of the room. He quickly moved to the wall beyond the door and admired what he took to be Haitian figures gathered at an outdoor marketplace. Before he could finish his tour of

Malcolm's residential gallery, Duke felt Malcolm's hand on his shoulder.

"Some wild craft, huh?" Malcolm asked.

"It's a striking collection of beautiful work. Seriously," Duke offered.

"Thank you, man. Thank you." Malcolm returned to his seat.

"So, you pray the requisite times a day?" Duke took his seat too.

"Not always, but when I can. But let's be clear. I'm not that devout. Prayer does help clear my head, though."

"So, how do you think your imam would like your scheme?" Duke held his beer bottle to his lips.

Malcolm reflected in silence for a couple of minutes. "Probably the way your pastor would. Negative. No question. But I've compartmentalized my faith from other parts of my life," he said with quiet conviction.

Duke said, "I did go to church during the campaign. Certain passages of the New Testament forced me to reflect on how I'd blocked out God when I looked down the barrel of my rifle at some Taliban creep. I still haven't really resolved the dilemma we faced in war—taking lives to defend our country. I mean, I'm not positive God takes sides, you know?"

"Quiet as it's kept over here, most Muslims don't believe in jihad. We're taught to treat other men like you Christians are. No, my imam would definitely not condone my scheme." Malcolm seemed to be focused on some other space, some other reality.

"So, why plan this scheme?" Duke persisted.

"Same reason as you. The evil being perpetrated, the destruction of institutions and norms that make our country work, the unfair distribution of pain and misery while the top one percent smile in your face and pile up their wealth.

There are limits, man. I can't wait for some just God to take action."

"So why pray, then?" Duke inquired honestly.

"Come on, man. You still got to struggle with what's right, good, and just. You telling me you don't compartmentalize what you need to do, as opposed to what you should do? Still got to look for guidance. I can't totally explain it, Duke. Can you?" For the first time, Malcolm looked slightly vulnerable.

"No. You're right. It's complicated. Seems like there's no easy merging of the good with the practical, the just with the achievable. What's it that Yankee Yogi Berra said? If you come to the fork in the road, you got to take it."

Both men howled.

Malcolm shook his head. "So, I ain't against religion. But some days it seems like we got more and more evangelists, megachurches, synagogues, mosques, gospel groups, religious influences on every corner. Yet look at how we treat each other. Men and women, average folks."

"I'm not sure there's any cause-effect relationship there," said Duke.

"Certainly got to be some correlation," insisted Malcolm. Silence.

Then Duke said, "Anyway, Malcolm, I'm glad you're also struggling with faith."

"I suppose the shit would be simpler if we were total believers. Totally put our faith in some scripture, some church, and some priest who helped apply it all to daily situations," Malcolm mused.

"It don't work that way. I don't know folks built like that."

Both men seemed pulled into some other consciousness for several silent minutes.

"Anyway, these dudes are wrecking the country we fought for, Duke." Malcolm offered what he believed was an undeniable truth. Then he stood to get his car keys. "I'll take you to the subway, man."

In the car, Malcolm said, "While you're thinking about this approach and how your organizing skills and contacts might help, think of the likely outcomes for your constituents, if they have to suffer through five more years of their savior. You want despair, you want violence? That's some serious, sho' nuff risk!"

"It's funny. We're both smart enough, experienced enough, and connected enough to have nice 'legitimate' careers. We could probably earn nice livings and celebrate all of the benefits of capitalism. Why are we so concerned about those who can't?" Duke asked, only partially expecting an answer.

" 'Cause we can't ignore bold-faced hypocrisy and injustice. We just can't. Not while we're young." Malcolm felt he spoke for both of them.

"All right, I promised to show you what resources I can bring to the table. Just let me think about it and make some calls. When we get back together, I'll be all in and have commitments—or I'll drop out." Duke exhaled. He knew he was in.

"Fair enough, my man," said Malcolm.

CHAPTER 5

2028

Malcolm settled into a corner table with a plate of beans, rice, and collard greens at Ben's Chili Bowl, a soul food restaurant along gentrified U Street in the District of Columbia. When his cup of steaming green tea arrived, he pulled his laptop from his knapsack, opened it, and began to make notes.

What is the ask? That's the question Duke and I need to nail. We've got an impressive set of events shaping up, and I'm positive we can scare those knuckleheads at the top of the government. We've figured how to cover our tracks, and I think we can remain anonymous for months. But what do we want to ask?

Otis Redding was singing "I've Got Dreams" through the ceiling speakers, and Malcolm looked around the restaurant for several minutes.

What do they have to offer? Legislation and appropriations.

"That's it," he thought.

He typed a couple of paragraphs outlining the environmental and educational policies and money they would demand.

"Don't ask for something that they can't give," he said to himself.

"Anything else, Mr. Mohammed?" asked a waitress.

"I'm good, baby. Thank you." Malcolm smiled.

Malcolm scrolled his emails and then looked at a notice that he had a new Snapchat message.

Listo para nuestra reunion [Ready to meet].

The thing is ready.

Malcolm deleted the message from visible electronic existence and closed his eyes. Jorge Blanco was a billionaire Mexican businessman, who had introduced himself to Malcolm after a speech he gave on the importance of maintaining free economic trade relations throughout the hemisphere at a Pan-Caribbean conference in Havana. Blanco was involved in some derivative of the petroleum business that had been damaged severely by the US antitrade, anti-immigrant policy toward its southern neighbor. To say that Blanco hated the current US leaders was to euphemize his feeling.

The two had stayed in touch and met in Texas and Mexico City over the last couple of years. Malcolm discovered that, although Blanco was a firm capitalist, he was also a proud Mexican patriot and staunch believer in social justice. After they became closer, Jorge revealed yet another, more personal reason for his anti-US-government sentiments.

His sister-in-law, his two young nieces, and his brother, Juan, had been killed by US Border Patrol when entering California at the Tijuana border. The guards mistook Jorge's brother for a drug-lord fugitive, whose electronic photo on a police notice resembled Juan Blanco. Juan had been driving and had stopped appropriately at the border crossing. He handed the officers his family's passports and paid only minor attention to the guard staring at him.

"Sir, pull the car over to the side, please," said one officer quickly in an exaggerated Brooklyn accent, after he conferred with a superior on his mobile.

Juan, not understanding US accents well, and not being accustomed to the New Yorker's version, looked at the officer questioningly.

The officer handed Juan all of the passports but his and said, "We need to inspect this vehicle. Pull over up ahead."

Juan, thinking he had been cleared and that he had all of their documents, rolled up the window, drove through the uplifted gate and headed up the highway.

"Motherfucker! That criminal is trying to drive away," the officer yelled to a colleague in the next stall. "He's the guy we've been trying to find for months. I'm still holding his goddammed passport."

"Blow his tires out," said his buddy, drawing his revolver.

The first officer yelled again for the car to stop, as it picked up speed. Then he leveled his pistol and fired several shots at the back of the sedan.

Juan, assuming he had been waved on, had turned up his radio. The music buffered the shouts of the officers from outside, so the last sound Juan ever heard was his exploding gas tank, as his vehicle scattered in flaming pieces across the highway. None of the passengers survived.

It was not clear why Jorge, a private man, had shared this story with Malcolm, other than the sense that he recognized Malcolm's anger and frustration with his own country. It was clear to Malcolm, however, that Jorge could be a solid benefactor to the scheme he had designed. Jorge had indeed been intrigued by the APOCALYPSE plan and had all but committed to major financial backing.

"You need something else, Mr. Mohammed?" The waitress bent over him.

"No, just talkin' to myself."

"OK then, sugar," she said.

Malcolm shut his computer.

***

Weeks later, Malcolm and Jorge finished a round of golf at a renovated East Potomac Park city course, across the inlet from the new four-star InterContinental Hotel at DC's

Wharf. While the golf was reasonably priced, and fitting the mediocre games of the two men, the three-hundred-dollar-per-night rooms at the hotel were of a different class altogether.

"We can shower in my suite and then have dinner at the Kith/Kin restaurant off the lobby. I hear the New Orleans cuisine is spectacular," offered Jorge.

"Sounds like a plan. You know the chef is of West African and Caribbean stock," said Malcolm, as they loaded their bags into the trunk of his Acura.

"Excellent combination."

As they entered the lobby, having left the car with a bellman, Malcolm couldn't help gawking at the ultramodern, industrial-feel, blond wood interior. Nothing seemed to impede the sense of open space and light, even though the lobby offered its share of lounges, chairs, and writing surfaces, and the ceiling was punctuated with cascading gold chandeliers. The men ascended to Jorge's fifth-floor suite overlooking the harbor, its myriad houseboats, and a couple of the fairways they had just left. Using the two bathrooms, they showered, changed, and descended quickly.

As they approached the restaurant, Malcolm looked up at the ceiling and gently touched Jorge's elbow. "My friend, follow me out to the front terrace for a moment," he said, as he turned for the front door.

Once out in the fresh air, leaning over a railing and out of range of any obvious cameras, microphones, or diners, he turned to Jorge. "I think we need to eat at a less conspicuous and less trendy place."

"But this is my treat and the food is supposed to be extraordinary," protested Jorge.

"No doubt, but we don't want to be seen on any tape likely to be available to authorities later. You're registered under your real name, right?" Malcolm waited.

"Yes. You're probably right. As much as I think I'm well-thought-of by these turkeys, it is possible that they may actually do some homework after *el Proyecto* happens. They will naturally wonder how it was financed and who had motive."

"And if they see you dining with me, they could get suspicious," said Malcolm.

"Even though they're so arrogant, so incompetent, and biased against Mexicans that they're unlikely to connect me to my deceased family and uncover motive," Jorge sputtered.

"We've got my car, so I can drive us up to a spot north of Petworth, in the Brightwood section of town," said Malcolm.

"You know, *mi amigo*, now you've got me being cautious. I'll grab a Lyft and meet you there." Jorge laughed.

"Smart," said Malcolm.

Forty minutes later, the colleagues were in Moreland's Tavern on Fourteenth Street, a funky bar/restaurant half filled with gentrifying neighborhood patrons. With tequila and Coke in hand, they delved into the final arrangements.

"To be clear," said Jorge, "I'm paying five million dollars to have you put some threatening signs up around the Capitol offices, cause and/or take credit for a Metro train derailment, stage some virtual reality episodes around blowing up that damn border wall in the Southwest and some industrial buildings in the former Speaker's district, and actually cause a mini tsunami at the president's Royal Flush Resort, in South Carolina?"

"Right, but . . ." Malcolm couldn't finish his thought.

"And this is supposed to scare the president, ex-Speaker and the majority leader into passing legislation on environment, education, and other *mierda*?" Jorge looked skeptical. "Oh, and the explosions at their kids' schools? Right? Now, that will piss somebody off."

Malcolm sucked on an ice cube floating in Coke.

"I've been to Royal Flush, its course, and the golf course up the road. Yeah, that would be some destruction. There's close to a billion dollars invested in that little retreat. Probably take some lives of Latino help. Like to avoid that. But, yeah, that would shake the arrogant SOB if he couldn't figure out who did it, might even scare him. Also his darling little princess would get shook if her classroom was torched." It was Jorge's turn to suck on ice. Floating in tequila.

Malcolm fidgeted and chewed a piece of fried calamari.

"So, you and your partner orchestrate the destruction and 'fake news,' demand the legislative fix, and hope it comes quick—like emergency legislation. You go underground. You'll have to leave the country for a bit, 'cause even if you get legislation, they won't stop until they track you down."

"We thought we'd disappear in Mexico for a spell," Malcolm said, looking over the brim of his glass.

"Mexico? Not *la Capital?*" Jorge choked on a lime rind.

"Don't worry. We'd go to another spot first, then blend into the continental expat scene in some place like Puerto Vallarta. Safe, particularly given the outstanding intergovernmental relations now enjoyed between Washington and Mexico City." Malcolm smiled at his own sarcasm.

Jorge downed his tequila and signaled the waiter for another.

"I got to go to the restroom. You wear me out, *mi amigo, moreno,*" Jorge grumbled.

Malcolm thought he was away for a long time and began to wonder if he'd been stiffed.

Then Jorge returned.

"I stopped in the kitchen to find out what the specialty of this joint is, and ordered two steaks. You eat meat, don't you, Malcolm?"

"Yes. Are we done, brother man?" asked Malcolm.

"I had to think. It's a lot of money. I'll have to set up a trust, untraceable, of course. It's a risky plan that relies on perfect execution on the ground. But, on reflection, I think I get the sort of revenge I want. I don't know if you'll get your legislation, but I like the disruption, chaos, and angst I think your scheme will cause." He gave Malcolm a shrewd look. "Yes, *mi amigo*, we have a deal. Over to you. Let's eat."

CHAPTER 6

2028

"**W**ell, how did it go with Morton? Is he out of the picture?" Duke Wallace looked over his shot glass at Malcolm Mohammed, who was nursing an iced tea.

"Don't have to worry about our boy. He got the message that we can reach him anywhere and that he should forget our association. I'm sure he got the message," Malcolm said.

"You sure? I mean, we can't have . . ."

"I said, it's taken care of. Move on, Duke."

Duke knew not to press his colleague further. His tone and glare conveyed the extent of his annoyance.

"OK. Moving along . . . So, we still need to find somebody who can pull off the APOCALYPSE 'War of the Worlds' type of virtual-reality threat."

"Right, 'cause not all of this shit can be real. We don't have the resources. Or the time."

"Do you remember Kutar, Omar Kutar?" asked Duke.

"Can't say as I do," said Malcolm.

"Yeah, the smartest dude I knew at Duke. Never seemed to book it but aced every single exam. Graduated somewhere in top five in our whole fuckin' class." Duke's eyes sparkled with intensity.

"So? What's he got to do with . . .?"

"Goes back to India, sets up a business, sort of . . ." Duke paused.

"So, there were plenty of smart foreign dudes in the class," said Malcolm, trying to assess where Duke was headed.

"I've stayed in touch. Interested to see what he was up to. Remember that IRS scam and those fake 'help desk' schemes targeting seniors a couple of years back?"

"Yeah, didn't the police arrest a few dudes at some call center in Delhi?" Malcolm asked, hesitantly.

"Right. Omar wasn't arrested, but he mysteriously got richer. And I've seen some of the sophisticated game shit he's produced. This guy has legitimate virtual-reality talent. Also, he's just greedy and lends his talents to a cyber-scam here and there. Never gets caught," Duke said, matter-of-factly.

"So, I'm still not feelin' this," said Malcolm.

"Those scams where he escaped arrest? Those folks, elderly Westerners, believed the IRS had contacted them or that an Apple technical services group was fixing their computer. People were so sucked in that the money requested in supposed fees or in service costs would normally have alerted them as fraud, but Omar had captured them in an alternative reality, had them suspend disbelief, and almost reached into their pockets before they realized the hoax."

"Sounds like some of the pols we need to displace," said Malcolm, smiling.

"He can create an environment, a reality that sucks you in emotionally and physically, like a dream, or . . . some kind of suffocating virus. Omar writes script, finds actors, creates dialogue, and coordinates it all with computerized audiovisuals that put you in the center of some other space, a space he's created and controls. I'm telling you," Duke went on, "I've randomly run into victims of his shit who felt so vulnerable that it took them weeks to get over how they had been duped. Dude's a genius."

"So, you think this Arab, sorry, Indian could make a couple of our cataclysmic events happen in the news and cause enough confusion to have the Congress and White House believing they are actually happening?" Malcolm was edging toward acceptance.

"Have you ever been in a small movie theater with really high-definition video and surround sound audio where the content, dialogue, and scenery were so gripping that you felt like you were in the midst of the imaginary reality not just on the screen, but in the space surrounding you? You were actually in some other reality and not in a movie theater seat?"

"Yeah, I suppose. But these viewers won't be in a theater, they won't have on virtual reality goggles—they'll be at home, at the office, or on the street. They'll see a phone, or at most a TV screen." Malcolm Mohammed was still not convinced.

"I'm telling you, man, some of Omar's shit is so real, players need a few minutes after they remove their headsets to decompress, to come back to earth, so to speak." Duke sat back and let his picture sink in.

"Again, folks won't have on headsets," Malcolm persisted.

"Let's get him in for a demo. You should be convinced before we move on this," Duke said confidently.

"OK. Let's have him do the Midwest factory explosion and the collapse of the border wall. See how real he makes those." Malcolm rose to leave.

"No problem. I'll have him set it up in the next couple of weeks."

"Duke, hold up. Is this cat a believer? Is he a fervent jihadist?" Malcolm asked.

"To be honest, I don't think he's into politics or religion. He gets a kick out of using technology in innovative ways.

And he likes to spend. If the price is right, he'll be all in. The problem won't be technical. We need perfect salespeople for the network TV access. Once the video feed is on their equipment, Omar will control what goes over the air. With fake reporters, reality TV videos of the action, and a few fake eyewitness interviews, it will take a day for those not on the scene to know the story was bogus. But since the South Carolina incident is to be authentic, real first responders rushing to the devastation, the legislative demands streamed across the screen, lawmakers freaking out, the chaos will be palpable. People will be primed to believe Omar's stuff is real as well. They won't know what to focus on, and some administration and congressional staff will have to follow our demand prompts—because they won't know if more is to come—should they fail to introduce the legislation we want." Duke said out loud what had been spinning in his mind for days.

"I see the potential for a mix of real and cyber-manufactured event. But there are still loose ends. Divers to plant the explosives off the Carolina coast, border guards to detonate the wall, scripts for fake news people. By the way, what's the carrot for news and camera folks? No employed talent would take these assignments," said Malcolm.

"Right, but eager communications students, who think this is some kind of class assignment would love these 'opportunities.' I got another buddy that didn't make it through Navy training, who's a stone cynic and teaches media at some community college in Colorado. Let me figure out how to weave in a few of his students."

"Let's hope they're cool. Well, we've got calls to make and shit to do. I'm actually intrigued about your Omar cat," said Malcolm, as he finished his iced tea and stood up to leave.

A few weeks later, Malcolm received a cryptic text message from Duke:

Meeting O at Juilliard 65th off Broadway 3PM next Saturday. See you there.

"Julliard School of Music? Weird," thought Malcolm. He bought an Acela ticket and continued his digital recruitment of onscreen student talent for their schemes.

No matter how many times he exited Penn Station or caught a game at Madison Square Garden, Malcolm Mohammed felt chills inhaling the urban chaos and vitality of midtown Manhattan. It was only about one thirty Saturday afternoon, so he decided to walk up to Columbus Circle on Broadway, grabbing a sandwich on the way. When he entered Julliard's main lobby and saw Duke, Malcolm thought he recognized the casually dressed man of color with him.

"Nice to see you again, Mr. Mohammed," said Omar, offering his hand.

"It's Malcolm, and I can't say as I would have picked you out of a crowd of Duke alums, but hey . . ." laughed Malcolm.

As they chatted, while walking over to a studio space that Omar Kutar had somehow procured, Malcolm studied the man dressed in jeans, white business shirt, and Mexican-looking serape. His hair was jet black, skin a little lighter brown than Malcolm's, and his face was handsome with Caucasian features. Omar spoke with a slight British accent, but without the heavy tongue that Mohammad had come to associate with the few Indians he knew.

The door to the space he had obtained was secured with a combination panel-lock. Inside, the three men entered a small auditorium facing a large screen, with a fully equipped, ultramodern sound studio on the side of the auditorium seats. Omar motioned to his guests to sit in the front row, while he manned the controls in the studio.

"Can you hear me OK?" Omar asked through the sound system.

"Like in the movies," said Duke.

"By the way, Omar, how did we get access to this facility?" Malcolm asked of the blank screen.

"I donated it to the school." Omar chuckled.

"Cool," said Malcolm, raising his eyebrows and catching a smile on Duke's face.

"Yeah, I'm a big fan of supporting young musicians, particularly jazz. But we can talk about me tonight. We only have the space for a bit over an hour."

"So, I know you didn't have time to get a crew out to Wisconsin. What are we about to see?" Duke cued Omar to offer an introduction.

"Right. This scene is 'shot' at a lake town near Jaipur, so the architecture of the warehouses and on some of the commercial streets doesn't really approximate the Midwest of your country, but you should get an idea of the technology's capability. Sit back and imagine you're in your living room."

The screen panned a waterfront with three rectangular warehouse structures, parking lots surrounding the buildings, and a small shopping center set back from the lake at the far end of the site. A news reporter appeared superimposed on the setting, holding a mike in one hand and, with the other, clasping the unbuttoned lapels of a linen Nehru jacket against the wind. Malcolm and Duke had to sit up to watch the reporter's lips because his accent was not as polished as Omar's.

"This is Lake Michigan at, Muskegon, Michigan, at about eight this morning," recited the reporter.

The background dissolved, leaving the reporter in front of what appeared to be a live setting. The buildings were crumpled and scattered over the parking lot, clearly having been devastated by explosion. The steel frame of one of the three buildings remained, while the other two were heaps of construction material. A road previously visible at the end of the site near the shopping center was being drowned in a four-foot wall of water, fast approaching the reporter. As the remains of the farthest warehouse were engulfed in the whirlpool-like turbulence of water and debris, the sound of rushing water flooded the theater. The sight of the onrushing wall of brownish water was real enough to force Malcolm to rise in his seat, looking for an exit. Duke's knuckles turned white as he gripped the arm of his theater seat.

"This scene of destruction is now, twenty minutes after explosions leveled this waterfront industrial park. We have to get in the van and leave," yelled the reporter.

A camera showed the reporter hopping into a local news channel van. As the vehicle accelerated toward the back end of the industrial park, a wave of filthy lake water, whose brackish odor permeated the theater, overtook and overturned the van. One could hear screams for help and then the screen went dark.

Omar came back into the auditorium as the lights were slowly raised, and he saw his two guests pinned against the backs of their seats, like six-year-old children who've seen their first modern horror movie.

Malcolm wiped the sweat from his brow, and Duke loosened the underpants from his crotch.

"Sorry it's so unpolished, but it's the best we could do on short notice," said Omar.

"Hey, man. Don't apologize. I'm almost glad you didn't have time to create a polished version. That convinced and scared the shit out of me," said Malcolm.

"Dude, that reached me. You need to offer seat belts with your shit. Damn," whispered Duke.

"Right. So, the real test is writing a script, finding competent actors, accessing network electronics, and then producing a piece that keeps folks not at the site believing that what they saw was real for at least several hours, right?" Omar settled into a theater seat.

"Can you do that?" asked Malcolm, regaining some of his composure.

"With lead time and a few well-placed actors, absolutely. And, it sounds like you'll have prepped an edgy, audience, ready to believe. That helps. So, yeah, we can frighten a whole lot of folks," said Omar with confidence.

Duke looked at Malcolm, but didn't have to say a word.

"So, I guess we Blue Devils have to stick together," said Malcolm. Smiling, the three men shook hands.

"Our hour is up, so let me clean my stuff out of here. Oh, by the way, how about dinner and a little jazz tonight? I have tickets to a show a friend of mine—a legit dude—is doing at Jazz at Lincoln Center tonight," Omar said, as he reentered the control room. "That would give me a chance to write out a few details and work up some numbers for you."

"Sounds good. What time?" asked Duke.

"Say, eight? We can eat there and look over my offer before the show."

"Your friend wouldn't be Vijay Iyer, would he?" asked Malcolm.

"Yeah. Smart. You know his music?" Omar peeked out of the door of the control room.

"Yeah. He's a bit out there. Studied Monk, Trane, McCoy Tyner, Andrew Hill . . ."

"Among others. But yeah, his shit is not 'Light Jazz,' " Omar said with a smile.

Duke looked on with amusement at the two would-be musicologists.

That evening, Duke and Malcolm met in the downstairs office lobby of the old Dizzy's Club and took the elevator up to the penthouse club.

"What did you do this afternoon?" Duke asked Malcolm to fill time.

"I tried to catch up on some sleep, but I couldn't get the images of that warehouse destruction out of my head. That shit looked real as a heart attack."

"Told you the boy is good."

"I'm curious to see how much over the thirty thousand we have budgeted for the Midwest part of this he goes," said Malcolm.

"It will depend on how much he values putting a scare into the Congress. That, and whether or not he wants credit, which I doubt," Duke said with confidence.

Omar was sipping a drink and eating some hummus at a corner table, while some recorded Oscar Peterson piano riffs bounced back and forth between the ceiling speakers. Malcolm and Duke ordered a Coke and Scotch, respectively, as they passed the waitress on their way to the table.

"This is nice, Omar," said Duke.

"Wait 'til you hear the live sound. It's a great place to hear a trio or quartet," Omar said, leaning back.

The décor was cherry wood wall panels, picture widows opening out onto Columbus Circle, a bar and stools affixed to the back wall forming a crescent, and blue tableclothed mini dinner tables encircling the bandstand. The "house" closed the window drapes and lit pine-scented votive candles after sunset.

"So, Omar, what you got for us?" Malcolm got straight to the point after a sip of Coke.

"Right, well, you said you have two primary audiences—the president and House members. The president is a piece of cake, given his addiction to cable and his audio-video preference for learning. For the ex-Speaker, the fake follow-up news interviews will be more important, but still not too tough. Duke, you've been a friend, and this crew in Washington really does deserve to be shaken up and eventually replaced. So, this is partially a public service," Omar said.

"Don't need to go too far, my man. I understand that you are at heart a businessperson." Malcolm smiled.

"Roger that. A certain discreet type. One who doesn't publicly market his services." Omar smiled back. "Anyway, if you help with actor recruitment, I can do it for twenty-five thousand dollars." Omar took a long sip and looked both alumni in the eyes.

Malcolm and Duke looked at each other, as practiced.

"Twenty, and you got a deal," said Mohammed.

"Now, I thought I was the crook here," said Omar.

"We don't have big backers for this, and the Midwest piece is being coordinated with two other events requiring cash. Besides, how often do you get to one-up a reality TV star?" Duke said, straight-faced.

"Split the difference. Twenty-two five. That's tight, a gift, but . . ." said Omar

The other two again feigned consultation, and Malcolm said, "Done."

HARRY

CHAPTER 7

1996

"**Y**ou look like you been flyin' a good while, mister," said the cabbie carrying Harry Morton from Dulles Airport to his Northwest Washington home.

On tired autopilot, Harry responded, "It's been a long Asia trip. What's been happening here in DC?"

"Well, you know Marion Barry is back in as mayor. Always somethin' goin' on 'bout President Clinton, but he got renominated. Everybody's talkin' 'bout the upcoming OJ Simpson trial. Tornado hit over in Maryland and did a lot of damage. Of course, us sports nuts is all excited 'bout the coming Atlanta Olympics."

The driver was happy to rattle on, but he could see in the rearview mirror that his passenger had nodded off at the Clinton news.

Harry tipped him, grabbed his bags, and was relieved to exit. Halfway up the front steps, however, the sense of dread he'd experienced off and on during his return trip from Hong Kong rose up again, causing his stomach acid to boil. He wondered how much, if anything, about the collapse of his CTRED real estate deal had hit the *Washington Post*'s Business section. If other news had been plentiful over the last week, then it might have been designated a nonstory. If news was slow, though, some reporting might have appeared. It also depended on the extent of the leak provided by Bao Li, the quietly irate Hong Kong tycoon who was husband to the female CEO with whom Harry had had an affair. Did Mr. Bao fabricate a plausible business reason, or did he allude to the affair Harry had had with his wife, Wong Xi? Also, he might have only communicated with Harry's company, Masterfield Consulting, and not with the media, as he had threatened. Harry could be worried for no good reason, or he could have a lot of shuffling and explaining to do.

"Anybody home?" Harry called out as he opened his front door.

"Hello, Daddy. Glad you're finally back." Ten-year-old son Mark ran into his father's embrace.

"Welcome home, dear." Mary Morton placed a warm but not enthusiastic peck on Harry's cheek.

"What's been happening, young man?" Harry stayed on safe ground by focusing on Mark.

"School's been good, sports are great, friends are cool. Life's good. How was your trip, Daddy?" Mark's attention was already on some early evening TV preview of the coming pro football season. Normally, his parents would insist that he sit with them during the dinner hour, but he and Mary had already eaten.

"Go on, boy. Your father and I need to catch up," Mary said pleasantly.

"Do you want some warmed-up lasagna?" she asked Harry as they stood around the kitchen table.

"That would be great. I'll just drop my bag up in the bedroom," Harry said.

Both adults sipped a glass of Pinot Grigio, and Harry slowly worked through a bowl of microwaved Italian pasta.

"Well, you certainly had an eventful business trip." Each of Mary's words was coated in ice.

"Oh. You mean because the deal fell through?"

"Harry, that's the story in the *Post* business section, but I received a direct call from a Mr. Bao. Bao Li. I believe you know him."

"Yes, he's the contact with CTRED, the company that wanted to buy commercial space in DC." Harry wasn't going to give up any information unless forced to.

"Apparently, Harry, you had a Bill Clinton moment and got caught with a CTRED employee. That indiscretion is what killed the deal." Mary's left eyebrow arched and her blood boiled.

Harry breathed out. Bao had evidently not told her the real story. Obviously, he wanted to protect his wife, so he made up some affair that Harry was supposed to have had with an insignificant female employee at a nonexistent company. The story was true as allegory only. Harry had slept with the powerful CEO of SRI (Silk Road, Inc.), while successfully helping with its merger with a mainland clothing company, South China Apparel. She happened to be Bao Li's wife. When he discovered the affair, Bao invented a real estate deal to lure Harry back to Hong Kong, revealed that the deal was fabricated, and then informed him that the news of the deal's collapse and his indiscretion would be spread in strategic locations upon Harry's return to Washington.

"*The story Bao told Mary was damaging enough, but not as bad as the truth,*" thought Harry.

"I was stupid, and I can only apologize," Harry whispered.

"How could you be so dumb? Was our relationship so unfulfilling?" Mary was worked up, but could muster only so much indignation, given her own recent tryst.

"You know very well that we've been drifting apart for quite a while. But this had nothing to do with us. I am truly sorry," Harry said.

"You're right. You are truly sorry. Men and their zippers . . ."

"OK. So, can we move on?" Harry didn't want to compound the discussion by mentioning that his friend, George Birch, had overheard his wife, Mabel, whispering on the phone to Mary about her dalliance in NYC.

Harry knew that their affairs might be a sign that, indeed, their marriage was heading down a slippery slope. His immediate thought, though, was to persevere—try to work out a way to get back to a more harmonious relationship, work on it, etc. Under no circumstance did he want Mark to suffer, so he willed himself to recommit to the marriage and to move on.

By the time Harry left for work the next day, the atmosphere at home had become gray and cloudy. Driving into town, however, he smiled at the warm sunny streets, grinned even further at some of the silly jokes on Tom Joyner's "The Morning Show," and broke out laughing at some of the crazy scores reported on the US men's Olympic basketball team and the trial times of Michael Johnson in the two hundred meters. At his office, his old team from the successful Hong Kong SRI deal was glad to see him, and only his executive assistant, Hazel Marsh, mentioned the collapsed CTRED deal.

"Welcome back, boss. Sorry to see that the real estate deal fell through. Confusing article in the *Post*, but even you have to lose one now and then," Hazel said with a smile.

"Good to be back, Hazel. Thank you." Harry slipped by her desk heading toward his office.

He threw his jacket over a pedestal-style coat hanger and settled into his swivel chair. Looking out on K Street, a downtown power-office corridor, Harry felt like he had dodged a major bullet. Then Hazel buzzed him.

"Harry, Don would like to see you when you get a moment."

"I'll head over to his office in a sec."

He strode the two-minute walk through Masterfield's executive suite to the glass-enclosed inner sanctum of the CEO of its international division.

"Well, you don't look any the worse for wear. Welcome back, old man." Don Bartram stood and warmly gripped Harry's hand. "Let's sit by the coffee table. There are two fresh cups."

Once they were seated, the room's atmosphere went from sunny to cloudy to stormy.

"Harry, I'll get right to it, so that we can navigate through the issue."

"To what are you referring, Don?" Harry's stomach tightened.

"Well, we both know that the CTRED deal didn't fall apart because you were somehow unprepared. I got a call from a Mr. Bao, on behalf of CTRED. He said that you were indiscreet in getting involved with one of their employees and that killed the deal." Don took a sip from his cup of cream and sugar with some coffee flavor.

Putting down his mug of black coffee, Harry thought for a moment.

"That's all he said?" Harry asked.

"Basically. That was enough."

"Yes. I understand. Don, that's not exactly what happened, but close enough. I fucked up."

They looked at each other.

"It looks like Bao wants to keep this a story about professional screwups or differences, given what he told the press. So, there's no immediate harm. And, because they asked for your involvement in an area that's not our sweet spot, they'd be ill-advised to drag this out. Make some big deal of it. Nevertheless—" Don was cut off.

"So, what are you really saying, old buddy?" Harry was tense.

"I think we should move your retirement contract up a few months. We'll pay you till the end, but, thinking purely of the company's interest, it would be best if you announced you've decided to further curtail your schedule and leave the company. Travel's no longer fun, the SRI deal was a hallmark, nothing left to prove or accomplish, etc. If it had been real, the CTRED deal would have been nice, but not all that significant. Your "body of work," as they say, is outstanding. Nobody is going to think more of it at this point."

"Wow. Not sure I saw that coming. But, on reflection, thinking from the company's perspective, it makes sense. Why risk any more exposure?" Harry said, matter-of-factly.

"If this were the middle of your phenomenal career, the risk would be totally worth it, but . . ." Don trailed off.

"I got you. Well, let me come in a few more days so that it looks like I'm making a decision, if you really want to allow that illusion," said Harry.

"Perfect. Sorry, old man. But you see the picture and you're a pro," said Don, extending his hand.

Harry gathered himself, smiled, and went back to his office to pretend to work.

"What was that about?" asked a curious Hazel Marsh.

"Nothing much. He just wanted to brief me on possible next assignments, but I need to spend a few days catching up on paperwork. The usual." Harry smiled and swaggered convincingly.

The rest of the work week was uneventful, with several catch-up meetings around the division. Monday morning, Harry told Hazel that the trips had finally taken their toll and that he really needed to step back for a while. He let her think that family demands were driving his decision. He then drafted a formal retirement announcement suggesting that travel had finally caught up to him, that he was going to take a real work break and spend more time with his family before taking on a slimmer, domestically focused, independent portfolio. He framed the announcement as a second retirement because he had, in fact, semi-retired when he sold his company to Masterfield but had agreed to stay on and manage some contracts for a couple of additional years with the parent company.

At Masterfield, only Don Bartram knew the real reason for his early resignation. After a few months, the DC business community pretty much forgot about the one-time superstar. Those who did think about him, remembered Harry's long international career, the tales of astonishing deals he had concluded, the prominent local civic contributions.

At home, however, memories were not so generous, nor skies so blue.

***

"Well, of course, I'm sorry that Masterfield has decided to part ways. I can't say, however, that I'm surprised. Nor can you be, really. And don't look for sympathy here," said Mary. She and Harry were sitting on their backyard deck, so that Mark would not be able to hear them.

"I don't expect sympathy, but remember, I didn't jump up and down and get hysterical when you had that London affair," replied Harry, sipping a Scotch.

Mary blinked several times, trying to determine when Harry had found out about her liaison with her old friend Max Dupree in Europe.

"Who's getting hysterical? I just think what you did was stupid. Did you even have any feeling for the woman?" Mary stayed on the offensive.

Harry ignored the question but concurred, "It was stupid."

Robins, sparrows, and an occasional cardinal provided the soundtrack for their early-evening confrontation. Harry and Mary gazed alternatively at the fall foliage and each other.

"Harry, you were winding down anyway. And, given your accomplishments, you should be able to consult, teach, write, whatever. I mean, the public knowledge of why the deal fell through is so benign. And you're hardly the only powerful business guy who has failed to consummate a deal with the Chinese these days." Mary chuckled into her glass.

"True, but how many have been so-called 'high profile' African Americans? Sure, I can bounce back professionally, but one always wants to negotiate from total strength. Now, what do I tell Mark?"

"The boy's not even in high school yet, so I don't think you really have to say much of anything, other than you're changing jobs. Plus, we've saved for Mark, so we don't absolutely need the same level of income," said Mary.

"Lord, you're so practical sometimes. Thank you."

"Harry, don't thank me. I think our relationship is in trouble, and I'm very unclear what to do to work it out. You and I both know that we've been drifting apart emotionally for a while."

Their gazes reflected understanding, tolerance, even empathy, but a warmth considerably shy of love. Harry reached out and grasped Mary's hand, and they smiled at one another. But neither accomplished, talented, emotionally intelligent parent felt comfortable forecasting their future as a couple.

"Are you guys coming in to dinner?" Mark's call from the kitchen door broke the spell.

Harry easily found consulting contracts with troubled business cultures, merging firms, or downsizing businesses, and he followed up on a long-standing invitation to teach about global business cultures at Georgetown's business school. To his surprise and relief, Bao Li had had to keep his story about the collapse of the CTRED deal more innocuous than he had threatened because of the damage any sordid specifics might do to his wife's status. Thus, only Don Bartram and Mary Morton had been given the damaging information about an affair. Even they were not told with whom Harry had been so indiscreet, so there was no public stigma associated with Harry's retirement from Masterfield.

At first, ten-year-old Mark Morton didn't notice any difference in his parents' behavior after his father began working solely out of his home office. One change was that he and his father spent more time together in the late afternoons. They attended ballgames with Mark's friends or by themselves on weekends. Sunday church service or trips to various Smithsonian museums were with his mother. The family occasionally ate Chinese or Mexican food at restaurants in downtown Silver Spring, usually after a weekend movie. If Mark had an important game or was in a play at school, both senior Mortons would attend. Over the year, however, he felt that his parents began to spend more time with him individually and that they did fewer things together, as a family.

Mark couldn't articulate the difference he felt at the dinner table, other than that meals seemed to go faster, and that his parents appeared to escape more quickly to different parts of the house when the dishes were done. At first, none of these changes seemed to have any noticeable effect on the youngster. Slowly, however, Mark lost interest in some of his school subjects, and he became less intense about competing in sports.

Mary focused on her labor-market studies at Brookings Institution but began to take more weekend trips by herself to New York. She had girlfriends with whom she loved to attend theater, go to galleries, and simply hang out. Earlier in their relationship, she and Harry would have gotten a babysitter and left Mark, or made the trip a family affair. But when she was in DC, Mary still loved spending time with her son and fully enjoyed her work. Her anger toward Harry had morphed into disinterest.

The Mortons drifted in place for a little more than two years after Harry left Masterfield. When Mark finished sixth grade in 1998, Mary and Harry agreed that they would separate. Harry rented an apartment in the Shaw neighborhood, closer to the revitalizing center of town, but near enough that he could easily maintain a frequent visiting schedule with Mark. The separation was what counselors or columnists would describe as "amicable."

For young Mark, however, the impact was dramatic. It was as if he recognized or appreciated for the first time how comfortable and supportive his home environment had been, even with traveling professional parents. He suddenly missed weekend visits to Philadelphia or New York that the family had not taken for many years. Summer car trips down South or out West that they hadn't taken since he was five years old now seemed meaningful. The knowledge that at least half of his classmates were in single-parent households or adjusting to a new step-parent was of no solace to Mark.

Mark was polite and outwardly thoughtful with his parents, but he began to feel that he was alone in the world in a way he had never before contemplated. With his parents wrapped up in their careers, he felt that as long as he continued to get very good grades, no one really cared what was happening with him—inside.

In seventh grade, Mark was enrolled in an elite DC private school, where he had to make further emotional adjustment to more privileged kids from all over the region. He felt like he had lost close contact with his father and now was losing contact with his best friends. The isolated youngster turned inward and became more serious about his studies, as well as about current events and economic issues that he had been exposed to through his mother's profession.

Harry and Mary were cordial, but by the time Mark entered his last semester and prepared to leave for Harvard, the family ties were thin. Mark loved his mother and enjoyed talking politics with her—Anthony William's mayoral administration, President Clinton's impeachment, the 9/11 attacks, and the invasion in Iraq. They were sort of buddies, though Mary waited until late in Mark's senior year to share information about her growing relationship with an old flame from London, who'd also taken an apartment in New York.

Mark felt less close to his father, although they spent as much time together—at games, at meals, hanging out at Harry's apartment—as any father and son in a similar situation. Mark simply felt his father didn't care as much as he should. Nothing specific, but he grew to blame his father for the dissolution of the family. Then, one week during 2004, Mark's senior year, before he got his driver's permit, his relationship with Harry turned ugly.

One Saturday morning, Mary drove Mark over to her friend Viola Gregory's because Mark was spending the weekend with her son. Roger was a classmate and one of Mark's few close friends. Mary dropped Mark off in front of the Gregorys' and pulled out from the curb. As she looked back to see that Mark had gained their porch and Roger had come to the front door, she noticed a sports car in their driveway that resembled Harry's. Mary wondered about it for a moment, dismissed it as coincidental and drove off.

"Good morning, Mrs. Gregory. It's nice . . ." Mark stopped mid-sentence, for through the door to the kitchen, Mark saw his father approaching with a glass of orange juice.

"Hello, Mark. Well, you boys have a great weekend," Harry said, awkwardly. He deposited the glass, gave Viola a peck on the cheek and left.

Mark made small talk with Roger and his single mother until the boys were alone in the Gregory's TV room/den.

"What the hell was my father doing here, dude?"

"What do you think? He and Mom have been seeing each other for a few weeks. They're both single adults, you know." Roger was more embarrassed that his friend didn't know than that the two parents were having a relationship.

"I know, but your mom is a friend of my mom's and you'd think he would find some other . . . I don't know, it just feels strange to me," said Mark. "And somehow wrong." After a minute, he continued, "But you're right; I guess they are free consenting adults."

"Let's hit the gym. Exercise will do you good," Roger urged.

When Mark was dropped off at home on Sunday night, Mary said something about having seen Harry's car, but Mark didn't admit that he'd seen him with Viola.

During the week, Harry called Viola at her office. "Well, that was awkward Saturday morning . . ."

"Tell me about it. I know I was supposed to have said something to Mary—not ask for permission, but sort of check to see that she was comfortable about it. I guess I didn't think there was any urgency about it; it's still early days. I just haven't gotten around to it. My fault," said Viola.

"No one's fault. I'm sure after a few bruised moments, she'll be OK. As you say, it's not like we have reached the serious stage. I guess I'll see next weekend when I pick up Mark." Harry sighed and hung up.

The next weekend, Harry appeared uncharacteristically nervous when he arrived to pick up Mark. Before Harry and Mark could leave, Mary asked him point blank if he had been at Viola's the previous weekend. Silence filled the room like a combustible gas.

"I don't see how that's any of your business. In case you forgot, we are no longer married," Harry said without anger, but defensively.

"It is my business, if you are sleeping with my friend and carrying on an affair in front of our son." Hands on hips, Mary prepared for battle.

"I don't tell you who to see, who you should associate with." Harry's voice rose.

"I have sense enough to be discreet, and I think of others' feelings," Mary yelled back.

Mark stood uncomfortably near his parents. He had never heard them confront each other with such vehemence.

"Well, aren't you just the perfect little Miss Goody Two Shoes? You know what, you're just a selfish bitch—" Harry stopped as Mary stepped toward him, yelling through tears.

"I would never be so thoughtless as you. It's like what happened in Hong Kong. You just can't control your zipper, can you?" Mary practically spat venom in Harry's face.

In a rage, Harry raised his right hand. But, before he could strike, Mark stepped between them and pushed his father backward. Harry dropped his hands to his side and backed further way.

Angered, dismayed and deflated, Harry looked at his feet, then Mark, and finally Mary. "I'm sorry. I'm sorry," he said, just above a whisper.

"Dad, you should go," said Mark in muzzled anger.

As Harry left his old house for the last time, Mark embraced his shaking mother.

Harry attended Mark's high school graduation but received a cool reception when he congratulated his son. He left after the ceremony feeling that he'd been dismissed from both Mary and Mark's lives.

After Mark moved away to college, Mary announced that she was making arrangements to move to New York. Harry told himself that he, too, needed a change of scenery. He suppressed his anger and sense of loss, telling himself that these were "normal" feelings for a father to have after a divorce and separation from a child. He explored places where he could immerse himself in a different, more exotic environment. Not a total cultural departure from DC, yet truly different. On reflection, he recalled the excitement he'd enjoyed while working on Asian assignments. He suspected, however, that moving to Japan, China, Singapore, or India would mean giving up his US anchor and might eventually create too drastic a sense of isolation. Maybe, he thought, a move to San Francisco, LA, or Seattle would provide the sort of change he needed. Then, after several months of discussion and contemplation, Harry decided to move his consulting practice to Honolulu and to accept an invitation to teach at the University of Hawaii's East-West Center.

CHAPTER 8

2018

Harry was excited to see that the late afternoon waves off Sandy Beach were growing in size. At sixty-eight, he was still a powerfully built and athletically agile man, and he loved the ocean. Harry respected the power of the Pacific and in the years since he had "retired" to Oahu, he had spent countless hours swimming, wading, floating in, and simply staring at the innumerable shades of blue, green, and white that she could offer. The majesty of her thunderous tides, the geometry of wave formation and dissolution, and the pungent aroma of freshly discarded seaweed on morning beaches never grew old for Harry.

But, as he mounted his boogie board to catch a half-hour's worth of medium-sized breakers, Harry wasn't thinking about the cacophonous sound of cascading waves or the beauty of towering curled arcs of blue-green tunnels. He was thinking about the exhilaration of being pushed along the crest of the next wave clinging to a flat bullet of fiberglass at what felt like fifty miles per hour. Each year, he had been pushing himself a bit further out beyond the shore, toward the launching area of the more experienced surfers. The young men and women who sat atop their boards waiting for their next ride joked with him that he might as well learn to surf, rather than continue to lie flat on his boogie board. But Harry had no intention of trying these waters while standing up. While he was an excellent swimmer, Harry knew that the beating one's body could take when knocked off a rocketing surfboard and the quarts of seawater one could swallow before surfacing were more than he could safely absorb. And, excellent shape or not, he was still not a young man. No, his current thirty- to sixty-second rides down ten- to fifteen-foot waves were enough of a challenge and immensely rewarding.

"Here's one for you, 'old school'!" shouted one of the teenagers as he paddled by Harry and mounted his surfboard.

Harry turned into the path of a small mountain of aqua-colored foam, grasped the front of his board, checked over his shoulder, tightened his forearms to gain better control and waited for the initial surge that thrust him forward.

"This is a beauty," Harry sang to himself as he catapulted across the grain of the wave.

After several seconds heading laterally to the shore, the wave began to subside, so Harry pulled up on the left tip of his board to steer it into a turn. In an instant, a freight train-like wall of water heading directly at Harry overturned his board, pummeled him deep below the surface and spun his body around so that he lost all sense of spatial orientation. He regained some control and saw that the surface was at least twenty feet above him and that the wave was still pounding the sea's surface. With strong kicks and crawl strokes, he was able to surface after ingesting enough salt water to fill a small bathtub. Bobbing on the surface, Harry looked for his board, which had been torn from his ankle lash. It was hard to see beyond the new set of cascading waves, and Harry could not locate surfers, boards or shoreline. The confluence of waves that had knocked him off his board also pushed him into a current that propelled him away from the shore.

After about two minutes, Harry located the beach. "OK," he thought, "I can take my time and swim in."

Harry began making his way to shore, alternating between crawl and breast stroke, interspersed with periods of treading water. While his strength was diminished, Harry felt that he that could easily make it to the line of figures bobbing on the surface, less than fifty yards in front of him. He achieved a patch of relatively calm sea and stopped to tread water to recover his leg strength. He thought he could make out voices, but they weren't from the surfers still far off in front. Then he turned back toward the open ocean and thought he saw a boat, a canoe. Before he could focus, or wave, or call, he caught sight of something on the surface that sent paralyzing flashes of fear greater than any wave had caused. Harry saw a large black triangle cutting through the water ahead of a large wave. Both were heading in his direction.

Acting on reflex, Harry took a deep breath, plunged under the surface and stared in the direction of the big fish with an extra wide head swimming right at him. He started screaming underwater and prepared to hit the nose of the animal as it approached and opened its jaws to reveal a cavity that looked as big as Harry's torso. They collided and Harry felt like he was being run over by a small truck from the waist down, and twisted by a tornado from the belly up. The remaining air forced itself out of Harry's lungs, producing a crimson stream of bubbles, and then Harry's life went black.

"You'll be good, now," Harry thought he heard from above.

Can this be the afterlife? he wondered.

"Can you hear me?" asked a diminutive Brown man leaning over Harry.

"I can, but where am I?" Harry tried to sit up, but the large canoe on whose bottom he lay rolled to the right suddenly, and he fell back down.

"Just take it easy and relax. We're taking you back into shore, but the sea is a little rough," said the man.

Harry held onto the gunnel and lifted himself into an upright position. He looked along the length of a twelve-foot *ho'o* carved out of an island palm. There were three other men, all closer to Harry's size, in the boat. They were paddling in unison, as the craft perfectly rode each successive swell into the beach.

"What's your name?" asked the pilot, never taking his eyes off of the surf.

"I'm Harry Morton."

"Ah. The new fellow at the East-West Center." The silver-haired pilot offered a quick smile.

"Have we met? How do you know . . .?"

"It's a long story, Mr. Morton. Some other time. I'm Kiki Kahuku, by the way. And, this is my son, Mano, our friends Luau Jones and Danny Aka. Luckily for you we were coming back from an afternoon outing when we spotted you getting bounced by those converging waves. I thought nothing of it, but Mano spotted the scalloped hammerhead shark when we were coming in and thought we ought to wait to see where you surfaced. We must have gotten to you and knocked the shark away before he decided what to do with you, if anything. Anyway, we got you into the boat about five minutes ago and you've been resting ever since. Luckily, you only have a few cuts, but nothing deep or serious."

"Needless to say, I'm deeply indebted to all of you. How can I pay you back?" Harry was fully conscious and beginning to recover, as they got within twenty yards of the beach.

"Well, I'm also at the university, and am interested in some of your business collaboration theories. So, maybe we could grab lunch sometime?" said Kiki.

"My pleasure. Absolutely."

"In the meantime, you might take a lesson or two on reading the waves if you're going to board so far out," Luau Jones offered with a smile.

"Great advice. I will." Harry stuck his hand out to the younger man, who resembled the chiseled Samoan linebackers recruited from the islands by West Coast colleges.

After the *ho'o* navigated the shore-breaking waves and came to a halt on the beach near one of the red flags signaling dangerous current, Harry parted from his new acquaintances, didn't bother looking for his board, and headed up the small dune to the parking lot. As he neared his car, someone tapped him on the shoulder. It was Mano, standing behind him, extending a hand with Harry's board.

"This washed up only a few yards up the beach. You might want to preserve it for the bite mark—you don't see ten- to twelve-foot hammerheads off this part of the island often. That baby could have been two hundred pounds or more." The youngster was more in awe of the animal than of Harry's escape. With a friendly smile, Mano Kahuku jogged back toward the beach.

Thus began Harry's relationship with one of the most significant family guardians of Hawaiian people and culture in the state.

On his way back home, up the coast highway, up the cliffs toward Hanauma Bay, Harry noticed that the tiny parking lot for the "blow hole" overlook was empty. He turned in, killed the engine, got out of his car and sat, legs dangling over the stone wall, absorbing dusk over the Pacific.

Harry smiled because the day's escape had, in no insignificant way, been exhilarating. He thought about how privileged he was to escape his throttling existence in Washington, a depressingly lonely life in a city whose love had turned sour, and to be offered the chance to begin again on this idyllic island. Harry's age, his diminished reflexes, clearly prevented him from responding to physical challenges as effectively as even ten years earlier. But these islands offered him a chance to experience adventure and excitement that he could still safely appreciate.

He became more pensive. *Can I afford to simply drift wherever this island life leads me? Or will that lead to another type of isolation if I don't figure out where to steer?*

Harry again looked out at the Pacific, fluffy clouds accenting azure sky and frothy whitecaps skipping across aquamarine waters. *I think I have time to figure that one out.*

He couldn't hold back the smile that spread across his face.

***

More than half a year later, they met after a lecture Kiki Kahuku gave at the East-West Center on the pertinence of the "Hawaiian Renaissance" to Pacific trade, as China, Japan, India, and other South Asian economies continued to expand and play new roles on the world economic stage.

"Kiki, that was a compelling case for all nations to recommit to values of collaboration with people, as well as with nature," Harry said, as they descended the marble steps and headed for a small faculty parking lot to retrieve Kiki's Toyota Corolla.

"So, today you were speaking as board member of the Kamehameha Schools, founder of the Polynesian Voyager Society, cofounder of that Native Hawaiian Health Center, major Hawaiian Airlines investor or part-time UH lecturer?" Harry said, smiling.

"I see you have been doing a bit of research. No, I'm now just an interested activist on behalf of the Hawaiian people, an average Joe. Laila and I stay pretty much close to home now, compared to our younger days."

After Harry had climbed into the passenger seat, Kiki turned to him. "I want to show you a part of the island I don't think you yet know," he said, with one of his rare smiles.

Kiki headed south on University Avenue and then west on Highway H-1, the island's major shoreline road from Pearl

Harbor through Honolulu and to the Kailua area. He exited after the airport, headed toward the ocean along Farrington Highway to Wakaka Beach.

"Well, you're right," said Harry. "I've not gotten off the main road over here, on the leeward side, and come down to the beach. It's beautiful." He inhaled fragrant plumeria and took in extensive stretches of pristine sand beaches.

"Just hold your horses, cowboy. We're not there yet," cautioned Kiki.

They pulled off the road before a grove of low-growing ribbon ferns and white hibiscus, got out and walked along a grassy path, heading toward the beach. The path took a right turn, back up toward the road and Harry stopped in his tracks.

"Wow. Where did all this litter . . .? These tents look like Waimanalo, out beyond Sandy Beach, back beyond Diamond Head," Harry whispered. He gingerly stepped around bottles, cans, waste paper, and patches of crab grass. In bushes set back from the shore, he could see a few tents, clothes hung from lines between wind-blown seven-foot trees, with torn T-shirts and ripped plastic sandals scattered about the area between tents.

"Welcome to the Wai'anae Coast. You haven't seen the town yet, but this is the heaviest concentration of Oahu's collateral damage—Native Hawaiians, Pacific Islanders, and Filipinos. I'm sure you can identify similar communities on the mainland. This land, from the beaches, through the town, up into the once fertile hillsides, used to be totally self-sustaining. Then the White sugar plantation owners 'bought' community property and farmed it, sucked it dry of its nutrients and grew fabulously wealthy."

"The damage you speak of . . ." Harry interrupted.

"Yes, I'm talking about the homelessness here on the beach, the rampant alcoholism, the horrible childhood obesity, the unforgivable domestic violence . . . it all sets back any strides toward progress over here," Kiki said.

"Kiki, why are you showing me this?" Harry asked as they returned to the car.

"Hold on, my friend. *E kali'oe.* It will be revealed soon," said Kiki, smiling again.

They drove back down the highway, toward Pearl Harbor, and turned left at Pokui Bay Beach Park up into the Lualualei Homestead. The modest housing units enjoyed little landscaping, paving, or any of the exotic aesthetics mainlanders associate with Hawaii. Kiki drove slowly in a loop and parked at a Starbucks before Leihoku Streett rejoined the highway.

"Coffee, Harry?"

"No thanks, Kiki, I'll just sit, if you want to get a cup."

"I'll be right back," Kiki said as he stepped toward the coffee shop.

Boys and girls were playing in dusty streets, while teenagers milled around in front of a run-down restaurant swaying slowly to some Caribbean/Hawaiian pop music pounding the speakers of a 1970 vintage Chevrolet convertible. Harry closed his eyes, inhaled deeply, and imagined he was parked near a sandy beach near Ocho Rios, Jamaica. The salty breeze, crashing waves, floral-scented air, and musical beat seemed magnificently global. The street banter, however, was not Calypso but a form of Hawaiian pidgin.

"You've not been to Leihoku Street before, yet I bet you have been here many times," said Kiki, stepping onto the Toyota with his latte.

"If you mean that I've been to poor beachfront tropical communities, then yes. I have been to similar places. Of course, history, culture, habits, education, and so on make each community different. But you know that, Kiki." Harry leaned into his host. "I'm still wondering why I'm here."

"I've attended several of your sessions over the past few years, and have been impressed with your understanding of culture. Yes, you sometimes emphasize hard-core, almost

Machiavellian negotiation techniques, Harry. But the core of your message is always about justice. You tell your students that no deal is safe if participants feel cheated. *He mea pono keia?* 'Is it beneficial for all?' As we would ask," Kiki said.

"Of course, I'm addressing business, and sometimes national political negotiations—"

"Clearly, Harry. But are not some of the principles the same for interpersonal or institutional or group interactions?" Kiki slowly placed the vehicle in gear.

"As you very well know, it depends."

"Ah, yes. This is the nub of trouble in paradise. It all depends on whose perspective one takes. You know that while the kingdom was still strong, even after we were 'discovered' by Captain Cook but before annexation, Hawaiian culture and the local economy provided a wonderful lifestyle for our people," continued a professorial Kiki. "Although my wife would say that it wasn't so wonderful post-domination of the sugar and pineapple barons, or the destruction of sea-focused religions by the Christian missionaries."

"Anyway," he continued, "by the early twentieth century, haole visitors had imported Asian laborers and put all non-Whites to work building their empire and destroying our island way of life. Like your Native Americans on the mainland, language and customs were denigrated, schools focused on Christian values as opposed to appropriate tools of the intellect, and land was privatized. Asians, particularly Japanese, were able to maintain cultural discipline and adapt to Western economic requirements, and, until the huge World War II setback, began to create a successful political and business class. Filipinos and Chinese seem to have taken longer." Kiki paused.

"So," Harry inserted, "I know you are leading up to the woeful state of twentieth-century Hawaiian public education, but at least here you don't have to recover from the destruction of family that we had with mainland slavery."

"You know, Harry, if you look at achievement scores and economic well-being, I don't think the treatment of Hawaiians since annexation and the lingering effects on family have left Hawaiians any better off than the effects of slavery has left its descendants. That's the perspective I see now," said Kiki. Then he added: "And one of the few outlets youngsters continued to find was surfing. But do you realize that, initially, haoles didn't permit Hawaiians to compete in contests off of our own beaches? Look at pictures of early surf contests and you won't see dark-skinned competitors. Our own beaches!"

With a smile, Harry said, "So, you're telling me that our paradise of 'sun and fun,' our racial harmony, the symphony of Pan-Asian collaboration, even the extensive intermarrying we see all around us is not reality?" Before Kiki could answer, Harry continued, "Don't worry. I've seen signs that all's not what appears in the tourist brochures." Harry tapped the knee of his friend. "I know, for example, that if you get into and graduate from Punahou, or Iolani, you are likely headed for an economically comfortable life. From regular island schools, not so much."

"You're a keen observer, Harry. We are all here on this earth but a speck of time, but when generations of a once-independent people are subjected to economic and social deprivation in their own land, the steam of resentment builds. We don't know when the volcanoes on Kauai or Hawaii will blow, but we know they will. The same here, my friend." He paused to look over at Harry. "The 'Hawaiian Renaissance' you've heard about means that our language and culture are no longer forbidden in schools. And even though some Hawaiians out here lack some of the habits needed to succeed in school and later at work, *ke au hou keia*—it's a new era. Things will change on the islands."

"OK. I see your point, in general. Yes, there are similar themes in the discussions at the Center. And I am glad you brought me over here, but I sense you think I can somehow do something to bring about change."

"I think, Harry, that you are a leader—that although you have no formal title as such, your influence among participants, faculty, and administrators at the East-West Center is undeniable and will continue to grow. I merely ask that you keep an open mind about roles that may enable you to help with our move toward justice in the tropics." Kiki pulled up to a parking space on campus.

"I am, indeed, flattered Kiki. But, really, I'm just an adjunct professor, a semiretired businessman. You have much more powerful and effective allies in Congress." Harry offered a warm smile.

"A thought we have not overlooked. But, as for you, my friend, *E ho 'omanawanui.* Give yourself time. I have a feeling you will be called upon to be a leader again." Kiki returned the smile.

***

Over the next few years, Harry settled into a relaxing semiretirement lifestyle. His routines and discipline permitted him to maintain a physique, demeanor, and temperament that suggested to most that he was ten years younger. Although, recently, he'd noticed that his memory and energy were informing him that he was, indeed, getting older. Several years' lecturing at the University of Hawaii's East-West Center, occasional international consultancies, and a relaxed island social life had all but erased memories of Harry's previous life as a successful and very rich "man about town" in Washington, DC.

Harry often sat on the veranda of his three-story condo in Oahu's Diamond Head district overlooking a fairly calm Pacific Ocean. Cumulus clouds, bending palms, a flock of pelicans, and some windsurfing terns might be the only interruptions to the peaceful meeting of robin's-egg sky and turquoise sea. So began his comfortable morning ritual. He'd walk a couple of miles along the Pacific and around Diamond Head Park, swim several laps in his pool, take a brisk shower, meditate for half an hour, and enjoy a breakfast of papaya and blueberries, toast and guava jam, and granola in yogurt. He'd finish his routine by reading the *New York Times* and Hong Kong's *South China Morning Post* on his laptop between sips of dark-roasted Hawaiian coffee, flavored with macadamia nuts.

The pelicans and terns might be joined by albatrosses, able to complete perfect twenty-five-yard aerial ovals, and execute swooping dives toward the sea.

Harry occasionally reflected on Kiki's comments and questioned whether he would ever again personally engage the visceral justice issues confronting poor communities. Or, did retirement really mean his contributions would remain intellectual queries offered from a comfortable and safe Hawaiian academic perch?

When not teaching, participating in a conference, or working on a consulting deadline, Harry would pour another cup of coffee, stretch his legs up over the balcony railing and think about the adrenaline-generating close calls with shady characters he'd had in his international career. Images of his previously adopted home—Washington, DC—sometimes also flickered across his mind's eye.

Reconnecting with his son, Mark, was about the only draw Harry could envision getting him back to DC. Hawaii offered intellectual stimulus through the university, plenty of cultural and entertainment activities, more business travel opportunities than he chose to accept, and as active a social life as a semiretired single guy could absorb. He had dear friends from his previous consulting life and new colleagues from his East-West Center involvement. He often had coffee with an ethnically mixed group of retired acquaintances, former business, political, and academic men.

He also regularly played golf with a group of retired African American military buddies. Rounds occasionally included a vacationing President Obama. So, as he often said to mainland or Asian visitors, "What's not to like?"

Harry only heard about Mark through irregular contact with his mother, and, at that moment, he had no idea of his career goals or any significant details about Mark's life. When Mark got married, Harry received a last-minute wedding invitation, sent through the US mail. Unfortunately, he was on assignment in Hunan Province, China. So, by the time he opened the invitation, the event had already happened. Losing his wife after the China affair had been difficult, although they had been growing apart for some time. He never seriously entertained the idea of remarriage once he moved to Hawaii. But, having his son continue to slip from his life was perpetually painful.

ALAKA'I

CHAPTER 9

2018

Alaka'i Liu sat crossed-legged on his hard foam mattress, looking out at the rain sprinkling onto the fern and hibiscus leaves after escaping the broad palm branches that dotted the hill behind the house. He had only been home a week from Caltech and was already feeling hemmed in. He loved his parents but was anxious to explore options for his next step in life. He occupied that space in which a young person is so much more mature than a new high school graduate, yet not experienced enough in the ways of the real world to be sure about choosing a career. His adaptation to the world of work would prove more extended than would have been forecast by his first three years of college. For all of his brilliance, Al proved extremely undisciplined and only mildly dedicated to important tasks, such as graduation. While he stayed at school for four years, he never successfully completed his credit requirements.

Summer jobs with firms in Honolulu and companies in Silicon Valley had taught Alaka'i that he was quite independent, didn't adjust easily to office protocols, learned quickly through his own experimentation, and was far more talented than most older graduate engineering students.

As a child, he'd been something of a mathematical prodigy. Along the way, Al had also indulged his curiosity and filled his brain with bits of knowledge from innumerable fields—natural sciences, computer science, physics, mathematics, US and Asian history, political theory, natural history, and environmental science. However, he was far more interested in satisfying his curiosity than complying with others' reporting requirements.

College had permitted Al to explore his own ethnicity, to the degree that he understood his background. He had been adopted by the Lius when he was just a baby, in Hong Kong, and all he knew about his birth parentage was that one parent was of mixed Caucasian and Han descent, the other mixed African, possibly Native American, and some Caucasian. The Lius had given him the name Alaka'i, which is Hawaiian for "leader." At Caltech, he had gone out of his way to make friends with African Americans, Chinese and Japanese Americans, Pacific Islanders and European Americans, as well as foreign students from every continent. He was fascinated by students with what he considered exotic histories.

With some classmates, he spent his free time playing and dissecting computer games; with others, he spent late nights discussing family traditions, religious and cultural values, individual aspirations, and perceived barriers. He drew few conclusions other than that group categorizations were risky, because the kids he met brought so many varied personal experiences, personalities, and tendencies to college. Ethnic backgrounds, even DNA, were but a portion of the algorithm making up each individual.

The childhood stigma of being too bright or brainy disappeared, and he found young people alienated from their pasts for reasons he'd never considered or worried about. Now, back home in Hawaii, he was no more tolerant of what he judged to be Hawaiian ethnic prejudice and classism, but the notion of being a mixed-race outcast no longer weighed on him nor tied his stomach in knots, as it had when he was a child. His college years liberated Alaka'i the way that newfound religion did some of his classmates. It gave him a way to appreciate his home culture from a more intellectual and relaxed vantage point. He felt less confused and more at home with who he was, even though he still had no idea who his birth parents were. And he also began to appreciate even more the loving support and parental guidance his adoptive parents, Tommy and Donna Liu, had given him for the past twenty years.

As he looked out at the late-morning drizzle, Al's mind wandered to the weather, and then to the climate changes he'd studied in college and witnessed himself in the storms and tides of Hawaii. As he'd studied climate science at Caltech, watched YouTube videos, and heard stories from international students from other island and coastal countries, the trajectory of earth's changing climate had truly frightened him.

Turf battles, gang squabbles, terrorism, even wars were disturbing and stupid, he felt; educated people with power could at least mitigate these events, if they so choose. But melting ice caps, Pacific typhoons, sinking islands, serial forest fires, and perpetual flooding might not be avoidable any longer. They certainly were not yet controlled, and they exempted no race, no class, no ideology, no particular type of human or mammal. Humans, however, might be able to mitigate the worst effects, if those in power acted rationally and invested in and worked with scientific realities. If the greedy class acted in the interest of the planet, if the United States caught up with the rest of the world in its recognition of the reality of climate change, then maybe many forms of life could be saved. Maybe.

But, for the foreseeable future, Al was a college dropout with lots of computer skills. He stayed at home initially but needed to earn cash for an apartment and to feed his large surfing appetite. He talked his way into an Apple Store help desk job, read about climate, surfed, and hung out with a few friends. After being back a few weeks, he got a text message from an old friend, Peter Hung.

How about coffee at old café on Kapiolani near University at about 11:30?

Al and Peter had been the closest thing to best friends since elementary school, where they both had become math standouts in a class of math wizzes. Peter had stayed on Oahu to go to the University of Hawaii, Manoa, so they had seen each other only occasionally, when Al returned for summer breaks.

Be there! Al typed back.

He closed his computer, slipped on a fresh T-shirt, slid into his Crocs flip-flops, went out the front door, and jumped in the beat-up faded green 1986 Jeep Laredo his parents had bought for him. It was a sleepy, wet day in crawling traffic, but Al's car radio played Maroon 5's album "V" and the excitement of seeing his old pal elevated his mood dramatically.

At the café, he spotted Peter in a corner seat looking out the window onto Kapiolani Boulevard, the area's main drag.

"So, I come home to ponder my future, play with these crazy options swirling around in my brain, and find you're all set, cool as can be, heading to Stanford Law School. Maybe I should have stayed and gone to UH," said Alaka'i as he approached his friend.

"Or maybe I should have gone to the mainland for undergrad and figured out how to start a business and eliminate the need for grad school," the bespectacled, studious-looking boy responded.

Both ordered sandwiches and fruit juices, and Peter dove in.

"Yeah, law school—that's part of what I wanted to talk to you about, actually. I've hardly ever left Oahu, let alone

Hawaii. What I know about California could fit on the head of a Beats earbud. Do you think Stanford is a good place for me?" Peter took off his glasses, rubbed his eyes and stared at his friend.

"Dude, I'm the last person to ask. One, I screwed around my last year, couldn't focus or finish. So, no cap and gown. So, I'm at the Apple Store doing tech grunt work. Besides, I know only a tiny bit about Southern California and nothing about the Bay Area or Silicon Valley. I don't know where you want law school to take you. I mean, are you interested in representing corporations and big money, are you still interested in social justice, or are you just looking for a ticket to let you career-shop later?" Alaka'i drained his lychee juice.

"OK. Good questions. But, wait a minute. You didn't graduate? What happened to the ace student from Punahou? Dude, you're kiddin' me." Peter's jaw hung open.

"I wish I were, but I'd get into some subject, see an interesting angle to study and not do the paper or not prepare for the test. I don't know if it was pressure, laziness, or what," said Al.

"Well, maybe you'll pull a Steve Jobs or Bill Gates. Drop out and create some amazing company." Peter tried to be reassuring.

"Right. But, back to you. Where are you headed?" Al redirected the conversation.

"I'm interested in social justice. I want to help level the playing field for poorer Hawaiians and others on Oahu. But, homie, I don't want to live in poverty myself. And you know very well there are family expectations. Being a professional, and all," said Peter.

"So, like, no specific way you want to address inequality, other than through the law? I mean, are you thinking of running for office?" Al asked.

"You know, it's possible. Like, I just don't know yet. I know I'm good with numbers, but I can't picture stomaching

B-School, nor can I see being a banker or starting a business. Wrong crowd, I think. I was hoping to figure some of that out in law school," said Peter.

"Well, given that I'm not a lawyer, never been to law school . . ."

"Alaka'i, I'm asking for your opinion, not requesting a definitive probability," sighed Peter.

"OK, OK. Seems to me that you're going to need contacts, you will need to sharpen 'critical thinking skills' as they call them, and you'll need a credential. Absent some other alternative, and assuming they give you money, Stanford Law seems like a reasonable choice."

"Cool. That's helpful, dude. I had an attack of self-doubt," said Peter, turning his attention to his sandwich. "So," he said, through a mouthful, "tell me more about how you'll spend your time."

"Well. Funny you should call today. Like, you know how I used to really obsess about how mixed-race kids and non-Haole, nonwealthy Chinese are treated here?" Al sat back in his chair and looked out the window.

"Do I know? I had to listen to you fret and blow off steam for hours. Remember?" Peter laughed.

"Well. Thank god, I'm over that raw stage. But I'm now much more concerned that the same class of folks, the ruling class, here and on the mainland, are so obtuse about climate change that they're going to literally sink us all. Without understanding climate dangers and without strong advocacy for sensible regulations, then ethnic, class, religious, whatever differences won't matter. We'll all be destroyed," Al preached.

"Like, yeah, and . . .? So, Stevie Wonder, Helen Keller, and Ray Charles could see that. Your point is?" Peter said, smiling.

"Well, my strength is programming. My real talent is designing games. I just don't know if my skills can make enough of an impact to change minds—or, more importantly, change behavior. So, for now I'm reading stuff and I'll tinker with the environmental games that are out there, maybe go to some conferences. But, as my last year at Cal Tech showed, I'm in no hurry."

"That's awesome, dude," responded Peter.

"Awesome? What are you talking about? What's awesome?"

"Well, you breeze through and almost graduate Caltech, have a way to join fun with something important, can articulate a vision better than techies I've met, AND you're asking me if you have enough to make a significant contribution? Man, that's like asking if LeBron has what it takes to be in the NBA." Peter patted his friend on the arm. "Look. You were born around 1996, right?"

"Yeah. Same as you. And, you are reading a whole hell of a lot of content into this 'vision' than exists." Al looked at him quizzically.

"So, think about the tech changes in our lifetime and the impact they've had. Since 2001: iPod propels e-music, Firefox opens the browser competition, Facebook explodes social media, YouTube punches TV in the gut, iPhone revolutionizes the cell, Tinder helps nerds like me get dates . . . Shall I keep going?" Peter munched his sandwich.

"You forgot Nintendo's Wii and the gaming revolution. Yeah—point made. Like, I wish talking to regular dudes or investors was this easy," said Al.

"Dude, I just read this article on changes caused by 1.6 degrees Centigrade in the global atmosphere over the last hundred years. You probably know this, but there's a chain reaction that touches stuff I never thought of. Stuff that you could model in your game." Peter's arms flailed enthusiastically.

"Like what?"

"Well, crop production is curtailed, so food prices in poor countries rise; therefore, children get less nutrition and are more susceptible to deadly disease. Increasingly hot summers mean wildfires in California, but globally more elderly deaths in congested, poorly ventilated urban slums, and rural residents are more vulnerable because there aren't enough first responders to provide emergency assistance. The dominoes in this article kept falling, man." Peter looked, for a minute, like a youngster frightened by his first night of thunder and lightning.

"You're right. Those effects are well documented and not high enough in the public's consciousness. I have thought about some of them but can absolutely use more scenarios. There's stuff to play with. But, I have to get my surfing chops back, so I can enjoy North Shore. Some place other than around all of these tourists." Al laughed, hugged his friend and left.

As he bounced back into the house and headed for his room, Alaka'i's father, Tommy Liu, called out to him. The boy sighed, thinking he was in for another minilecture on his duties around the house and the yard.

"Al, if you've got a moment, can you come into the study?"

"Dad, I'm sort of busy now," was Al's reflexive response.

"Doing what? The dishes, wash, and lawn are all done, and it's too wet to do other yard work right now. Unless there's some hot job-related task I'm not aware of . . ." Tommy said with slight annoyance.

"OK, Dad. But can I bring my own music, so we don't have to have opera in the background?"

"What's wrong with opera?" Tommy didn't sound offended. "OK, fine."

Al kicked off his flip-flops, pulled his phone from his back pocket. and backtracked through the living room to his father's study, where the background noise was, indeed, Verdi's *Aida*.

"I just want to get caught up on where you are with your school or work plans," said Tommy, settling back into a thick black leather chair.

"Do you mind if I . . ."

"Oh right. Do you have a CD you want to put on?"

"Dad, I'll just use my phone and AirPlay," said Al, smiling.

"Air who?"

"I just have to push a button on your receiver, find the playlist on my phone, change its output to AirPlay, and presto, some nice 'Marshmello.' "

"Nice for you. Turn that down, please. I'm not even going to ask what genre that mess is," Tommy said, grimacing.

"It's techno."

"Great. Anyway, the last time we really talked, you were thinking about saving for an apartment with room to house a workshop."

"Still the case," Al said, looking at the jammed bookshelves lining the study walls. "I have some sketchy ideas about making a game on the climate crisis."

"And this is the game that projects calamitous climatic conditions?"

"Awesome. You've got it, Dad."

"What I don't have is how this will make you money."

"Well, no question that I need to stay at the store for a couple of years, but over time I can work on a concept, research content, and build a prototype. Then, I'll look for financing, investors. But, Dad, I'm like at ground zero. I'm not even sure I want to do this."

"Al, you know we'll support whatever you decide to do, but at some point you have to stick to your plans," Tommy said.

"Yeah. In terms of making money, have you ever heard of *BioShock* or the *Elder Scrolls*—some of the biggest selling . . ." Al tried to find a connection.

"I can honestly say, no," Tommy said, straight-faced.

"How about Wii, *Gravity Rush* or *Heartstone*?" asked Al with slight exasperation.

"Wii. That may be familiar. Use a handheld baton?" Tommy searched for something to grasp onto.

"Yes. I got it. *FIFA* or *Madden Football?*" Al's eyes opened wide in anticipation of an "aha" from his father.

"Of course, everyone knows about them. Although I've never played," Tommy admitted.

"But you can you imagine, right, that with their TV advertising, those games recoup millions?"

"I suppose," conceded Tommy.

"Well, there are annual conventions, like IndieCade in LA, where entrepreneurs, investors, gamers, the whole industry gathers to review the latest innovations. It's a multibillion-dollar industry. And, with all modesty, I'm good at playing and designing the type of innovations you'd see there." Al beat his palms on the arms of the chair to the music's rhythm.

"OK. Sounds like you have at least a partial plan. Not what I'd call employment, but we'll wait and see." Tommy smiled at his son.

The older Liu shifted his legs in the chair, looked away for a second and then bore down on Al again.

"Son, how can you take that noise? It's so crude and so very misogynistic." Tommy frowned.

"Dad, that's Kendrick Lamar. He's just reflecting cultural frustration using ghetto slang," Al retorted.

"Well, he needs to find other slang. It's quite offensive." Tommy opened his study windows wider, allowing the odor of white ginger to capture the room.

"Dad, I don't think he's targeting your demographic as his audience."

"He's smart there," said Tommy.

Father and son laughed together.

CHAPTER 10

2022

As the students filed out of the classroom onto a sunlit balcony connecting interior spaces, Tommy Liu caught up to Harry Morton and asked if he might speak with him for a moment. Harry suggested they drop into a tea house across University Avenue from the campus.

Morton was familiar with the professor of urban studies, but they had never really talked extensively, nor even thought about developing anything other than a cordial professional relationship. He knew that Tommy was of Chinese and Hawaiian parentage, had grown up in Northern California, was a lawyer, city planner, and urban development specialist. He had migrated to Hawaii exactly ten years before Harry came. Based on the faculty group contact he'd had with Liu, Harry had noted that he was well read and seemed to have a particular interest in "strong men" like Robert Moses of New York, Richard Daley of Chicago, and Lee Kwan Yew of Singapore. Harry had seen Tommy at casual East-West Center social events with his wife, Donna.

"Let me buy you a pot of Dragon Well, unless you'd like something stronger," said Tommy, looking for the waitress.

"Long Jing is quite fresh here. That would be perfect, thank you." Harry opened the collar of his short-sleeve shirt another button.

"I have only caught your general level discussions a couple of times over the years, but have always found them interesting," Tommy began.

"Thank you. I must confess that while I've heard great things about your courses, I haven't yet dropped in. I will," Harry offered genuinely.

"Well, I'd welcome you."

The tea came. After allowing the pot to steep, both men poured steaming cups and let them sit.

"Harry, I have a personal request that is probably out of line, so be honest and feel free to refuse."

"Personal requests are the fastest paths to friendship— and deal-making," said Harry, taking his first fragrant sip.

"My wife and I adopted a two-year-old boy from Hong Kong four years after we moved here, in 1998. Our wonderful son, Alaka'i, has all-but graduated from Caltech and is now thinking about some sort of entrepreneurial future. He's somewhat shy, wedded to social media, and a computer genius, literally. He is, however, somewhat disorganized and has completion issues. I think he could learn a great deal about the human side of strategy, the importance of relationships in business, intellectual discipline, and the value of learning about culture from just talking to you or sitting in on some of your classes." Tommy brought the cup to his lips and inhaled the fragrance.

"Wow, I'm flattered. But you really think he's interested in business theory? And, it sounds like he needs to find his own motivation. 'All-but graduated' you say?" Harry's brow emphasized his skepticism.

"He's pursuing patents on computer games he's already invented, has won every software development contest he's ever entered, has read stacks of management texts, and has an off-the-charts IQ. But, like some of his friends, he lacks confidence, and he needs to learn to appreciate and to engage in the world of face-to-face diplomacy." Tommy continued, "Full disclosure, Harry. Al is mixed race: African-something and Chinese. It's clear that he hasn't quite come to grips with his own identity yet. College helped him a great deal, and he seems to have met kids from so many more demographic backgrounds than my wife and I knew in Northern California. It's been wonderful for Al. But, we feel he'd benefit even further from the mentorship of a successful grown-up of African-American background."

"I think I understand. Well, why not? Let's give it a try. Why don't you have him come and meet me after class next week?" Harry responded on instinct.

That evening, Tommy was in professorial mode, suggesting a list of biographies Al might read. "You know, one of the reasons I assign these biographies to my urban studies classes is that I want students to see that even the most accomplished leaders have doubts, anxieties, and weaknesses that they build from or compensate for. You could skim through Caro's book on Robert Moses, *The Power Broker* . . . or better yet, Doris Kearns Goodwin's biography of Lincoln, *A Team of Rivals*. The point is that they had their own obstacles, which seemed enormous to them at the time, to overcome."

"I recognize the point from all that stuff you've had me read on Martin Luther King, Mandela, even Obama. But, few human beings have those sorts of genes," Al retorted. "And I don't even know what my own genes are. When you know your parents, you can find out about their backgrounds, their struggles, their dreams and disappointments. I can't do that." Al's lips tightened.

"True, but we raised you, and you can know those things about us." Tommy's eyes moistened behind his rimless glasses.

"Dad, I love you and Mom and appreciate all you've done for me. And I recognize that you wanted to find out more about my birth parents. It's not your fault. It's just a fact that I don't know what most kids do about their background, and that void creates a sense of loss that stays with me. Not as big, by any means, as before college, but . . ." Al looked away.

"I hope you'll outgrow that feeling, but I can understand it. You know, my being part Chinese and part Hawaiian hasn't always drawn favorable reviews in my life. And, as you know, there's plenty of bigotry to go around here. Learning to live together is one of our clear challenges on the islands, but—"

"I get it. And I do want to know more about your and Mom's background. But being Black and Chinese has its special negatives out here. There's no Afro community to speak of, Dad. I mean there's military folks, but most of them are really transient and part of a special community on the island," Al continued.

"True. But the average person has no idea of your background, other than you look mixed Asian and something." Tommy reached out to touch his son's shoulder. "Al, have you ever thought of talking to my colleague, Harry Morton, at the University? I ran into him earlier today, told him about your interests in gaming and environmental degradation, and he was interested in meeting you."

"Are you crazy, Dad? He's been a world-class business leader. I'm an unproven entrepreneur 'wanna-be.' "

"One of the reasons he teaches, and doesn't just write and consult, I'll bet, is because he values contact with younger people," Tommy suggested. "I don't know his story, but I'll bet he'd have some interesting things to say. Give it a try, son. What do you have to lose?"

***

A few of weeks later, Alaka'i had worked up the courage to ask to meet Harry Morton after his lecture on "Alternatives to Machiavellian Power," which he had given Al permission to audit.

"Ah, Al. Would you mind meeting out toward Kahala Mall? It's near my home, and I have a dinner appointment that I have to prepare for later," said Harry, checking the time on his phone.

"That's cool with me—where exactly?"

"You have a vehicle?" Harry asked. Al nodded.

"Then, let's meet at the bar at Kahala Hotel. I insist it's my treat, since you're doing me a favor to come out my way." Harry started for the door.

"OK. I think I know where it is, but I've never been inside. So I don't know the bar," Al said hesitantly.

"Follow me. And if we get separated, ask for me inside the front door. I've got a little sports car and will meet you at the University Avenue gate nearest the bottom of the hill."

Without waiting for an answer, Harry slung a satchel over his shoulder and headed for his faculty parking space.

Al trotted to the side street on which he'd parked and drove to the rendezvous point at the stone gate. He pulled over, turned on some electronic music and waited. A few minutes later, Harry pulled out of the gate in front of him and headed down University Avenue.

A Z-car. That's bad. Hope I can keep up, Al thought as Harry led them past downtown, through Kaimuki and onto Kahala Avenue, behind the golf course where Al thought the PGA played the Sony Open golf tournament.

When they pulled around the circle in front of the hotel, Al saw Harry say something to the bellman, pointing to Al's jeep.

"Come on, they'll take care of the vehicle," said Harry, leaning through Al's passenger side window.

"I'd better go back out and find space on the street," said cost-conscious Al.

"I got this," said Harry, strolling toward the glass doors.

Al stopped inside the lobby to take in the gorgeous view of the bay out beyond the hotel. The azure ocean, the palms, the heliconia, the pink ginger, the waterfall against the stone walls of the open interior created a setting exceeding any interior design Al had ever experienced. The scents, natural beauty, and relative quiet overwhelmed his senses.

"I don't think I've been in a place like this. I'm not sure I knew it existed," said the young man.

"Keep plugging away at your climate game idea and one day you'll not only have made good money, but you'll have saved scenic views like this around the world for the average person to enjoy. Come on, what will you have?"

Harry was dressed more casually than the few patrons having afternoon drinks, but his carriage and the recognition of him by staff told Al that he clearly belonged.

Al ordered a beer, Harry a gin and tonic, and Harry insisted on Al trying the pepper and onion-fried calamari. They settled into comfortable bamboo-framed chairs, and Harry took off his sunglasses. Al had never looked directly into the professor's light brown eyes before. Certainly, he had not experienced the intensity of Harry's full attention.

"Well. Thank you for agreeing to see me. I, uh . . ." Al took a sip of beer as if to gather courage, and then continued. "I talk to my parents, but I'm not sure they fully get what I'm talking about. I . . ."

"So, you're talking about race and how it affects modern-day Hawaii," Harry cut in.

"Yes. How did you know? Did Dad mention . . .?"

"He didn't have to, Al. And I do have a little experience in this area." Harry sipped and smiled.

"Well," said Al, gaining courage, "I know you're big on collaborative decision-making and pretty hard on totalitarian approaches to leadership, but look at what that approach has gained haoles over the last couple of hundred years here. They bribe and cheat native Hawaiians. They bring Koreans, Filipinos, Japanese, Chinese over for slave wages. They house them in plantation shacks and try to pit groups against one another to gain the 'massa's' favor. It took the Depression, two World Wars, and slowly built grassroots movements before they finally lost political power, but of course they still have the military in every corner of this island . . ."

"And, your question is?" Harry never diverted his glance from the intense young man.

"Blacks don't even figure in the equation because our numbers are so small. How do you deal with this? I gather, from your bio, that you used to live where there was a sizable African American population and culture. Yet you moved here, when you could have retired in the Caribbean or anywhere?" Al's face was open with curiosity.

"Well, that's a long story for another day. But I will tell you that reading Hawaiian history, meeting Hawaiians of all backgrounds, and just keeping my eyes open, I agree with the facts you present. However, don't discount the large number of European-stock folk who are equally sensitive to that history and who are as decent as any. The question is how one chooses to deal with other truths about life here.

"In simplistic terms, is the glass half full or half empty? I suppose, at this stage in my life, I've found that the half-full perspective serves me better. I've also had the benefit of exposure to many cultures around the world, and find that humans have similar tendencies wherever. Unfortunately, there's oppression, distrust, barbarism to spare. You've been affected by European Christians, but a few years back you might have been more pissed off at Japanese. You're part Chinese, right?"

Al nodded, again.

"Well, while you don't look African, you don't look pure Han either. You might have had a rough time growing up in China. Several nations in east or west Africa might also have made your childhood uncomfortable. As for my folks on the mainland, some of us have adopted bad habits from former masters. Prejudices about color, hair, facial features, vocabulary, and so on. And, like many Americans, we have developed a strong class prejudice. So, my guess is you might have had to deal with more than most single-race kids living in a culture where they are the majority or the most powerful." Harry spoke softly, but seriously.

"So, that sounds more like a half-empty point of view."

"Well, I haven't told you how I see navigating. Just as there are lots of assholes, there are many, many wonderful, caring and interesting folks in almost every place I've been. Second, most youngsters, whether in a majority or not, grow up adjusting to issues they find vexing to them. *I'm too short, not handsome, not quick-witted, not a good athlete, don't have a magnetic personality, not smart,* on and on. To each kid, those obstacles can seem monstrous.

"Third, most—not all—folks that discover and develop a talent, work hard, are open to other reasonable people, and grab good luck when it comes end up. Those who make big contributions or lots of money aren't necessarily the autocrats. Finally, the goal, I would think, is happiness, after learning to cope with the shit life is going to throw your way." Harry paused.

"Yeah, but it seems like people of color get heavier doses of shit."

"Maybe. But if you intend to change the situation, you'll have a better shot if you are comfortable with who you are. And, from the little I know of you, Al, you have a lot going for you. Your parents are great folks, you have a solid set of values, you're clearly super smart, you're curious. Look at your mixed background as an opportunity to learn from and experience multiple cultures. Man, that's a plus.

"Folks that give you a hard time because of shallow things are assholes and should be pitied, not feared. Keep your eye on them, but they are not likely to be the type of folks you'll want to emulate, in any event." Harry took a long drink.

"But you didn't have to face these Hawaii-type biases from your own people growing up. It had to be easier." Al was courageously assertive.

Harry looked away from the earnest youngster for a second.

"Remember, I said most kids have their own barriers? Mine weren't yours, but similar. Soft bullies abound. I grew up before and during the civil rights movement. So there were institutional barriers and prejudices that enforced the majority's bigotry. Breaking out of certain norms meant making friends with folks that 'our people' disapproved of. So, there was substantial White bias and anticipation that Blacks would fail on the one hand, yet resistance and disdain by Blacks for us going to 'White schools,' or socializing with Whites or non-Blacks on the other," Harry said matter-of-factly.

"But why not just do as other middle-class Blacks and enjoy a community of support. Why antagonize your own folks?" Al asked earnestly.

"Al, you don't know your birth parents and have had to grow your own identity in an adopted home. I had no choice early on about accepting the status quo. My parents were humanists, globalist before their time. Both were reared in segregated environments, but both feeling there was no reason to live by stupid rules, whether created by Whites to suppress, or by Blacks to survive. They truly believed all of us are equal before God. And they believed in a Christian God. They lived their faith and insisted their boys adopt that philosophy while in their house." Harry stared out past the bar's plant boxes, at the calm ocean beyond, as if staring back in time.

"Religious, huh? Sounds like my mom," Al mumbled.

"Tell me about it. Uncomfortable sometimes, but once I absorbed their basic tenets—half full, my man. That perspective made me a better consultant than lots of my competition, and it enabled me to appreciate and feel comfortable in many more situations than I might have, had I had a different upbringing." Harry fixed a steely look on Al.

"Yeah, but me, I've never got into all of the symbolism and pageantry of church . . ."

"You might try Buddhism. Less pageantry, very self-regulated. It might appeal to you." Harry relaxed his stare. "There are plenty of temples on the island. Formal religion, or not, I have a suspicion you'll find exploration of your spiritual side helpful." Harry didn't push the point.

"Sometimes, I think my anger at the injustices here is fed partly by my inability to be able to ask my birth parents what they went through, why they got together, you know?" Al stared out of the window, addressing no one in particular.

"Al, I can't pretend to know what it's like not to know one's birth parents. But I can assure you that many kids with two parents, myself included, were never mature enough, or never found the time to ask all they later wanted to know, when it was too late. It's not the same, I know, but you have two terrific adoptive parents. Learn from them, while you can."

"I hope you don't mind me asking these questions. I barely know you, but Dad didn't think you'd mind."

"He's right. Let's get together, from time to time. I'm pretty sure, though, your business will take off and you'll find your own sea legs. You've got tons going for you, and I'm betting that the issues you now see as impediments will recede in importance, as you age and experience more.

You'll be able to appreciate positive unique aspects of different cultures, and you'll quite naturally get good at code switching."

Harry finished his gin and tonic and began to rise. "Oh, and before you get immersed in some computer coding job or designing your own game, you might find a way to volunteer as a math tutor to a few native Hawaiian kids. There are programs all over the island, there's obvious need, and you might learn as much about yourself as you do about others." Without thinking, Harry gave the youngster a big hug and they exchanged '60s soul handshakes before heading for the lobby door.

"Half full!" Al said as they got into their vehicles.

That night, while scanning the ads for apartments downtown, Al reflected on his conversation with Harry, feeling happier and more sanguine about his decision to return to Hawaii to start the next phase of his life. Though he was more engaged at work since he had started as a salesman at a game store, it was his research and tinkering on his own project that gave him the most satisfaction. In his last semester at Caltech, Al had come up with an idea—a way, he thought, that he could close the circle and use his programming skills to address his interest in environmental sanity. He had been inspired by a book he'd recently read, *Ready Player One*, which described an immersive virtual-reality environment into which players could step and become totally absorbed.

He was outgrowing his parents' house and needed to find more privacy and more space. So, he slowly initiated his apartment search.

Buoyed by his conversation with Harry, Al headed out to one of his favorite beaches to catch a few waves and to sit alone and develop a plan for is future. He knew that he couldn't remain indefinitely as a game store salesman and felt that his tinkering with a climate crisis game was not only fun but could eventually lead to a business. He thought his main barrier was funding, so as was his practice, he filed his infantile "plan" in a remote corner of his mind, climbed on his board and caught several long afternoon swells.

Over the next several months, Al's new sense of urgency dissipated. Months turned into years. Game ideas and spare parts multiplied, as did a collection of articles, videos, podcasts, and conference websites on climate issues. Nothing, however, stimulated Al to develop a real business plan and aggressively seek funding. He had settled into a young adult's comfortable island life. Neither prods from his parents, encouragement from mentor Harry Morton, nor pushes from buddy and prospective attorney Peter Hung moved Al out of his comfort zone.

One afternoon in 2025 after work, Al, Peter, and Gretchen Okamoto approached Sunset Beach. Gretchen was a young environmental activist Peter had befriended in law school, who was now a close friend of both men. They had hoped to catch waves stirred by a recent storm in the Pacific.

"What the . . ." Al stopped at the water's edge. The beach was cluttered with kelp, seaweed, plastic trash and dead fish for as far as the eye could see.

"Some of this is just from the storm, but the trash and dead marine life is pollution. We see it more and more on the other islands," said Gretchen.

"This will take days to clear. Let's drive farther north," said Peter.

Gretchen and Peter started back to Al's jeep.

"What happened to Al?" asked Gretchen looking back at the beach.

Hidden from them by a crest in a small dune, Al was at the shoreline, picking up debris.

"Buddy, what are you doing? You can't clean enough of that stuff by yourself to make a difference. Let's go," said Peter, after having retreated back to the beach.

"This is worse than I've seen. It's like one of the many scenes I've sketched out in my game. If what I've read is accurate, this is just a portent of some of the massive pollution we'll soon be experiencing," Al said.

"Al, what do you think we've been protesting downtown all of these weekends? Guess what? It's not just fires in California, hurricanes in Louisiana, massive snowstorms in the East. The climate is hitting on all fronts." Gretchen's tone evidenced incredulity and frustration.

"I know. I've been . . ." Al was cut off.

"You've been messing around, procrastinating, and playing at life since you moved back. We love you, man, but you've been in a productivity funk for years," Peter cut him off.

"Al, you say you love the islands and the natural world like we do. But, Peter's going to be taking polluters to court, I'm organizing sit-ins against major companies. When are you going to get serious about getting in the fray? With your talent, you could be reaching millions of people, influencing a whole generation of climate deniers. Dear Al, if you don't like what's happening to the beaches, to the islands, get in the game," Gretchen practically exploded.

"Wow, where did all this come from?" a stunned Al asked.

"We've seen it for years, but figured if you wanted to play at building a game, that was your business. But, as you crabbed more and more about corporate irresponsibility, about tourists' insensitivity to our island, we've wondered when you would recognize your own indirect complicity. You got skills, bro. Time to get to work." Peter gave his friend a gentle shove.

When they reached the jeep, Al sheepishly asked his friends if they still wanted to surf. Laughing to release tension, they both said, "Let's head north."

Within a week of his confrontation on the beach, Al sent out dozens of inquiries to potential funders, and he contacted some of his classmates from Caltech about exhibiting at upcoming gaming conferences. One former student, who was working at Apple in Cupertino, California, said he was welcomed to hang out at a booth he was manning at a Los Angeles conference.

While perusing the conference agenda, Al came across a popular session given by guest lecturer and tech entrepreneur David Oweke. On a gut feeling, he approached the lecturer who looked more like a model from a GQ fashion executive than a scruffy techie from Silicon Valley. Al lost his shyness in pitching an environmental game whose outcomes could produce horrific climate changes, unless players took certain political and economic actions. The avatars and effects he described were so realistic that Oweke cautioned Alaka'i to seek legal advice as to the type of insurance he was going to need to protect against claims from players who were freaked out after participating in the game.

"I normally don't respond to student ideas unless we've struck a contractual arrangement. But, I think you really have something here," the young Nigerian said. "In fact, I think you should really be talking to a colleague of mine on the East Coast who's looking to fund tech game projects. Send me an outline, a proposal. I'll pass it on to my buddy, Mark, back east."

"Oh, that would be snap. Thank you so much. Technically, I'm no longer a student," Alaka'i responded.

David merely smiled and shook his hand. "Get it to me whenever you can. It can take investors like Mark more than a minute to respond. Here's my contact information. Nice to meet you, Al," David said warmly.

Back home, Al began in earnest to think through his idea for "Earth Reclaimed." Every time he felt he was ready to polish off a proposal, he thought of a new scene or new issue he felt the game should reflect. After a frustrating few months, he shared a draft with Peter and Gretchen. While their initial response reflected concern that he was trying to do too much, countless nights over beer and pizza talking out scenarios helped him focus on a few that he could neatly place into a tight proposal. After four months, he forwarded the proposal to David. Then, after finally having organized his concepts, scenarios, technology, budget, and skeletal marketing ideas, Al had to fight his desire to hear back from the investor. But, Mark Morton's plate was full, and he and his firm couldn't get to Al's proposal for months. Al continued to query other investors but didn't receive any encouraging feedback. He began to accompany Gretchen to some of her rallies to maintain contact with issues on the island and to avoid falling back into old defeatist habits.

Several weeks after New Year's 2026, the rain in Manoa began to fall hard. Al's mood was grim, and he pondered how long he should wait to hear from Oweke or Morton. *Too soon, too anxious*, he wondered. As he leaned back against his pillow and punched the keys to open *Gravity Rush 2* on his laptop, his Snapchat pinged. It was a text message.

Call me; good news on project. Mark.

Al shoved his chopsticks into the take-out box, picked up his phone, checked the time and called Mark Morton. It would be almost midnight back East, but he couldn't stop his anxious fingers.

"Wow. That was fast," said Mark. "I'm headed to bed, so I'll be quick. We're funding your game and providing all of the start-up cash you requested. We want to do the fund development, packaging, and marketing of the project. Investors and our board are jazzed about your concept. I'll forward the details in a day or so."

Al stood up from his chair, speechless. Then he managed to choke out, "Dope. That's amazing. Thank you. I don't know what to say . . ."

"Welcome to our portfolio. We're all very excited about what you've laid out. Chat with you later." Mark rang off.

Within a few weeks, Al's start-up was buzzing. His intellect, creativity, emotion, and ambition had finally kicked in together. It was as if his schooling, work experience, technological experimentation, and climate research finally clicked a switch, and Al Liu was reborn. While he was the primary creator, programmer, and producer, he had hired artists, an audio producer, story line writers, software engineers, a tech researcher to track new developments in the gaming world, and a Caltech classmate to be business manager. He purchased workstations, contracted with some local parts manufacturers, and leased old warehouse space to fit up as a workshop/office. He was energized and paddling hard, no longer just surfing through life.

CHAPTER 11

2026

"Tommy, come and look at this letter that's just come," called Donna Liu from their kitchen.

Tommy Liu sauntered in from their living room overlooking part of Manoa Valley, above the University of Hawaii's main campus. His dragging slippers suggested that he hadn't fully awakened from the Saturday nap his wife had interrupted.

"Pull up a bar stool, dear. This looks interesting. I had to sign for it, and it's from Hong Kong. I think it might be from that adoption agency where we got Alaka'i," whispered Donna, as if there was someone else in the house besides the two of them.

"Well, why don't you open it, love?"

"I am nervous for some reason. Maybe, I should burn a joss stick or say a prayer to the garden buddha," Donna said, handing the envelope to Tommy.

"Oh, superstitious. Let's see." Tommy, fully awake, took and opened the letter.

July 29, 2026

Dear Mr. & Mrs. Liu,

I hope this communication finds you well, and I pray that your son Alaka'i is also prospering. We have received a bit of sad news that is fortuitous for your son. His birth mother has recently passed away from cancer. She never had other children, although she has younger relatives, particularly on her deceased husband's side of the family, who will inherit some of her fortune. During future proceedings, you will learn of her identity. She never forgot that she had a son through a relationship that she felt had to remain secret. Alaka'i's mother wants him to know more about her, why she put him up for adoption, and that she has bequeathed to him a considerable fortune.

The specific details will be revealed in private proceedings handled by the Honolulu office of Zhou & Zhou, a major Hong Kong law firm handling the estate.

Most Sincerely,

Nancy Barton

Executive Director, Hong Kong Families Agency

Tommy and Donna sat facing each other in stunned silence. Tommy's mouth hung open, his back stiff and straight, as if he'd been struck by lightning.

Donna looked more worried. "He's had such a time finding himself, getting his feet on the ground, growing into a mature adult. I hope this doesn't overwhelm him. And how much is a 'considerable fortune,' anyway?" She sat on the edge of her chair and looked at her husband in confusion.

"Dear, there are a lot of questions, but Al's a very capable young man. Better he wrestle with a fortune than struggle in poverty, right?" Tommy tried to hide his own confusion.

"He's hardly poor after his start-up investment from back East. Besides, there is an in-between, Tommy, surely," said Donna, regaining some equilibrium.

"Bottom line really is 'Wow. Our son's from money.' It will be fascinating to find out who she was . . ." Tommy was thinking aloud.

"I just hope Al doesn't freak out when he has to digest this news," said Donna. "Do you think we should wait until the law firm contacts us, so Al doesn't stew over this?"

"OK, I admit, this could be overwhelming for all of us. I've never really dealt with lawyers, certainly not about any inheritance. But let's take it a step at a time. After all, if the agency had had his address, they would have probably contacted him directly. No, we should tell him and see what the gift actually is. Take it a step at a time." Tommy sounded more convinced than he actually felt.

"OK, well, I'll text him to see if he can come to dinner tonight or tomorrow," Donna said, nervously picking up her phone.

"Take your time, dear. Breathe. We should be cool, as Al would say." Tommy gave his wife a long hug.

When her phone pinged with a reply, Donna exhaled and stared out at the plants cascading up the hillside beyond their kitchen window. "He said tomorrow would be super, since we haven't seen each other for a bit." By now, Al had moved to a small and sparsely furnished apartment of his own, nearer the warehouse offices of his new start-up, Pua'ena Games.

"I'll barbeque some of that up-island pork and pineapple he loves," said Tommy.

"Good, and I'll pick up some corn on the cob and fix some potato salad," said Donna.

The next morning, the Honolulu office of Zhou & Zhou called to arrange for a meeting with Alaka'i, but his parents said he'd get back to them in a day or so.

Al spent the day with his friend Peter riding waves and hanging out at the beach. He felt that he needed a break from working on the game prototype.

His own office was modest because Al spent substantial time alongside his creative team's workstations and in meetings around the space. It was a small, glass-enclosed space, dominated by large color posters of *Star Wars* and *Ready Player One* movie releases, and a huge black-and-white photo of Hawaiian surfing legend, Duke Kahanamoku. An L-shaped blond wooden table served as his desk, and every available wall space was covered in IKEA-constructed bookshelves. The cartons of computer games, business management books, and science fiction paperbacks by Terry Brooks, Isaac Asimov, and Ursula Le Guin could be expected. But the tomes on Buddhism, Chinese history, and African American and African literature revealed the multidimensional curiosity of the young entrepreneur. Al had incorporated his game development company as "*Pua'ena Games*," named for the North Shore promontory and beach area where he often went to kayak, swim, surf, or simply gaze out at the Pacific.

The view was special to Al because he could see out beyond the waves to the horizon where bluish-purple sky met greenish-blue sea. Pua'ena's vista was, to him, a live painting representing all the horrific dangers, yet all the beautiful potential of man's future stewardship of the environment. Carelessly treat the earth and risk Armageddon; handle it with care and survive to enjoy its beauty for another era. His game would have to project both visions.

Al had rejected suggestions from Mark and investors that he relocate to the San Francisco Bay area because the Hawaii pace and lifestyle were in his blood. He was still discovering who he was professionally and what he wanted to accomplish, but, at thirty, he was now finally more comfortable and on better defined track.

Late in the afternoon, he drove directly to Manoa Valley in his functional Jeep Laredo. As he entered his parents' house, Al smelled the unmistakable aroma of roasting pork.

"Aloha. Anyone home?" asked the young entrepreneur, shuffling through the living room into the family room/kitchen.

"Hello, Alaka'i. How's your day? Grab a beer and let's go sit out in the garden," Tommy said, Chardonnay in hand.

Donna joined the men, carrying her Pinot Noir, with the letter stuck in her apron pocket.

"My *keiki kane*. It's so good to see you smiling and finally committed to something you really want to do, something that will allow you to contribute as well as to make a living," said his mother. She glanced at her husband, who seized the moment.

"Al, we have a surprise to share with you," said Tommy.

"OK. Is this some bad news? Is that why you wanted to be together, and cooked pork, and . . . I'm a little nervous here," said Al.

"No, son. On the contrary. This is, in many ways, a gift from God," offered Donna.

"OK, Mom. Don't get religious on me."

"Dear, why not just give him the letter and let him absorb it himself?" Tommy said.

Donna handed the agency letter to her son. Alaka'i read silently, placed the letter on the glass coffee table and stared at the miniature waterfall nestled into the rocky wall framing the corner of their back patio. For a few moments, he could do no more than follow the trickle of water as it splashed into a stone basin surrounded by ferns in the garden. He occasionally gazed on the stone Buddha at the base of the pond. Then, he imagined a prototypical *qipao*-clad Chinese model looking down at a baby being held by a Mongolian-looking peasant woman. The model then turned and walked away from the nanny and baby.

Al blinked his eyes, turned to his parents, and asked, "What am I supposed to think? I'm lost right now."

No tears, no sighs, just a puzzled stare.

"Yes, to hear all this at once is a huge shock, I know. Neither of us know any more than you've read. The firm, Zhou & Zhou, has already called to set up the appointment, but you should be the one to contact them. We'd obviously like to be there," said Tommy.

"I mean, out of the blue. Why now? Like, OK, the inheritance—but why give me anything? I'm not sure I want anything from her." Al spoke rapidly, his thoughts jumbled and confused.

"Well, whatever God your birth mother believed in somehow made her feel she had to reach out, even if in death," Donna suggested.

"What about my father? Is he alive? Where is he?" Al's voice rose.

"We don't know anything other than he has African, Native American and some Caucasian blood. He could be living anywhere, or may be dead. Depending on the circumstances, we may find that he doesn't even know you exist. Let's see what the papers say at the lawyers." Tommy tried to calm and comfort both of them.

"Well, no matter what, you are my true *makuahine* and *makua kane*. You're all I know," Al said with warm certainty.

***

Several days later, the Lius sat in the posh waiting area of Zhou & Zhou on the top floor of a new Chinese-built office building on Kapiolani Boulevard, near the Ala Moana shopping center in downtown Honolulu. Everything from the marble foo dogs and jade table ornaments to the ornate teak carving above the main door projected money and success. The building had drawn strong and vociferous protest from non-Chinese Hawaiians who resented the recent incursion of mainland Chinese wealth building towering condos, often held vacant, in this part of town.

Tommy, Donna, and Al sat erect and tense.

"Hello, Mr. and Mrs. Liu. And you must be Alaka'i." An attractive young mixed-race Asian woman came from a door at the end of the room, behind the reception desk. "My name is Joy and I'll be taking you into Jack Wong, who's the lead attorney in the Honolulu office. This way, please."

Al and his parents looked at each other with quizzical expressions and followed the young lady into a small but similarly appointed conference room. There were several stacks of neatly piled documents in the center of a large oak table. Five velvet-cushioned chairs were bunched at the end of the table nearest to the stack. Almost before they could settle into their seats, a side door opened and Jack Wong entered, followed by a legal assistant.

After greetings and preliminaries about Al's proof of identity, Wong outlined the core document.

"I realize this is quite a shock to all of you, and let me assure you that you can call on the firm, free of charge, at any time in the future to clarify any of the terms of the agreement. We are here to administer the estate and to ensure that its provisions are carried out as intended by your birth mother," said Wong. "So, while you can read the documents at your leisure if you like, I can summarize the main provisions of your inheritance, Alaka'i."

"Fine, but first can you tell me who my birth mother was?" asked Alaka'i.

"Absolutely, I'll describe what I can within the outline she has stipulated," Wong said, raising a pair of rimless reading glasses to the bridge of his nose. "Your birth mother's name was Wong Xi. No relation to me. Her mother was a Caucasian British journalist and her father a prominent Han businessman from Shanghai. She married a very successful banker from Shanghai, Bao Li. Ms. Wong built a successful company whose value exploded after she acquired a mainland fabric company. She became one of the most successful and wealthiest taipans in Hong Kong, thus in Asia. Her life was her business and the social engagements required of her position. While her husband was alive, they were an influential and very visible social couple on the island. They contributed heavily to the arts and to social causes, but steered clear of volatile Hong Kong politics. All this information you can find on Google.

"But what I am about to tell you has remained a secret between Ms. Wong, her aunt Wong Jianying, who raised her, and now our firm, as executors and caretakers of the estate. Ms. Wong had an affair and became pregnant early in her business career. She loved the child but realized that she had to choose between the high-profile career she had started in Hong Kong and divorcing her husband to raise the child. She chose the former. Her trusted aunt took care of Ms. Wong during her pregnancy, found an adoption agency, and handled the particulars when her niece went back to work.

"Nothing has been offered about your birth father other than his racial background, which you already know. Mr. Bao knew of the affair, but was apparently unaware of the child. Ms. Wong and her aunt eventually went to their graves maintaining the father's identity in secret. However, after she became sick with breast cancer, Ms. Wong contacted us to handle the estate and wanted to be sure that you were contacted and provided what I'm about to describe. With me so far?" Jack Wong looked up and paused.

"I'm here," said a stoic Al.

"Your birth mother lamented not having ever contacted you or the Lius, even though that was her choice. She knew that you were in Hawaii, but, well, she stayed focused on the Hong Kong life she had chosen. In the end, however, she must have done some soul-searching, as I believe you Americans say.

"So, in four years, on your thirty-fourth birthday I believe, Alaka'i, you will inherit five hundred million dollars. By that time, you are to develop plans for a program or foundation to help Chinese children of mixed-race background. The programs are to help this population deal with psychological or emotional problems they may encounter stemming from their mixed ethnicity. This can be part research and part service, structured and administered as you see fit. One fifth of your inheritance is to be for this project. I should also mention that a benefit to using our firm is that in many of our offices, worldwide, we have at least one attorney who doubles as a sort of cultural attaché. The younger Mr. Zhou had studied cultural anthropology and fostered an interest in researching the diaspora wherever he established major offices.

"Your plan need not be too detailed, but it should be a solid business plan that we have to approve. So, at thirty-four, after we approve the plan, which we will gladly help you develop, we will deposit four hundred million dollars into your bank account and deposit fifty million dollars in an account you set up for the foundation. Once the project is underway, no more than two years after inception, the remaining fifty million will be deposited into its account." Jack Wong paused.

"So, like, by age thirty-four develop a plan; receive four hundred million dollars for my personal account and fifty million dollars for the mixed-race kids' project; within two years, another fifty million to the project. Do I have that right?" asked Al, stunned.

"Essentially, that's it," said Jack.

"This is quite a bit to absorb," said Donna, pale with shock.

Tommy requested a glass of water and Donna pulled out a tissue, unable to hold back the tears of joy, shock, and disbelief. They each grasped one of Al's hands, as he sat erect, unable to speak. For a moment, Al felt as if he were in an isolation booth, behind glass, cut off from all surroundings, in a zone by himself.

"Well, take these documents. There are only three that have to be signed now, confirming that the inheritance in concept has been explained, that the documents have been given to you, and that Alaka'i is willing to abide by the general provisions. The rest can be signed and brought back to us at your leisure. You have several years before your thirty-fourth birthday, I believe." Jack Wong stood.

Al sat numbly looking at the three pieces of paper with yellow tabs for his signature. "Amazing," he said. "I'm still back at who my birth mother was."

"No hurry, look them over and sign before you leave. Ask the receptionist to call Joy, and she'll give you copies of the signed documents and you can take them and this whole package with you. When you've read and thought about the proposal, come on back and we will finalize what we've discussed. Fair enough?

"I know it's a lot and that your feelings are probably mixed right now. All over the place. But when it settles in that you are a very rich man, who can do a great deal of good in this world, you may feel a bit softer about your birth mother. I met her, and I know that she was hoping you would be able to do some of what she was unable to in her life.

"It was a pleasure meeting all of you. Until the next time." Jack Wong bowed and left the Lius to digest the news.

After he left his parents at their house, Al picked up a double mocha expresso and headed for the peaceful sand plateau at Ala Moana Beach Park. Sitting with his legs pulled into his chest and tears trickling from his cheek, Al tried to imagine his birth mother. Regal, cold, and distant. Had she felt guilty? Had she been sorry that she chose her career and husband over him? Of course not. How should he feel about her? How should he feel about taking her money? It was all too much to process. He wept silently.

Al looked over the flat, calm ocean and tried to clear his mind. He tried to solely absorb the beauty of the horizon. He pushed the wealthy, glamorous image he had of his mother from his mind, he submerged the business plans he was implementing from consciousness, he even blanked out the warm image of his adoring adoptive parents. Alaka'i simply tried to become one with the horizon above the surf. He remained quiet for over half an hour.

Back at his apartment, a calm Al Liu spread the contents of the legal folder on his dining-room table and carefully read the proposal and the few documents he had to sign. Then, he took the background materials on Wong Xi into his little study/bedroom, collapsed into his reading chair, and pieced together the life of a fantastically successful Eurasian Hong Kong taipan.

There was not much written about the struggles he imagined she must have endured as a mixed-race childless Chinese woman, in a cutthroat male business world. Nothing about the strength she must have had, just a vague allusion to prejudices against professional women in the marketplace. To have become a taipan, she had to have had phenomenal skill, endurance, and considerable luck. He searched Google and read the Wikipedia entry but found little more detail about her personal story there. The total absence of any information about his father was understandable, but frustrating nonetheless.

When he got a Snapchat message from Peter simply inquiring how he was doing, Al suggested they have a drink later that evening, mentioning that he had some news from China. Peter replied that he was busy, but said they should have breakfast at one of their favorite spots. Al thought of calling Gretchen Okamoto, but instead threw himself into some design issues he was facing with the gaming project, *Earth Reclaimed.* Unable to focus either on his work or on the major life change before him, Al fell asleep with new songs by DJ Kaskade pounding in his earbuds.

The next morning, Al showered, slipped on some faded cargo shorts and a University of Hawaii T-shirt, got in his Jeep, and drove over to the neighborhood restaurant near

Ala Moana Shopping Center. He had just settled on one of the worn wood benches and ordered a coffee when Peter rushed through the door.

"Well? What's all of this hush-hush stuff about China?" Peter asked, as if he had another important meeting in fifteen minutes.

"Good morning, Mr. Hung. How is work at the firm, and how was your day yesterday?" asked Al with a smile.

"Oh, stuff it, Al. What's happening? You've met the perfect girl? Some California Asian honey that came over for a vacation, met you surfing, and wants to stay?" Peter rambled on.

"I wish. No, I haven't met, much less dated that many hot girls since I left LA. Why don't we order first? I'm starved," said Al, sounding more on top of the world than he actually felt.

Peter ordered the strawberry shortcake stack and a black coffee, Al the avocado and scrambled egg "Sammy," with more coffee. Then he looked at his friend.

"OK. So, my friend, my buddy, you are looking at one of the future richest mixed-race surfer-programmers on the island. No, in the state. Make that in the country."

"Al, you sold your company without even finishing the *Earth Reclaimed*?" Peter leaned forward in astonishment.

"Nope."

"Come on. Like, you don't need to drag this out. You came into some money? So, you can accelerate game production, you can rent a better apartment, you can afford to fly some of those California ladies over for long weekends . . . What?" Peter began to look over his shoulder for his food.

"OK, since you're my best . . . actually, my only real friend, I'll let you know what's to happen over the next four years." Al told Peter the gist of his inheritance, what he had learned about his birth mother, what he had to do with a fifth of the money, and how he had no good idea what he was going to do after he signed and turned in the papers.

"Dude, you need to hire me as your lawyer. That's number one." Peter cupped his coffee and leaned back in his bench, feeling much older than when he entered the restaurant.

"Excuse me, bro, but you do environmental law." Al laughed.

"Like, I'll be ready. Totally!" Peter extended his hand to fist-bump his pal.

"Well, we'll see," said Al.

"Like, seriously, Al, why should you change anything, other than work with the firm to put a plan for Chinese mixed-race kids together? You still need the investors for *Earth Reclaimed*, you still need to finish the game and test it, and you don't yet have a cent to live much differently than you do now. You probably can't advertise the gift, so you can't borrow against it yet. But you sure won't have to worry about student loan debt. " Peter smiled as he saw, then smelled his pancakes.

"I suppose. But I don't really have a clue about Chinese kids of mixed ethnicity, their problems, what sort of help is available, what geographic areas to focus on, nothing! In case you haven't noticed, those of us with some Chinese blood are in every major location around the globe."

"OMG, excuse me, but who's always moaning about racism toward Black-Chinese-Hawaiians? Who's spent hours assessing different ways to contribute to a saner culture on the islands? Who's—" Peter bubbled with excitement for his friend.

"I know, but this is serious cash and I have no idea about the Chinese diaspora outside the western US," Al interrupted.

"It's a good thing I'm your friend, dude. Number one: Your birth mother didn't specify where in the world this work had to be. And, duh, you use some of the cash to study the very questions you posed. Finally, why would you think kids in Asia face a much different type of discrimination than you have? Your birth mother must have been quite a lady. This is made for you, dude. Eat!" Peter appeared more excited than his best friend, the heir.

After he had driven by the warehouse office later that morning, Al opened his laptop to work on the game. Atypically, he couldn't concentrate on story line riddles, avatars, scenery, and other computer graphics. Should he return the *Earth Reclaimed* investment and forget the whole idea about a socially challenging and hopefully politically provocative game about saving the planet? Should he borrow money and travel to China to find out more about his birth mother? Should he take courses in modern Chinese history and travel to China to get a jump on understanding the status of mixed-race children in China? Should he start researching what was required to set up the foundation he would need to create?

Al knew himself well enough to know that he needed time by himself in his favorite environment: the Pacific. He grabbed his surfboard, tossed it in his Jeep and headed for Sandy Beach, just past Hanauma Bay.

The mid-afternoon surf was high enough to allow surfers to catch waves without having to swim too far out, so, within forty-five minutes of leaving his office, Al was seated on his board, relaxing. With cumulus clouds on the horizon, frothy ten-foot waves gathering, Al, a very strong swimmer, focused on his first good ride. Navigating the small blue-green tunnel absorbed his full attention, and once he completed his first ride, Al swam back through breakers to catch his next. After almost an hour in the water, Al Liu strode up the narrow beach, found a clear spot and lay down on his board. The sun not only felt good as it dried his skin but was therapeutic in wiping out any anxiety he had carried with him.

Too bad I can't simply be content being a global surfer with my new wealth, he thought.

For quite a while, Al listened to the surf, sat up and watched the ocean, and enjoyed breathing in the smell of brine and beached sea vegetation. The laughter of other beachgoers became background noise, and Al cleared his mind so that he was truly only conscious of the sand, sky, and the ocean.

After about an hour of this meditative trance, Al smiled to himself.

Why complicate life? he thought. *I'm in a position to pursue several aims at the same time. I've already started to design a tsunami scene for Shanghai in* "Earth Reclaimed—A Climate Simulator," *so I can legitimately use my travel budget to go there. My birth mother is from there, so I might find out more about her, and it's supposed to be extremely cosmopolitan, so I can begin to look into the situation of mixed-race kids.*

For once, Al didn't mind the afternoon traffic on the coast highway, as he excitedly played with the possibilities of a trip to Shanghai.

When he dropped by his parents' house with the signed papers and told them about his idea for a trip to China, Tommy welcomed his son's new enthusiasm. Donna was more cautious.

"Shanghai is much different from when your birth mother or even I grew up there," she said.

"That's a good thing," said Tommy.

"I mean with China severely tightening up on dissent— with Tiananmen, Hong Kong, and Taiwan. It can be dangerous," continued Donna.

"My love, he's not going to protest or to challenge the Communist Party. He's simply an overseas Chinese going as a tourist," said Tommy.

Somewhat reassured, Donna reflected on her cheerful childhood, her parents' decision to leave during Mao and her eventual happy adaptation to the United States. She looked at Al and realized that he had matured beyond the insecure young boy into an independent and prosperous young adult. After a few minutes with her own thoughts and without forethought about the family budget, Donna said, "We could go as a family. Both your father and I have relatives in Shanghai that we've not seen since we were kids."

Tommy, however, noted that Alaka'i's expression suggested that he needed to take this step, commit to this adventure, on his own.

"Maybe the next trip would be good for a family vacation. I think Al needs to find some things out on his own first. Given the inheritance he's due, I suspect he'll be able to treat us later," Tommy said, encircling his wife in his arms.

"Thanks, Dad. That is sort of the way I feel."

When Al called Mark Morton to run the "research trip" idea by him, Mark's only response was that he thought it was a great idea and to joke that he looked forward to the Shutterfly album of Shanghai attractions. Al applied for his visa, contacted the law firm to get more information on his mother's Shanghai roots, and made sure there was adequate work for his staff and contractors for the next several weeks. His mother was able to contact a distant cousin who insisted Al stay with her during his visit. His father cobbled together a list of articles and books on modern Shanghai that were accessible online. Almost overnight, Al's angst about his identity and concern for what he had perceived as an unrooted personal history had been displaced by excitement about discovering more of his origin and possibly gaining insight into a culture to which he felt only tangentially attached. Al had to wait longer than he expected to leave because relations between the Chinese government and the United States were quite frosty. The Chinese embassy took two months to issue his visa. So early in 2027, Al finally left on his journey of discovery.

CHAPTER 12

2027

Al's ten-hour China Eastern Airlines flight to Shanghai was his first international flight, so he had loaded up his laptop with articles, music, and recordings of Chinese phrases. During much of the time, however, he reflected on his own personal experiences with and feelings about his Asian heritage. His family never really celebrated holidays, other than Chinese New Year, and his parents no longer spoke Mandarin around the house, although they had done so when he was young in order to start him out as a bilingual child. He had an academic appreciation for China's long cultural history, for the omnipresence of the diaspora, and for the tortuous beginnings of the early Chinese laborers on Hawaii. His parents had occasionally spoken of some of the hardship and horrors relatives and family friends had endured during Mao's Cultural Revolution, but they had tried to shield Al from the visceral antagonism and anguish they both felt about the mother country pre–Deng Xiaoping. While some of his schoolmates were outwardly hostile to the recent influx of rich Chinese buying up major chunks of commercial real estate in downtown Honolulu, Al was more embarrassed at what he perceived as foreign insensitivity to local politics and customs.

Al had read enough about the policies of Xi Jinping, his oppression of Uighurs and aggression in the South China Sea and Hong Kong to be nervous that "Big Brother" China was capable of swallowing up overly inquisitive foreigners. But the purpose of his inquiries, the government's marketing to overseas Chinese encouraging visits to the homeland, and the scale of Al's first overseas adventure dissolved his apprehension. Without much further reflection, Al suspected that the number of uninformed opinions he had about modern China was probably vast.

At almost three p.m. Wednesday—about nine a.m. Tuesday in Honolulu—Al's flight taxied into its gate at Shanghai's Pudong International Airport. As he rolled his carry-on through the airport, the efficient customs lines, and into the reception hall, Al had to check himself from gawking at the geometrically appealing steel and glass interior, fountains, and colorful artwork that adorned the mega indoor shopping center/airport. He had read of obstinate Chinese officials holding up entry to overseas Chinese upon reentry to the motherland, but Al found himself in the brightly lit reception hall without having to utter more than minimal phrases of Mandarin. Before he had a chance to arrange his knapsack on top of his carry-on, a bespectacled, gray-haired, pleasant-looking woman holding a cardboard sign approached him. Her sign read: *Liu Alaka'i*. She asked and greeted him simultaneously, "Are you Liu Alaka'i?"

"*Ni hao*, Feng Ying." Al bowed to his older cousin, recognizable from the photos forwarded to his phone.

She led the way through the airport to an ultramodern-looking train station, handed Al a ticket to be pushed into a slot at the entry booth, and they entered a waiting sleek train, which looked to Al like something from a sci-fi movie. The Metro took about fifty minutes to deposit Ying and Al at West Nanjing Road Station, and from there, a younger male cousin grabbed Al's bag and escorted them on a short walk to Ying's brick townhouse, nestled among the towering new apartments in the Bubbling Well Road Apartments in the Jing An section of Shanghai. Tidy restaurants and shops, mid-sized and compact cars, and streetscapes shaded by overhanging plane trees gave the district a small-town feel that Al imagined one might find in some New England college village.

On the trip in, Al had been too busy gazing at the passing urban landscape to engage his distant cousin in conversation or to worry about being hassled or arrested by whimsical officials. But, settled into her comfortable living room/dining room with a steaming cup of green tea, he used halting Chinese phrases to begin to learn about his hostess and her city. After the young cousin, who obviously lived nearby, bid them a good day, Al and Ying sat around a small glass-topped end table with a pot of Dragon Well tea between them.

"When did you last see my mother?" he asked her. To Al's delight, once Ying was comfortable with her young cousin, her English was far superior to his Mandarin. So, they communicated easily.

"We were both about ten years old when Donna visited Shanghai with her parents. So, I do not remember much about her other than she was playmate for a summer, and that her parents were seen as successful Americans," said Ying.

"So she spoke adequate Mandarin at the time?"

"More than adequate. It was clear early on that my mother's younger cousin, *biao mei*, was very smart. She picked up language and identified new customs very quickly. We would often say later that she would do better in US because not so many barriers for women to succeed. Although, she could have become a doctor in China, as well." Ying smiled warmly, as if remembering a dear, dear friend.

"She often speaks fondly of her Shanghai family, although I don't think she has seen any of you since her parents moved from California to Hawaii many years ago. I promised to take pictures to show her family," Al said.

Al looked around the room, framed in dark wood, adorned with calligraphy and Chinese watercolors depicting urban gardens and countryside meadows, and furnished with bookcases, tables and chairs similar to but sturdier than those Al had seen in various import stores on Oahu. There were small Buddhas, vases with joss sticks and square table linens embroidered with multicolored flowers. The air throughout the house had a slight hint of cinnamon and sandalwood. He breathed deeply, then realized that he had drifted off while soaking in the intoxicating interior.

"You must go and rest. The journey was long. But please give me some brief idea of what you would like to see while in Shanghai," said Ying.

"So, there are so many interesting and historic parts of the city. The Mao residence, the Jing An and Jade Buddha Temples, Lujiazui Park and all of Pudong, city planning exhibit in Shanghai History Museum, the French Concession and British Concession, maybe go to Suzhou to see the canals . . ." Al took a breath.

"But you are here only for a couple of weeks," interrupted Feng Ying.

"I don't know. Perhaps you can make suggestions for itinerary. I don't want to impose." Al's light brown complexion reddened.

"With pleasure. I am pleased that you have studied enough to know some of famous sights," said Ying.

"Oh, and my father, who was here once many years ago, said I should see Yu Garden and go to the Oriental Pearl TV Tower. The first, he remembers as an intoxicating garden and tea house; the second, which was built after his visit, he says must be a wonderful place from which to check out views of the city," said Al, fighting sleepiness.

"Well, let me see what we can arrange. What about the question of your birth mother? Donna said you have some leads, but seek more information. As long as you have letter from agency and identification, we can go to the registry in the English Concession to see what's recorded. I am former history teacher and remember reading about her spectacular career—early female business hero." Ying grinned proudly.

"That would be cool, yes."

"And now, young man, let me show you to my modest guest room," said Ying.

The next morning, after a breakfast of pork buns, noodles, and tea, Al gave Ying some blouses, sandals, and a handbag, which his mother had picked out as gifts for her.

"No need to bring such gifts," said his cousin. But she was visibly pleased.

Al set out to explore the Jing An neighborhood and the French Concession. He had his cell phone with an international chip, but Ying had insisted he take a marked-up street map and some transit cards. She promised to have a younger, English-speaking cousin available to accompany him as he continued his exploration later in the week.

The cobblestone streets around Ying's house were lined with small houses, tiny gardens, convenience shops, and street vendors. Once Al reached West Nanjing Road, however, a modern, twenty-first-century, high-rise glass and steel megalopolis opened before him. Al had read enough in guidebooks, talked to his parents, and been online enough to have a sense of what Shanghai would be like, but now that he was in it, on the ground, he was overwhelmed, as if the city had exploded into brilliant three-dimensional Technicolor for him. He furiously snapped photos.

Part of me, he thought, *in a real way, is of this place, from these people.*

Al noted that some shop owners, café waiters, and ticket-takers looked at him sometimes for a fraction of a second longer than he felt was normal. Older people on that first day were either too busy tending to their own appointed rounds, slightly haughty, or disinterested, but universally polite when addressed. Young people seemed eager to assist him if he appeared lost, studying his phone or paper map too long. A fair number tried their classroom English once they heard his halting Mandarin. He occasionally looked at his reflection in shop windows and confirmed that his almond-shaped eyes, his flat cheeks and his straight black hair came from Chinese genes. But his mocha skin color, slightly broad nose and ever so puffy lips were clearly non-Chinese.

There were Chinese with Mongolian blood, or a Malaysian strain that looked foreign, but frankly, Al couldn't tell where so many people he saw were from that he soon forgot about his own appearance. He was mixed-race, but might easily have been born in Shanghai. Faulty Mandarin aside, Alaka'i was comfortable—just another newcomer to Shanghai.

Once on West Nanjing Road, Al was again astounded at the number of modern high-rise buildings. He had expected row after row of 1950s Soviet-style concrete towers. But many of the blocks, interspersed with shopping centers, recreation areas, and geometrically planned green streetscapes, made Honolulu seem like a village designed in a much earlier age. Not unlike Hawaii, however, the look and feel of Shanghai had been shaped by invasions from around the globe. It was a major trading city in the late thirteenth century, resisted Japanese invasion in the mid-sixteenth, and didn't succumb to British invasion until the mid-nineteenth-century Opium Wars and the Treaty of Nanking (1843).

Al was a tourist in a city of twenty-four million that has been a trading center for many thousands of years, while he was native to a city of three hundred thousand that was first an island settlement in the eleventh century, the capital of a kingdom in 1845, and then capital of a US territory in

1906. As he walked around, Al reflected on the interesting similarities between Hawaii and China in terms of attempted Japanese and European invasions and multiethnic legacies, yet the stark differences between the Chinese and Polynesian core cultures.

After stopping at a street vendor for a bowl of broad noodles in a spicy broth and at another stall for sweet pork in a steaming bun, Al wandered in and out of temples, old curio shops, and an ultramodern shopping center. Luckily, his Chinese was adequate for him to read subway maps and negotiate the vast underground transit system. He heard but could not identify many distinct Chinese dialects, Japanese, some French, and British. And, in the Yu Garden, where he stopped for late afternoon tea, Al noted scores of Chinese twenty- and thirty-somethings speaking US English. Remembering the news stories about ever-present surveillance and citizen spies, Al hesitated. But, they were young and reminded him of friends back home. Overcoming his shyness and wariness, Al approached one.

"Excuse me, but are you American?" he asked a stranger.

"Oh, no. My friends and I are from Shanghai, but we all studied and worked in the States for a while. The tech and finance jobs are now better for us here," said the stranger.

"So, are you in the tech world?" Al's interest was piqued in between sips of fragrant Oolong tea.

"I'm an engineer working for Alibaba. Things are changing here so fast that it's hard not to get excited about life here. Once you get through the cutthroat school-university-grad school gauntlet and land with a major company, life is sweet. Materially, that is. My name is Ding Panchen, by the way." The young bespectacled engineer offered Al a genuine, but soft handshake.

"Al Liu, or Liu Al in Chinese. Call me Al. I'm a video reality game designer, but I'm here visiting relatives." He tried, unsuccessfully, to meet his new acquaintance's eyes.

Panchen was staring at his phone. "I've got to run, but if you like, we could hook up later in the week and my friends and I can show you some of the cool nontourist parts of our city," said Panchen, as he rose from his stool and was able to meet Al's gaze for a moment.

"That would be fantastic. I will contact you later next week." Using their phones, they beamed each other contact information.

"By the way, if you're walking around with that knapsack, you might want to rent a moped. Cheapest, quickest way to get around town, unless you're just traveling between tram stops. You can rent them right outside the Yu Yuan gates. Do it all on your phone." With a quick nod, Panchen left the tea house.

Al spent a few minutes scanning some tourist pamphlets he'd picked up, and then took Panchen's advice about the moped. He headed for the Shanghai Museum to see what he might like to see later in a more thorough visit. Getting used to the bike was easy, but Al had to adjust to crisscrossing vehicular traffic at large intersections. Several times he found himself starting to turn the wrong way down some street. But Panchen had been right. Between his paper maps, Google maps and his *Lonely Planet* guidebook, Al soon mastered navigating his new environment.

That evening, Ying had prepared several noodle dishes and a sumptuous soft-shelled turtle filled with ginger and diced scallions. She had also splurged and bought a bottle of plum-scented rice wine. Between carefully savored bites of food and sips of wine, Al told his cousin of his first full day.

"Ah, renting the moped is an excellent suggestion. Of course, you are young and can adapt to the traffic. I would never have thought of this way to get around . . . Perhaps tomorrow I can take you to the police and the old neighborhood committee in the British Concession where you can begin looking for the registry entries on your mother. That way, if the research requires more time, you will still have many days."

"Perfect. And if you are more comfortable, we can take a cab." Al returned Ying's smile.

"Yes, thank you, but I am comfortable on a moped, do not worry," she said.

Before bed, Al walked around his cousin's neighborhood. Music from clubs, aromas from street-side restaurants, boisterous and tipsy young adults hailing taxis or crowding into Uber-like cabs filled his senses more intensely than he had ever experienced. He momentarily envisioned groups of wealthy techies heading off to lavish parties, like the ones captured in the movie *Crazy Rich Asians*.

Hello. Shanghai is not Singapore, he reminded himself.

Al's walk did, however, fill his head with scenes he might incorporate into his video game. He fell asleep smiling.

In the morning, although initially not so comfortable with his cousin attached to his back on the moped, Al was immensely thankful to have her navigate preliminary questions about his mother at the police station. A neighborhood committee office in the old English Concession was a dead end, but the octogenarian attending them directed Ying and Al to a local police station, which seemed to have some records, and even acknowledged recognition of famous banker Wong Shi and his pioneering daughter, Wong Xi. Most files of interest, however, had been destroyed in a twenty-first-century digitizing effort.

When Ying mentioned that Al might be a relative of the taipan, the officer looked quickly at Al, as if for the first time.

"Not possible. Wong Xi was mixed blood, but English, not Malay," said the confident policeman.

A long moment's silence followed, and Al feared that his quest had come to an abrupt end. Feng Ying thanked the officer, took Al's arm and headed for the imposing cast-iron door.

"You should also try the library at Shanghai International Studies University. They have good research on such matters," added the officer, as they reached the door.

Down cobblestone side streets, he could see ladies carrying laundry on bamboo poles, as some students wove past them on flashy skateboards. As they approached Luxun Park, a large heavily planted and well-landscaped city green space protected by a large stone gate, Ying insisted they stop at a curbside noodle stand and sample egg noodles covered in soy sauce-braised tripe. Al wanted to hold his nose, but was surprised and delighted at the flavor of the dish. He pushed out of his mind the thought that thousands of others had eaten from this bowl, with minimal dishwashing.

Soon, Al began noticing the numbers of young people on bikes, motos, skateboards, and on foot.

"So, we must be entering the university?" he said over his shoulder.

"This part of Shanghai has many universities: Fudan, International Studies, University of Science, University of Finance and Economics. So, lots of apartments and spaces for students," said Ying.

Once on the campus, Al easily located the library.

"Wow, this tops our U of H campus. It's amazing," Al remarked, as he parked the moped, taking in the impressive landscaping, with its lakes, bridges, and waterfalls.

"Do you also have young girls with skirts too short and too tight to be seen in public, walking around as if they wanted to distract scholarly males from their jobs—studying?" Ying's disgust was clear.

"Cousin, that style is global, I think," Al laughed.

"They diet to stay skinny and focus on studies so they can find wealthy husband."

"I think many of them will become wealthy in their own right, cousin," Al said, as if he had some authoritative source.

"Unfortunately, Shanghai has long ago forgotten the values of the revolution and become obsessed with money," she sneered. "Your birth mother became wealthy without publicly losing class or face."

Inside, it didn't take them long to find material on Wong Shi; the library had a room set aside for both paper and digitized documents on famous Shanghai natives. From several sources, Al read that his grandfather was born in 1916 of common parents and was a gifted student. He rose in banking to be head of the Shanghai branch of Shanghai Commercial Bank. He was a Communist Party member, but not an active officer. He had been permitted more concessions, even as the Cultural Revolution approached, because the government recognized the critical role played by big banks in trade and in building revenues for the state. His marriage to the British *Daily Telegraph*'s Far East correspondent, Katherine Harris, received little attention. Some Shanghai newspaper clips did, however, reveal the stir that their union caused in upper-crust Shanghai society. It was evident to Al and Ying that the couple had to have been extremely strong and very much in love.

Ying found an article that mentioned Harris' early death from smallpox not long after the birth of a girl child. The girl was brought up in Shanghai and later in Hong Kong by her father's sister, her aunt Wong Jianying. Her father had moved to Hong Kong to run China International Bank and to escape the Cultural Revolution on the mainland. Though a "mongrel" and a reclusive child, Wong Xi had the brains of her father, the charm of her mother, and the political savoir faire that surpassed them both, according to the article. Al found several other biographies that heralded his mother's rise and dominance as a taipan in Hong Kong. They all mentioned her marriage to Bao Li, another finance genius. The couple was childless, and there was, of course, no mention of any affairs or indiscretions.

Al found a few business articles heralding his mother's development of SRI, its 1996 merger with the mainland company South China Apparel, its subsequent dominance of the Asian fabric and fashion markets. He even discovered a business biography that alluded to the discriminatory treatment Wong Xi had received as a youngster after arriving with her father in 1965, and highlighted the "star couple" attention she and her older husband, Bao Li, received in a modernizing twenty-first-century Asia. After Deng Xiaoping declared that China had evolved a "Socialism with Chinese characteristics" and that "to get rich is glorious," mainland leaders were anxious to consult with their famous Shanghai native.

The library visit whet Al's appetite to see the city. Ying directed their return along the Huangpu River, taking them by monasteries, synagogues, the financial district (Bund), and even the Oriental Pearl TV Tower. She insisted they cruise past the streets and alleys of the French Concession, although Ying seemed more interested in the souvenir, T-shirt, jewelry and jade shops, cafes and bars, and smartly dressed shoppers than was Al. Exhilarating as the ride was, Al's mind remained occupied with his primary mission.

When they reached her house, he had made a decision.

"Ying, this was a fantastic day. You have shown me part of a city I want to visit often. I love Shanghai," said Al.

"But you have only begun to explore . . ." she began.

"I know, and I will return many times. But I have to find out more about my mother. What the library revealed is that she was biracial, child of a single parent, super smart, overcame many odds, and became a business icon. I'm honored and proud to be her son. But . . ."

"But you don't know how you fit in, what were circumstances of your birth." Ying finished his thought.

"Exactly. It's clear that her aunt, Wong Jianying, raised my mother. I need to find her."

"Alaka'i, I doubt she's still alive. And, if she is, she's in Hong Kong."

"I have to go to the adoption agency where she took me, and from which my American parents adopted me. They must have more information. I can't appreciate this magnificent place, this land of my ancestors, until I know more about my mother. Do you understand, Ying?"

She looked at him for several seconds, then smiled. "Of course. You are a curious son. A good son."

Al felt badly about not being more of a gracious guest. He promised to return and leisurely visit all the architectural and historical highlights that Ying had recommended.

Ying was able to convince Al to spend another day exploring Pudong and some of the urban lakes and waterways scattered throughout the city. She suggested that his notion of a tsunami swamping Shanghai directly from the Pacific was one he should investigate because the actual Pacific Ocean was over a thousand miles away.

That evening, Al spent hours of computer time studying the geography of Shanghai and was reassured that a tsunami out in the East China Sea might sweep over the southern tip of Japan, up the Yangtze River Delta, flooding the banks of the Huangpu River and smaller tributaries. The damage would be extensive to urban Shanghai, which is built primarily on flat plains. The next day, he photographed key locations along the river and around lakes and streams, as well as iconic buildings and avenues up and down Shanghai coastal areas. He envisioned scenes of a dystopian destruction that would greatly enhance the terror portrayed in *Earth Reclaimed*.

He was also concerned about regional factors that he would not have time to study on this trip, but which he knew could heavily influence the believability of his game. Al made note to research North Korean military and naval activity, Chinese moves to increase control over coastal waters, industrial and agricultural effluents polluting the ocean, and political stances that could destabilize the region. On a more philosophical front, he felt he needed a better grasp of the role Eastern religions were playing in shaping perspectives and policies toward growth in the region. He recognized that for insight on these issues, he would need to do much more research and reflection. The East-West Center, he thought, would be a perfect resource.

Before he left the next day, Al found a thank-you card at a little shop near Feng Ying. Inside, he drew a sketch of a beach with palm trees and a banner stretched across the top, saying: "Welcome to Hawaii, cousin Ying."

He left the note on his bed.

Al hugged his older relative as he prepared to leave.

"And now, let me call a cousin in Hong Kong, so you—"

"Thank you, Ying, but I need to be alone in a hotel and at this agency until I figure this out," Al interrupted her.

"Well, at least I can phone the YMCA on Kowloon. It's reasonable, centrally located, and very nice," Ying insisted.

After checking in at the YMCA near Hong Kong's famous Peninsula Hotel on Kowloon, Al dropped his bags on his bed, checked the foggy view across Victoria Harbor to Hong Kong Island, and descended fifteen floors for a quick walk up Nathan Road. Having spent some short time in Shanghai, Al was not overwhelmed by the modern structures, hectic traffic, crowded sidewalks, pervasive commerce, or the international cosmopolitan environment of Hong Kong. But as he strolled among late-afternoon pedestrians, his fully engaged senses absorbed the twilight over the island, sea breezes off of the shimmering harbor, and the fog horns of cargo ships and fishing junks. Hong Kong had a similar, but more concentrated, more intense urban feel than Shanghai. Al knew he was in yet another world within China, one even more recently controlled by the British, yet a space truly unique, in ways Al sensed but could not yet finger.

Al could see signs of tension with police in some areas, sidewalk and storefront scars from scuffles between crowds and police in others, and boarded storefronts on some side streets. Otherwise, the vibe of Hong Kong seemed by and large similar to other world commercial capitals Al had seen in videos.

The address of the Hong Kong Families Agency was off of Queen's Way, not far from the Peak Tram on the Hong Kong Island side of Victoria Harbor. So, the next morning, after a bread, tea, and rice porridge breakfast in a little café near the famous Star Ferry terminal, Al boarded the boat with hundreds of commuters headed into "Central." Though overwhelmingly Chinese, the crowds were also Hindi, Sikh, Malay, Philippine, Japanese, Korean, European, African, Australian, and Russian. Those were the looks and tongues that Al recognized; he knew there were many more. As he wound his way through parks and public gardens, glancing up at ultramodern office towers and low-rise brick and concrete colonial mansions, Al inhaled the city. In contrast to the control and surveillance he had partially feared, Al felt liberated.

The adoption agency was in a random mid-rise office building on the third floor. Rather than wait for the slow elevators, Al ascended the steps, two at a time. When he found the correct door, Al looked down a hallway of about six suites, turned to the wall opposite his destination, sat on a window sill whose bay window overlooked a standard granite paved courtyard and closed his eyes.

Am I nuts? he asked himself. *I'm halfway around the world in a foreign metropolis looking for clues about my insignificant self from a place where a woman who didn't want me had me deposited. Even if this Nancy Barton is still working here, is in, and is willing to see me, she may not have any more information about my mother, or my father for that matter.*

Al reflected on what he had seen in the last few days. The majesty and urban wonder of two historic, significant capitals of global culture, economy and power. *To have lived in, overcome prejudice in, and then prospered in Hong Kong, my mother . . .* Al couldn't finish his thought before he began to tear up.

"May I help you, sir?" A young Han Chinese woman was about to open the agency's door as she addressed Al in British English.

"Ah, yes. Sorry. I'd like to see Ms. Nancy Barton, please, if she is still working here." Al wiped his face with a sleeve, stood, and approached the bespectacled woman.

"Do you have an appointment?" She motioned him into a small anteroom.

"I'm sorry, but I don't. But I have come all the way from the United States."

"I'll see if Ms. Barton can see you. Your name?"

Al gave her his name and sat next to a table of magazines, while the woman went down a hall and entered an interior office.

She returned and sat facing Al, who realized that she was staring. *Without the glasses, she would be very attractive.* He looked up and caught her quick turn of the head back toward her desktop. A minute later, she openly turned to him.

"Please forgive me for being impolite, Mr. Liu. But I don't often meet young Americans and am wondering what is your impression of Hong Kong."

"My impression?"

"I am so sorry to bother you. But we are going through major political discussions, have had significant government changes, and so many in Hong Kong wish for freedoms they thought had been promised. Many have visited your country and feel envy. So, sorry. My name is Hung Meije." Meije looked quickly toward the door of her boss, Nancy Barton.

"Nice to meet you, Meije. Well, I've only been here one day so far, and less than a week on the mainland."

"Yes, but do you see differences between here and the mainland? Do you notice more, how you say, anxiety among young people?" Meije pressed ahead.

"Well, I really don't think I have been here long enough, or met enough people to draw that type of conclusion." Al shifted in his seat, facing Meije more directly.

"It is not my place, but we need our overseas cousins to understand what we are going through here." Meije became more at ease as she spoke.

"But, if I'm correct, China never promised that Hong Kong would be 'free,' like in the West, did it?" Al tried to remain objective.

"Not like in the West, but more than on the mainland. Anyway, forgive me for bringing it up. This is not what you are here for. Please, forgive me." She returned to her computer.

About fifteen minutes later, Al sat facing a matronly looking, wrinkled, Yorkshire-sounding and perfectly coiffed Nancy Barton. Her stiff and starchy appearance, however, was but a cover for a very warm and engaging executive.

"You've come quite a way, Mr. Liu. I hope Meije didn't disturb you with lots of questions. These are trying times, particularly for people of your generation in Hong Kong," said Nancy Barton.

"Not at all. She was quite enlightening," Al tried to reassure her.

"Please, give my regards to your parents. They are such a lovely couple."

"Thank you again for seeing me. I must admit that my life before I found out about this inheritance seems like a decade ago, and more than four thousand miles away."

"I can imagine. I can, perhaps, give you a bit more information about your birth mother, but I have nothing about your father, nor about the circumstances that led Wong Xi to have her aunt bring you to us."

"Sorry, but is Wong Jianying still alive?" Al interrupted.

"My guess is that she died several years ago. She was already getting on in years when she brought you to us. And, if she were still alive, I'd have no way of finding her." said

Barton. "What little I know is from short conversations with her, contacts in our business community, and commonly known stories about your mother's side of your family. Much of it has been conveyed to the law firm with whom you met."

Al listened as Nancy Barton repeated much of what he had already read, but added some illuminating detail. Like Al, his birth mother had had different coloring than her classmates. Her brownish hair and olive skin were cause for teasing when she was young. Even though Jianying looked after Xi as if she were her daughter, she was no substitute for playmates. The young girl turned inward and discovered that she loved reading and had a talent for learning foreign languages, perhaps inherited from her mother. She also was brilliant with numbers, a talent passed on from her father. After her father moved them to Hong Kong, where there were more children of mixed blood, Xi seemed to acquire some friends and be a happier child, though still very much a loner. As her father, Shi, grew more and more prominent in the business community, people became more accepting of his daughter.

Though she was as rich as other kids in prestigious Hong Kong schools, Xi's father insisted that she walk to the bus, rather than be chauffeured, learn to cook, study history and politics and be able to discuss current topics with adults. She was not treated differently than if she had been his son. Above all, she was not allowed to forget that her roots were from the multicultural, ethnically complex, politically complicated society that was mainland Shanghai.

"As you know," Nancy continued, "your mother became one of the most successful and influential taipans in Hong Kong, thus in Asia. So, you see, Al, you come from a line of very strong, very successful, culturally mixed people." She smiled at her young visitor.

"Mixed with European is not mixed with Black," Al said matter-of-factly.

"That is true, but you are from a new generation, a new country—one which has already had a globally admired mixed-race African Hawaiian president."

Al had other concerns. "Can you tell me how I came to be born?" he pressed.

"I wish I could, but Jianying had no information on your birth father, or on the circumstances that led to your birth. Suffice it to say that your birth mother wanted to ensure that you had a chance to grow up in an environment free of Chinese prejudice."

"And in one that would not embarrass her," Al said with slight bitterness.

"Clearly, she did not want to disrupt her own career. However, given what I see of you and the financial gift she has left you, she must have loved you and made a choice that will stand you in very good stead indeed."

Al sat for several minutes, not sure how to respond. After reflecting, he stood, extended his hand and said, "Thank you for the part you have played. I love my Hawaiian family, and I very much appreciate your filling me in on my birth mother."

"Mr. Liu, thank you for coming this far. I have a feeling that the world will hear from you, and that your mother will be proud."

Nancy Barton resisted the temptation to advise that he adopt patience and reflection, and develop understanding. She strongly sensed that this young man would become exceptional in his own way, in his own time.

CHAPTER 13

2027–28

After Al's China trip, Donna and Tommy sensed their son had grown more secure in his identity. Though he didn't say anything specifically that conveyed this, he spoke more matter-of-factly about his prospective wealth, about his Chinese heritage, about the immediate and longer-term projects he had, and about his thankfulness at being Hawaiian and their son.

"He seems more comfortable in his skin. And more appreciative of how far the mainland has come since Mao," Tommy said to Donna over a late morning coffee.

"What? You think he anticipated people in big cone-shaped straw hats pulling each other around in rickshaws?" Donna laughed.

"I'm just glad that he's less anxious about who he is and doesn't seem overwhelmed by the prospect of becoming a very wealthy young man."

"Who would have thought that our trip of a lifetime to adopt a baby in Hong Kong would have taken us along this path?" asked Donna, shaking her head in amazement.

Miles away, off the shore of Sandy Beach, the whitecaps, foam, and crashing breakers justified the dangerous red danger flag lifeguards had stuck in the sand that morning.

Al and the other water babies looked for paths in the surf that would permit only the most experienced native swimmers to push their surfboards out beyond the waves. He sat on his board for at least twenty minutes looking back at the emerald green cliffs beyond the beach, at the blue ocean out past his board, at the albatross and terns surveying the water for lunch, and he inhaled long fulfilling breaths.

"This is where I belong," he thought. "Money is irrelevant out here. Ethnicity, class, academic smarts don't mean a thing out here. This ocean is the most powerful and magnificent ruler on earth. And I get to enjoy it for free."

Al had grown up in the ocean the way mainland US kids do shooting baskets on playgrounds, kicking a soccer ball, or swinging a bat on open fields. Every muscle, tendon, and nerve had been conditioned to respond to wave force, direction, height, and speed. On his best days, Al imagined his body to be one with the energy of the ocean. *"Don't fight it; find it and flow with it,"* he had been taught.

He chose three championship waves to ride over the next couple of hours, and then rode onto the beach on a modest breaker. He lay down in the sun and quickly fell asleep.

"You're pretty good out there. Ever compete on North Shore?" A familiar voice snapped Al back to consciousness.

He looked up into the noon sun and could only see the figure of a powerfully built dark-skinned man.

"Professor Morton?" he asked, shading his eyes.

"It's Harry. Sorry to disturb you."

"Not a problem. I should be heading in to get some lunch, anyway. I'm taking some mental health hours," said Al.

"You're your own boss now. Let me buy you a sandwich? We both are heading back past Hawaii Kai. You know those water-side lunch places in there?" Harry offered Al a hand up off the sand.

Al didn't have a firm plan until later in the day, and it occurred to him that his mentor might have some ideas about his new mixed-race assignment. He thought for a minute about how much to tell him of his inheritance.

What can it hurt? he reasoned.

"I'm in the corner of the lot. Meet you down there? You know, I really admire the way you attack the big ones. You really could compete, I think," Harry said.

"I may have grown up out here, but I didn't spend all of my time in the ocean like the really good surfers. Thanks, but I know my limits out there."

"Well, you're smarter than me. I almost didn't make it back one time."

"Monster wave?" asked Al.

"No. Shark," said Harry. "I was lucky that a man, who's now a friend, pulled me out. Anyway— let's head out. I'm hungry, too."

Driving along the coast highway behind Harry, Al reflected on Shanghai, on the radical turn of events in his life. Even though he had a major decision to make in terms of a project to satisfy his birth mother's wishes, even though he would soon have more money than he could imagine using in a lifetime, and even though he still knew little about his birth mother's private life and nothing of his real father's identity, Al was more at peace than he'd been for a long while. Perhaps it was being in China, experiencing the enormity and excitement of modern megalopolises— Shanghai and Hong Kong. Maybe it was the warm reception by his mother's cousin, or, strangely, the sense of belonging in a culture both foreign and familiar to his millennial Honolulu. Or perhaps it was simply being back in the Pacific.

Whatever the cause, Al knew that he was a lucky guy able to enjoy the life rolling out before him. Being part Chinese and enjoying solving puzzles, working hard and caring about family didn't make him so terribly unusual within the framework of a global diaspora. That he had slim tolerance for organizational structures and procedures, which he perceived to obstruct achievement and innovation, placed him in the mainstream of young twenty-first-century entrepreneurs. At this point, his major worry was that older generations were going to destroy the planet, leaving a wasteland of cinders, ashes, sand dunes, and swamps for younger generations.

On reflection, he thought there were two salient, interesting distinctions between him and his mainland Chinese contemporaries. Having been admitted to Caltech or a similar Chinese university, no mainland student would experiment during his senior year and fail to graduate. On the other hand, Al surmised that he felt more of an obligation to help minority kids of color on the islands than he perceived young tech-savvy affluent Chinese did for their rural cousins. In fact, even the sense of duty and obligation to family appeared to have lessened from the days reflected in stories from when Donna was a child. It wasn't just the super-rich portrayed in Singapore writer Kevin Kwan's novels who were consumed with acquiring grown-up toys in urban China. He thought that recent young Chinese immigrants to Hawaii acted as if family responsibility, particularly for one's parents and grandparents, was old school. The value of the community over the individual, so pronounced in his older Chinese relatives, was clearly diminished in his generation. Just a cultural observation. Not some determinant of future outcomes, he thought.

As they pulled into the parking lot of a dockside Asian bistro on the fringe of the Hawaii Kai neighborhood, Al was more comfortable with where and who he was than during his early association with Harry. He was comforted that their meetings, though infrequent had remained interesting and enjoyable, and he hoped that he would continue to be able to learn from him.

"So, how was China? Was this a video-game business trip?" Harry asked, sipping iced tea as they waited for Korean barbeque and kimchi.

"Partially, yes. As you know, Shanghai and Hong Kong are quite distinctive, and I really only touched the surface. There are so many parts of each city. Obviously, if my Mandarin up north and my nonexistent Cantonese in the south had been adequate, I could have explored much more. Still, I met friends of my mother's cousin and a few random young people. So it wasn't all sightseeing." Al waited to see if Morton would press for more detail. He was hesitant to share the real reason for the trip.

"So, remind me how China fits into this environmental game you're designing," asked Harry.

"Yes. There's a major cataclysmic event that affects Shanghai."

The food came, Harry took a bite of his meat, sat back and smiled, as if daydreaming about something.

"You probably don't know, but one of my last big consulting gigs was in Hong Kong. Not the most significant, but unusual and full of intrigue." Harry took another bite.

"Intrigue?" asked Al, suspending his chopsticks in midair.

"Yes. It started as a consulting assignment to help with a merger, but before it was completed, there was more than the normal tension and fighting and at least one nonprincipal was murdered." Harry chuckled.

"You're kidding. Murdered over a merger?" Al was now transfixed.

"You have to remember that this was in the early days of the CCP (Chinese Communist Party) and the People's Republic's transition to capitalism. The National Army chieftains wanted to get first dibs on lucrative business opportunities, and Hong Kong had already experienced violence around the opium trade, as well as a tradition of triads. So the town, a portal to the West, was ripe for struggles over power and wealth."

"But your lectures and writings all suggest that you sought cooperative, collaborative business solutions. How did that square with—?"

"I tried those approaches at first, but I was able to recognize when other tactics were needed to bolster an overall strategy. Nothing is ever as clean as a case study." Harry laughed.

Al stared. This guru of process and procedures, of formats and formulas, was more practical, more into "action," than Al had thought.

The two were silent for a while, concentrating on their lunch. Then Harry looked up at Al.

"So, successful trip?" he asked innocently.

"Yes, well, pretty much." Al hesitated.

Harry simply looked and waited.

"The real purpose of the trip was to find out about my birth mother."

"Oh. She was from one of those cities?" Harry expressed polite curiosity.

"Yes, born in Shanghai and spent most of her life in Hong Kong."

"Interesting. How did you track her down? I thought the background details of birth parents were usually closely held by agencies," Harry continued, following his natural curiosity.

Al shoveled in several quick portions of food with his chopsticks. He looked at Harry and tried to assess the probability that telling him the full truth about his inheritance could lead to personal or professional embarrassment. It was low, he concluded.

"Professor, Mr. Morton . . . I mean, Harry." Al hesitated.

"Yes. What's going on here?" Harry's curiosity was now piqued.

"It's that I'm not used to talking about personal stuff, like I'm about to tell you. I mean not face to face. That's what social media is for, in my world." Al tried to maintain eye contact with Harry.

"Well, would you rather text me?" Harry said, in jest.

"No. I trust you, and I wouldn't mind sharing this with someone who knows a lot about modern China." Al relaxed a bit. "It turns out that my birth mother was a very successful businesswoman—exceptionally successful."

"You mean like the head of some product line or an import company?"

"I mean successful enough as a CEO that she was able to leave me, her only heir, half a billion dollars." He stopped to let the figure sink in.

"That's billion with a B? Wow. But you never met her, right?" Harry proceeded as if he were an investigative reporter.

"That's right. I found out about her when my parents were contacted by a big Chinese law firm representing the Hong Kong adoption agency where I had been placed as a baby." Al then told Harry about the terms of his inheritance, the project he had to create, and the little bit of background he had found on his birth mother.

"But did you find out why she put you up for adoption in the first place?" Harry's curiosity was still almost academic.

"Well, she must have had a relationship with an African diplomat or something, and felt that having the child would kill her marriage and career, plus make for an arduous childhood for the kid—me. From a detached perspective, I suppose I can't blame her," said Al.

Harry reflected on Al's story and then froze. He stopped chewing, put down his glass, looked deep into the young man's eyes and asked, "Alaka'i, did you happen to find out the name of your mother's company?"

"Sure. SRI, Silk Road, Inc. Did you ever hear of it?" Al hadn't noticed Harry's suddenly rigid posture.

Harry reached for his iced tea to drown the acid reflux creeping up his esophagus. He slowly folded his napkin and mopped the sweat beading on his brow.

"Are you OK, Harry? You look a bit weird . . ."

"I'm fine. I just have to run to the restroom a second." And, without waiting for a response, Harry stood up and quickly strode to the men's room. He splashed cold water on his face and stared at himself in the mirror.

Over thirty years later. Why had it never occurred to me that Xi might get pregnant? I assumed, stupidly, that she had used some form of fail-safe birth control. Now what?

His emotions were tightly wound into a knot, squeezing his gut tighter by the minute. Joy, fear, surprise, apprehension, even anger paralyzed Harry from head to foot. *Do I tell him? If so, when?*

Another patron entered the restroom to use the urinal, so Harry took a deep breath, dried his face and left to return to the table. He had not made a decision. A voice on one side of his brain argued for delay, to enable a planned decision and time to analyze the likely and unintended consequences of revealing the truth. Another internal advocate lobbied for immediate disclosure and a joint struggle with Al about the future.

He sat down.

"Wow. I'm sorry. It must have been the peppers. Got caught in my throat," said Harry, displaying full composure.

"You had me worried for a moment. You looked like you couldn't get your breath," said Al.

"OK, so, where were we? You have basically two years to research and design this project to help mixed-blood Chinese kids, then you can spend your life running it . . ."

"No, the project will only be part of my life. I'm sure I'll hire a staff. The gaming company will still be my main focus. Climate change isn't going away easily, and certainly not any time soon." Al glanced at his phone, lying on the table. "Oh wow, sorry, I have to get back to the office. Thanks for lunch and for listening."

They stood, hugged, and Harry said, "Anytime. Sounds like you've got some exciting times ahead. Feel free to share whatever you'd like whenever."

Driving back to his house, Harry realized that the stomach tension had been replaced by a vise of pain in the back of his neck. As he entered his living room, the sweet fragrance of his night-blooming cereus almost made him throw up. He changed into bathing trunks and running shoes and headed for a twilight run along the beach. He tried to clear his mind, but after a long hot shower, a few sips of ice-cold Pinot Grigio, and a quick peek at his emails, Harry settled on his ocean-front balcony to allow his emotions to surface.

He reflected on his relationship with Xi and how it had been a pleasure stimulated by taboos and exotic circumstances. He didn't regret its brevity, but he wondered how she had felt bearing a child, and whether she had, even for a moment, thought of contacting him. He wondered if she had been tempted to find Al over the last thirty years. No, he thought, she would have filed that chapter away and assiduously moved on with her life. How ironic, he thought, that the consequences of his affair had eventually cost Harry his marriage and his son, yet this progeny might, if he was lucky, offer him another chance at being a kind of father. The real question now was how to break the news to Al, and then how to build a deeper relationship, if he was willing.

Later that evening, Harry sent an email to the Lius asking if they'd join him for breakfast the next morning. They were not free for a couple of days but agreed to come by his place two days out. Harry asked his house help to leave some rolls, meats and cheese that would nicely accompany juice and coffee in the morning.

"Wow, this is quite a view out beyond Kapiolani Beach. Hidden back here at the foot of Diamond Head," said Tommy, savoring a cup of black Kona coffee.

"This is a gorgeous scene. And your house is lovely. Lots of light," added Donna.

"Well, you are too kind. And thank you so much for coming on short notice. Why don't we take our plates and sit in the living room?" Harry ushered the Lius off the balcony, so they could face each other as they dealt with his bombshell.

"Tommy, I don't know if Al's told you, but he has come to me every now and then for advice on his company. So, over the years, I've become somewhat of a mentor to him." Harry paused.

"I couldn't have wished for anything more," said Tommy, raising a glass of juice in a toast.

"Mentorship is, perhaps, too formal. A friendship," Harry continued.

"Even better," said Donna.

"I don't know if he'd want me to tell you, but he shared the news of his trip to China, his inheritance, and the discoveries he's made about his birth mother."

"If he chose to share, that's his decision," said Tommy. "Actually, I'm glad he has because I'm not sure we'll be much help assisting him with his project. Although, I think his birth mother wanted to give him wide latitude to be as ambitious as he is comfortable."

"Yes, well, I'll bet there are experiences you've had growing up as Chinese Hawaiian here and in California that can inform Al's perspective and his project," said Harry.

"Maybe, but we're his parents and so he doesn't always look to us for advice." Tommy squeezed Donna's hand and chuckled.

"Well, I would hope he'd mature enough over time to seek both of your counsel," said Harry.

Donna and Tommy clasped their hands together in front and bowed.

"Anyway, what I haven't shared with Al, nor any other person, until now, is this." Harry took a deep breath. "During my last job in China, I had an affair with a client. Her husband found out and eventually told my wife. The relationship with the Chinese woman ended with the job,

and, partly due to the affair, my marriage fell apart and I became estranged from my son, Mark. I put it all behind me, started teaching in DC, retired, sort of, and moved out here."

Harry noticed that the Lius shared skeptical questioning looks, as if to say: "Why are you telling us your private stuff?"

"That affair was about thirty-two years ago, but I found out the other day that the woman had a child and placed him for adoption." He paused, gathering his courage. "That child is Alaka'i, your son."

Silence.

Donna stood, clasped her hands, walked to the picture widow opening out to the Pacific, and stared. Tommy looked at Harry with his jaw open.

For minutes, no one said anything.

Tommy broke the silence. "How is this even possible? The odds must be less than one in a million. He's born in Hong Kong, you don't know about him, we travel to Hong Kong to adopt a two-year-old; later, we ask you to mentor him . . . I mean, no way," he stammered, more confused and bewildered than angry, yet upset and wanting to complain to somebody.

"And you think God doesn't have a plan for us?" asked Donna, softly. "I am just deeply concerned that this will be way too much for Al to handle at this point."

"I know. I thought long and hard about keeping this to myself. But, on balance, maybe selfishly, I concluded he would want to know," Harry offered sheepishly.

Tommy blurted out, "I mean, what do you think is your responsibility beyond informing him? How do you think this will affect our relationship with him? Damn, there are so many questions to figure out. You can't just walk away from this." As soon as Tommy uttered the words, he realized that his anger had gotten the better of him. "I know you wouldn't do that. Sorry." He raised his hands in a sign of peace.

Donna remained quiet, but was processing the news. She blocked out Tommy and Harry and entered into prayer in her own private space.

"Dear, tell me, what do you think?" Tommy broke in.

"Well," she responded calmly, "I think there will be a positive side. It will take some getting used to, but I can envision happy outcomes. After all, it's not like Harry purposely abandoned our son, or his birth mother, for that matter. Let's talk it through."

"Look, I haven't told anyone but you two. So, we can just keep it between us and not burden Al with this information. This is my doing, so I will assume whatever responsibility is best for the boy. I don't want to burden you . . . and, while I didn't plan to have another son, I did. I understand your anger. Why don't we leave it for now, not say any more about it?" Harry rocked back and forth in agitation.

Tommy stared at Harry, his brown eyes boring a hole in the taller man. After a few moments, his intensity dissipated. He saw the contorted agony and sorrow on Harry's face.

Another long silence.

Donna lifted her head, as if released from the grip of deep meditation, rose from her chair and walked toward Harry, who stood defensively. Then she embraced him.

"You have given us the most precious present in our lives. And you never even knew it," she said.

"But you have a right to be disgusted!" Harry sputtered.

As if jolted back to his normal "can do" personality, Tommy brightened.

"Disgusted? We're adults, Harry. Affairs happen. It's not like you fathered a son and neglected him. You just now found out he had been born, and that you happen to know him. I'm not disgusted. When I take a breath and think about it, I'm happy that our son will get to know one of his birth parents and can put the final pieces together about his natural heritage. Although I think he's beginning to understand that he already knows much of who he is." Tommy embraced Harry, whose tears wet Tommy's shoulder.

"You are amazing. I so dreaded telling you, and at first I thought I'd made a terrible mistake in telling you. I certainly wouldn't blame you if you wanted to keep this news in this room. But I really hoped we could find an accommodation that would satisfy everyone. He's your son, you raised him. I would just like to be some part of his life, if he chooses."

"Yes, it is up to Al to decide. So, you didn't tell him anything yet?" asked Donna.

"No. First, I was shocked to find out that Xi, his birth mother, had had a child. Then I had to be sure that what Al was telling me meant that I am his birth father. Finally, I needed time to consider the various consequences, primarily to him, of telling him the truth."

"Well, now that I've had a moment, I'm so glad you decided to tell us first. But I do think it's your responsibility to tell him. Then, we go from there," said Tommy.

"You know, Al's always chafing at my religious notions, but in fact he's never had a godfather. If he decides the idea could work, then how would you feel about that role?" Donna asked, tentatively.

"Donna, it's almost too good to be true, that you would be comfortable with me in that role for your son . . . Tommy?" Harry looked questioningly at him.

Tommy simply gave Harry a big smile and a thumbs up.

"Wow. Well, let's see what Al thinks. I don't want to get out ahead of him. This has to be his wish. But thank you two." They clinked glasses, all three still in a state of shock.

Harry waited a couple of days before texting Al that he'd like to meet for a coffee to talk about his mixed-race project. They agreed to meet at the beachfront restaurant of the Otani Hotel at the end of Waikiki. Harry arrived first, having walked down the hill from his house, and ordered a pot of green tea. He sat looking out at the late-afternoon horizon, planning what to say, and wondering about the whereabouts of his other son, Mark.

"Sorry to be late. I already ordered a latte, on the way in," said Al as he sat down. "Wow," he said, smiling as he leaned back and absorbed the view, "I've only been here for Sunday brunch, but it really is peaceful at this time of day. Thanks for thinking of it."

"Al. I've been thinking about your project and how I might help," Harry began.

"Thanks, but I didn't expect you to put any real effort into this. After all, I have a couple of years and legal advisors. And it's not something that I'm spending much time on yet myself."

"Understood. But before I get into my ideas, I have to confess something to you," said Harry.

Al was marginally better at reading people face to face than the average millennial, but he had no idea where Harry was headed.

"Al, when you told me what you had discovered about your birth mother, I made a discovery myself. One that I wasn't sure I could or should share with you." Harry hesitated.

"You actually knew her?" Al asked excitedly.

Harry sucked in his breath, let it out and avoided the young man's gaze for a moment.

"Thirty-two years ago, I had a brief affair with a client, a rising business tycoon named Wong Xi, your biological mother. I wasn't proud of it, but until the other day, I thought the only consequence of our tryst was my broken marriage and the alienation from my son in DC. Now I realize, Al, that I . . . I am . . . your birth father."

The two men stared at each other.

Al gasped for breath and he broke away from Harry, stood up abruptly, left the restaurant and walked to the beach beyond the hedges. Harry threw some cash on the table, waved to the waitress and rushed out after his son.

When he caught up to him, the youngster turned to him and whispered, "I have never felt so confused . . . so angry and happy . . . so anxious and relieved all at the same time." He collapsed on the sand, legs folded and wept.

Harry, not sure of his own emotions, of what boundaries to cross, hesitated and then embraced his son on the beach.

After at least ten minutes, Al wiped his face and began. "For so many years, I wondered who both of my parents were and why they had put me up for adoption. I finally discovered my mother and have grown to accept her actions, at least intellectually. Now, a person I greatly admire turns out to be my birth father. But he never knew it. Heavy doesn't begin to describe this, this feeling . . ." Al's sobs slowed and he took deeper breaths.

"I debated not telling you, feeling you had enough emotional adjustment to handle at the moment. But I talked to Tommy and Donna, and we all felt that you are now a man who's about to collect an enormous fortune, and you should be able to face that future having had the opportunity to know as much as possible about your original parents." Harry sat back, elbows in the sand and exhaled.

"God, there is so much I want to know about you, your background, your estranged family, and my birth mother, of course."

Harry gave Al a capsule biography of his life growing up in Philadelphia, his political and professional career, his marriage to Mary and his relationship to Mark. He told him briefly about selling his firm and about the SRI deal that took him to Hong Kong. Without much detail, he told him of his fascination with and attraction to Xi, of her husband's discovery, and the end of Harry's Washington consulting career.

Al listened intently, processing the story. "It will take me some time to digest this all. I mean, all in all, I'm glad to know the truth. It's just such a shock right now. And," he added, hesitantly, "what do I even call you?"

"Harry, just like you do now," Harry said matter-of-factly.

"No, I mean Dad, Father . . ."

"How about sticking with Harry? We could say I'm your uncle, as in a godfather. I'm comfortable with that. After all, Donna and Tommy are, in every sense but biological, your mother and father, don't you think?"

"I'm good with that, too."

Both men smiled broadly for the first time since leaving the restaurant.

They moved off the beach to a stone wall separating the sand from a small grassy park and sat.

"Now that you know who your birth mother is, you don't have a desire to find more of her family?" asked Harry.

"No. I think my trip satisfied that need. She showed no interest, during her life, in knowing what happened to me. And it's purely by accident that I found out about you. Well, she reached out in spirit, I suppose," Al said.

"Yes, but, of course, I never knew that Xi was pregnant, let alone gave birth."

"What would you have done had you known?" Al's question had a slight accusatory tone.

"I would have brought you home to DC, with the rest of the family."

"I'll bet your wife would have had something to say about it . . ."

"You're right. Given the choices, however, it would have been the right thing to do. No way I'd have left you in China without any natural parent," said Harry with confidence.

Al stared out at the ocean for a while, then turned to Harry and said, "So, I'm curious to know more about your family—what your parents were like?"

"Well, I had strong, loving parents who gave me solid values, lessons in civility, coping, and toughness that I only fully appreciated as my adult years unfolded. For the short time he was alive, I was close to Pierce, my talented brother.

We were quite different in our gifts and in our challenges, but the hole dug out of my soul when he died can never be filled." Harry stared out at the ocean for a long moment. "But, on the whole, home and school gave me a pretty solid platform from which to jump into adulthood."

"So, how did your brother die?" asked Al.

"He was driving on a slippery road near home, in Philadelphia, and lost control. He hit a tree and was gone," said Harry.

"Wow. I'm sorry," said Al.

"Thank you. Tough as it was losing Peirce, I didn't know how well-off I was until college and then the service. The more I encountered adversity, the more I felt disrespected by others, the stronger those values and that preparation emerged. Yeah, even though I spent all those years in Washington, Philadelphia will always be home for me." Harry smiled at Al.

"What about your father?" Al asked.

"Well, I really never got to know him, since he died of a heart attack while I was in the service. He had a rough youth in the deep South, had a brother lynched, and had to work after school ever since he was eleven. He was academically talented, so he went to Howard University and then Ohio State for graduate school in English literature. Then he settled in Philadelphia, met my mother, began a career in teaching and social work.

"He seemed to always be working or doing fix-up stuff around the house, so he never got to our ball games. He did go with us to church and occasional cultural events. He was a stickler for speaking English correctly, for reading voluminously, upholding Christian values, and for being thankful for the gifts we were given by God. Everyone who knew him, young or old, thought he was the most kind and thoughtful adult around.

"Though he was quite accomplished, he apparently felt that he never achieved the economic or social status that made him equal to the private-school parents or church elders with whom he and Mom interacted. I know he suffered from depression a few years before he died, but again, unfortunately, I was away during those years." Harry paused, and a look of nostalgia came over his face. "And he had a few sayings that I'll always remember: Read, read, read. Pay attention to details. Always aspire to be your best. You're a child of God. Be proud of being a Morton. Prejudice is the problem of the biased, insecure person. Don't buy into it."

Harry wiped a tiny bit of moisture from the corner of his eye. "I'm glad that I am one of his sons and feel that some of my good fortune is due to the love he gave us while my brother and I were youngsters. I'm sad that I never really got to know him."

"Wow," said Al, not sure how to respond.

"Sorry to unload on you. I don't think I've ever told anyone that much about my father."

"No, thank you. Seriously. He sounds like an inspirational guy," said Al.

Harry didn't respond.

They walked along the beach in silence, past the Aquarium, toward the more active parts of Waikiki.

"One thing is for sure, Al. I'm very happy and feel extremely lucky to have discovered that you are my son and are in my life—here in your home," Harry said.

"I'm glad too." After a few minutes of contemplation, Al continued, "It seems like you had a solid family environment surrounding you. Doesn't sound like you had an ethnic identity crisis to deal with . . ."

"Al, you are right. But one thing you learn as you get out here in the world is that most people have some issues that are serious to them. I, for example, knew who I was, but I had to learn to appreciate that I was as good as anybody on this earth. Knowing that I was African American was little solace when ball players on the other teams called me 'nigger.' Knowing that my parents were smart as anybody and as accomplished as the next didn't help my confidence when White kids ignored me in our lunch room. Being the son of two Howard University alumni didn't carry much water when other seniors in high school were legacies at Yale, Harvard, Haverford, and so on.

"I was cool being Black; it's just that the White school environment I grew up in didn't know what my parents knew. They didn't know we are all created equal and that you and I are as good as anybody else that God put on this earth. My parents, particularly Mom, preached it, believed it, and practiced daily life as if it was the unshakable creed of all mankind. In her eyes, anybody who didn't act accordingly was not to be feared, but pitied and prayed for. Whether my brother and I were treated fairly or not, nobody in that school wanted to see Elena Morton pushing through the front door of the administration building. Eventually, we learned to make it on our own and felt pretty comfortable after our adolescence.

"So, the advantage I may have had over you as a kid was not that I was all Black and you were mixed, but that I had parents who never bought into inferiority in front of us, who never met a person of any race or position in society to whom they acted inferior. And that's the strength and toughness they tried to impart to us."

"That's dope. To be fair, Donna and Tommy have given me a pretty strong anchor, too."

"I think you'll find, as you age, that you've got more than you think. I'm not saying that there isn't substantial bigotry and stupidity abroad. I'm saying you have what it takes to be centered and secure as you move about your complex world. Plus, Al, you'll have a hell of a lot of money."

Father and son roared with laughter.

CHAPTER 14

2028

A s the big 737 banked over Oahu, Mark thought he recognized the sunken Naval monument in Pearl Harbor. He'd only seen pictures of the USS Arizona, or of anything else in Hawaii. Even if his suspicions about Malcolm Mohammed proved a wild goose chase, his first visit to the fiftieth state and a reunion with his father might be worth the expense of the trip.

After he exited the luggage area with his medium-sized canvas bag, Mark saw his father waiting just inside the sliding doors. He was grayer, more wrinkled and with a slower gait than what Mark remembered, but the man was unmistakably Harry Morton. They approached each other warily, looked carefully at one another and hugged; both men struggling with mixed emotions—joy, anger, anxiety, relief. They gripped one another for several minutes.

Before Mark could stop him, Harry grabbed his bag and started walking out of the terminal toward a parking lot. Trailing him, Mark noted that his father looked like he was in his fifties, not seventies: tall, erect, buff, and with a slow bounce in his gait. He couldn't help but smile.

"How was the flight, son? Are you tired?" Harry wanted to keep preliminaries light and cordial.

"I'm a little tired, but this weather, and the smell of the ocean, and the blue sky, and whatever flowers I'm smelling have my attention. I'm awake," said Mark as they entered the lot.

"Good. I thought I'd give you a little view of this side of the island before we went home. I also need to pick up a gift a friend has insisted on personally giving you. You game?"

"Let's do it," Mark said.

They drove quietly in Harry's open-topped Z-car along Oahu's major road, Interstate H-1. Mark couldn't help smiling. The hills to his left were green and dotted with homes, and he could occasionally see beyond the industrial roadside structures to his right to the palm-bordered low-scale pastel buildings downtown and out to the ocean.

As they exited the downtown fringes of Honolulu and drove toward the Kahuku spread in suburban Nui Valley, Harry told Mark a little about the geography of Oahu and of the different ethnic groups composing its population. Then, he briefed him on Kiki and Laila's family, their background and Hawaiian roots, current activities toward restoring rights for native Hawaiians, the Polynesian Voyaging Society, various conservation initiatives, and custodians of Hawaiian cultural traditions.. He also mentioned that the Kahukus had saved his life early on in his stay in Honolulu.

The sports car rolled past what looked to Mark like California ranch-style modest houses on quarter acre or smaller lots. Pastel stucco exteriors reminded him of single-family suburbs along the east side of San Francisco Bay.

"That fragrance you mentioned when we were at the airport? Here you'll find all sorts of tropical plants and trees. Just on this short ride, you'll see kikuyu, monkeypod, eucalyptus, golden shower, hibiscus, an occasional koa, a banyan tree, all interspersed with flowering plants." Harry waved at trees as they drove by.

As they approached a hand-crafted gate of barbed wire and koa branches, Mark thought, *This is definitely beyond California.*

A couple of friendly dogs greeted the car as it wheeled slowly up to the main ranch-style home, passing four modest houses set back from the dirt and gravel road. A thin, elderly white-haired lady, looking quite fit, swung down off of a chestnut stallion to greet the pair.

"Hi, I'm Laila," said Kiki's wife, offering a firm grip and placing a lei of freshly cut, aromatic flowers around Mark's neck. "Welcome to Hawaii. Aloha," she said.

"Thank you. Very nice to meet you, Laila." He felt a bit shy in this lovely, bucolic place among totally new acquaintances.

"We are so happy to finally meet you and are delighted you could stop by on your way to Harry's," said Laila.

From the other side of the deck, a wiry, short, white-haired Japanese-Pacific Island-looking older man strode toward the Mortons.

"Welcome. I'm Kiki," said the handsome host, offering a vise-like handshake.

They mounted blanched wooden steps to a porch that encircled the open-air house. To one side were green foothills on whose tops Mark could see cliff-hanging modern mansions overlooking the valley. Behind the house were ascending pastures ideal for unlimited grazing by the Kahukus' three horses. Looking back down the gravel road and beyond the residential neighborhood outside their fence, one could see over a half mile of low-rise houses out to the Pacific Ocean.

"Wow, it's a wonder anybody ever leaves your spot, except to go to the beach. This is spectacular," said Mark, accepting a glass of iced tea.

"We like it, and the kids each have their own houses, as you saw coming in. So the notion of the close Hawaiian family can be realized," said Laila.

"We're extremely fortunate in many ways," agreed Kiki.

"What about you, Mark? We know and love your father, but don't really know much about you," said Laila, sitting on a bench built into the railing around the deck.

Mark took a sip of tea, inhaled and looked around again while deciding how much to share. *I'm starting anew with Dad, and these folks are obviously close, but I can only say so much*, he decided.

He told them about his schooling, his business, the statehood project, and about Sonya. When they sat absorbing his story, but not pressing him, Mark continued to tell about his tight relationship with his mom. And, finally, he talked about being happy that he and Harry were reunited and beginning an adult relationship. As he talked, he realized that it was nervousness, not anger, that accompanied his exhaustion. His father had been one of two solid anchors in Mark's youth. Who and what would he be now?

Harry merely smiled and nodded.

"Thank you for sharing all of that. I think you'll find that your father is eager to be back in your life, eager for you to learn to love Hawaii. And I know he's overjoyed that you have come out here," said Laila.

"You should also feel that whenever you're in Oahu, you are welcome to stay with us. Our kids and their families are rarely all here at the same time, so we have lots of room. And we'd love to get to know you," added Kiki, sipping a Budweiser.

"Speaking of loving Hawaii, I want to give you this history. I think you'll find it fascinating." Kiki handed Mark a copy of Lawrence Fuchs' *Hawaii Pono*, a popular tome documenting the several centuries of Hawaiian culture and history.

"Wow. Thank you. Will I read about the Kahukus in it?" Mark grinned.

"No, but you'll see the basis of our work and commitment." The deep voice belonged to a handsome reddish-brown, medium-build, forty-something man, who mounted the steps, approached him and gave him a hug.

"Mark, I'm Mano, Mano Kahuku. Welcome to Hawaii. Dad and Mom are modest. She's a ubiquitous conservationist, even got a World Heritage Site designation for one of our coral reefs after years of fighting. Her side of the family has been involved in social welfare for generations, probably the reason explorer Alexander Adams gave two thousand acres of what's now Nui Valley to her great grandmother. Harry's probably told you of Dad's work for kids via the schools."

"Well, I know you two have a bit of catching up to do, so I've packed a few sandwiches, some fruit and a couple of beers for you to have after you get back to Harry's. And we'll expect you over here for dinner before you go back to the mainland, Mark," said Laila.

"Thank you all. We'll talk soon," said Harry, as they all walked to his car.

"I might text sooner," said Mark, smiling.

The route Harry took back toward Diamond Head and his condo gave Mark views of the ocean from sea level and then from cliffs hundreds of feet above the surf. Harry let his son breathe in the environment.

"They are very special, wonderful folks," said Harry.

"Yeah, I can see that. It would be great to spend more time with them," sighed Mark.

"This scenery is also special. All of the hype about 'paradise,' really doesn't do Oahu justice," Mark said.

"It's more laid-back than DC, for sure, but we've got our tensions and conflicts not too far below the surface. I can tell you about that later, if you'd like," cautioned Harry.

As they mounted Harry's steps and deposited Mark's bag and knapsack in an ocean-facing guest room, Mark took in the details of his father's home. "Well, I recognize some of the paintings and the carvings. Must be from your early travels, when we were all together."

"There are some new pieces—but you're right, I do still cherish things that remind me of my earlier life," Harry admitted.

They sat in deep chairs facing the glass wall, looking past the ferns on the balcony, past the treetops across the highway, and out to the blue-black sky and ocean. Both men sipped beers, minds racing about how to break through and reconnect. Both happy, yet cautious.

"I'm really happy that you called and decided to come," Harry started.

"So am I, Dad." Mark set down his bottle. "To be honest, Mom and Sonya pushed me to come, to reconnect and not waste any more of my adult life being angry at you. And to get your advice about an issue I'm facing that may have serious national implications. But, first, I really don't know who you are, what you do, how you feel about me. So many questions . . ."

"Well, you can probably check Wikipedia to find out the resume-type background. I teach international dispute resolution as an adjunct professor at UH and do a bit of management consulting with large international corporations." Harry paused, then plunged in. "I was quite hurt when you cut me off when I separated from your mother. I certainly understood your perspective, but nonetheless it was painful. And the longer you kept your distance during the years in college and the summers in DC, the more I began to feel like I needed to start a new phase, if you will. So, after a while, I leapt at the opportunity to move here.

"I do see women, but I've never remarried. I'm happy that Mary seems to have found a soulmate in Max . . . Otherwise, I go to theater, check out occasional concerts and movies, read like I always did, see friends, like the Kahukus, play golf and travel a bit."

"Wow, you still play golf?" Mark asked awkwardly.

"Absolutely, mostly with a group of ex-military brothers. I swim and boogie board, but my knees don't tolerate running or hoops any more. And my reduced energy level means that everything happens a lot more slowly. Sometimes, life's like those movies where the audio and the visual of the actors' lips are out of sync. I'm a second or so behind the action. Pretty boring semi-retired life. But, I'm happy." Harry smiled. "What about you, son? Tell me about your work and your wife."

"Hold up a sec. I just want to know how you felt about breaking up with Mom. Did you feel guilty?" Mark held his father's gaze.

"I suppose that's a fair question. No, guilt is not what I felt. Sorrow, that we didn't still have what we'd had for almost two decades, but our relationship had been heading south for a while. It might be hard to believe, but deep down, I'll always love your mother.

"Anyway, we both had affairs. Mine got more exposure, but still, we had both drifted. My constant travel may have added to our demise. I'm not sure. I was sure, however, that I wanted to maintain a relationship with you." Harry stopped.

Mark wanted to bring up Viola Gregory, the mother of his friend with whom Harry had an affair, but realized that he couldn't press further. He steered the conversation toward his own story.

"Well, as you know, I felt like Mom was my only real parent after you moved out. It was rough. I was only in sixth grade. Once I moved away to school and met other kids who were from long-term single-parent households, I was able to suppress my anger at you for having broken up our family. Then, you moved out here, so 'out of sight, out of mind,' I guess.

"After Harvard Law, I went to work for a bank in New York. Then met this great lady from Spelman and Stanford, who was working in the US delegation at the United

Nations. Sonya's mother is Mexican and her father's African American.

"I got a DC job with this investment firm, Walden & Rockefeller, in 2016 and quickly developed an expertise in tech start-ups. Even though I studied law, you may remember that back in the day I was pretty good at math and fascinated with computers. Sonya got a job at the World Bank, moved to DC, and we got married in 2017."

Mark stood up to stretch.

"Yes. Thanks for the invitation, by the way," Harry said, matter-of-factly.

"I didn't think about you that much, but when I did, was still pissed, so . . ."

"Any babies?" Harry redirected the conversation.

"Not yet. But, when we do, I want them to know their grandfather," Mark said, smiling.

"And, for fun?" asked Harry.

"Well, I recently spent a lot of time with a group working on DC home rule, statehood. I'll tell you more about that later. Sonya and I watch movies at home with friends, go to some concerts, ride bikes together, treat ourselves to restaurants, go back up to 'The City' to catch a play or to see friends. I still play b-ball with buddies, and I'll jog a bit. Sonya's in a book club, but I like reading techie stuff online. Gen-X stuff, I guess."

Harry squeezed Mark's shoulder. "Thanks, son," he said. "I appreciate your sharing and being honest. I really hope we can remain honest with each other from here on out."

"So do I, Dad," said Mark.

"Well, you must be tired, I could use some sleep myself. What say we go for a swim right out here at the end of Waikiki in the morning, then drive into Kailua, where President Obama used to hang, up to the North Shore and Sunset Beach, where I can show you real waves that attract the world's best international surfers? Then we can have a late outdoors lunch

at a nice fish place in Haleiwa, fun little village. You can tell me all about this issue that's confronting you."

"That sounds perfect," said Mark.

At about two-thirty the next afternoon, the two Mortons rolled into the parking lot of the Haleiwa Beach House. After being seated on the upstairs balcony overlooking the Pacific, Harry ordered a glass of Pinot Grigio and Mark a Cucumber Cooler.

"I'm going to get the tuna club, but if you want something just a little different, I'd recommend the fish and chips. Fresh like you've probably not had," suggested Harry.

"God, those were huge waves around the bend at that beach. It's hard to imagine getting on a board, much less riding those bad boys," said Mark.

"The history of surfing is interesting here. It used to be the province of pure Hawaiians, until California beach boys and Aussies 'discovered' the beaches. Then haoles, as they called Whites, forbade Brown natives from competing in international events. Off their own beaches! But that's history. Not too distant history, but history nonetheless. Anyway," said Harry, changing the subject, "why don't you tell me about this issue troubling you? I know you sent me something, but might as well start from the beginning."

For the next hour, Mark told Harry all about the Home Rule Project, Duke Wallace and Malcolm Mohammed, and the steam room and Metro incidents. As Mark recounted his tale, Harry prodded him for detail, then said, thoughtfully, "Well, without further corroboration, my first reaction is that there is no conspiracy, there's random coincidence. But, given the potential consequences, if your gut is correct, I'd say it's certainly worth keeping your eyes open. You say you got no real help from the DC police or the FBI? Not surprising. In fact, I might make some calls to alert a few trustworthy friends. The most challenging part of your story, of course, is this twenty-first-century 'War of the Worlds' scenario."

"Funny thing about that is that I've funded a geek out here on Oahu, who's a genius at creating virtual reality games," said Mark. "Young kid, barely out of Caltech, but brilliant."

Harry froze. Until that moment, he had not thought about Alaka'i, Mark's half-brother. He had to be the "geek" Mark was funding?

"He's creating a powerful simulation of climate-change disasters," Mark added.

Harry's mind began to spin. It had to be Al. But, what were the odds? And how would his newly repairing relationship with Mark suffer when he found out about Al? How would Al react to learning that his initial business benefactor was actually his big brother? It was all too overwhelming.

"Dad, are you OK?"

"Yes, fine. It's just . . . There are a lot of people I'd like you to meet, but this is a short visit. We're just getting to know each other. I can think of a few folks I trust to put on alert about your would-be domestic terrorists in case they really are planning something. Then we can worry about what to do if they plan on trying something big." Harry reclaimed his composure.

"I got it. You look like you just 'woke,' " said Mark, smiling.

"I what? Oh, yeah, woke." Harry laughed at the current terminology. "Mark, there's somebody else I'd like you to meet in the next few days. You leave day after tomorrow, right?"

"Yep. Late morning. Let me pay, Dad." Mark reached for his wallet.

"Absolutely not. This is on me, all the way."

For a moment, as they left the restaurant, they had their arms around each other's shoulders.

"Any particular music you want to hear?" Harry asked, as they climbed into his Z-car. "We've got satellite radio out here, you know."

"Well, I remember how the house used to be filled with bop. You know Bird, Trane, Miles, Oscar. I like Keith Jarrett." Mark settled into the soft leather seats, pulled down his shades and looked out the side window. Harry punched in his Spotify playlist and melodies from Keith Jarrett's trio quietly floated through the car.

Harry took a route through old pineapple plantation country and the center of the island back to Honolulu. Mark spent a few minutes reflecting on how happy he was that his mother and wife had insisted he come. Harry spent the entire trip mulling over several ways to introduce his sons to each other. All of them awkward.

Early next morning, as Mark slept in, Harry finished a long walk on the beach and settled down at an Otani Hotel table with a cup of coffee.

"Tommy? Sorry to get you so early, but I need your advice," said Harry into his cell.

"No problem. I just finished some stretching," said Tommy Liu.

"I don't remember if I told you that my son Mark, my estranged son, is out here for a quick visit."

"Yes, you mentioned it."

"Well, we seem to be on the road to reconciliation, in no small part due to help he needs with a problem both his wife and mother said I might be able to help him with. A bit of desperation there. Nonetheless, he's here and it's terrific to be reconnected."

"You have quite a few family surprises all at once," Tommy chuckled.

"Well, yes, and that's why I'm calling. It turns out that Mark is the big venture funder of Al's company. They've dealt with each other electronically. But neither knows about their family connection. Mark hasn't expressed a pressing desire to meet his client on this trip, but at some point they will meet and find out the connection."

"Come on. Who's scripting this? Sorry to react, but isn't this a bit too coincidental? I mean, really." Tommy took a few minutes to absorb the new twist. "Ok. You're trying to figure out whether now is the best time?" Tommy anticipated Harry's question.

"Exactly. I don't know either of them well enough to know how to best do this. Normally, I'd say let it rest. But if Mark gets back to the mainland and finds out about Al, I don't know . . ."

"Well, I'd suggest getting them together and take the deep dive sooner rather than later. It may be upsetting, but I think at least one of them will react badly if you wait because you now know the situation."

A long silence.

"Harry, are you there?" asked Tommy.

"Oh, I'm here. You're right, of course. I just hate to ruin the good vibe with Mark that's taken two decades to recapture. And I'm only beginning to build a real relationship with your son. I have this disquieting feeling that I'm never going to fully pay for the Hong Kong affair. It keeps cropping up in ruinous ways."

"Understood—but are you thinking about what's easiest for you or what's best in the long term for the boys?" Tommy asked, rhetorically.

Another long silence.

"Why don't Donna and I try to get Al over for dinner tonight, and you guys drop by to say hello at about eight? I'll let you know if he can't make it," Tommy suggested.

"Well, I guess . . . That will give me time to tell Mark about Al and see if he's willing to meet. I can text you if he's not receptive."

"OK. I hope to see you later."

Back at his condo, Harry found Mark awake, swilling a glass of guava juice and eating some cut-up papaya and pineapple.

"Good morning, son. How'd you sleep?"

"Great. The ocean air is so refreshing and waking up to the fragrance those flowers outside is heaven." Mark's face sparkled with joy.

"Good. Those are plumeria. So, listen, I have some things to do at the university this morning. How about you drop me and then take the car into Waikiki, park, and walk around? Maybe do some of the shopping for Sonya and Mary. I'll show you good spots on a paper map, then you can navigate with the car's system or use your phone."

"That sounds great. When should I pick you up?" Mark asked.

"Let's say two to two thirty."

***

Later that afternoon, they dug into sandwiches at a restaurant in the Sheraton Waikiki.

"This morning was great," said Mark. "I picked up some jewelry for the ladies. I love that the beach is right across the street from the main drag. But I do see why you residents would easily tire of the beach-town commercialism down here."

Harry nodded, then said, "Son, this has been fabulous. You being here. And of course I'll be glad to help in any way I can if your Mohammed and Wallace characters actually do attempt something."

"Thanks, Dad. I have to admit, I really wasn't sure how this would work out myself. But, yeah, I'm glad I took the leap."

"I hesitate to bring up another subject that may bear on our relationship, but I think I have to." Harry took a long drink of ice water. He maintained eye contact but took a deep breath.

"OK, fire away," said Mark confidently.

"Well, you know that the final trigger to your mother and me separating was an affair I had in Hong Kong?"

"How could I not know? But, actually, your fling with Mrs. Gregory and then your fight with Mom was what sent it over the top," said Mark, with more than a touch of bitterness.

"Fair enough. I was an ass; you're right," Harry conceded. "Anyway, I never contacted the Hong Kong woman after I returned to the US. And I understand that she died of cancer recently." Harry turned in his seat to face his son directly.

"Sorry to hear that, but how's that concern me, if it was over when I was in sixth grade?"

"Well, I recently learned that she . . . we . . . had a child that she immediately gave up for adoption. She was one of the most powerful, most visible businesspeople in Hong Kong and decided that an out-of-wedlock child would strain the tolerance of even the most forward-thinking Chinese. Not to mention that of her husband. In her situation, she also assumed that having a mixed-race child would kill her career quickly. She had been the product of a White British journalist and a prominent Shanghai businessman and had had enough of a taste of Chinese prejudice growing up herself."

Again, Harry paused.

"Dad, this is fascinating, but we're past your indiscretion. Kids happen. And, as we know, Mom had her own tryst with Max, before they married. So . . ." Mark relaxed a bit.

"The boy was adopted by a Chinese-Hawaiian couple and grew up here on Oahu." Harry took another sip.

"And, you met him?" Mark's eyes grew wide.

"Actually, within the last few years his adoptive parents, not knowing of the relationship, had me begin sort of mentoring him. Long story short—his birth mother died and left him a fortune, which he can't touch until he's thirty-four. So, he went to China to see what he could learn of the Asian part of his background. When he was telling me about his trip, it became clear to me that his birth mother was the woman with whom I'd had an affair." Harry took a breath. "Talk about a shock."

"So, what you are saying is that I have a half-brother?" Mark asked, stunned.

"Yes."

"And, since I'm here, you want to introduce me to this, this 'mistake'?" Hostility had now entered Mark's voice.

"It's even more complicated," said Harry.

"Oh, I can't wait," said Mark, pushing away a half-finished club sandwich.

"My newly discovered son, your half-brother, went to Caltech and turned out to be a software genius. He started a gaming company . . ."

"No. No way. He's not Alaka'i Liu?"

"Yes. The company you financed is owned and run by your half-brother."

Mark fidgeted in his chair for a minute, stared at Harry, then out at the ocean. He dropped his head into his palms and held that position for several minutes. When he raised his head and looked at his father again, Mark's complexion had reddened.

"Can you pick up the bill, Dad? I need to walk out there on the beach. Get my feet wet," Mark said, as he pushed back from the table and strolled down a hotel path to the beach.

As he walked, he lost his balance and almost fell into the shallow tide. He couldn't tell if it was sunny, hot and humid, or overcast, chilly and dry. Mark Morton was enveloped in an emotional fog. He shed his T-shirt, folded it around his flip-flops, waded out beyond the breakwater barrier and dove into the first small wave.

Back at the restaurant, having paid the bill, Harry texted Tommy: *Not tonight, thanks. Too much info at once.*

He looked down the beach in the direction Mark had walked, but saw no trace of him. *Could he have gotten that far already?* Harry started down the beach at a slow trot, scanning shore and surf. After several minutes, he came upon Mark's shirt and shoes, but no sign of his son. Out of breath, Harry looked for a lifeguard, then asked two bathers if they'd seen his son. They hadn't. He shuffled on, pushing up waves of sand until he stopped, exhausted. He plopped down in the sand and scanned the horizon in vein. After several more minutes, he decided to call the police.

Meanwhile, hundreds of yards out in the bay and several hotel beaches up the coast from where he entered, Mark tried to float in order to rest, and build up his air supply. The water was not yet chilly and, out beyond the breakers, Mark could easily float on his back. His mother's voice replayed in his mind, declaring that she forgave Harry long ago and accepted who he was. But, Mark thought, she couldn't know about Al, if Harry only just found out. Probably wouldn't change anything for her, though—he wasn't important to her future.

Mark wrestled with endless questions as he slowly drifted further out. He rolled over onto his stomach and started swimming back into shore. His strength was tested because the tide was now more forcibly rushing out to sea. It took him twenty minutes and all of his energy to return to the beach. As he swam, Mark imagined and envied the strength of those surfers up on the North Shore, navigating powerful waters and gigantic waves.

Standing on the beach, Mark welcomed the packed sand between his toes and began trudging, then jogging back toward his clothes.

As he finally reached an officer on the phone, Harry saw Mark coming back down the beach and sighed an audible breath of relief. He thanked the police, told them Mark had surfaced, and clicked off.

"Dad. I can't stay. I need to get back home and sort things out," Mark said, as he approached Harry.

"I can understand not wanting to meet Al yet, but don't go." Harry caught himself before he extended his plea. "Well,

OK, if that's what you want, I'll take you to the airport in the morning."

"No need; I can get an Uber or Lyft."

"Mark. Let's not go back to where we were three days ago."

Back at Harry's, Mark changed his flight online to one early the next day, had a quick dinner with Harry, and retired early. Harry dropped Mark at the airport before eight o'clock in the morning.

At the airport, Mark focused on his return to DC and tried to put his confusing, disturbing, whirlwind Hawaiian reunion behind him. After checking in and going through security, he glanced up at a departure board. It announced that his flight was delayed.

Mark browsed in several shops, stopped to pick up a cup of coffee, and then settled into a seat at his gate. He tried to read an IT journal, but couldn't focus. So he called Sonya's cell.

"Baby, it's three thirty in the morning . . .You're coming home now? So soon? Oh no, what happened? "said Sonya, rubbing sleep from her eyes.

Mark gave her a capsule version of his stay and the revelation about Al.

Sonya didn't respond immediately, but she smiled at the news that Mark had discovered he had a brother.

"Hmmn," said Sonya, "I think you should think on this a bit. It's not Al's fault that Harry's his father. And it sounds like Harry is really trying to turn a tough situation into something positive. Also, from the little you said about working with Al as a client, way before you knew you were related, you liked him." She added, hastily, "Look, love, I have to go. I need to sleep. You, stay and work something out." The line went dead.

Mark started scrolling through his emails, when the attendant at the gate podium apologized over the PA system for having to tell the passengers that the flight was now cancelled, due to mechanical problems. Rather than argue with United Airlines personnel, Mark went to their lounge, booked a flight for the next day, and got a voucher for a hotel he thought was at the airport.

The hotel was a nondescript tourist motel near Ala Moana Shopping Center, back in Honolulu. Mark grabbed a salad and glass of wine at a California chain restaurant, and wandered the neighborhood near the center before sitting for an hour on the beach at Ala Moana Park. He tried to answer email traffic but couldn't concentrate, so he called Sonya again at about one thirty in the afternoon.

"Mark, do you realize it's still just seven thirty in the morning?"

"Sorry, babe, but I really need to talk this through."

"Mark, you make multimillion-dollar decisions with less analysis than you're putting into this. Meet your half-brother. You don't have to love each other. Think about what a tizzy he's in after discovering that a mentor is actually his birth father. How's he going to feel when he discovers that his major investor was out there, found out they are brothers, and didn't try to meet him? It's not just your feelings that count in this." Sonya sat up in bed and blinked the sleep from her eyes. "Baby, you're not that fragile, *aye Dios!*"

"OK, trying to shame me into it, great." Mark tried to sound angry. But he recognized that his most trusted advisor was right.

For whatever reason—genes or training—Sonya always seemed so balanced to Mark. She appeared totally comfortable with herself no matter the setting or audience. The only thing that visibly bothered her was her inability to master foreign languages, particularly Spanish. Mark knew that she had had a few intimidating incidents at Spelman College. One student had charged that she wasn't really Black nor did she speak Spanish fluently. Sonya was bummed out for a day and then recognized that her inability to carry a tune resulted from the same poor ear that impeded her language ability. No course work would radically improve her ear. She finally accepted that limitation. In a day, her self-confidence was back in gear.

Neither said anything for minutes.

"Sweetheart, you know how you claim we're global, multicultural, blah, blah, blah? Well, don't you think having a part Chinese half-brother might be interesting? Don't you think his growing up in Hawaii and having only recently found out about his birth parents would be nice to know about? He might want to talk out some conflicts himself. Like it or not, you have the same father . . . Maybe the two of you can hit the beach in a day or so, and enjoy a sunrise in Hawaii, a new beginning."

"OK, OK. Points made. I'll stay and meet him. You are right." Mark started to hang up. "Sonya, thank you, my love."

"Goodbye, love," Sonya said softly.

As she hung up, she thought that it was fortunate they had not yet decided to have kids because her life seemed full of emotional challenges at the moment. Work, aging parents, Mark, and terrorist attacks were enough for now. Her tension didn't show like Mark's, but Sonya now feared the activities of Wallace and Mohammed were possibly more dangerous than even Mark suspected. So, she sensed Mark needed to resolve his complex new family relationships in order to be happier about his father but also because she worried that someone of his experience and connections might be crucial, at some point, with the radicals.

Mark rescheduled his early morning flight for a few days later and notified his office that he was going to see one of their investments. Later, he texted his father to ask if he could have the Lius set up the meeting with Al in the next couple of days.

Delighted. Glad you are staying, was Harry's quick response.

CHAPTER 15

2028

Al looked across the small pond in front of Byodo-In Temple, off Kahekili Highway in the center of the island, northwest from Kailua. No one else was praying, meditating, or visiting the Japanese temple and gardens, so the peace and sense of isolation allowed Al to shed all tension, worry, and distraction. He focused on the pond, its stillness and its beauty. He subsumed thoughts about his business, his new wealth, the mixed-race project, and his newly discovered father as he sat in lotus position in one of the temple's kiosks. If someone had asked the young entrepreneur what he was doing sitting there, he might have responded, "Nothing. Absolutely nothing."

For an undisturbed hour, as Al contemplated the water, he attempted to meditate on the oneness of all being in nature. He didn't attempt to "figure out" his challenges; that would come with time. He consciously tried to embrace what was before him. No analysis, just acceptance. When he finally moved and uncoiled, he felt that he had successfully transferred the focus of his energy from tension and anxiety about all the changes in his life to positive anticipation about his future.

As he drove back to his office, Al received a text from his father asking him to dinner with Harry Morton the next evening, to which he responded with a quick OK.

Mark had asked Harry where he would recommend he explore, if he wanted a quick day-long getaway to see some beautiful part of Hawaii. Harry thought about a quick trip to Kauai for a round of golf; then, instead, suggested he check with the Kahukus, for some more informed recommendations.

"Perfect timing. Our son Mano is going over to our cabin on the Big Island later today and will be spending at least a half day tomorrow in a kayak photographing the lava flow of Kilauea from the boat off Apua Point. The two-person kayak is pretty safe, and he might enjoy the company. Shall I ask him?" inquired Laila Kahuku.

"Wow. That would be great. Thank you," said Mark.

By mid-morning, Mark had been booked on an interisland flight to Hilo airport with the eldest Kahuku son. After driving the family car, stored on the Big Island, up toward the western side of the volcano to deposit their knapsacks, Mark and Mano inspected the kayak. They then made a trip to the market to get several days supplies for Mano's extended stay. Mano drove Mark through the national park and down the winding road as far as vehicles were permitted, not too far from the active lava flows closest to the ocean. It was there, after hiking over hardened, cooled black lava, that Mark peered out along the coast at some of the newly formed cliffs, dripping molten red lava.

"I've seen fantastic photos of this activity, but getting this close on land is amazing," he said.

"Wait until you see it tomorrow morning from out in the ocean," Mano replied.

"I mean, right now, the sunset framing the molten rock is spectacular."

"This is part of why we can't imagine living anyplace else. It's part of why I do what I do," Mano whispered.

They hiked up from the hardened lava fields to the car and rode out to the cabin as dusk turned to ink, then starlit silence.

After dinner, they sat around a fire with glasses of Chardonnay, and Mano explained his work to Mark.

"As a youngster, I was fascinated to learn all I could about my Hawaiian heritage. So, I first studied cultural anthropology and was going to teach Hawaiian history to our high schoolers and at the university. That got boring and kept me away from the ocean for longer than was healthy for me. So, I got another master's in marine biology and spent a few years working with my father retracing original Polynesian journeys to these islands. I loved it, particularly the voyaging down to Polynesia in perfect replica canoes.

"After a bit, I felt my family needed more income security, so I convinced a couple of Hawaiian brothers to join me in a business. 'Historical Hawaiian Tours' does as the name implies: takes visitors on ocean-going kayak tours of these islands. We get a chance to convey history; discuss current issues affecting native Hawaiians; sail, dive, and surf a bit; hike and keep up with our spectacular flora and fauna. And there are plenty of Japanese, Chinese, and US ecotourists willing to pay handsomely for the experience." Mano permitted a slight smile to crease his handsome weather-tested face.

The next morning, they left a small landing off the rocky southern shore of Hawaii and paddled for almost an hour to a spot where they could see and hear the hissing vapor rise from the sea, as the fiery red globs of molten rock dropped into the ocean.

As they sat in relative quiet looking at the molten formation of new land mass, Mark felt the kayak rock forward and almost lost his balance. In a panic, he grabbed the side of the boat and lost his paddle overboard. Mano calmly steered the kayak to the floating oar and retrieved it. A frightened Mark asked, "What was that? Some large fish?"

"Oh, I doubt it. Probably the result of chilly ocean current colliding with the heated water from the volcano. Nothing to worry about," said Mano.

Mark felt silly and vulnerable. He was relieved when they started paddling back to their launch point. Watching Mano's strong, smooth, confident strokes he reflected on the Kahuku's family dynamic, particularly on Mano's relationship with his father.

"Mano, how do you handle being the son of a legend, an icon? Living right next to him?" he asked.

"Easy. He's been super supportive. Besides, I'm not trying to be a second Kiki, and there's plenty of room and space both in our compound and in the islands. Most of the time, we come and go and don't see each other for days. Why, do you and Harry have issues?" Mano asked, not having been privy to any discussions about the Harry-Mark schism.

"Let's just say that we're still working some things out," said Mark.

Mano showed no interest in pursuing the topic.

Later that afternoon, when Mano drove Mark to the airport, the mainlander thanked his host.

"Yesterday and this morning just whetted my appetite for seeing more of the natural diversity of the islands and increased my respect for the power and beauty of the sea. Thank you."

"Come back and take one of our five-day tours. We'd love to show you more. Then, maybe, you'll decide to join your father and move out here. We have lots of start-up financing needs here too," said Mano.

"Yes. I know. Although this is a whole new world for me."

"*E ho 'omanawanui*. Give yourself time," Mano said, as they parted.

Al arrived at his parents' house a half hour before Harry was due to arrive. He helped with setting the table, fixing hors d'oeuvres, and selecting the wine. He was excited to be with the only people, other than Peter and Zhou & Zhou, who knew about his new discoveries and wild opportunities.

"Mom, did you miscount?" he asked, noticing the extra table setting. "You've set five places, instead of four."

"No, son, your godfather is bringing a guest," said Donna.

"Wow. My godfather. I'm so still getting used to that title," said Al, smiling and unconcerned.

"Well, it's a nice adjustment for all of us," said Tommy, giving his wife a quick smile.

***

"You still OK with this, son?" Harry asked Mark as they approached the Lius' house.

"I'm pretty sure it's the right thing to do, even though I'm not thrilled with having to face another jolt right now. Yeah, let's get it on," said Mark.

Tommy Liu came to the door. "Welcome, Mark. Very nice to meet you. And, Harry, always good to see you."

Before Mark could finish saying hello and thanking Tommy for inviting him, Donna came into the vestibule and placed another fresh flower lei over Mark's neck. She pulled him by the neck down to her level and planted a kiss on each cheek.

"Welcome to Hawaii, Mark. I'm Donna."

Mark, a bit embarrassed, repeated his thanks.

"Let's go out on the back lanai to have drinks," Tommy said, ushering the guests out onto the patio.

Before they were even introduced, Mark recognized something about the nose and cheekbones of the handsome mixed-race youth arranging chairs outside.

"Mark, this is our son, Alaka'i," said Donna. "Al, this is Mark Morton."

Extending a friendly hand in greeting, Al registered recognition of the name. "From DC? You're my angel investor! Mahalo. God, great to meet you." Then he looked puzzled. "But what brings you here?"

Al stepped back, confused. "What, how . . .? I don't get it."

Rather than wait, and in an attempt to get past the elephant in the room, Harry took a deep breath and said, "Al, Mark is also my son. You two are half-brothers."

Al stepped back in shock and looked more intently at Mark. Silence pervaded the lanai for an eternity.

"Um," Donna finally said, "shall I get the drinks? We might all enjoy one. Mark, what would you have?"

"What? Oh, a beer, please," Mark managed to respond.

"Dear, I'll come and help you," said Tommy, eager to give the Mortons some space.

Turning to Harry, Al asked calmly, "So, how long have you known?"

"Mark and I have been incommunicado for many years, so I didn't focus on you two being related until this week, when he came to visit," offered Harry.

"And I just found out two days ago," said Mark.

"Snap. I got to sit for a minute," said Al sinking into a chair. He gazed at the little waterfall in his parents' garden. Emotions and visions fell turbulently in his head. He thought about his Shanghai trip and the revelations about his birth mother. He thought about Harry's new status in his life. Pushing both of these images aside was the live image of this new young relative. For several minutes, Al struggled to process all of this new information. He felt a bit dizzy, but didn't know if he should be angry, happy, or simply bewildered. He knew that he would need to get away by himself and slowly evaluate what had happened. For now, he followed his body's instincts, stood and approached Mark, arms extended.

As they embraced, Al said, "Nice to meet you brother."

"It will take some getting used to. I've never had a real brother before," said Mark through tears.

"Well, for most of my life, I didn't know who my birth parents were. And now, it feels like in the blink of an eye, I discover I had a famous mother, a famous mentor who's my birth father, and a hot-shot investor who's my half-brother. You think *you* have something to get used to?" Al laughed to relieve the tension.

"To say the least, I've not been a good father to either of you. I'm hoping I can make it up as a godfather to you, Al, and a participating father to you, Mark," said Harry, wrapping long arms around both young men.

Most of the rest of the evening was spent swapping fairly impersonal stories of their lives. It took a couple of days of hanging out before the brothers were able to begin to trust each other, and their father. Al gave Mark a tour of his office to see some of his techie toys and meet the staff he'd assembled, and they attended a seminar Harry led at the university. All three of them ate spicy Asian and traditional Hawaiian meals at downtown restaurants, and they caught a jazz performance at the Blue Note in Waikiki. After a long chilly swim a few mornings later, their storytelling continued with more openness over breakfast at Harry's.

Finally, Mark briefed Al on his concerns about Malcolm Mohammed and Duke Wallace—the reason for his visit to Hawaii in the first place. Harry still felt that it was premature to do anything because it wasn't yet clear what, if anything, the conspirators' plan was. In addition, any attempt to use chits to garner attention from the government would likely only be successful once a real threat was evident. He suggested that Mark casually refresh any strategic contacts he had in Washington, in case they needed to get to Homeland Security or NSA folks quickly, and he promised to do the same through his current network. Al noted that portraying certain destructive events in a virtual reality space was definitely possible, but that controlling the audience's environment to reinforce the fiction would be a severe challenge. Before Mark boarded his flight for the mainland, all agreed to keep their eyes and ears open for any developments signaling a major threat.

Back at his condo, Harry took a slow walk around the neighborhood streets of Diamond Head, had a long, steaming shower, and stretched out on his lounge facing the Pacific. He felt confident that, should he be asked and sanctioned, he had the investigative, analytical, and emotional skills to help track down the terrorists. His energy couldn't match that of earlier years, but he thought wisdom could make up for that shortcoming. Yet he didn't know if his sons possessed the skills and temperament that might be required for such an assignment—and he was hesitant to expose them to danger and risk, potentially losing his recently reconstituted and fragile family. At the same time, he recognized that Mark was actually the linchpin for providing critical intelligence on the suspects, and that Al could be invaluable if cyber/IT resources were needed. *They are men, after all,* Harry thought. Still, Harry's predominant instinct was to keep them safe and fly by himself to DC, if asked.

After a quick nap, and then quiet reflection, Harry reasoned that the probability was very low that any Morton would be asked to get involved.

THINGS FALL
APART

2029

CHAPTER 16

n the summer of 2029, a series of unusual events began to rattle the nation's capital.

Sunday, July 8, after an extended raucous Independence Day celebration, maintenance crew members to the Russell Senate Office Building and Cannon House Office Building on Capitol Hill stopped for morning coffee at their normal breakfast trucks parked along Independence Avenue at the bottom of the Hill. They were casual in their pace up the hill, as no members and very few staff would be coming in later. No hurry.

As they approached their respective buildings, two crew members, the heads of the Cannon and the Russell crews, suddenly felt a bit woozy. They sat to rest on the majestic marble steps to side entrances, waving their colleagues on, assuring them that the nausea was passing and that they'd soon join them inside. The nausea did pass, but both men soon lost consciousness and crumpled over on the steps. Each was quickly attended to by a passerby, who dragged the limp bodies into waiting sedans. Within minutes, men reemerged from the cars and marched up the steps to resume their morning tasks. Strangely, they left the buildings within a half hour, slipped back into the vehicles, and were then carried back out to the steps, apparently deep in sleep. They were discovered by their colleagues after the morning shift.

Meanwhile, the substitutes jumped back into the cars and sped off as dawn began to break over the Capitol.

Minority Leader of the House Ryan Trane beat his staff into the office that Monday after the long weekend. When he opened the door to his inner office, he froze. Propped up on his desk was a large placard that read, "Guard your children, for this is 2029." After a moment of paralyzing shock, Trane laughed and dismissed the sign as a weird joke, probably played by the staff of one of the congressmen who had lost out to him in the bruising battle for minority leader.

More sour grapes, but whatever, he thought. *I'm definitely out of this place in November.*

When Ken Ditch, majority leader of the Senate, arrived at his Russell Building office, his chief of staff stood in the doorway.

"Good morning Alice. What's going on?"

"Sir, we're not sure, but we're finding out," she said, stepping aside.

Ditch's head snapped back when he saw a banner draped over the picture window of his office.

Tequila, cattle, horses and football are toys for you Texas bluebloods. But can you protect your grandkids in 2029?

"What the hell . . .? Did anybody else get one of these?" Ditch screamed at his staff.

"It looks like Mr. Trane got a similar sign," said Alice Mormon.

"Let me know as soon as the Capitol Hill police track this sucker down. Probably start with the maintenance crew. I never did trust that bunch," Ditch barked.

The Senate majority leader had to wait a couple of days to be notified that the crew leader had, somehow, been drugged, and someone had taken his badge and entered the office over the weekend. Ditch's chief of staff talked him out of having the legitimate worker fired. And, with the crush of preelection schedules, both the Senate majority leader and the House minority leader soon had more pressing concerns than threatening banners, which they dismissed as pranks.

Many young congressional staff who lived more than biking distance from the office took the Metro's Blue, Orange, and Silver lines from Maryland and Virginia suburbs to the Hill every morning. The L'Enfant Plaza stop was always particularly busy, as a transfer stop for the Green and Yellow lines, bringing additional travelers from Maryland suburbs and the District. So the following Friday's rush hour found those lines jammed with members, staff, other government employees, and tourists. No one panicked when Blue, Silver, and Orange line trains all stalled between L'Enfant Plaza and Capitol South stations, their internal lights flickering. Announcers explained that there was a delay on the tracks ahead, that they would all be "moving momentarily."

"Par for the course, these days," explained one congressional staffer to a French tourist holding the pole next to her.

As the time passed, and riders began to sweat and become short of breath in the thinning air, the French tourist almost fainted, tottering into the staffer. The staffer held the tourist up until he regained his equilibrium. It was then that the staffer noticed the smoke seeping through the car door. The tunnel outside the car was dark, so no one could tell anything about the source of the smoke, but people began to try to open the doors, pushing and shoving, as mild hysteria broke out. Minutes passed as riders sought to move to cars toward the front of the train. Finally, in response to someone tapping the emergency lever, an announcer said it was safe to exit on the right side of the train and walk along the tracks to the next platform, Federal Center SW.

Metro employees with bright orange vests guided passengers from the three trains to the nearest station platform, and, as they exited, travelers were relatively orderly, since they were so relieved to escape the congestion and death-trap-like feel of the smoky cars.

A new panic spread as the procession to the stations closest to the Hill reached their would-be exits. Each had smoldering fires at the bottom of their staircases and escalators. Someone had lit piles of trash and alcohol-soaked rags, forcing crowds to await Metro police and DC firefighters, who, once on the scene, easily extinguished the blazes.

The whole series of incidents lasted about an hour, and no one died. Several hundred patrons suffered from smoke inhalation and a few sustained minor bruised limbs. But tension and anxiety were rampant. And mid-morning news reports further inflamed those emotions because all major media outlets and social media sources had received and posted this message: "Your government is in control and keeping you safe from terror. Ha! Ha!—Welcome to APOCALYPSE 2029." By the evenings news cycle, the metro scare was circulating nationally.

After extensive cyber investigation, federal national security teams could only report that the message emanated from South Asia, somewhere. The mayor of the District promised to have Metro get to the bottom of the incident, however, the president was reported to be annoyed at the news releases implying a weakness in national security. By Saturday afternoon, however, Metro patrons, Hill staff, and members were back to their normal weekend activities. Other than the security agencies, few held the veiled APOCALYPSE threat at the top of consciousness.

***

Georgetown Day School is one of the most competitive academic private schools in the District, rivaling internationally famous Sidwell Friends, choice of presidential children for decades. Tucked away near the American

University campus and close to the Tenleytown Metro station, the high school rests in an affluent, yet accessible corner of Northwest Washington. This was where fifteen-year-old Stephanie Trane spent her weekdays.

Late Sunday afternoon, in early August at the beginning of the school year only a drowsy security guard and seven students studying for the national History Bowl competition occupied the halls and one classroom. None of them had noticed that a window on the Forty-Second Street NW side of the campus had been jimmied open, nor did they notice two young hooded men tinkering around the boiler room below the assembly hall of the main building. While the guard patrolled part of the athletic fields and the students peppered each other with questions on European history, the two interlopers finished attaching a timing device to the boiler, mounted the stairs and slipped back out the window.

Several miles north on River Road, in the tony suburban town of Potomac, Maryland, is the campus of the Bullis School, another highly rated area prep school. The president's daughter, Floral, was a student at its high school. That same afternoon, there was no one studying or using any of the library facilities among the blue and gold banners and pine tabletops of the Marriot Family Library. No one, except for an uninvited visitor, who was fiddling with the fuse box that powered the whole building. The stranger set a timer to a device he installed and boldly walked out of the building, knowing where to step to avoid security cameras.

The offspring of another US government leader attended a third prestigious private school in the area. Nellie Ditch, the granddaughter of Senate Majority Leader Ken Ditch, attended the Madeira School in bucolic McLean, Virginia. This Sunday, its campus was also practically deserted; most girls had not yet returned from off-campus weekends. Being a girl's boarding school, the campus boasted more sophisticated security than the others. With its expensive security contract, parents rarely had to worry about outside intrusion. Their main anxiety was wondering which top-ten university would admit their daughters.

No one paid attention to a mature-looking blonde dressed in faded Aéropostale jeans, an unmemorable Forever 21 blouse, and a lightweight Hollister hoody. Had anyone paid her any mind, they would have seen her emerge from the woods separating the campus from the Potomac River. Pretending to scan her cell phone, she caught the door being held open by a student to one of the two-story dorms.

"Thanks," she murmured to the student.

Not recognizing the girl, the senior student asked, "You must be new. Can I help you find anything?"

"Oh, no thanks. I'm waiting for my cousin, Nellie Ditch," said the blonde, avoiding the student's eyes.

"Cool. Her room's on the second floor."

"Great. Yeah, I visited last year," lied the blonde.

The student bounded up the stairs, and the blonde watched her disappear into a room far down the hall. The blonde then retreated to the stairs and back down to a vacant lounge/study area on the first floor. It took her only five minutes to locate a wooden credenza in a far corner of the room, remove a black box from her backpack, and install a small timer-driven device. She pretended to read the *New York Times* headlines and flip through a few magazines on a circular end table next to one of the deep couches dotting the room. Then she casually flipped on her hood and walked out of the campus back into the woods.

Her movements in the dorm were later studied on the tape from building security cameras, but she had managed her posture so that her face was never fully captured on any recording device. And no camera captured her as she uncovered the kayak she had hidden in the brush near the river bank, paddled out between Hermit and Perry Islands to the Maryland shore, carved holes in the boat and set it adrift downstream. She found her early model Prius on a residential road in the Avenel Estates. She threw her sweatshirt and blond wig in the trunk, brushed her brunette hair and applied some blush that darkened her complexion. Within five minutes, she merged into traffic on River Road heading back into Washington.

Monday morning news on every area station carried horrific pictures of burning wreckage from predawn explosions that destroyed sections of buildings at the schools of Stephanie Trane, Nellie Ditch, and Floral Spade. The reporters quickly speculated about a connection to the earlier "pranks" on Capitol Hill and in the Metro.

"Somebody is going after government leaders. Luckily, no one was killed this morning, but people are wondering how safe we are. The panic is beginning to approximate what we experienced with the John Allen Muhammad serial killings back in 2002," a local newswoman declared.

As press secretaries for the president, House minority leader and Senate majority leader were preparing to issue generic statements condemning the violence and vowing to find, apprehend, and punish the culprits, news outlets received another brief notice.

Time to deliver on campaign promises to America. Where are the jobs, immigrant justice, religious freedom, cleaner environment, and equitable education??? Until delivery, neither your police violence, your border walls, your assumed supremacy, your God, or the NRA can protect your privileged leaders.

APOCALYPSE 2029

"What the hell is going on, Ron?" President Robert Spade demanded of his chief of staff.

"Sir, we have FBI, Homeland Security, and local police on this. We'll find them," said Ronald Barker.

"This shit is not subtle. They are playing with us and making this personal. We don't even know what they want.

They think we can wave a magic wand and get rid of poverty, for God's sake? Is this all about the election? Are these damned Muslims? Damn, they got into Trane and Ditch's offices. Now they get our kids' schools. It's clear they're just toying with us, 'cause they could have blown up people but didn't. Not yet, anyway. And, for all our crack security bozos know, this could be an inside job!" The president was red-hot. "Well, don't just stand there, Ron. Go get some answers," said the commander in chief.

As the chief of staff exited the Oval Office, a rare visitor stood in the doorway.

"I'm taking Floral to Royal Flush for a few days. It's not safe up here right now," the First Lady said.

An irritated president had to agree.

CHAPTER 17

"**S**eriously, Duke? You're listening to Bob Dylan?" Malcolm Mohammed had just entered the doorway of a two-story, two-bedroom Airbnb house that Duke Wallace had rented in the Washington suburb of Arlington, Virginia.

"Crazy as it may be, but some of the poetry he was writing in the '60s and '70s speaks to the crazy shit we're seeing right now," Duke responded, as he stood from his armchair to turn down his iPhone that was sending his playlist to the house's stereo system.

"I'm glad you didn't say 'singing,' 'cause the noise that dude made with his throat and harmonica hurt my ears."

"He might be an acquired taste," Duke said, laughing.

"Well, you sure 'nough got to do something to cut the tension up in here. I don't know if it's smart to wait around 'til they either pass some legislation or the other major shoe drops on September eleventh. They already caught the cat you had do the House signs, and looks like they closing in on the dude who planted the Bullis School piece," said Malcolm.

"Yeah, but there's so much distance and many untraceable links between the front-line soldiers and us that it will take a year before they figure shit out. We're good, 'cause we chose sponsors who chose individuals who cared more about the cash they earned than about ideology. No, we're good—but

I still can't wait until we can blow this town. I don't like having to look over my shoulder every time I go out," Duke said.

"Look here, my man, you might as well get used to having to do that, 'cause even when we split the US, we going to have to be careful for a minute," Malcolm said matter-of-factly.

"Yeah, but even though the people we recruited are top-notch, they've conducted dry runs to the extent possible, and their funds are ready to be wired, I still wonder if the big day will force the action we need . . ."

"That's why we allowed a couple of weeks between the Metro and school attacks and the big day. Let them worry. Let them fret. Let the anxiety build. By now, they got to be wondering if this is jihadists, crazy crackers, Proud Boys, reconstituted Black Panthers, MS-13, or just some wacko MF's. When they can't get anywhere by questioning a couple of captives, they'll know this is not a rinky-dink operation. The fact that we haven't taken any lives yet also has to be worrisome, 'cause it's got to feel to some like real violence is just around the corner. And the fact that we could get to the president's daughter's school has got to have ol' Captain America tied up in knots of fury." Malcolm smiled to himself.

"Yeah, he seemed to love playing with the press and the haters when he escaped impeachment, but my money says, this is going to make the bully nervous. Because he knows now that all the social media in the world won't protect him from physical destruction, loss of property, and possibly loss of life of someone close to him. He knows his physical protection is not invincible. Whole different ball game." Duke sipped a beer.

"I can tell, it's gettin' good to you, partner. But we got a few days to sweat this out. One trail could lead the feds to Al-Shabaab and another to the Klan, but nothing directly to our virtual crew." Malcolm tried to reassure them both.

"Still. They might get lucky and trace something we didn't think of." Duke changed the music to Reba McEntire.

"Well, we just got a couple more days to be cool. I must admit, I'll be glad to get off this fried chicken and pizza diet. We don't need to communicate until we meet at the Montreal airport in three days, right?" Duke asked.

"Snap. Don't forget to leave that ISIS recruiting video, like we said. Scrub down the place with those throwaway gloves."

"And don't forget to leave those two paperbacks you bought," Duke said.

"*Taliban* and *Black Flags*, right?" checked Malcolm.

"No, not the second one. That bio of the recruited French journalist."

"Oh, yeah. *In the Skin of a Jihadist*, Anna Erelle. Scary, man." Malcolm hugged his shoulders in feigned fright. "OK. Think I'll roll on back to DC. Be cool." They bumped fists.

"Nothin' else to be . . ." Duke walked Malcolm to the door, looked up and down the street and let him out.

CHAPTER 18

"**O**h, my lord, it's them. That's got to be Malcolm and Duke." Mark Morton stared at CNN's *Out Front* nightly segment, which recapped what *The Situation Room* had been reporting an hour before. He and Sonya had finished a light dinner and were looking at the news before turning their attention to the stacks of memos, emails, and reports each had to cover that night.

"I can see more of their strategy now. These office, school, and Metro attacks are not the main components, I'm sure. They definitely have something bigger, something national in scope planned." Mark ran his fingers through his hair and tapped nervously on the arm of the sofa. "Sonya, can you put me in touch with that colleague of yours at Homeland Security?"

"You're sure of this, sweetie?"

"No, but I'd rather cry wolf than witness some catastrophe that I might have helped avoid. And, somebody in the government has to at least listen to us."

"I'll set you up with Monica Breslow. I think she's an executive assistant to the director. What should I say it's about?" Sonya asked Mark.

"That is key, isn't it? Just say I have some leads on these APOCALYPSE 2029 episodes and need to speak confidentially with her boss."

"Oookay. I'll give it a shot," Sonya responded with a raised eyebrow.

Late morning the next day, Mark called his father in Honolulu.

"Dad, I know it's early, but have you been following the subway disruption and school bombings by this APOCALYPSE 2029? "

"Damn, son, I haven't even been awakened by my clock radio, much less had wake-up coffee," Harry said groggily.

"This stuff has been going on for the last several days." Mark wasn't sure whether or not to be frustrated with his father.

"Yep. Of course, I've followed it. Hard not to," said Harry, sounding a little more focused.

"Well, I'm pretty sure this 'Apocalypse' is those guys Malcolm and Duke that I told you and Al about. What's worse is that I'm sure that if it is them, they have much more severe action planned soon. And my guess is that they'll target the president, the Senate majority leader and the House minority leader, if they don't quickly get some action in the Congress."

"So, what are you suggesting we do, son?"

"Well, I've tried to get a meeting or phone call with the head of Homeland Security to no avail so far. Can you rouse any contacts? The least we can do is tell somebody high up in the administration's national security apparatus what we suspect."

"Before we get too far, might as well patch Al in here," Harry suggested.

After Al was patched into a Face Time conversation, Harry sat staring at the computer screen.

"You OK, Pop?" Mark asked.

"I'm fine, but let's think through the implications of more involvement. I mean, I believe you, Mark. The feds, however, are likely to thumb their noses at your theory.

The best we can hope for is that they put some low-level spooks on alert to monitor Mohammed and Wallace," Harry theorized out loud.

"What if we do nothing and they initiate some sort of cataclysmic strike? That's what I worry about," said Mark.

Al chimed in, "You don't really think they have some kind of 9/11 capability, do you?"

"I am positive that whatever they have planned, it will be worse than the school fires, locking me in a steam room, or claiming responsibility for a Metro incident," Mark contended.

"OK, boys. We're all independent adults. So I am not trying to pull rank. But here's what's bothering this old man. I now agree that these guys are extremely dangerous: any of these parties can come after you and your families. You're young and you have future careers and possibly growing family to think of. Al, you have an inheritance with a considerable mission laid out for part of your future. We know this administration can turn on folks in a minute, and Malcolm and Duke may have already passed the point of no return with respect to willingness to press some deadly agenda. Point is, you could easily become collateral damage in this dynamic." Harry stared into his screen.

"So, you think we ought to back off?" Mark asked.

"You should consider it," Harry responded in a stern tone. "What do you have to offer that the feds don't or won't have?"

"Information about how they, well, how Malcolm thinks," Mark offered.

"Trust me, son, once the feds decide these guys are real perps, they'll have much more info about them and their contacts than we do."

"But that's just it. They have to come around to taking Mohammed and Wallace seriously. A lot of lives could be lost before then." Mark gave no quarter.

"I hear you, but recognize that being seen as an 'obstruction' to the formal investigation doesn't fit well on the resume," Harry said.

"Obstruction? That would be ironic coming from this White House."

"Nevertheless, you and Al are rookies at this, and there won't be much room for error, I suspect. And I'm an over-the-hill management consultant. I use up my daily energy supply walking on the beach," Harry declared in jest.

"Please, Uncle Harry. I've seen you swim and surf. Try that on someone else," Al said, jovially. "Anyway, I'm happy to help with analysis, cyber and IT support, but the feds are likely to have whatever I can offer in spades," he added.

"Clever," Mark laughed.

"Having the resources and possessing the commitment and smarts to use them effectively are quite separate things. But I guess we can wait to see what the feds do." Mark yielded to Harry's argument.

"If they get desperate, they know how to find us," said Al.

"Depending on the timing, we may not be able to bring value to a solution," Mark quickly added.

"Let's hope that's not a risk we have to take," said Harry.

"OK. Now that we've talked out the risks for you youngsters, I don't think we have to be totally idle." Harry signaled that he wasn't altogether against helping. He had already concluded that APOCALYPSE could cause major harm, if the government failed to take them seriously and throw substantial resources into finding them soon.

"The problem is that most of my contacts have retired, died, or are in the wrong party. I can try to get you a meeting with an old State Department colleague, who I think still does some consulting on Asian affairs. He might have some pull. Let me text David Lee. Expect a call from him. I think he settled in the DC area after his last China stint. It's certainly worth a shot because from what I read and see, the 'Great Americans' are not even close to finding out who is causing this ruckus," Harry concluded.

Al and Mark each wore a smile of satisfaction as they ended the meeting.

After lunch, Mark received a text from David Lee asking if he'd like to meet for coffee late the next afternoon.

Seated in a booth, Mark watched the door of the Panera coffee shop in Tenleytown at the appointed time. No one caught his eye. For some reason, he paid no attention to the white-haired Asian man walking with a cane until he walked up to Mark.

"Are you Mr. Morton?" asked David Lee.

Mark slid from his seat and shook the man's hand. "Forgive me, sir. I should have been more alert."

After a few pleasantries and exchanging a brief summary of Mark's bio for the story of how David Lee knew Harry in high school and then in China, Mark settled in to tell what he knew of and suspected from Mohammed and Wallace.

David Lee sipped his chai thoughtfully as he listened to Mark. "Sounds like your hunch is worth alerting the administration," he said at last. "Although the secretary of state is not fully involved in this, I'll notify him. I'm sure he can contact the others and maybe the president. Given the level of arrogance over there, however, I would not expect any response. But at least if they don't make much headway on their own, you'll have gotten on one of the outer circle radar screens."

"Thank you, sir. That's all we can expect. They have the resources to try to track them down, if they so decide." Mark's declaration was more of a question.

"That's right. Anyway, say hello to your father. Nice to meet you, Mark." And, with that, David Lee rose and limped from the coffee shop.

CHAPTER 19

"What you got for me, Charlie? We got FBI, Homeland Security, National Security team, and us scrambling to make heads or tails of this threat. Give me something I can take to the president." Martin Pickett, head of the CIA, had been recruited to help because the president's team suspected there were foreign elements involved with the terrorists. He was spending more time with his cybersecurity team than he normally did, or than he liked. He was well over seventy, should have retired years ago, but the administration had created a special personnel classification to keep him on due to the ongoing threat of terrorism.

"Hitler, Pol Pot, and Kaddafi can all creep out of the grave and march on Washington in December," he continued, "but in January, I'm gone. I'm too old for this crap. My chiropractor says I'll be feeding her meter as long as I have this work tension in my neck." An avuncular Pickett placed his oversized right hand on the shoulder of his studious and frail-looking aide, Charles Stanton.

"Well, sir, I've got good news and bad news. Which—"

"Usually, the bad first. Good is for dessert. Oh, for the hell of it, tell me good first today," interrupted Pickett.

"OK. We've traced the warnings to a relay station in Germany, and we think they emanate from a cell located in Delhi, India. Probably a call center."

"That's perfect. India's a strong ally. We'll get them to arrest the culprits and we'll expedite." Pickett almost knocked Stanton over with a congratulatory slap on the back.

"Hold on. The bad news is that the sender went dark and shut down before we could get a specific location," Stanton hastily added.

"Well, can't you get some close coordinates and have the Indians raid a couple of joints?"

"The area in question has dozens of internet businesses. Even if we could pinpoint the right one, we still would have to get legal authority to seize equipment and scan hard drives. These guys are sophisticated enough that they have already scrubbed and destroyed any evidence," Charlie assured Pickett.

Martin Pickett strolled back to his office, while texting the other department heads involved. His information was the most current.

"Even though it's not actionable, better give the boss some news. At least it will feel like we're making headway," advised the FBI head. Pickett put a call in at once.

"Pickett. You guys ready to take some scumbag out yet? Give me an excuse to bomb the shit out of Iran," President Spade said, only partly in jest.

"Sir, we know that the messages came from a call center in Delhi, India."

"India? Hell, they're supposed to be allies. Have them take 'em out," ordered the president.

"Not that simple, sir."

"God, it never is around here. What's the issue?" The president made no attempt to hide his contempt.

"Essentially, the signal went dead before we could identify the building, much less the group, or the machine. And it's in an area loaded with internet companies. But if they send other messages, we'll be able to target the user more quickly." Pickett hoped the added statement was true, for it did mollify the president's anxiety a bit.

"OK. Keep on it, Marty."

Pickett grimaced and hung up.

***

"Come in, Mr. Morton. I'm Sheila Baxter, special assistant to the secretary of Homeland Security. He asked me to listen to your information about the recent arson at the schools of key members' children."

Mark took a seat opposite the younger thirty-something woman, seated in the standard government-issue wooden armchair squeezed between the desk and her door.

"Thank you for taking the time to see me on such short notice." Mark opened the conversation.

"Absolutely. Everyone is anxious to stop these attacks and get the terrorists behind bars."

"Well, I'm pretty sure this is not your garden-variety terrorist." Mark instinctively jumped to the offensive. He then gave Ms. Baxter a truncated, sanitized version of his involvement with Malcolm Mohammed and Duke Wallace.

The pert young staffer quickly responded, "Very interesting, but you don't actually have any proof to back these assertions. They merely threw out hypotheticals to your own radical group."

"My group, as you call it, was hardly radical. These outside guys expressed their specific ideas to me only. And, yes, the strategies they offered were hypothetical. And, no, I don't have proof that they carried anything out, but Congressional office graffiti, school attacks, and the Metro fire seem too similar to scenarios they described to be unrelated." Mark tried to suppress his annoyance at being subjected to the third degree by staff that looked no older than a summer intern.

"Well, thank you, Mr. Morton. I'll pass your alert on to the secretary." Ms. Baxter rose, indicating that the pro forma meeting was over.

Mark cordially shook her hand and left. He tried to put the meeting out of his mind, but remained annoyed for a couple of hours at what he viewed as dismissive treatment. Back at his office, Mark sent a cryptic text to his father.

Sheila Baxter sent the homeland security secretary a two-sentence email summarizing the Mark Morton theory, which the secretary read and quickly deleted.

Amateur detectives with power connections wasting taxpayer time with their stupid suspicions, he thought. He knew the White House was concerned about the attacks, particularly the school fires. But neither CIA, FBI, nor White House staff would take seriously the young man's assertions, no matter who his father happened to be.

Soon, the second week of September would alter everyone's view of the seriousness of the APOCALYPSE claims and demands.

CHAPTER 20

On September 11, 2029, Congressman Ryan Trane had finished a morning run, showered, enjoyed a late breakfast, and was alternately looking through news items and staff memos on his PC. Today, he planned to visit several new plants in his district, Michigan's Second Congressional District. So he knew that he had another hour to catch up before a staff aide came by his home to pick him up. Their kids were at school nearby their home in North Muskegon, Michigan. His wife was at her office across the lake in Roosevelt Park, near the Muskegon County Airport. The house was peaceful.

At eleven a.m. eastern time, Trane thought he heard an explosion and looked out a living-room window facing southwest, toward the state park. Other than a swarm of crows and starlings cackling loudly, the scene looked normal. He checked a side window, facing other houses on the cul-de-sac. There were no loose branches on his lawn from the fall poplars, nor were there cracks in the street's asphalt, nor whiffs of gas from underground pipes. *Must be my imagination*, he thought.

Just as he was turning away, he heard muffled explosions off in the distance toward the east, across Lake Muskegon. A plume of heavy gray smoke rose over the city of Muskegon, miles away. Had one of the vacant plants near Muskegon

Heights or one of the new facilities in Manistee had a gas explosion?

He hurriedly walked back to his den and the laptop he'd been using. The newsfeeds and staff memos that had occupied both sides of his split screen were gone. In their place was one panel that flashed live newsfeeds of a burning SRS Industries aluminum facility in Ludington. An old Heinz Pickle factory in Holland appeared as a smoldering pile of crumpled steel and concrete, followed by live feeds of cratered streets and highways leading to lakefront towns. Roads and bridges in his district looked as if they'd been attacked by IEDs in Iraq or Afghanistan. The congressman tried to click away from the images, but every site he tried had the same footage.

As he reached for his phone to call his local office, the screen changed. Running across the middle of the screen in large white block letters at twenty-second intervals was a message:

YOUR FEDERAL GOVERNMENT'S NEW JOBS PROGRAM. CALL YOUR REPRESENTATIVE NOW TO APPLY FOR INFRASTRUCTURE CONSTRUCTION POSITIONS. WELCOME TO APOCALYPSE 2029.

"What the . . . ?" asked the congressman, as he waited futilely for the dial tone on his cell phone.

Meanwhile, at nine a.m. mountain time, Victor Johnson, MD, had turned off Loop 375 Express in El Paso, heading north on Route 54 on his way to his office at University Medical Center, when he felt the road shake and heard a thunderous boom behind him toward the south. As he slammed on the brakes to avoid slowed traffic in front of him, Johnson thought he spotted several chimpanzees jumping on car roofs and a half dozen lion-sized cats up ahead on the right side of the road. He was able to pull over onto the shoulder. The rumbling in the earth stopped, but wild animals continued to stream across the highway.

Shaken, all he could think was that there had been some kind of accident at the nearby zoo. He reached out and switched the radio from his country music station to the news.

"Our aerial crew is approaching the border with Ciudad Juarez to follow up on reports of explosions along the wall at the Mexican border," said an excited reporter. "Oh, my goodness! The Stanton Street Bridge crossing the Rio Grande is gone, fallen into the river and the industrial area below. Up ahead, the new wall looks as though mortar shells have peppered it for several miles to the west. It's totally destroyed!"

Dr. Johnson opened his briefcase and flipped the lid on his laptop. He clicked on CNN and held his breath. Pictures were streaming of El Paso directly to his south, but most of the shots of the landscape along the Mexican border were unrecognizable. It looked as if the "wall" had been located directly over an active fault line whose tectonic plates had just collided. Then, as he watched in shock, these words streamed across the screen:

MAKE AMERICA THE BEST AGAIN –BRING BACK THE NATIVE PEOPLES AND THE MEXICANS— APOCALYPSE 2029

Further west, in Nogales, Arizona, also at nine a.m., Doris Flores, professor of elementary education, was pulling into the staff parking lot at University of Arizona, Santa Cruz, when she felt her car skid uncontrollably and saw the large first-floor glass walls of the administration building shatter. Her car slammed into a concrete parking barrier and stopped. She turned off her motor, took several deep breaths, closed her eyes and tried to understand what might have caused the loud concussive explosion. Students and faculty members were fleeing the campus building and milling around in the parking lot, afraid to drive on the local streets, which were pulling apart in reaction to the explosion. She recognized a fellow professor, blood dripping from a facial cut, staggering toward her.

"John, John, are you all right?" she asked, climbing out of her vehicle.

"Hi, Doris. Yes, I'll be fine. A few others inside have cuts from flying glass, but yes . . . It's strange. Did you hear or see what happened?" John Porter spoke slowly and his eyes couldn't focus on anything in particular.

"I haven't heard or seen any news, and the explosion happened behind me. I did see columns of smoke in my rear-view mirror. So . . ." Doris reached out to steady her colleague.

"Well, the news says that the fence between Nogales, Arizona, and Nogales, Mexico, has been blown to bits. On the monitor in the lobby is flashing something about 'opening up America' with APOCALYPSE 2029. I didn't have time to really read it and understand what they were getting at. But whatever this is about, it seems to be a man-made event that's targeted the border."

Around the same time, Wilhelm Boll, superstar executive at Deutsche Bank of New York, was standing on the seventeenth tee, having made the turn at Spade International Golf Club on Daufuskie Island, South Carolina. He was taking a day off before flying to Washington to meet with Prince Spade, son of the president of the United States. Until very recently, Spade had acted as titular head of the nation's largest tech office park and vacation-home developers. The firm was one of Deutsche Bank's largest clients worldwide. The Spade Company had only recently finished redeveloping the golf course and a nearby luxury conference center, country club, and vacation home community. Royal Flush, the highly leveraged project, was a prize in the bank's loan portfolio.

So, between his quite average golf game and his pending business meeting, Boll's concentration offered little room for outside disturbances.

The roar that broke his concentration was thunderous. And, as the sound appeared to be approaching, Boll stepped from the tee box and looked over the palm trees to the adjacent fairway. Then he looked north toward the Harbour Town airport on Hilton Head Island. *Maybe some flotilla of military aircraft is conducting maneuvers off the coast or some new monstrous Airbus had to make an emergency landing. Perhaps the sound traveled all the way from Marine training at Parris Island.* Boll had only seconds to speculate.

The skies were empty, but the roar continued to grow, now clearly from the east, the Atlantic Ocean. Boll looked at his watch, as if his Apple product could give him a quick answer. He only had time to register the hour, eleven a.m., before his eye caught sight of a huge wall of water tumbling his way, less than a quarter of a mile out to sea. No time to get to his car and up to Royal Flush, where he was staying. The twenty-five-foot wave swept in over the southern tip of Hilton Head, then onto Daufuskie, washing over roads, Royal Flush, and Haig Point Golf Course, crushing well-appointed villas and homes, and uprooting an historic nature reserve. Nothing within a mile of the shore was spared.

His golf cart could not outrun the wave, so Boll abandoned his very expensive clubs and began sprinting toward the clubhouse. Still a young man in excellent athletic shape, he reached the eighteenth tee box, and cast a glance over his shoulder. The wave's height had crested to well over thirty-five feet, but was dropping fast and its speed had begun to diminish. *I'll make it*, he told himself.

Wilhelm Boll was a soccer and lacrosse athlete who had grown up in landlocked European suburbs, vacationing around mountain lakes in Germany and Switzerland. As a young man, he had not spent much time on the ocean, nor had he paid much attention to the dimensions of its power. A half minute later, Boll had the eighteenth green and the clubhouse beyond in sight. He summoned up a final burst of energy and strength. Within seconds, however, he was sent tumbling into a sand trap and over the green, ricocheting off bushes and palm trees that offered no resistance to the wave. His rag-doll-like body was drowned before it reached the stone wall only momentarily protecting the clubhouse.

Several minutes earlier, the president's chief of staff had tapped his boss on the sleeve to interrupt a phone call and pointed to a Fox News scene on a monitor in the Oval Office. They watched in astonishment and then anger as the infrastructural implosions in Michigan and the explosions at the "wall" in Texas and Arizona rained physical and psychological damage on key administration achievements. The commentators' coverage of those events had only just begun when the station switched to the devastation in South Carolina.

An airborne Coast Guard camera had caught the beginning of an apparent tsunami off the coast of Hilton Head and followed its destructive path as it washed over the president's "vacation home" at Royal Flush, crossed pristine beach homes and natural preserves, then pummeled the president's country club resort and swallowed up his world-class golf course. The water continued as far south as Little Tybee Island and caused damage twenty to twenty-five miles inland. As the pictures rolled on and the wave subsided, the TV screen posted a message that ran laterally, like a banner behind a small airplane:

> CLIMATE CHANGE IS A HOAX, RIGHT? THESE WAVES MUST BE FAKE NEWS. OH, YEAH. MAYBE THE NRA CAN PROVIDE ENOUGH WEAPONS TO SHOOT BACK THE WAVES. IF ONLY . . .— APOCALYPSE 2029

In the White House, President Spade flipped between Fox News, CNN, and several DC-area network affiliates. He even caught current YouTube videos. All confirming, to his horror, that symbols of his wealth, accomplishments, and stature—of his greatness—were under unfettered attack.

"What the hell is going on? How can there be a tsunami off South Carolina? Where's the security around the wall? Didn't we stop those damn jihadist attacks planned for O'Hare and Dulles and the Capital Building?" screamed the president.

"That's right, sir. The FBI was all over it," stuttered the chief of staff.

"Pull in the goddamned National Security team," ordered Spade.

As the chief of staff hurried out, the president's counselor charged into his office. Before she could say a word, he waved her off. Staring at the monitor, the president said, "I need a few minutes here."

Who could do this? Not the Russians. That would trigger WW III! ISIS? The North Koreans? He's crazy enough. The Chinese? What's left of the 2021 January rally? Not likely? Some left-wing crazies? They'd like to have that capability. Jesus, Royal Flush Resort! I just escaped major damage with that hurricane Cortez, only to get wiped out with some tidal wave two years later? Not Royal Flush!

The president of the United States buried his copious mane in his palms. His eyes twitched from tension, his face flushed, and his lips curled in anger. After a few moments, he sat up, took a deep breath, and stretched his legs out onto his historic desk. He grabbed some chips, swilled a Diet Pepsi and addressed himself. *This is some freakish test. Don't show weakness! Remember, nobody gave me a chance of being here. Always being underestimated.*

He glanced around the Oval Office and smiled to himself. There was a large photo of a new technology office park outside Hong Kong, completed by Prince before China had clamped down on foreign real estate activity. The Spade Company was fast catching up to Paul Allen's Vulcan as top tech office park developer in the world. Next to it, a glossy shot of a luxury vacation home development on the Caspian Sea, used by Russian top brass. Below that, he loved the architectural drawings of the world's largest technology office park on the outskirts of Dubai. His company had skillfully placated authoritarian governments around the world, becoming the leading global developer.

I need to get back to the brand and doing what I love, he thought. *This diplomatic stuff is bullshit.*

He looked down at the leather-bound family pictures on his desk: Queenie, the First Lady; Prince, his son and heir to the business; and young Floral, his high-school-age daughter. Hopefully, she'd be tough enough to survive the next four years in DC.

As he turned around to look out at the grounds beyond the White House back portico, the president stopped to admire one more wall-mounted photo collage. It showed before and after photos of his two properties on Daufuskie Island: old Bloody Point Golf Club and new Spade International; old Daufuskie Island Resort and new Spade Resort. He smiled as he thought of the market share he had already taken from his northern luxury developer competitors on Hilton Head. The smile turned to a scowl as he reflected on the images of the destructive tidal wave.

I'll throw the whole goddamned government against these friggin' terrorists. This time they challenged the wrong guy. Buoyed by his own pep talk, the president stood up, straightened his crimson silk tie, and strode toward the large oak door to take command of the crisis.

***

The president called an emergency meeting of what he labeled his "detective force," national security advisor, Homeland

Security chief, attorney general, CIA and FBI heads, and his own chief of staff. As he waited for the men to assemble, he burned with slow rage at the tweets of concern from former close allies—Canada, Britain, and France—and the emails of solidarity from sympathizers in the Kremlin, North Korea, Turkey, and the Philippines

They're the only ones who really understand power and the isolation it can create, Spade thought, self-pityingly.

"They're here, sir," his aide said over the desktop speaker.

"Send 'em in," he said, moving to the U-shaped conference area to the side of his Oval Office desk. He could barely contain himself until everyone was seated.

"Tell me you have some good news about this unbelievable breach!" he almost shouted.

Eyes rolled and stares went round the room, but no one spoke.

"Well, Travis? You're Homeland. Surely you at least know who's doing this," yelled Spade.

"No, sir—not yet," responded Travis Roy. "But at least the loss of life is well under one hundred," he added in a whisper.

"We have some unconfirmed theories, but nothing solid yet," said CIA head Martin Pickett.

"Unless my Fox guys are wrong, unless CNN and damn PBS, even MSNBC, are off, somebody purposely caused that tsunami in South Carolina, bombed the shit out of a chunk of the Texas wall, and destroyed factories in the former Speaker's town. And we have no clues?" The president was building up steam.

Homeland Security and FBI had strong evidence that the Midwest explosion was partially a hoax: a real explosion, with smoke created by a large rubbish pile, emulated in an industrial park, but a simulated catastrophe simulcast to all TV news stations. But no one offered that conclusion yet. Let him cool down first, they thought.

"My wife and kid were supposed to be at Royal Flush this morning, and I'm due there tonight. Shit, imagine, you would have had President Nickle by midnight. That idiot." The president laughed at the notion of Vice President Dick Nickle sitting in the big chair and trying to make deals.

"We're looking at possible Latino and Black terrorist groups, some of the nihilists out west, and we're checking the radical mosques," offered Attorney General Hardy Stennis with confidence.

"Oh, fine, Hardy. And where would that stellar group get the sophistication to cause a tidal wave? Shit, at least the Secret Service is on it and has doubled protection around my wife and the family," the red-faced commander in chief snapped dismissively.

Before anyone could respond, Travis Roy's loss-of-life estimate registered, belatedly, with the president. "Did you say under a hundred? That's still a catastrophe!"

"Sir, there has not been any credible foreign agent or jihadist activity in the last week, so—" Martin Pickett was cut off.

"No credible activity, huh. Well how the fuck did a valuable, strategic part of the state of South Carolina get washed away by a fake tsunami? Explain that to me." The president slammed the palms of his hands on the arm of his chair. "OK, I'm going down there to fly over the area later. You idiots find who did this stuff. You guys are making Bush, Obama, Trump, and my predecessor look competent. Get out of here. Find me some bad guys."

After the room cleared and the president had had a few minutes to stew in private, call his daughter and grown son, Chief of Staff Ronald Barker stepped into the Oval Office.

"You know boss, we can't assume this is domestic or even Muslim. We've been cutting deals with some crazy folks recently. The Chinese leader, 'Rocket Man' in North Korea, even that thug in the Philippines have reach and means in this country," Barker suggested.

"They are straight-up and know I'd bomb the shit out of their shithole countries," the president barked.

"No offense, sir, but they all have access to immense firepower and have shown willingness to wipe out enemies in a heartbeat."

"But I'm not their enemy!"

"Sir, I'm just saying, they've been at this international poker game for a long time. You've acknowledged that there's a whole other level of chutzpah when you're dealing with national security, rather than major real estate deals. Remember, we and the Soviet Union almost blew each other to smithereens over Cuba." Barker held the president's stare.

"Yeah. You're right, Ron. I just can't believe that Russia or China would risk war. And if they did, the shit would be so well disguised, not a whiff of fingerprints or DNA. You'd never find evidence. This isn't obvious, like their hackers during our elections, or some British food poisoning. No, the big boys aren't in this. OK, you stay on those guys. Send out condolences to the Arizona and Texas people and the Midwest folks."

"Right, and I'll have staff prepare special condolences for the Carolina victims," said Barker as he closed the door.

The president gripped a putter and began tapping golf balls into a cup on the carpet edge furthest from his desk. *Shit, I can't show weakness here. Everybody knows that the Obamas got dozens of threats from trash in my base. To their credit, they never flinched in public.* He thought about the urging of his son to hold it together when he went and saw the devastation that night.

After a week of following leads, questioning activists of every stripe, and reaching dead ends, the executive branch departments involved were all bursting with tension and reflecting the paranoid behavior of the boss. Most staff no longer offered theories or suggestions for fear of intimidating tongue lashings. Finger-pointing about collegial incompetence became standard operating procedure in all but the highest levels of government. And the White House communications staff had to dig deep to find new deflections of the queries about why it seemed to be taking so long to find out who APOCALYPSE 2029 was.

Pressure on the Congress and the White House continued to ratchet up, as DC traffic gridlocked at all hours because commuters shied away from the Metro.

Queenie Spade kept Floral home from school and, along with Marjorie Trane and Tracy Ditch, began making plans to home-school their children, while lobbying their husbands to have their families return to their home districts. The president was initially sympathetic but balked when he received feedback from conservative media implying weakness of leadership. Then Majority Leader Ditch checked into Walter Reed Hospital with chest pains.

Sheila Baxter found herself breaking out in hives from the pressure of dealing with her uptight boss at Homeland Security. She put in for vacation, with the intention of renting a room at the shore and just chilling for a week. Travis Roy laughed at her email request and called her into his office.

"No one's going anywhere until this puzzle is solved, when we find the spics, rag heads, crackers, or nigs responsible," said the former Alabama senator from behind circular tortoiseshell glasses.

Sheila loved her job but hated her boss's occasional outbreaks of pure bigotry, so she stood to go. She took two steps, without saying another word, then stopped. "Nigs," she thought. *What if that young man who had come in with that wild story about a Muslim and a redneck really knew something?*

"Sir, do you remember that story about the young man who claimed to be certain about who was planning something?"

"No, I really don't, Sheila."

"You know, the young Black . . ."

"Oh, yeah. What about it?" Roy was already scrolling through his emails on his phone.

"Well, suppose he's right? I mean, at least it's names to investigate."

"I suppose . . . We sure don't have anything else, at this point. Can you get him in here?"

"I'll try."

"Try? It's his nation and president at stake, goddamn it." Roy stared at his aide.

Sheila left to try and reconstruct the information she had on Mark Morton. She knew that she hadn't written anything down and hoped that she had at least made some note on her laptop's memo pad. No. She couldn't find anything there. She tried the various online search engines, found his firm, Walden & Rockefeller, and a general phone number, which she dialed immediately.

"This is Marcia Dexter, Mr. Morton's assistant. He's not here at the moment. May I take a message?" Marcia said while staring at Mark, who was motioning that he was out with his thumb.

"Would you please have him contact the Homeland Security secretary's office, Sheila Baxter?"

Sheila waited a couple of hours before calling again, getting the same result. She was unaccustomed to being put off after having invoked the secretary's name. She knew their response to Morton's initial outreach had been perfunctory, but surely he couldn't hold that against a cabinet secretary. She had a notion that he might not see helping the president, the nation, in the same patriotic terms as did the administration. But certainly he'd respond.

"Well?" Travis Roy was leaning over Sheila's desk, hands behind his back.

"Sir, they haven't been able to reach Mr. Morton," Sheila looked up and responded nervously.

"Don't they have cell phones? What, is he on a submarine beneath a polar ice cap or something?"

"No, sir. I'll keep trying," she said, picking up the phone.

Mark had told Sheila to tell the assistant that he was in a meeting but could be pulled out, if the secretary was on the line. When a more frantic Sheila Baxter called again, the message was delivered in an oh-so-friendly tone. Two minutes later, she called back and asked if Mr. Morton was available for Secretary Roy.

"This is Mark Morton. How may I help you, Mr. Secretary?" Mark said with flat affect.

"I'm sorry that it took so long to respond to your inquiry, Mr. Morton. Would you be available tomorrow morning to come in and discuss the information you offered about the recent, ah, activities?" Roy didn't like being put in the position of supplicant. But he had no choice. He had no viable leads, and the president was ready to blow—more so than usual.

"That would be fine, sir. And, if you don't mind, I'd like to conference in my father," said Mark.

"Your father?"

"Yes. Harry Morton. He's been consulted on this matter."

"Harry Morton, the Masterfield International consultant?"

"That's the one."

"Why, why yes, certainly." The secretary could find no easy or legitimate reason to keeping out a former favorite Democratic strategist. The president's family was at risk.

Eight o'clock the next morning at a corner table at the Mayflower Hotel, with Harry Morton yawning on Mark's laptop screen, Travis Roy listened attentively to Mark's tale of interaction with Wallace and Mohammed.

"So, you really think they had access to explosives or depth charges to set off the Carolina tidal wave, explosives and personnel for the schools fires, and cyber expertise for the Michigan bombing?" Roy asked Mark.

"I obviously don't know for a fact, but all of those events are similar to tactics Mohammed discussed with me. Tactics which I rejected as far too radical and destructive for our purposes." Mark looked at the image of his father on the laptop.

"Not to mention treasonous. Anyway, this is enough for us to begin to track them down, arrest them, and bring them in for questioning. Thank you." Roy motioned to the waiter, got the bill and stood to go.

"Mr. Secretary. Without being presumptuous, should you need assistance in finding these fellows, could we count on agency cooperation?" Harry asked through a bad connection.

A bit taken aback, Roy said, "I hardly think that will be necessary. We'll take it from here. But thanks for the concern. Y'all have a nice day."

After Roy left the restaurant, Mark motioned to his father to stay connected and got a coffee refill.

"So, what do you think, Dad?"

"Well, I think I'll go back to bed," Harry said.

"No, I mean . . ."

"I know what you mean, son." Harry chuckled. "Look, if Mohammed and Wallace did organize this 9/11 repeat, that jokester we just talked to will never get close to finding them. Now, the attorney general, the FBI, or CIA may find them. My guess, however, is that these guys have thought this caper out and are out of the country laughing their butts off in one of the regions that this administration has alienated. But that's just a hunch."

"So, what do you think we should do?" Mark sounded dejected.

"Well, you should reconnect with your Statehood crowd, review all of the contacts they had with Malcolm Mohammed. Also, see what you can dig up on Duke Wallace;

he can't be too invisible. I'll get Al to look into this fake cyber-generated attack, and I'll see if any of my old contacts can discover what the feds have found out. Then, I'd say you might want to come out to visit your Honolulu investment again, if you can swing it."

"So, you really think we could find them, Dad?" Mark asked, genuinely skeptical.

"Let me put it this way. If that clown, Roy, is leading the most important agency in this search, and if it's possible that your boy Malcolm Mohammed isn't done with APOCALYPSE 2029, we *need* to try to find them. See you soon, son."

***

After a few days of intense activity—evaluating airport video, tracing random phone conversations, and checking TSA and State Department records—the virtual federal task force working on the APOCALYPSE 2029 events was able to assemble a partial picture of the principals' activities.

"OK, boys and girls, what do we have?" Chief of Staff Ronald Barker asked, settling into an office armchair down the hall from the Oval Office.

"Go ahead, Martin." The secretary of Homeland Security deferred to CIA's Martin Pickett, while nodding at National Security Advisor Rachel Jones.

After a long drag of iced tea, Pickett flashed on a screen a few bullet points prepared by staff:

- Duke Wallace, former classmate of Malcolm Mohammed at Duke University, started out on finance career working for an auto exec, but became organizer with various White nationalist groups a few years before 2016 campaign. Did some work for us in 2024.
- Wallace had been a Navy Seal, trained at Coronado, and Mohammed an Army Ranger, so they had lethal training.

- Mohammed worked for NGOs in Africa after college, some UN community-building type work. Has established extensive international leftist contacts, but not with most violent Islamist groups.
- Somehow, the two reunited in DC a couple of years ago and began recruiting associates for some sort of activity, but they left no detailed trail.
- We found one Salvadoran workman who they paid to leave a message in one of the congressional offices and some Kentucky drifter who set explosive at president's daughter's prep school for a fee.
  - o Unlikely these two are hiding any further information.
- No connections to the tidal wave, but US Geological Survey confirmed that the explosions at sea likely triggered slippage along the Helena Banks Fault, in turn causing the wave.
- The Texas explosions and the Midwest partial cyber event are still mysteries.
  - o No trace of involvement or travel . . .
- Suspect connected to Indian IT talent in Delhi, but no real leads from the one communication intercepted.
- Identified and searched recent apartments of suspects and found material on ISIS, Al-Shabaab; appears they're doing Islamic terrorist bidding.
- Last week, camera at Montreal airport caught them boarding a plane to Camaguey, Cuba.
  - o The trail is dark since then.

The four principals sat in silence for a few minutes.

"Well, it seems Wallace and Mohammed have some direct involvement in the local events, but that doesn't mean they are part of a national or international conspiracy," said a more reflective Rachel Jones.

"Save for the use of the hashtag 'APOCALYPSE 2029,' " responded Pickett.

"Yeah, but that could be a copycat stunt," Travis Roy pointed out.

"Well, I hate to go in again with partial info. You know how he flies off the handle and jumps to tweetable conclusions," pondered the chief of staff.

"Wait a minute. This might help. Got a text here from Hardy Stennis. He says FBI just took some ex-Seal into custody who may have set off tsunami explosion," said Martin Pickett, quickly scanning a message from the attorney general.

"OK, here's an email with more detail. By chance, they spotted some guy in fatigues at a couple of antigun rallies acting strange. Turns out, this guy runs a charter boat business in Pompano Beach and had a daughter seriously wounded in the 2018 high school shootings over in Parkland, Florida. He'd been suffering PTSD symptoms after his last Seal deployment in Afghanistan. The Stoneman Douglas school shooting sent him back to the VA hospital for weeks. In an interview yesterday, he told the Bureau that the feds have dragged their feet too long on serious gun control for nonmilitary, nonpolice, or nonhunting use. That's what's allowing crazies to shoot up schools, shopping centers, etc., he said." Pickett paused.

"So? Still seems a stretch to prove he colluded with Duke Wallace to drown out half of South Carolina," said Rachel Jones.

"Guess where he trained and with whom he shipped out on his last tour?" Pickett raised an eyebrow.

"Clearly, trained in Coronado and served with Wallace," answered Barker, grim-faced.

"There's enough pieces here that the FBI is holding the guy. Not a slam dunk, but I'm just sayin'." Pickett put down his phone.

"Yeah, but this is close to the most solid information to date, so . . ." Travis Roy hesitated.

"I think we really need time to connect some of the scattered dots. There's definitely something here, in all of this data," Rachel Jones cautioned.

"The problem is time. In case you haven't noticed, the country is freaking out. Our guys are starting to panic and voters want answers," said Roy.

"So, it's better to give him something to show progress. This is definitely more concrete." Barker finished Roy's thought.

The president was indeed displeased that they hadn't captured the masterminds, but seemed partially satisfied with the FBI progress. He exercised uncommon restraint in a tweet bragging that his team was hot on the trail of the responsible terrorists. Aides winced at one line insisting that those responsible were definitely allied with ISIS.

Only after he fired off his tweets did it strike the president that Cuba had zero incentive to help, and that US intelligence capabilities on the island were a bare minimum.

CHAPTER 21

Mark Morton stared at a Snapchat message from his *Boston Globe* friend Gabriel Marquez, summarizing the Martin Pickett slide show.

If these guys hadn't pissed off so many White House staff, maybe they could keep a secret. Must be hell inside the puzzle palace, Mark thought.

He wasn't surprised that the operation behind these recent 9/11 events was a mystery to the feds. The suspects were nothing if not strategic, smart, and detail-oriented.

He checked the time and called his brother.

"Good evening to you, Al," he whispered.

"My word—what is it, one in the morning back East?" Al put down a cup of tea and turned from his laptop's screen. "I've read the stuff you sent me. Looks like your pals are the culprits, huh?"

"Not my pals, bro," laughed Mark. "Could the Michigan scene really be a cyber event, and could someone hoodwink the media for half a day?"

"Absolutely. Except for the smoke. They might have burned actual rubbish piles to dot the horizon. I can put together a demo for you," Al said.

"If you get a chance, look around to see who might have helped them put that event together. They're not AI or gaming guys that I can identify, but some talent must have helped."

"There's thousands, maybe millions of guys who could do it. You got to give me something more to narrow down the field," said Al.

"So, let's see. You could check their units when they were in the Navy Seals and the Army Rangers. Maybe they met some geek in college, at Duke. Sorry, no offense," said Mark.

"We're good. Well, that narrows it down a bit. I'll see what I can scope out."

"Great. Thanks. I think I will have to come out there to see how the investment is doing. On a plane tomorrow," said Mark.

"Dad told me. Glad to meet you at the airport. Lookin' forward to it." Al hung up.

As Mark left the United luggage carousel, stepped out of the Honolulu overseas terminal, and rolled his bag down the open outdoor path connecting to the main terminal, he inhaled warm plumeria-scented ocean air. Even though he couldn't see it, he now knew the Pacific was minutes' drive from the concrete, glass, and steel airport infrastructure. The tension he had carried on the flight escaped his body with every step. As he left the main building, he grinned widely when he saw the open Jeep, Al standing by the door.

They hugged.

"I wonder if all mainlanders get this buoyant feeling when they deplane here," Mark said, as he dropped his bag in the back and hopped into Al's front bucket-style passenger seat.

"Well, Harry says he does. Most of the folks I work with on the project from the West Coast, my classmates from Caltech who visit, say they do. So, yeah, I guess so," said Al.

"My spot is a little tight for more than overnight, so we hope it's all right if you stay at Harry's."

"That's cool, but I got a hotel room. I have to keep working on a bunch of stuff while I'm out here."

"Remember, he's got tons of room, he's close to the beach, and he's good at not bothering you. I crash there on occasion these days. It's like a deluxe B&B," Al assured him.

"OK, cool. I'll cancel the hotel. This is all still wild to me. First, reuniting with my father, then discovering a great brother. My wife thinks she needs to come next time because I'm having too much fun."

"Truly, we'd all love to meet her. You got to do it, dude." Al patted his brother's shoulder.

For the next two days, the three Mortons reviewed what Mark and Harry had been able to piece together from Washington and Boston contacts about Mohammed and Wallace. What had initially seemed like disparate data began to form a picture of a very odd couple engaged in a very dangerous plan. They didn't know enough details to comprehend the full implications of their New York City meeting with their IT magnate, or how each's military background played a part in this scheme. But the school and Metro fires, the claim of access to a capable national network of disaffected colleagues, and their sudden disappearance after the 9/11 events seemed likely to be related.

On the second afternoon, Al hosted Harry and Mark at a makeshift studio he had constructed in his warehouse office space. As they sat down for Al's presentation, a colleague interrupted and pulled Al aside. After a few minutes of whispering, he rejoined Mark and Harry.

"Well, Mark, there's good and bad news about who might have helped develop the Michigan cyber theater," said Al.

"Good news first," Mark said quickly.

"Well, it seems that one of the top students their senior year at Duke is an IT prodigy named Omar Kutar. Assuming he continued in a related field, he could have easily developed the capability to produce the sort of phenomenon I'm about to show you," Al said with an expressionless face.

"Assuming?" asked Harry.

"Right. The bad news is that he returned to India after graduation, went into business and sort of disappeared from any professional social media, conferences, or publications. One article suggests that he may have had some role in some international hacking, but nothing definitive, and no clue as to where he is now residing," said Al.

"Well, maybe even that tidbit will be useful to us or the feds later. Thanks for researching that much," said Mark, turning to the front of the room.

Al stood in front of them and assumed a confident, professional demeanor that even Harry had never witnessed.

"So, imagine that a few major media correspondents assigned to Honolulu all received Facebook feeds, followed by phone calls from supposed on-the-ground reporters relaying the same message. An explosion at Ala Moana shopping center and a warehouse district further west, toward Pearl Harbor. Additionally, someone hacked the airport's communications, suggesting a bomb is planted on the runways. Say the Facebook feed ran the video you're about to see, and someone lit a harmless fire at each site, which gave off a plume of black smoke, visible from miles away."

Without waiting for a response, Al started a video in an Imax-like space that showed the destruction of the shopping mall: cars, steel girders, and bodies flying in all directions among orange and red flames that the three could not simply hear and see but feel. The warehouse destruction was similarly catastrophic and realistic. And the airport tape successfully faked tower communications to incoming flights, redirecting traffic, and to terminal personnel telling them to seek and stay in sheltered areas.

"Now, further imagine that electronic communication to key news executives at each of the major networks had been compromised and that orders were given to run the story with accompanying videos immediately," Al said.

Harry and Mark sat in silence for several minutes, each slightly wet with nervous perspiration.

Harry spoke first. "That's all believable—tricky to pull off, but possible. What's not believable is that no one would check the on-the-ground reality and report a hoax."

Mark nodded his head in agreement.

"Remember the context, now," said Al. "There have actually been real school bombings, real Metro fires, a real Carolina tsunami, and threats of more to come. Sure, eventually the truth would surface. But the public is so fickle today—with all of the fake news—and networks are so anxious to get the jump on competition that these stories would have a good run on the mainland. AND, when the hoax was revealed, hysteria would still prevail, given the apparently ubiquitous reach of the terrorist group to manufacture events and control TV and social media reporting."

"So, your point is . . ." Mark began to think out loud.

"My point is that the Michigan caper could have been fake, in whole or in part, and, combined with the other real events claimed by the group, Michigan would effectively add to the hysteria. APOCALYPSE 2029 doesn't need an army to do what they are doing. Pay some key talent through intermediaries to perform isolated tasks that they know will have the effect of a coordinated attack. Like casting for a movie or commercial." Al turned the lights back on.

Then Harry spoke up. "I've been thinking about the tsunami 'cause we've had a few in the Pacific. Some well-placed explosives near a fault line could do the trick. With his Navy background, Wallace might have access to disaffected people and material. He could have coaxed someone to create enough of a wave to scare the coastline and paid a second diver to do the same a mile or so away on the same fault. The divers may not have known of each other's activity, but Wallace could have synchronized the charges to create a larger wave. A wild theory, admittedly, but these guys seem to have wild and creative imaginations."

"But what about their requests? The demand for environmental and immigration legislation seem unrealistic. What's the point?" asked Mark.

"I disagree, son. What's the one thing those leaders targeted can affect? Votes in the Congress. Even if it's emergency legislation, and they later retract it, they can pass laws. If they truly believe APOCALYPSE has the reach to get at their families, and they have already destroyed a presidential property, then these are threats that could have significant impact. Remember, we've heard that the First Lady was to have been at Royal Flush when the tsunami hit. She and their daughter would have been fatalities for sure. What we hear from the White House is that the bully in chief is acting much more on edge than normal, with 'normal' already being more agitated than the average human being." The three laughed.

"Anyway," Harry added, "Wallace and Mohammed don't have to be in the country to collect ransom, don't have to communicate through cyberspace to coordinate, and can check the news safely from any corner of the globe to see if legislation is passed. It may be a brilliant strategy."

"OK, so if we've convinced ourselves that APOCALYPSE 2029 is our boys, what do we do now?" asked Al.

"Well, I propose we wrap up for the day and head to the beach for a nice swim or surf before dinner," said Harry, standing.

"I need a nap. This future tech stuff is getting close to home. No one is supposed to actually use AI and the new audiovisual technology for such sinister purposes," said Al.

"That's the problem with technology, if you don't mind my saying so. It is a tool to be used for good, for evil, or for neutral purposes," Mark responded.

"Of course," said Al. "That's something I wrestle with all the time. Well, anyway, I'm exhausted," he repeated.

"Why don't you catch some winks on the beach, while we swim?" said Harry.

Al drove the trio east along the coast highway to Makapu'u Beach, beyond Sandy Beach and before the town of Waimanalo.

"OK, how's this?" asked Al, pulling into the beach parking lot.

"Well, this is fine for you and me, but Mark may be intimidated by the waves," cautioned Harry.

"Hey. I've got good genes, and I'm game," responded an enthusiastic Mark.

"I'll take a quick plunge and hang out on the beach," said Al.

"Right," Harry and Mark said in unison.

Harry and Mark swam through the big waves out far enough to sit comfortably on their boards and wait to select medium-height crests. Mark was, indeed, not intimidated, but he instantly recognized that the waves in this part of the Pacific demanded more respect than anything he'd negotiated off Martha's Vineyard during summer vacations, or even those he played in with his parents as a kid during Los Angeles vacations. Harry picked a couple of moderate-sized waves, pushed his board expertly toward a crest, grabbed the front and began traversing the powerful mountain of seawater. Mark followed but wiped out after a couple of turns. As they sat astride their boards awaiting a third wave, Harry offered encouragement, saying that Mark was doing super for a first time in these waters.

Mark was the clear beneficiary of regular hours in the gym, with flat stomach muscles and well-defined strong arms. His father, not so much. But Mark recognized a sinewy athletic ability, quick reflexes, and tempered-steel resolve beneath Harry's loose-skin frame.

Meanwhile, Al drifted off into a sunbaked reverie, with the breaking of the surf as background. He slipped into an uneasy dream, imagining that he was still in the ocean, treading water thirty yards from Mark. Suddenly, in his dream, Al saw a seal beyond his brother. What caught his attention was the unnatural way in which it jerked through the surf toward Mark and Harry. Al stared for a minute and then surveyed the ocean around his family. He looked at the beach, and then returned his attention to the seal.

"Harry, is that a seal out beyond Mark?" he shouted.

"Cool," responded Mark, instead.

Al thought, for a second, that he had rarely seen a seal off this beach. Then, still treading water, he looked up to a cliff promontory that rose more than a hundred feet above the beach. On that bluff, he saw a person holding something—like he was guiding a model airplane or drone. Al scanned the horizon looking for a plane. Nothing. He dismissed the strange figure and returned his gaze to Harry and Mark. Suddenly, something *else* in the water beyond them caught his attention. There appeared to be a shark's dorsal fin tracking the seal. Endangered Hawaiian monk seals were favorite meals for tiger sharks, but they generally fed at night. Yet the seal was now heading for Mark's board and a ten-foot tiger shark was closing in on the seal.

Al's eyes widened in terror and he called to Mark to hit the wave that was forming behind him. Instinctively, he pointed his board at the nose of the shark. Al saw its eyes roll back and its mouth open seconds before it tried to bite the robotic seal and himself. He launched the pointed end of his board into the open death chamber. The sound of teeth on fiberglass was terrifying, the turbulence created by the missile passing across his chest sent Al spiraling underwater, and salt solution began to fill his lungs. For a moment, his world went black.

Al sat up, choking and coughing as he woke from his dream. In a panic, he looked out to sea and located Mark and

Harry slowly swimming back into shore, boards in tow. No sharks or robotic seals in sight.

'You all right, Al? You look like you've seen a ghost?" Mark laughed as he toweled off.

"Just a bad dream. You guys have fun out there?" Al quickly changed the subject.

"The water was fantastic. However, I sense it's that time. Anybody use a drink?" Harry said, stretching his long legs in the front passenger side of the jeep.

"Snap. Let's go," Mark barked.

They headed back toward Diamond Head and Harry's house, the radio blaring some sort of calypso/rap, tension and fear exiting into the wind with each enjoyable curve of the highway.

Al showed Mark where his cooler with bottles of cold Gatorade was stashed. "It's a good idea to rehydrate after sustained exposure to beach and sun," Al advised.

A little after Sandy Beach, but before Hanauma Bay, as he drained his bottle of fluid, Al checked his rear-view mirror and saw a swift motorcycle cruising up to his bumper.

"We've got company, dudes," he said.

The other two Mortons turned as the black-clad cyclist pulled his vehicle alongside and tried to nudge the jeep off the road. Al remained calm and accelerated as a car approached from the ocean side of the two-lane highway. The bike had to drop back. It stayed twenty-five or so yards behind, waiting for the next stretch of straight road.

Harry thought fast. "Al, you know the overlook/turnaround about a quarter of a mile up on the left?" he asked.

"Yeah," said Al, gripping the steering wheel more tightly.

"OK. Let the bike get alongside of us right before it. Then brake hard and spin across the road into the lot," Harry said, as if calmly giving driving lessons.

"If no one is coming the other direction . . ." Al stuttered.

"Most cars are slow there because they are coming out of the curve after the Hanauma Bay parking lot. And hopefully, they'll brake." Harry's grin was reassuring.

"OK. Then what?" Mark asked, holding fast to the side of his back seat.

"The rider will either pass and we can turn the tables by following, or, more likely, he'll instinctively try to turn and lose control. For some reason, there's always extra gravel on the road in that area. If he spills and lives, I think the three of us can take him." Harry didn't feel seventy, at that moment.

"Here it comes. And here we go." Al perfectly executed the brake and spin-out maneuver, and safely skidded into the parking lot ahead of an oncoming, horn-blaring sedan.

The motorcyclist tried to make a quick left turn spin, then tried to pull out of it, lost control and skidded over a barrier just beyond the parking lot. The rider and bike bounced a few feet to a precipice, then fell several hundred feet down the granite hill and into the pounding surf below.

"You OK, boys?" asked Harry after a moment of shocked silence.

"My palms are drenched, my stomach is a knot and I have a crushing headache—but otherwise, I guess I'm OK," whispered Al.

"I'm not. That was some scary shit. What the hell?" said Mark.

The shaken trio got out of the jeep and walked to the edge of the cliff. The wreck below left little doubt that neither cycle nor rider survived. The Mortons immediately called the police, who responded quickly, but not until a sizable crowd had gathered around the site. The officer who questioned them accepted the description of the incident given by the Mortons and corroborated by witnesses at the overlook. He even agreed to notify Harry if they could identify the body.

Half an hour later, Al was still more visibly shaken by the incident than his brother or father. Nevertheless, when the police said they could go, he slid behind the steering wheel, took a deep breath and started the engine.

"You OK, bro?" asked Mark.

"Fine. Thanks," was Al's perfunctory response.

Mark looked up at the hill across the road from the parking lot and caught a glimpse of a goose-like bird with a dark brown striped back, speckled black and white belly and a bright yellow patch on its neck. "Wow. Up on the hill. Check out that bird," he said pointing.

"That's the state bird, nene. It's not seen in this area often," said Al.

"But it's a good sign, an omen, 'he hoailona ke ia, because its name means 'fearless.' Nice," offered Harry.

"Impressive, Uncle Harry. And, nice pronunciation," said Al, as he pulled onto the road.

Later that night, the precinct captain called Harry to tell him that the fingerprints of the dead motorcyclist didn't match anyone they had on the state database. Afterward, as he sipped aged and expensive Japanese Scotch, Harry looked out at the Pacific from his balcony and spoke to his two sons, who also had drinks in their hands.

"Well, I'd say this was an attempt by nervous pseudo-terrorists to buy time. This was not the feds trying to keep us away from the case. They clearly don't have a handle on more than disparate facts. Let's hope this is the last effort that Mohammed and Wallace set in motion to silence Mark before they fled. Hopefully, they'll have bigger worries than being fingered by an investor/activist from DC.

"They must calculate that even this administration will eventually catch some witness, view some surveillance tapes, and deduce where they exited the country, if not where they landed. So, we have to be cautious, but let's hope that was the last bullet we'll have to dodge from them."

Harry's intention was to calm his sons because he was by no means confident that Mohammed and Wallace had fully turned their attention elsewhere.

"I don't know, Pop. I wish I could be sure this was their last shot. I'm worn out," Mark confessed, draining his Scotch.

Almost suffocating in a steam room, being caught in a stranded subway, and now almost becoming a traffic fatality on a winding cliffside highway on Oahu, had a cumulative effect on Mark's anxiety. He feared he was becoming paranoid, and seeing assailants where none existed. Being with Harry and Al was reassuring, but he knew he would soon be heading home and have no such protection.

Al nodded. "I'm ready to go back to finishing my game, putting together my organization, and living 'the life.' "

Al's stomach felt like those twisted seaman's knots he'd seen at the docks. He quickly drank a couple of glasses of water to keep his digestive tract from erupting. While he was extremely confident and comfortable in the ocean, the dream had shaken him, and the motorcycle incident had scared him more than his face revealed. Helping solve some cyber puzzle or defeating avatars in a computer game was one thing, but facing down killers, real thugs, required a totally different temperament. He felt this was now a job for the government pros, competent or not.

Harry saw the fear and anxiety in his sons' faces. As he continued to sip, he conjured up a last attempt to allay their fears.

"I thoroughly understand your hesitancy now. But suppose, for a moment, that these characters have more plans in store to hurt innocent people, not just the obnoxious clowns in government? Their resources have got to remain focused on their target, particularly as they are on the run."

Neither son looked convinced.

"Look, they know that Mark is a well-meaning 'do-gooder' with no police or military experience. I'm

confident that they assume Mark's either dead or frightened to death—off the case."

Mark raised his hand and nodded his head. "They would be spot on."

Harry smiled, and continued. "I suspect they will take at least one more pass at government leaders. They have generated mass paranoia, stirred up the public, but they haven't secured their legislation yet. So, it's likely that they have at least another trick ready to be triggered."

"Like you say, their primary target is the feds. If they think we're out of the way, they most likely will focus on the big boys," Mark agreed, relaxing a bit.

"Now, those 'big boys' couldn't find Mohammed and Wallace after the school bombings, after the Metro mess, and now . . ." Harry stopped.

"But, like you say, they've more than likely been driven abroad, where it will be harder to coordinate any strikes. Although they clearly have resources. Even so, I'm beginning to think they're done," Al said. Thinking and talking out odds, probabilities, and options helped relieve his fear and engage his mathematical genes.

Silence. Feet up. Ocean-gazing. Brains calculating. Scotch-sipping.

"OK. I suppose we could do a little more digging. But, at some point, I'm out of this. I think I've learned my limits," said Mark.

"Bingo, my thoughts exactly," said Al.

"Look, I can't pretend that I had a career dealing with this type of physical danger, but I am much more used to it than you two. As your father, I'd fully understand and even applaud your decision to pull out." Harry switched tactics and tested his sons.

Neither young man could now countenance letting their stubborn aging father go on alone. After a moment, pride, nascent family loyalty, and a moderate sense of obligation overcame fear, anxiety, and hesitation.

"Not now. I do want to finish this and see these suckers captured," said Mark firmly.

"I'm still in, for now," said Al.

"OK then, gentlemen, we've been invited to join Al's parents for a friendly dinner at the Kahukus' in honor of Mark's coming out to visit. No talk of conspiracies, although we will have to have some answer for the motorcycle accident. The media will have stories on all the local channels. Shall we?" Harry finished his drink and ushered his sons into his car.

***

The usual family of friendly dogs greeted Harry's car when he opened the gate to the Kahukus' property. Not all of the family houses were visible in the twilight engulfing the valley. Mark could see horses behind the L-shaped one-story house at the end of the driveway and noticed another modern glass structure on a hill to the right of the gravel patch where Harry parked his car.

"Welcome back, Mark," said Laila.

"Thank you. It's great to see you again, and I love the open space, the mountains, the fruit trees . . . This is a wonderful paradise."

"Well, Laila's mother kept this valley, but actually owned much of the land that is now the subdivision you just drove through. She was a descendant of—" Kiki was cut off.

"Kiki. No one wants to hear about Hawaiian royalty. And, it's history. What's important is what we do today for people," Laila insisted.

"Actually, I would like to hear more," said Al.

"We'll have you boys over some other time, then," said Kiki.

"So, listen, I saw a brief news clip about some biker that went over a cliff near Hanauma Bay. And you guys were in it. Scary! I'm so glad to see you're OK. That must have been awful." Laila's face registered motherly concern. "But what happened? The report was light on details, just that he went over the cliff."

Harry gave a five-minute matter-of-fact report that omitted any theories of why the rider was trying to run them off the road. As Mark added a few supportive details, Tommy and Donna came in from the deck and listened as well. No one noticed Al, in the background, pulling out his phone. It was as if adrenaline had sustained him all afternoon, and now he was exhausted.

Another older couple rose from the bench bordering the deck and came to greet the Mortons. They knew Al and Harry, but Mark was new to them.

"Paul Tanaka, golfing buddy, this is my son Mark. And I take it you know my godson, Al," Harry said.

An attractive silver-haired woman dressed in a Hawaiian floral print stepped forward, hugged Harry and shook Mark's hand.

Before Harry could introduce them, Muriel said, "I am Muriel Tanaka, Paul's wife."

"Wonderful to see you Harry, and Al over there. Mark, welcome to Hawaii. Please, sit while Laila finishes up. You know, you take your life in your hands if you try to assist in her kitchen."

Harry sat in a wicker armchair facing the couple. He had researched a bit about the academic superstars, who, though native to Hawaii, had maintained extensive constructive relations with Japan. Muriel Tanaka had produced numerous social work projects focusing on indigenous Hawaiians. He had known that Paul was a leading historian focusing on twentieth- century trans-Pacific economic development. He had been one of the early pioneers of the East-West Center.

"Harry, I must admit that I and many of my colleagues, former colleagues, admire the dimensions on business collaboration you have recently brought to the Center," said Muriel, sipping a chilled white wine.

"This is a magnificent place to work on, research, and explore collaboration of any type. I am blessed to have this opportunity," Harry returned.

"Mark, the Tanakas have done more for the improvement of the status of Hawaiians than almost any non-Hawaiian reformers on the islands," Laila said, handing Harry a tall ginger ale with a dash of cranberry juice, his favorite daytime cocktail.

Kiki redirected the conversation. "Actually, we're here to celebrate Mark's return visit to Hawaii and Al's impressive new gaming business."

"And to think . . . isn't it wonderful that Mark is the major investor in Pua'ena Games?" Laila said, shaking her head in amazement.

After a kind of ceviche hors d'oeuvre, Laila started into the house to bring out the rest of the meal. Before she went in, she turned and said, "I want to hear more about the accident when we eat. It sounds terrifying." Then she disappeared inside the house to bring out a spread of roast pork, green beans, roasted corn, garlic mashed potatoes and home-baked bread.

"Harry, could you tell if it was a local lad?" quizzed Kiki.

"He was not. We know that much from the early police report."

Harry went on to try to dismiss it as some drunken kid from the mainland, joyriding. After a bit more speculation by the group, Harry was able to steer the conversation toward Mark and Al and the gaming industry. Al talked a bit about how he was hoping to get his generation motivated to action on climate change through his game. There was interest from the older set about the environmental aspect, but once Al turned to the technicalities of AI and gaming, long silences punctuated with "really" and "ah hah" prevailed.

As the group finished their corn on the cob, Kiki noted a strange car coming through the gate.

"Are we expecting someone else?" he asked, squinting.

"Maybe that's one of your kids," said Muriel.

"No. I'm sorry. I think that's an Uber for me. I have to apologize for leaving. But I guess the day tired me more than I thought . . . and I've got an early morning business meeting." After quickly hugging everyone, Al descended the steps and got into the Uber.

"Was it something I said?" asked Laila.

"No, of course not," said Harry. "It really has been a stressful day."

"And he's recently had to absorb a lot of life-changing events," added Tommy.

"It is a lot, but he's from good stock and is maturing fast. He'll be fine," Kiki said, reassuringly.

"Come on friends—we have a feast to finish," said Donna, linking arms with Laila.

MORTONS JOIN THE CHASE

2029

CHAPTER 22

The Uber deposited Al at Harry's, where he retrieved his jeep and headed back out. There was no answer at Peter's apartment, so Al risked driving to his parents' house. He pulled into the driveway of the Hungs. Their spacious beige ranch-style house sat atop a hill in one of Hawaii Kai's suburban neighborhoods, with a view over a subdivision sitting on a lower hill. Beyond that hill, one could see, though not hear, a wide blue expanse of the Pacific. Al didn't see any of the picturesque environment. He was fixated on catching his friend at home, hopefully not busy. He knocked.

A casually dressed Chinese woman of about sixty-five opened the door.

"Well, hello, Al. Haven't seen you in a while. How are you, and how are your parents?"

"Everyone is fine, Mrs. Hung. Thanks for asking. I hope things are fine here with you and Mr. Hung."

Obligatory courtesies completed, Al asked, "Is Peter around?"

"He just came in. We're his laundry, you know. Can I get you some tea, a beer . . . ?"

"I'm fine. Thank you," said Al, standing in the marble foyer.

"Why don't you go to the TV room and I'll get Peter for you?" Alice Hung motioned Al to a room beyond the living room, which he knew well.

Al settled into a stiff couch, turned away from the large-screen TV, gazed out at a spare side yard of neatly trimmed lawn surrounding a weeping cherry tree. *This is way comfortable, but I can already tell that Peter wants to escape this life,* Al thought.

"Hey, dude. I thought you had some dinner for your brother," said Peter, embracing his friend.

"Sorry to disturb you man, but I had to talk to someone close, but not family."

"Understood. But what's up?" Peter sat in an armchair facing Al.

"While Harry and Mark were swimming, I had a dream that somebody tried to turn Mark into shark bait. Then, on the way back to Harry's, some hood on a motorbike actually tried to run Mark, Harry, and me off the road up near Hanauma Bay," Al blurted out.

"No way." Peter sat upright in his chair.

"Yeah. But scary as that is, that's just the kicker. The top of all the shit that's swirling in my head. I'm not used to so many emotional issues swirling around at one time. Nor am I ready for real-life cops and robbers," Al confessed.

He then told Peter about the Morton family relationship to the APOCALYPSE 2029 scare that was flooding social media and the major national networks.

"You're shitting me. You guys actually know these terrorists?" Peter gasped.

"Not really. Mark has met them, but there's a chance that we may have the best shot at finding them. That is assuming we've identified the right guys."

"Dude. That's awesome."

"Peter. Think about it. Even if we could help the feds find them, think for a minute about who gets helped and who gets hurt." Al sighed.

"I'm all ears, Al."

"The climate change-deniers. The keep-out-the-Brown and Muslim anti-immigrant fanatics. The ones who want to shred the safety net for poor Hawaiians, among others, marginalize women and LGBTQ folks. The right-to-White Christian Right. The folks who drilled holes in the ship and now cry out that it's sinking. *Those* are the assholes who this APOCALYPSE group is trying to unseat," Al said with uncharacteristic vehemence.

"So, dude, how do you really feel?" Peter laughed. "But you know, folks like my parents love what has happened to their taxes, investments—" Peter was cut off.

"Don't need to go there, Peter. You're not your parents. Anyway, the problem is that I think this terrorist approach is, in the long term, wrong and counterproductive."

"You think? So, on balance, you, an about-to-be-wealthier-than-Jack-Ma entrepreneur, think you need to help find terrorists who maybe, possibly, perhaps, could make the planet better? You, a mixed-race Black-Chinese-Hawaiian guy, who could do nice things for people of color around the world, want to risk it all in some wild goose chase for some jihadists that the feds likely will or won't catch without your assistance? Is that it?" Peter deadpanned.

"I sure don't want to help this horrible administration that has promulgated 'fake news' and buried facts, that is hoodwinking poor folks, capitalizing on ethnic rivalries and hatred that has destroyed nonpartisan governmental institutions and dismantled important international alliances—not to mention sucked the air out of a global economy. And this APOCALYPSE group sees that and has scared the shit out of these guys. That's hard not to like. At least they have guts and a strategy."

"So, you're siding with the terrorists who've shown no respect for human life?" Peter persisted.

"No. I'm saying that there's no easy choice. I mean, I recognize that their ends don't justify their means, and bottom line is that it's still our country—institutions and real civilians are being threatened. These leaders, however, don't deserve help. They're the reason why games like *Earth Reclaimed* are so critically necessary. But the everyday people do deserve help." Al seemed, to Peter, uncharacteristically confused. "I guess I sound like a preacher. Yeah. Crazy, huh?" Al looked at his friend for reassurance.

"Dude, it's not your fight. I don't see that it's your father or brother's either. No way you can support this jihadist shit. Their goals are as disastrous as climate change for the people. If you had to pick a side, you got to help the government—no brainer. On the other hand, last time I checked, you have zero military or intelligence bona fides. I think you'd be safe taking a pass, all of you. That said, you're the only one who lives inside that head of yours . . ." Peter looked down at his feet, then at his despondent friend.

"Hey, Harry Morton is a legitimate stud, and he does have military experience. What the hell. Go for it. Help find these creepy terrorists," said Peter after a long moment's contemplation.

"I'm tight as a drum on this, can't shut it out, having bad dreams. . . . This is way above my pay grade, dude. But, you're right—it's the only right choice, and I've basically committed to Harry and Mark." After another few moments, "You're a real friend. Thanks for letting me talk this out," Al said and fist-bumped Peter.

***

"Mrs. Sonya Morton? "We're trying to contact your husband or your father-in-law," Sheila Baxter barked into her phone.

"I'm sorry, but you are?" Sonya answered.

"Oh, I apologize. I'm Sheila Baxter, special assistant to Homeland Security Secretary, Travis Roy. Your husband has graciously offered to help us with this terrorist attack I'm sure you've read about." Sheila's voice became softer, yet more urgent.

"OK. Yes, I do know something about the attacks and Mark's assistance. My understanding, however, is that the government really doesn't need his help." Sonya enjoyed the silence on the other end.

"I'm sorry if Homeland, or any of the agencies involved, gave that impression, Mrs. Morton. We really do need to reach them." Sheila tried to sound solicitous and respectful.

"Well, my husband is in Honolulu. Here's his father's number. I suggest you try there." Sonya offered the number as minimal assistance.

"Thank you so much," said a partially relieved Baxter.

After she hung up, Sonya texted both Mark and Harry about the call.

As she dialed Harry Morton's home number, Sheila thought about how deeply and viciously divided the nation was, even in the face of a national threat. Of course, she realized that many people saw this threat as one directed solely at the president and Republican leadership, but not at the nation as a whole. Reactions were quite unlike what she had been told of the national unity in the wake of the 9/11 attacks in 2001.

Both the CIA's Martin Pickett and Chief of Staff Ronald Barker had cautioned Roy about any "good ol' boy" attempt at familiarity with Harry.

"Keep it friendly, but professional, Travis. We need their help and can't afford to offend him in any way," said Barker.

"Shit. Why so politically correct all of a sudden, Ron?"

"Why? Well, for starters, since you don't have a fucking clue where these terrorists are; and since they headed for a country with whom we have dog-shit relations, a country with a new security agreement with our good friends the Russians; and given that Morton has been around the block and would likely balk at any attempt to strong-arm him; and we have a boss who seems to be hunkered down and not even using his phone, and so we are living on borrowed time in terms of the stability of this government—I'd say being "politically correct" with this reluctant patriot is smart.

What do you think, huh?" Ron Barker's midtown New York City accent sharpened each phrase.

Earlier, the president's willingness to involve the Mortons had surprised Barker. When briefed, the president had said, "Harry Morton. I know that name. Back in the day, he was a hot shot M & A consultant. So he's got to be about my age."

"Same guy, I guess," said Barker

"Yeah, made a lot of money with his company, then sold to Masterfield. After a year or so, he semi-retired and went low profile. Hear his name on occasion. Smart guy, but playing detective on terrorist stuff is not his thing, I don't think. Although he did have some sort of intelligence clearance or status, 'cause I've heard he was periodically briefed on African and Asian political stuff. You know the lines between the business, the political, and the personal blur with a lot of these dictators. So, he can't hurt. He's certainly no dummy. And it appears we don't have solid leads." The president stared icily at his chief of staff and closed the conversation.

***

"So, Mr. Morton," said Travis Roy, on a secure line, "we appreciate the assistance you and your sons have provided. We're now sure that the two men you identified are, indeed, our main suspects. In fact, we have traced their movements to Havana, via Montreal. But we lost the trail in Cuba." Roy waited for a moment.

"OK. I hear you," was Harry's only response.

"So, we'd like to have you work more closely with us and perhaps even travel to Cuba to see if you can help find these guys." Another pause.

Harry did not respond.

"I've located an old Agency for Internatioinal Development contract you had with the government to which I can add an emergency extension to cover your work on this." Roy waited. He had not only retrieved the contract, but had a file of Harry's top-security consulting assignments in front of him, as he spoke.

After a long couple of minutes, Harry spoke.

"Send me three tickets and have the 'cost-plus' contract include Alaka'i Liu and Mark Morton, my sons. They've been working with me on this. I can get to DC in a couple of days." Harry readied to hang up.

"No problem with your sons, the tickets, or the contract. But, given the disruption this is causing, I'd like you to leave today. I realize that it's inconvenient, but things are nuts here."

Harry sensed that Travis Roy's anxiety, unlike his earlier chatter, was genuine.

"OK, get us the tickets and we'll see you tomorrow," Harry said and hung up.

***

"Thank you for agreeing to help the country, Mr. Morton—all three of you." Travis Roy ushered the Mortons to chairs around a conference table in his office. "This is not 9/11, but it's truly a crisis. We don't know when these guys will strike again. Let me introduce Rachel Jones, national security advisor, and Ron Barker, the president's chief of staff,"

"We've met a while back, when I was at Masterfield," Harry said, grasping Barker's hand. "A pleasure, ma'am, and these are my assistants and sons, Mark and Alaka'i," he added.

After they were all offered coffee to complement the bottles of water beside their chairs, Ronald Barker began. "Again, our deepest thanks for working with us on this, and I'm here to personally represent the president. So, here's what we know.

"The suspects organized and paid a troop of disconnected and unrelated individuals to do the school bombings, disrupt the Metro, even execute the South Carolina tidal wave, Michigan cyber events, and Southwest explosions. We then traced them, too late for capture, to a flight from Montreal to Havana three days after the attacks. As you might imagine, our intel in Cuba is not the strongest. We are not sure where they are today.

"So, even though we know the leaders have fled, we can't be sure that their destruction is finished. As I understand it, you narrowly escaped an attempt on your lives in Hawaii." Barker looked at Mark.

"Bad news travels fast," Mark responded.

"In my partially informed opinion," said Harry, "once they see movement in the Congress on their requests, or even if they feel stonewalled, they won't risk continuing to communicate with agents here."

"You could be right, but the president doesn't want to take chances. He's canceled campaign and other appearances. That's a first," Barker admitted.

"Understood. So, how can we help?" Harry settled back in his seat and sipped coffee.

As if awaiting a cue, Travis Roy said, "We think that with the information we possess, with your experience and language skills, Mr. Morton, with the familiarity that Mark here has with Mohammed, and with the on-the-ground intel we've got, you have a good chance of finding them."

"I see. But why not use your own agents? You've got to have a fair number of native Cubans or second-generation Miami agents who can do this," Harry said.

"We do. However, they have more than likely already been identified by the Cubans, particularly with their intelligence enhancements since their Russian agreement. You are not as likely to draw attention until you locate the suspects. We can take it from there," said Jones.

Harry knew this was the moment of commitment, the point beyond which there was no retreat. The whole situation seemed surreal. The nation at risk? Top officials calling on amateurs for assistance? He remained confident in his ability to be useful, but he still was hesitant to put his sons' lives further at risk.

Yet, even after the motorcycle attack, Mark seemed ready to get on with the assignment. Harry knew that Mark's knowledge of the terrorists' behavior, thin as it was, could be valuable in tracking them. Al was more nervous, he thought, but almost personally affronted by the tidal wave and cyber tactics. As if this nefarious use of science required his defense. The potential for domestic damage, global repercussions, accidental military actions continued to grow as long as these guys were at large, he felt. These characters had to be caught or neutralized.

Harry looked quickly at Al and Mark, to confirm that they were in.

"Well, we flew from the middle of the Pacific to come back East. So, I suppose we can stay and give it a shot," said Harry with a practiced smile.

In unison, the two officials said, "That's great. Thank you."

"I've arranged for you to get a much more thorough briefing, introduction to the resources you'll have in Havana, identification documents, cover story, etc.," Roy said. "There's a car downstairs that will take you to Langley to meet with the CIA brass that will run our part of the operation. Again, on behalf of the president, many thanks." Barker and Roy, frustrated and worn out, both expressed genuine gratitude.

After the more detailed briefing, the exhausted trio were given a ride to Mark's house. Harry and Al had met Sonya and inhaled the late dinner she prepared, and then retired to Mark's "man cave."

"What a terrible way to meet my daughter-in-law. I barely got a chance to say how happy I am to finally meet her," Harry lamented.

"I feel the same, brother," added Al.

"Don't worry, there'll be plenty of time once this business is over," Mark reassured them.

"Unfortunately, this may take more than a minute," said Harry.

"To be truthful, I don't think they're still in Cuba. My money's on Mexico," said Mark.

"Oh, why's that?" asked Harry.

"Well, Malcolm once said something about a trip to Puerto Vallarta, and it's got many more of the amenities he would want, if he were to become an expat. Plus, the difficulty of maintaining a sophisticated intel network in Mexico, given governmental relations these days, makes it very challenging for the United States. We still have diplomatic and trade relationships, but the current government has made its intent to operate as an independent entity very clear. But I'm just guessing," Mark admitted.

"Not my area of expertise, but what about San Miguel? I hear you don't need Spanish, lots of Canadian and US expats, and a great culture," Al said.

"Just for that reason. Too many expats—it's a logical place for our feds to look. I agree with Mark that Puerto Vallarta is more likely. That is, if they have left Cuba," said Harry, rubbing his eyes. "Well, let's go to Havana and see what we can find."

***

Ron Barker reported to the president about the meeting with the Mortons and got an unexpected reaction.

"That's great. Maybe they can flush these guys out. My sense from our intelligence is that these guys really are the head of the snake. Cut them off and we can reassure everybody that all's taken care of. Ron, I think we need to have party leaders approve emergency legislation giving this group some of what it wants." Spade looked out at the Rose Garden.

"But, Mr. President, you really thinks that's wise?" Barker was stunned. "You want to look like you're giving in to terrorists right before the election?"

"Look, I said 'emergency.' I think I can go on Fox and sell this as a temporary fix to begin addressing some of the issues. If I hold out and stonewall too much longer, and they attack again, take more lives, destroy infrastructure, some of the base might blame me. We've had some of our base indicate support for the environmental crap and react strongly to school gun violence. Even with immigration, I'll essentially repeat what we have said in the past, I'll just downplay detention of kids. I can even imply that some of the Republican Senate leadership wants some legislation. I'll sound tough, but empathetic. The actual legislation can be more specific.

"We reverse it once the election is over. By then, we should have captured or at least isolated these jerks. If we catch a break, the Congress will deliberate and not actually pass legislation for a couple of months. In the meantime, we catch these assholes and pull back the proposed emergency legislation. Face it, the base is nervous. They are traumatized, waiting for the next attack. We are responding to their top fear. Just make sure the right leaders know this is 'emergency,' temporary." The president grinned.

"I don't know, boss." Barker was unconvinced.

"Well, I do. Get Trane, Ditch . . . You know what? Reach out to the Dems leadership, as well. They don't need to know about the retraction strategy. They should want to stop this national nightmare. It will look good for all sides. Do it," said the president, turning away to the TV screen.

Barker quickly selected bright staff to craft environmental regs that essentially supported tenets of the rejected Paris

Accord, as well as specific gun measures that narrowed the use of military-type weapons and constrained ownership of weapons for residential and personal defense. Lawyers had a more difficult time envisioning how to relax recently deployed immigration restrictions. But, with staff working nonstop, day and night, emergency legislation was soon introduced.

Barker dreaded the organized reaction he felt some groups would mount, regardless of the president's reassurances. But he and White House communications had their orders, and they prepared an arsenal of spin messages.

At a bar near Union Station just off Massachusetts Avenue NE, Rachel Jones, Hardy Stennis, and Martin Pickett all sipped rare Scotch and stared gloomily at the sunset beyond the Capitol.

"I didn't sign up for a circus or to try to steer a runaway train," said Stennis.

"None of us did, but we have to keep the welfare of the country in mind," said Pickett.

"That's what I have been telling myself for almost four years. It's getting old," muttered Rachel Jones.

"Drink up, y'all. It's going to be a long winter. And we have to keep the president from totally losing it," Pickett said.

"I'm afraid that's a task that will require divine intervention," said Jones.

CHAPTER 23

"**D**uke, what does this area remind you of?" Malcolm asked his travel companion.

"Nothing, except some dried-up, dusty Southwestern town," said Duke, looking into the midday sun.

"Exactly, which is why we should take a taxi to the bus station and get the hell out of here," said a smiling Malcolm. "If we were spotted in Montreal, I doubt we got tracked to Camaguey. And even if we were, the bus station is an unlikely stakeout locale."

Seated inside an antique Plymouth taxi with the windows cranked down, the two Americans watched the pastel pink, green, and blue single-story houses and stores roll by. Malcolm, in his broken New York/Puerto Rican Spanish, asked the driver to slow down to allow them to watch some young uniformed kids practice mambo and salsa steps in a small park.

"For a few convertible pesos more, I can take you to Cuba's most beautiful church and park at Plaza Del Carmen," offered the driver, in Spanish.

"*No, gracias, mi amigo.* Some other time," quickly responded Duke.

Malcolm turned to him. "Not bad, gringo."

"How about the famous Casa de Arte Jover, for paintings, or the Casa de la Diversidad, the best museum in eastern Cuba?" the driver persisted.

Both Americans, in unison, said, "*No, gracias.*"

They were dropped at an unimpressive bus terminal in time to purchase their Havana tickets and grab a couple of chicken and avocado tortilla wraps, dipped a spicy pepper sauce.

"To be safe, let's sit in separate parts of the station," Malcolm said, looking around at the few patrons waiting on hardwood benches.

"So, you think that a fed, whether Cuban, Russian, or American, couldn't tell we were two traveling gringos with one eye-sweep of this room?" asked Duke, with a slight smirk.

"I suppose you're right. I just all of a sudden felt a wave of caution.'"

"Well, the fifteen folks I see here, assuming they are all waiting to board for Havana, are not in any way preoccupied with us. I'm just sayin'," Duke said, jokingly.

The 2:25 Viazul bus left at three o'clock for the nine-hour trip to Havana. As it rolled through cattle country and former sugar plantations, sage shrubbery, and low mountains, Duke and Malcolm slept. They pulled into the station a bit after midnight, hauled their carry-ons from the luggage racks, dismounted, and walked through the run-down main hall to the taxi stand.

"We look for a sign saying 'Sr. Dolores,' " said Malcolm.

"Dolores, as in pain?"

"It's a play on the word 'dollars.' Jorge Blanco has financed APOCALYPSE, but obviously doesn't want his name spread around, even in Cuba. Or ours. The cat who's picking us up will take us to a place like a B&B, where Blanco has covered us for the night. We have a midday flight tomorrow," said Malcolm, looking at a middle-aged man in a well-worn white dress shirt and pants, carrying a sign.

"Welcome to Havana, *señores*. I hope you have a pleasant night at Casa Colonial Yadilis & Yoel," their driver said in halting English.

After he deposited their bags at the B&B, the driver handed each of them a "welcome drink kit," containing a miniature bottle of rum, a lime and a Coke.

"Let's enjoy one old-fashioned Cuba Libre before we head in," said Malcolm, as they strolled down to a little late-night café next to their house.

"But you don't drink, bro." Duke stared at his colleague.

"I don't. But this is a rare celebration and it's a rum and Coke. That ain't drinking, dude," chortled Malcolm.

They ordered some chicharróns to go with their drinks, and with the accompanying guitar, bongos, and voices of the trio in the back of the café.

"You know, Malcolm, this was business for me in the beginning. Personal business to get even with pols and to help my people. You were, I got to admit, a convenient partner. That's it. But I'm glad we reconnected and did this together. Really. Thank you, man," said Duke.

"That about sums it up for me too, my man," said Malcolm.

They clinked their glasses in a toast.

"This place, though, this is the pits. Lefties idolize Havana, but really the little I've seen is enough. Reminds me of Alabama or northern Florida in the '70s. Paint peeling, run-down cars, Thomas Edison-era lights, streets look like they were last surfaced before Castro. Man, I need to get me to Western civilization," Duke complained.

"Homie, you forgetting the boycott?"

"I'm not casting blame. And I'll give you that the health care, the education, and the baseball may be terrific. I'm just sayin' I'm happy to be on my way to London." Duke drained his second glass.

"It's too many spades down here for you, my man," Malcolm challenged.

"That's rich, man. I'm headed ultimately for South Africa, remember?" Duke laughed.

The street life was now bustling and they watched lively attractive people of all shades, from vanilla to licorice, sashay past them. As they finished their drinks, they tried to sing along with the band. Back in their room, no sooner had they fallen asleep than they were awakened for a sumptuous breakfast of beans, eggs in a spicy tomato sauce, tortillas, and black coffee. Their driver picked them up early in the morning, after they had a chance to briefly walk around and take in the friendly sunrise street banter of storekeepers, street sweepers, and early-rising partiers.

The driver had been instructed to take them on a more circuitous route to the airport, in case they were followed.

"So, we don't communicate for a couple of weeks, right?" Duke reconfirmed with his partner.

"Right. The final job to remove the pesky DC brother has, by now, happened in the fiftieth state. Don't forget, I can handle our last APOCALYPSE surprise before I leave Mexico, unless there's legislation passed. If we get legislation, cool. If not, we've had a mean ride, have put the big boy assholes in a world of worry, put their fake promises concerning the needs of the 'little people' front and center and stimulated serious political debate. And, we got paid." Malcolm fist-bumped his partner.

"These last years have been crazy, man," said Duke. 'But I have to admit that this feeling right here, this sense that we finally got the mule's attention to do something other than screw those that he's twisted and hoodwinked with his self-serving racist emotional bullshit, this feels right. God, to think I helped get so many folks to vote for this mess . . . I don't know what's going to happen in Congress, but as long as we're at large, they have to worry that more unpredictable events will hit them. We may even benefit from some copycat left-wing or jihadist attacks."

"You already discount that some of your right-wing brothers won't get the message and take up the mantle?" Malcolm laughed.

"Maybe. Yeah, that's possible, too. Anyway, it's been good, my man. I've enjoyed it. By the way, please thank Blanco for me, too," said Duke.

"Yeah, bro. He took some big-time risk. Who'd have thunk it? A Mexican capitalist financier, a White supremacist and a Black nationalist trying to get a tiny bit of justice in Los Estados Unidos. Now, that's some shit." Mohammed's laugh drew the driver's gaze up to his rear-view mirror.

At the airport, they tipped and thanked the driver and headed for separate gates with tickets purchased by Jorge Blanco. Duke for London, England, and Malcolm for Los Cabos, Mexico.

On his way to the gate, Duke stepped into a men's room, changed from jeans into a lightweight gray business suit, donned a blond crew-cut wig, and unfolded a broad-brim Panama hat. With the large sunglasses and a dirty blonde 'quiff' or medium length 'blowout' haircut, he looked like Don Johnson of the 1980's TV show, Miami Vice. Duke was now David Hart, the person on his fake South African passport. He smiled, wondering if he'd recognize Malcolm if he saw him in the lounge. He knew that his partner, in another men's room near the gate for his Cabo flight, was changing into the person identified on the ticket provided by Jorge Blanco. Malcolm Mohammed was now Marty Martin, clean-shaven, close-cropped, dressed in an expensive baby blue cotton suit, with a pale pink striped shirt and white patent leather loafers.

Marty and David would have had to stare conspicuously to recognize Malcolm and Duke.

When the London flight was called, David Hart carefully surveyed the lounge and found no one paying him any particular attention. He enjoyed several relaxed days in

London, then traveled to Johannesburg and checked into a hotel in the Sandton section of the city. Hart had decided to explore the new South Africa with an open mind, leaving his racist past behind him. He met a group of expat Brits in business and the arts, and, since he had made enough from the APOCALYPSE 2029 caper to start a small winery, he began to befriend young vintners. He heard nothing from Malcolm and didn't find any news about congressional action.

Then, after a few weeks, he saw a news item that the Congress had passed some more lenient immigration legislation and reinforced Obama-era climate control regulations. The big item, however, was that the president, "on advice of his physicians," had pulled out of the electoral race mere weeks before the November election date. This threw the United States into constitutional turmoil because the president's party was not uniformly happy with his vice presidential heir.

David felt satisfied. But he couldn't help wonder what would befall his constituents, his people, after the election. Would they bear the brunt of liberal "payback" or simply be ignored once again? Well, he thought, those consequences would be dealt with by others. He helped rid the nation of a dangerous disingenuous parasite. He'd risked everything; it was time to relax.

Having found a modern apartment in a safe, conveniently located neighborhood, the former Duke Wallace found that life in Jo'burg was settling into a comfortable pattern. He noticed that the tension he had borne for the last decade had finally left his shoulders. One morning, a few weeks into his stay, he was fixated on his phone, reading the news, and didn't pay attention to his surroundings as he walked through a familiar shopping center in Sandton. He turned a corner to head for his favorite pastry shop and ran into the stiletto held by a hooded assassin. Duke Wallace and David Hart died in an ambulance on the way to the hospital.

The assailant was captured on high-resolution video in the shopping center corridor and later with his hood flung back as he entered his parked car. He was arrested by the police after a very brief escape attempt. Extradition to the United States was easily arranged because he was identified as a White nationalist from Kentucky who had worked with Duke Wallace during the 2016 election campaign. Circumstances around Duke's death remained mysterious, however, because his accused killer was shot by a sharpshooter while in police custody, as he was being transported to the Johannesburg airport to be returned to the US. The sharpshooter was not identified and remained at large.

***

As Marty Martin waited to board his flight to Los Cabos, a brown-skinned man in the area around his gate stepped away from the boarding line to speak into his phone, while keeping an eye on Martin.

"I'm not sure. I don't see Mohammed. This clean-cut guy could be him, but it's only a hunch. He only vaguely resembles him. But I'd have him checked at Cabo," the agent said.

Marty Martin smiled at the attendant as his boarding pass was approved for him to enter the jetway to his Aero Mexico flight. He turned around just as a man with dark glasses stepped from the line to consult his phone. Marty noted his red and white striped shirt and, after taking his seat, watched for the man to board. He didn't board.

When the flight attendant announced that they were approaching the tip of Baja California, Marty Martin grabbed his bag, brushed by a protesting attendant, and entered the restroom at the back of the plane. As he made the final adjustments to his dress, touched up with a bit of rouge, positioned his brunette wig and put on flats, Marty felt the plane descending quickly. He looked in the mirror and gave himself an approving wink.

The restroom door opened quickly as the plane leveled off in sight of the runway. An attendant stationed in the aisle looked aghast, for she had seen a man enter, but, clearly, a young woman was rushing to her seat. The attendant had to rush to her own seat, puzzled. She didn't mention the suspicious cross-dresser until well after the crew had deplaned. By then, none of her colleagues paid serious attention to what she had seen.

As Marty sat back in his seat and buckled his seat belt, the passenger in the next seat looked up and said, "I'm sorry, but there's someone in that seat."

"Oh, my husband switched with me," Marty said in a muffled falsetto.

"Oh, OK," the other passenger said.

The US agent looking for a clean-cut African American man dressed in expensive business-casual clothes never gave a second thought to the tall, brown-skinned, neatly coiffed woman deplaning from the Havana flight. Had relations with the Mexican government been cordial, as they were a few years back, the agent would have asked to see the passenger manifest, but he knew that the bureaucratic hassle that would follow such a request was unlikely to lead to a quick look at the list. Instead, he looked at a nearby arrivals board and saw that another Havana flight was due within a couple of hours, so he decided to wait and look at those deplaning passengers.

Malcolm found a restroom near the airport exit, entered and changed back to his Marty Martin outfit, and tossed the female get-up into a waste bin. He hailed a taxi and was at the pier for the hydrofoil to Mazatlán, on the mainland, within an hour. In Mazatlán, he boarded a bus with a ticket to Mexico City. When the bus pulled into the Guadalajara station, Malcolm went to the restroom, then walked out of the station and found the nearby car rental office. Deep in the night, Malcolm was driving west to Puerto Vallarta. As he drove, he sipped strong coffee and found a radio station that played hits from the '90s and 2000s. He was pleasantly surprised to recognize a few songs from the Guadalajara pop group, Maná.

If I have to be without jazz or hip-hop, I can dig this for a while, he thought.

He stayed at a hotel in the spiffy Nuevo Vallarta suburb his first night, but the next morning, he called a realtor who had been primed by Jorge Blanco's office.

"We have a gorgeous hillside villa above the arts district of the old city. It's walking distance from galleries, clubs, restaurants, and the beach. It reminds me of Venice Beach in your country. I'd love to show it to you, Mr. Martin."

"*Perfecto,*" Malcolm tried his Spanish accent.

After Malcolm had settled into his new digs, he stocked up on some basic supplies at a convenience store, and then checked his emails.

Welcome to P.V. Let's meet for a simple dinner at El Pollo Grande. It's a second floor restaurant near you, at the corner Insurgentes and Bardo Bacilio. About 8:30. JB

Malcolm walked around his hillside residential area and down to the beach, passing head shops, galleries, funky second-hand clothes outlets, bars and restaurants open to the street or beach. All emitted their own mix of mariachi, world, pop, or light jazz. He walked over to the Malecón and back up the hill to the restaurant. Malcolm spotted Jorge immediately. He looked more tan and relaxed than when they had met in DC. They embraced and sat at his table.

"I hope you don't mind this modest spot," said Jorge.

"This is my style, and I love this area. It's perfect, and I think I can be pretty inconspicuous here. Thank you," said Malcolm.

After Jorge ordered a tequila and Malcolm a Coke and a dish of guacamole and chips, they settled in at their round wooden table set back from the street front window.

"I see we have some partially promising legislative proposals, congressional leadership is scared to death, and the president has dropped out of the election for 'health reasons.' He's left town, and his party is in turmoil." Malcolm took a swig of Coke.

"If I recall, he hates to hang around all of those 'losers.' If we get nothing else, having that bastard quit is worth the fortune you've cost me." Jorge Blanco raised his glass.

"Yeah, and Duke is safely in South Africa by now. I'm going to be comfortably ensconced here for a while," said Malcolm.

"Even if you get traced here, our government's new security agreement with China, thanks to the brilliant 'deals' of your president, makes you pretty secure here in Mexico. I've even engaged the services of a top Chinese law firm, Zhou & Zhou, to assist me in various international transactions. So, you'll be fine, my friend," said Jorge.

"And the number of screens, accounts, passwords etc., between our activity and your identity makes it unlikely that they'll trace the project's financing to you before your grandkids grow up." It was Mohammed's turn to raise his glass.

"Let's hope. *Viva la revolución!*" Jorge grinned broadly.

"*Viva Mexico*," offered Malcolm in response.

CHAPTER 24

"**U**ncle Harry, is there something you're not telling us about your past that enables you such easy access through customs and all the paperwork?" Al asked as they waited for a taxi at the Camaguey airport.

"What do you mean, Al?"

"Well, they barely looked at your passport, then you pointed to us and said *familia* and we're through," noted Mark.

"Oh. Well, I did a bit of traveling as a consultant, and I had a number of government-sponsored Latin American and Caribbean trips," Harry said, without really thinking about the question.

"That's dope, but it doesn't make sense, given the current state of relations between the US and Cuba," observed Al.

"I suppose it's all the trips on reentry visas to China," Harry said, spotting a taxi.

"That's probably it," agreed Mark. "Cool."

As they rode to their hotel, Mark and Al were fascinated by the sparse urban layout, the pastel-colored buildings, and the number of churches. Then, after dumping their bags in their two rooms, the three men walked around the town's central area.

"Well, this is quaint, but I can't envision Malcolm or Duke hanging out here for more than an hour," said Mark.

"Yeah, my bet would be on Santiago de Cuba for this part of the island," said Harry.

"Why's that, Pop?" Mark asked.

"Well, for starters, it's got more of a mixed population, Spanish and Afro-Caribbean, so our travelers would blend in easily. It's got a million music festivals, so it's more 'happening.' More attractive, if a fella wants to lay low for a while. And it's got a population of almost half a million, and density's another factor aiding somebody trying to be inconspicuous."

"How'd you get so woke, Uncle Harry?" laughed Al.

"I'm not positive I know what 'woke' is, Al. Anyway, I may not have my old energy, but I remember how to research a location," said Harry, walking over to a sidewalk café.

"Sounds like we have travel plans for the morning," said Mark.

After they ordered beers and pork, beans, and rice, Mark ventured into a new subject.

"You know, it's weird experiencing you as a fellow adventurer, as someone who has spent a career figuring out foreign cultures for business purposes. To be honest, I'm so used to seeing you as the father who was never around." Mark held his father's gaze without animosity.

"That was a long time ago for me, but I understand. I can still picture you as the academically inquisitive boy who loved sports and had only slight interest in where I was traveling or what I was doing. Then the breakup with your mother, and you drifted away. I suppose you felt that I was even further removed from your life. There's so much I don't know . . ." Harry admitted.

"And I'm still getting over the fact that I experienced you as a mentor, only to find out that you're my birth father . . . On top of that, discovering that the sharp dude who's financial backer for *Earth Reclaimed* is my half-brother. It's deep, to say the least." Al sipped his beer.

"Not to mention that you also discovered that your birth mother was some Hong Kong taipan who has left you a fortune. Now, that's dope." Mark made them all laugh.

Before going to bed, Al scrolled through his messages, deleting most of them quickly. He stopped, however, at one from Tommy, because his father wasn't a frequent user of technology. He was forwarding a message from Jack Wong, Z&Z:

Please contact any one of our major offices as soon as possible. We apologize, but we forgot to have you sign one more document. It's quite perfunctory, but we need your signature to begin setting up accounts. If you are traveling, contact New York or DC office. Also have offices in many major foreign capitals.

Thank you

Al went online to see if Z&Z had a Mexico City office. They did.

Perhaps they'd also have one of those informal cultural attaché types whose brain he could pick about the diaspora in Latin America, he thought.

The next morning, they rented a car and drove to Santiago. The US Embassy in Havana had booked them into the newly refurbished Hotel Imperial, near a moderately calm Parque Cespedes, the oldest standing house in town (Casa de Diego Velazquez), and across the park from the lively Hotel Casa Grande. They immediately set out on foot to hit the key cultural spots, before starting their search for Mohammed and Wallace.

Three days later, having canvased real estate agents, talked to bar, restaurant and hotel managers, and checked in with the police, they sat in the bar at the Hotel Casa Grande.

"Well, we've covered a lot of territory. There's more to Santiago than I had expected, but we are nowhere in terms of finding our guys, and I am feeling my age," said Harry, sipping a mojito.

"No sign of them anywhere. But I'm going to have sweet dreams about that Bacardi Rum Factory," said Mark.

"You can imagine how this used to be a gem of an island. The Miami crowd tends to gloss over the fact that many immigrants 'escaped' a Cuba run by a dictator, under whom their families were doing quite well, thank you very much." Harry puffed on a postrevolutionary cigar.

"You got to wonder how these folks in Santiago will fare once Cuba opens up and the capitalist Miami tsunami rolls into town," Al thought out loud.

"Well, as a capitalist myself, I'd say a lot of what we've seen could benefit from some Miami ingenuity and type-A work ethic," said Mark.

"It will indeed be interesting," offered Harry, half listening while reading his emails. He looked up from his phone. "Well, I guess we can wrap this part of our hunt up. I just got a message from the embassy in Havana. They have current information on our fugitives and have sent e-tickets for us on a morning flight to Havana."

"And I never got to eat at Roy's Terrace Inn, the Rooftop Garden," lamented Mark.

"Let's go now," said Harry. "I know we can hoof it, but let's let the old man hail a taxi."

"No, let's not miss the street action. You can hang, Uncle Harry," said Al.

They walked through a bustling street with jazz musicians and impromptu dancers. An attractive young West-Indian-looking reveler hooked her arm through Al's and tried to get him to dance.

"*No, gracias, linda. Tenemos que ir.*" Harry leaned into her and spoke smoothly into her carnation-adorned ear.

"*Tal vez mañana, señor,*" she said, smiling broadly at Harry.

"Mark, looks like we need to keep close tabs on Harry. After seventy-plus years, the women's movement, and '#MeToo,' he's still got 'dog' in him," said Al. They all laughed out loud.

Later, as their plane banked over the crashing waves below, above long beaches, out over fertile coffee plantations, and sailed above the mountain range where much of the Cuban revolution was hatched, Al dreamt he was still thousands of feet below. He envisioned himself dancing through cobblestone streets with beautiful ladies in white blouses and red, yellow, and green banded skirts, swaying to music from the Buena Vista Social Club. Whether or not the Mortons found their fugitives, he was discovering yet another side of life. The last few months had exposed him to an explosion of new places, emotions, and sensations. Sensations his young engineer's mind had yet to fully understand.

Standing outside the front of José Martí Airport, the trio took a few minutes to look around and experience the sights and sounds of a bygone urban era.

"Maybe instead of a taxi we should get one of those horse-drawn carriages," Mark said, in jest.

"We have to get to the embassy—today," Harry quipped.

They piled into an old Chevy that looked like it wouldn't last more than a couple of blocks. It did, in fact, maneuver through moderate traffic, past inexpensively landscaped parks, down boulevards bordered by Spanish Colonial buildings in various stages of disrepair. An occasional steel and concrete structure built in postmodern rectangular style stood out as recent contributions to the cityscape.

During the ride, while his sons were enjoying the sights, Harry was growing anxious. This search had to bear fruit soon, he sensed.

At the embassy, they were briefed by a US intelligence officer. "I'm sorry that we couldn't be helpful earlier, but we were just permitted to review an airport tape showing Mohammed in a gate area where planes leave for Mexico. It's several days old, doesn't pinpoint which flight or what exact destination, but it's the best we could get from the government. Frankly, we're lucky to have any solid information, given the state of our relations," the officer said.

"Well, he could be anywhere in Mexico, but we'll—" Harry was interrupted.

"Sorry, but we were able to check arrivals from the Mexican side, and it's pretty clear that he didn't go to Mexico City, at least not directly. Given the schedules, he likely flew to Oaxaca, or La Paz, or Cabo. I've asked our people in Mexico City to review terminal records and videos more carefully. We definitely have more cooperation with that government than this one. Although, as the Chinese influence grows, ours diminishes."

"That, plus our immigration and trade policies can't help their willingness to cooperate," said Harry matter-of-factly.

"That too, I'm afraid. I've taken the liberty of getting you morning flights to Mexico City. You're booked tonight at the Hotel Saratoga, the best Havana has to offer, and a car will pick you up to get you back out to the airport at seven thirty a.m. tomorrow. Sorry we don't have more GQ. Enjoy the evening, gentlemen, and good luck in Mexico."

After they shook hands and the three headed for the door, Harry turned to the agent.

"Wait, you said 'he.' So what do you have on Wallace?"

"We've lost track of him. He's not traveling with Mohammed any more, and we think he's left the island for some other location. Sorry, that's all we know."

"OK. Well, thank you," said Harry.

As they enjoyed a delicious Cuban meal at the hotel, served by an attentive waitstaff, Harry and his sons discussed their next steps.

"Mark, you still feel he might be in Puerto Vallarta?" asked Harry.

"I have nothing more to go on, but yes, it's my gut feeling."

"Well, given that Mexico City is over nine million people, and the metro area is over twenty-one million, I don't think a door-to-door reconnaissance will get us too far," said Al.

"OK, OK. The key to solving many people problems is figuring out how the subject thinks. What would they do?" Harry said.

"Cool, Sherlock. What do we know about this dude?" Al sounded borderline frustrated.

"Well, Mark knows him best. But we know he wants to become invisible, for a while. We also know, from what Mark says, that he likes contact with and is good with all types of people, that he likes jazz and hip-hop, that he's well read, that he can only marginally communicate in Spanish. What else, Mark?" Harry focused on both sons.

"You've covered it, Dad. Oh, he played football and has a mean streak. He was in Iraq as an Army Ranger. So he's got some machismo in him. We don't know about his sexual preference, but I'm not sure how that info would help." Mark shoveled in more chicken in a dark chocolate sauce and swallowed a crisp cold white wine.

"Based on what you've said and what we've seen, he's not very IT savvy," added Al.

"So, let's see what the US guys have from the airport cams. See what resources, if any they can offer. Put our Mohammed mindsets on and check out some of the key cultural and music venues, and assess if it makes sense that he would stay in the capital, or leave for P.V. I'm not sure what else to suggest at this point," Harry said.

"Jeez, guys, finding a needle in a haystack would actually be easier," complained Al.

"Remember, we said we'd give it a shot. The feds don't seem to be any closer to finding them then we are. At least, no other shoe has dropped in the US. Well, as far as we know. I won't feel terrible if we can't track him down," said Mark.

"Well, let's not pack it in quite yet. There are still two dangerous guys out here who are capable of doing major damage to lots of innocent people," Harry cautioned.

"To *la Ciudad*!" Al offered a toast.

"*La Capital*!" Mark joined in.

"*Vamos a Mexico*!" Harry clinked glasses with his sons.

CHAPTER 25

On arrival in Mexico City, the Mortons went straight to the US Embassy to exchange notes with their contact agent. To date, US officials had not picked up any trace of either Wallace nor Mohammed entering the country, and the agent apologized for not having enough eyes on the ground.

"You can probably imagine that we're limited in staff by the Mexicans and in resources generally by Congress. It's not an easy time to conduct our needed surveillance here. The Chinese now have more personnel here than we do." He didn't hide his frustration.

After they left the embassy and checked into a large two-bedroom suite at the five-star St. Regis Hotel, they set out to explore museums, cathedrals, and parks in the center of the city. No one consciously planned downtime to bond, but the Mortons were learning to work together and to trust one another well beyond the bounds of a professional search team.

"Despite all of the negative stuff about cartels, crime, poverty, and all that, this is one of the most culturally rich and interesting cities in the world," said Harry, as they mounted the steps to the National Palace.

"Wow, now that's quite an endorsement," Mark remarked.

"Well, if other landmarks are as spectacular as the university campus and those Diego Rivera murals, I'd put it up there with Shanghai," said Al.

After about a half hour in the Palace, the tourists headed for a sidewalk café and cold sparkling water or iced tea. Reflecting on all the art he'd seen in their quick tour, Al suddenly sat up.

"That's it. That's what we've been missing," he said.

"What? What are you talking about? Did we pass by an Apple store, or something?" teased Mark.

"No. What stands out, what are the common themes in Diego Rivera's work?" asked Al.

"War, turmoil, class struggle," Mark quickly responded.

"And what else? Who else is he connected to in history?"

"Let's see. Frida Kahlo," Mark said.

"Right, and what do you notice about her in those murals?" Al grew more excited.

"Well, she's not portrayed as a sex object or lover. She's like the men standing up to the capitalists," Harry replied.

"OK. Cool. Where's this going?" Mark had grown impatient.

"Look, it's clear that the issues around oppression of the White, Black and maybe Brown underclass are what fuel Wallace and Mohammed's anger, at least in part," said Al.

"They're woke, as you would say," Mark said.

"Yes, but what about women? Do they have wives, girlfriends, male partners? We have no clue who the key emotional partners are for Wallace or Mohammed. The answer to that question might give us a lead on where they are or are headed."

"Bingo. Nice work Sherlock," said their father.

"And you got that from looking at those murals?" Mark shook his head, smiling. "You may be my brother, but you're weird, dude."

"I'd say, it's a good thing he's weird. If we can get real information or even dirt on any tight personal relationships, there's a prayer that we might find a clue about their location or destination. Blow some of the straw off of the hidden needle in this haystack," said Harry.

"You two have read too many detective novels," Mark said, laughing.

"Let's see if we can borrow one of those spiffy conference rooms at the Regis tomorrow morning to chart out what we do know," Harry said, ignoring Mark.

"That would help me," agreed Al.

Next morning, after a workout in the fitness center, Mark and Al showered and headed down to the lobby to meet their father.

"We've got a few minutes. Let's walk over to the park and get some fresh air," Mark suggested.

The two young men exited the revolving door, down a floral-bordered path and out onto busy Avenida Reforma.

"I never expected this city to be so green and colorful. It reminds me of some places back home, without the ocean or the palm trees." Al took a deep breath as they walked.

"So, it reminds you in what ways, then?" Mark raised an eyebrow.

Al got his sarcasm but answered sincerely. "Well, the feel, the array of colors on buildings, and the vibrancy, I guess."

" 'Cause it can't be the cosmopolitan feel. This bustle is more like New York," said Mark.

They walked in silence for a few minutes.

"So, how has he changed since you guys were sort of estranged?" Al asked.

"Dad, Harry? Wow, that was so long ago. I was just going off to college. Well, I suppose he's more relaxed—he doesn't seem so type A anymore. He doesn't have the extraordinary energy I remember he had, and his memory is not as amazing as it was. Other things seem as sharp as ever. But you have to remember, I never really saw him in a work situation during his heyday. He was just a dad, who was fun to be with when

I was a boy and an adolescent. I guess I never forgave him for splitting up with Mom and for then dating my friend's mom. He was an ass."

"But you stayed close to her, right?" Al pressed for more.

"Yeah. She moved to New York, married some old flame, and now goes back and forth between New York and London. Sonya and I get to see them maybe three or four times a year."

"Regardless of my birth circumstances, I'm now more at peace with me. Before, Harry was just an unknown sperm donor and my mother was a mythical carrier of a fertilized egg. Now that I get to have a relationship with Harry, and I know more about who Xi was, I feel lucky," mused Al.

"But, you know, the disappointment I felt when Harry was working and traveling wasn't that different from what many of my privileged classmates felt. So, I guess it wasn't that bad," said Mark.

"But your mom worked, right? And you haven't expressed any disappointment in her . . ."

"True. Yeah, somehow I felt she was always there for me. The hurt and anger I felt when they split was directed at Harry. Squarely. I thought he'd violated the 'till death do us part' clause. He was also callous and nasty about his right to date a friend of Mom's." Mark stopped short of describing his physical confrontation and looked away from his brother.

"For me, finding out about Xi and Harry made me appreciate, even more, my adoptive parents. The love, support, and space they've given me is phenomenal." Al paused. "You know, I need to learn more about their upbringings, their early lives on the mainland." It was his turn to look off into space.

"When you compare us to lots of folks, we've had lots of love. I hate to admit it." Mark shook his head.

"My mom would claim that God, like, saw our lives as some jigsaw puzzle whose pieces He could see and carefully put together. That's not my thinking, but I do believe there is an omniscient spiritual force, as in Buddhism," Al confessed.

"I guess I'm Christian, if anything. But I don't know how much that has to do with us finding each other, finding Harry, and having a chance to foil these terrorists. I'm more comfortable calling it fate," said Mark. "Crazy to think that I started out almost agreeing with Mohammed's objectives."

"Not so crazy given that DC statehood is all about social justice and equality. It's just that their means are over the top, and, ironically, likely to set back social justice."

"Damn, we sound like some flag-waving patriots," laughed Mark

"Not hardly, dude," said his brother, as they both laughed.

***

"How was the fitness center?" Harry looked up from the Mexican daily press as Mark and Al sauntered into the hotel restaurant.

"You're comfortable reading Mexican journalism in Spanish?" Al asked.

"That is the language down here. Where do you guys think you got our talent for languages, from Google?" Harry laughed.

"The fitness center is so-so. How was the extra hour of sleep?" asked Mark.

"Just what my old bod needed. Thank you." Harry turned to the waiter and ordered huevos rancheros.

"I think I'll get yogurt and some fruit from the salad bar," said Al.

"Snap. That sounds like a winner to me," said Mark.

After breakfast, they asked for coffee to be sent to their conference room and went up together in the elevator.

"Wow, this is amazing," said Al, looking out at the city as fog lifted over different segments of an expansive urban tapestry.

"OK. Let's use that whiteboard to identify categories of information we have so far." Harry grabbed a marker and moved to the board.

"After we've gotten our initial info down, I can use my laptop to capture and organize the data," Al said.

"Cool," said Mark. "So, in no particular order, I think we have these types of information:

- Motive
- Incentives for targets—president + Congress
- Analysis of their inaction to date
- Solutions sought by APOCALYPSE 2029
- Likely government response
- APOCALYPSE strategy to overcome initial government response
- Escape plan

"Does that cover it?" Mark paused.

"I think we can work to fill that in, yes," said Harry.

"So, let's just get down the central points of each. Motive." Mark stood at the whiteboard.

"Improve the well-being of underserved populations with whom they identify. Basically, get the federal government to address problems of the poor," Al said.

"Good enough, little brother," said Mark. "What incentives do they think have worked to move Congress and the president?"

"These guys obviously feel that normal lobbying and voter pressure haven't worked. They are narrowing in on violence and threats to person and property, financial loss, and loss of power. I sense the element of vindictiveness. It doesn't seem like they'd be satisfied if the government acceded to all of their demands tomorrow. They want leaders to experience anxiety, pain, and loss along the way." Harry assumed his professorial posture.

"Ok, so which of their tactics to date have worked?" Mark asked.

"Well, the attacks on kids' schools and the destruction of property in Carolina, Michigan, and Texas have created anxiety, pain, and loss of life. Coupled with the fact that they have avoided capture, their actions have successfully generated legislative action. For now, anyway." Al stated the obvious.

"So, that answers part of the question about what solution they're seeking. Have any demands beyond legislation been articulated?" Mark asked.

"Again, they are already exacting their pound of emotional flesh. But nothing else. And, that's strange because they could obviously be asking for funds to restore the federal budgets for science, food stamps, education, et cetera," Harry noted.

"The way I read their demands, those funds are expected to accompany the legislation," Al said.

"Agreed," said Mark. "OK. If the governmental response is weak, incomplete, or slow, the radicals must have a next level of action planned, right?"

"Well," said Harry, thinking aloud, "the administration could probably be counted on to ignore the protest, while putting forward some half-baked response. Or paint the actions as fake news, or blame the victims for distorting the devastation, or divert focus from the issues to another problem altogether, like the former president did a couple of years ago with the NFL players who took a knee. Spade's predecessor claimed they were somehow protesting the military or the flag. He obfuscated and drew attention away from the real problem—racist urban cops. Spade uses the same playbook."

"OK, so what strategy has APOCALYPSE indicated they will use to respond to initial administration roadblocks?" Mark continued.

"We don't know yet, really. But they have a lot of options . They could: Trigger recurring terror attacks. Focus phone calls, messages, and physical attacks on families of the key figures. Mix virtual and actual attacks. Take advantage of disruption caused by others, like ISIS does. Keep organization loose, so that no one knows all of the plans and tactics. Make threats with open-ended timetables, to keep the population on edge . . ."

Al took a breath to conjure up further examples.

"Wow, is this how you designed those explosive scenes in *Earth Reclaimed*?" Mark asked, jaw hanging open.

"Right, well, we can only conjecture at this point. What do we know about their escape plan?" Harry picked up the questioning.

"They obviously left the country, heading for Cuba before Congress or the president had a chance to respond, or to mount an effective search. If they came to Mexico, as we suspect of Mohammed, then they're choosing locations that currently have tortured relations with the US. Safe from extradition treaties. But I doubt they are together still. US intelligence here says they picked up visual on Wallace at Heathrow Airport. Whether Mohammed has a financial connection here, a romantic interest, or some familial tie, we don't know. And we can only guess where in Mexico he might be." Harry's voice tailed off.

Al thought for a moment. "Feels to me like my usefulness is about up on this gig. I need to be getting back to my business. After all, I have a financial backer who'll be expecting major progress at the end of the month." He smiled at Mark.

"We've all got stuff to do back home. Even those of us who're almost retired and only teach. I think we need to give it a bit more time. We still don't know, for example, what it is about these guys that drove them to act, to plan this operation. Precise, detailed, high risk. Why? There are plenty of Black, White, Christian, Muslim extremists who hate the government. Hell, one doesn't have to be an extremist. But those others didn't go this far, risk this much. So, what pushed these two?

"And then there's Al's question about possible love interests. If we figure out the emotional or personal motivation, we might be able to anticipate what they'll do next." Harry stood and walked to the windows overlooking the park.

"Ok. I'll try doing a more in-depth background search on publications, associations, activities of our targets," said Mark.

"Maybe I can dig into some of their email and other electronic communication to see who's financing their operation. I may not be able to find more than the feds have already told us, but it's worth the shot." Al's research enthusiasm suppressed his thoughts of leaving.

"Why don't we meet downstairs for dinner to see what we've learned?" Mark suggested.

"Let's make it noon tomorrow. I have an old contact in San Miguel de Allende, who might be able to shed light on the finance question. I doubt Mohammed or Wallace have deep enough pockets to fund this operation on their own. But I'll need time to arrange a flight, get there and impose on some of his time," Harry said.

"Cool. We two can hang out tonight, then," Al said to Mark.

"Just don't get arrested. Have a ball," Harry added.

Al found a quiet nook off the lobby, while Mark went back up to their suite to work. Primarily using search engines that Al recommended, Mark soon developed more information to supplement the Google-generated profiles and those provided by their federal contacts.

After college, Malcolm had thought he'd go into the foreign service. For some reason, he became attracted to the military and trained to be an Army Ranger. After the service, Malcolm worked for NGOs in Africa. He then put his international career on hold, returned to the US and next showed up working for the Library of Congress, but doing some speaking on campuses, challenging the US war efforts, and encouraging students to organize for more rights at home. He focused on themes of poverty, immigration, and climate change. He published a few articles in progressive magazines focusing on his three areas of interest. Mark noticed that the intensity of Malcolm's rhetoric, the frequency of his appearances, and the extent of his geographic reach picked up after the president's trashing of the Black athletes challenging White police brutality. He either took a leave of absence or was fired from the library. Not only did Malcolm develop ties to protesting professional athletes, but he seemed to appear more frequently with entertainers and writers of similar conscience.

Mark also noticed that, while Malcolm was scrupulous about avoiding news cameras, in several of the shots with activist writers he appeared next to the same attractive light brown-skinned woman. It took the better part of an hour, but Mark finally was able to find some biographic material in an *LA Times* article about Rosalie Artiste. Born to a Mexican journalist and a Dominican tennis player in New Orleans, she moved with her family to LA as a teenager. She studied music at the Berklee College in Boston and had built a career as a jazz pianist. She maintained homes in LA and Nuevo Vallarta, Mexico—near her mother's original home.

Mark checked in with Al, who was deep in concentration on streams of email, Facebook, and more ideological social media. Leaving Al to his laptop, Mark went for a swim in the hotel pool and then grabbed a sandwich on his way back to his temporary office.

Although Duke Wallace had not published much or hung out with as many high-profile celebrities as his buddy, he had left a trail that Mark was able to track. After his service career, Duke secured a finance position with a Detroit automaker. He left and took a job as a research assistant at the War College in DC, where he did some work in naval intelligence concerning the historical role of Navy Seals in counterterrorism. He developed an interest in national politics and joined the staff of a North Carolina senator before dropping out to become an activist and organizer of right-wing organizations in Kentucky. Mark found several articles in traditional media about Duke's organizing for a few alt-right groups leading up to the 2016 election. Then the trail ended, and he seemed to disappear from public view until he resurfaced as a strategist in the 2024 campaign of Robert Spade. Mark found no mention of love interests.

Using a few modest-priced apps, plus his own hacking skills, Al was able to follow numerous exchanges between the two radical colleagues and could verify that other contacts of interest were made. He was not able to hack the substance of some of the key exchanges, however. He noticed periods when Duke had frequent communication with a few of his Navy Seal colleagues and when he chatted with someone living in Delhi, India. Something happened to increase the volume of his communication after he visited Ohio in early 2017. It was impossible to tell from Al's analysis of communication exactly to whom Wallace was communicating in preparation for their 9/11/29 attacks, but it was clear that he maintained a wide network of contacts beyond White supremacy circles.

***

The forty-five-minute taxi ride from the Querétaro airport to the mountain hideaway of San Miguel de Allende forecast nothing of the quaint cobblestone streets lined with a smorgasbord of international restaurants, art galleries of every genre and quality, shops, and residential structures that Harry knew awaited him in town. The road was surrounded by fields, punctuated by occasional farms and rural homes nestled in the valleys below moderately high mountains.

Clouds hung over the lower-lying hills, breaking up the intensity of the late morning sun. The ride was quiet, and the driver's Mexican songs were turned low on the radio.

Harry had arranged to meet his old contact Herbert Cox at a local coffee shop near the university where Cox was in residence. It had been at least five years since Harry had seen Herbert, at the East-West Center, and Harry was grateful that his friend was able to see him. It would be a bonus if he could shed any light on their search, he thought.

"*Por Dios, hijo.* You haven't changed a lick. Must be the infamous rural water up here in the mountains," Harry said, embracing his friend.

"Well, it's not the ocean paradise with sweet sea breezes and erupting volcanoes. But, we try." Herbert Cox returned the banter.

"Thanks for seeing me on such short notice." Harry sat in a woven cane chair next to Herbert.

"I was hoping to get you to stay a day or two, so we could really catch up and I could show you the countryside," said Cox.

"That would be splendid, but I'll have to take a rain check. I've got my sons waiting on me, and we're in the middle of some work for the US administration, if you can believe that," Harry said.

"Well, first, how about some real Mexican tortilla soup, a sandwich, and a beer?" Herbert was already signaling for the waitress.

"Perfect," said Harry.

"So, what was that? Your sons, plural?"

"Yes. Since you were last out, I've reconnected with Mark, my investor son in DC. And, believe it or not, I've discovered that Al Liu, a sort of young protege, who's building an impressive computer gaming company, is my son by an affair I had years ago in Hong Kong. Long story for another time, but my emotions have had a workout—mostly joyful—over the last few months." *I am so fortunate to have this time with them*, Harry thought, as he said this. *They fill an emotional gap that I've long denied existed.*

"Well, that's amazing. And fantastic. God, I'm happy for you on both accounts. And it must be a shock—pleasant I hope—for the boys as well?" Herbert opened his arms, inviting Harry's response.

"Yeah. Like I say, and I promise to fill you in, a tale for another time." Harry stayed focused.

"OK. How can I help?" Herbert sipped his beer, took one spoonful of soup, and settled back in his chair.

Harry inhaled and took in his surroundings more carefully, as if scanning for curious ears, wall-mounted cameras, or professional spies. Although it was next to the sidewalk, their café patio was surrounded by five-foot hedges covered in reddish-purple bougainvillea and deep purple jacaranda. The opening back into the main room of the café was guarded by bouquets of red trumpet flowers. Customers at the other tables were all engaged in lively conversations of their own, or too far away to hear what Harry and Herbert were saying.

"Herbert, if I remember correctly, your adult students are primarily retired Mexicans, gringos, and Canadians, right?" Harry asked.

"Yes, for the most part."

"But from talking to you at the East-West Center, I know you stay up with international issues, and I got the sense that some of your students are current in hemispheric economics, politics, and strategic issues."

"That's pretty accurate. Yes, I think so." Herbert looked quizzically at Harry.

"Sorry for all of the preliminaries. The nub of what we are doing is trying to find a couple of terrorists who ignited a few horrific explosions this September."

"Of course, I read about it. But why look in Mexico? And why you and your boys?" Herbert asked, looking completely baffled.

"Through random connections, my son Mark had an affiliation with one of the perpetrators, who showed interest in Mexico before the terrorist acts occurred, and we're able to move about in Mexico more easily than our feds. I'm sure you can imagine the barriers to conducting official intelligence these days."

"Yes, it will take at least a decade to repair the damage that the last 'greatest of deal-making administrations' has wrought. But what, you are working with the Spade crew?"

"Country over party. I'm old school, baby." They both laughed heartily. "Anyway, we haven't made any progress on who might be financing this APOCALYPSE 2029 outfit. Whether it's the Chinese opportunism that we've both seen around the globe, or some regional discontented wealth. I thought you might have some ideas."

"Well, it's not something I've given any thought to, certainly. There is a growing number of businesspeople with increasing concern about their US investments, and others worried about US stakes here in Mexican companies. There's plenty of anxiety and a fair number of wealthy men and women who closely follow the utterances out of DC. Having told you the obvious, no one comes to mind who would venture so far as to finance terrorist activity up there. Down here? That might be different."

Herbert talked at length about how academics isolated themselves from the terror of drug gangs, how one could live a rich intellectual, social, and cultural life without coming in contact with the misery the cartels were spreading. They talked about how neither of them were big fans of Mexican or Hawaiian music, but how they admired the literary tradition of Mexico.

"These are fascinating, but radically different societies," exclaimed Herbert.

As the day wore on, Harry wished that Herbert was still teaching at the East-West Center so that they could meet more frequently. The two kindred souls chatted about sports, immigration politics, Herbert's work at the University, Harry's life in Hawaii. They sipped after-meal Modelo lagers—but it was clear that Herbert could offer no useful pointers on the APOCALYPSE financing.

"Well, it was worth the trip to see you, Herbert," said Harry at last. "And, whether here or in Honolulu, we'll make the next visit more cordial and extensive." Harry insisted on paying, embraced Herbert, and they walked arm-in-arm to the door.

"Let me at least call you a taxi, Harry."

"That's not necessary, Herbert."

"It's done. Here he comes. You should have an open road to the airport, since it's still before the end of siesta, four o'clock."

As Herbert opened the door for Harry, he suddenly stopped. "You know, it's a long shot, but you might want to consider . . ."

"What? Anything can help, at this point, Herbert."

"Well, there is a very bright inquisitive financial guy on the fringes of policy and active in trade debates. And he seems well connected to the new Chinese diplomatic folks. He's got the wealth to finance the sort of operation you describe, he's known to be sensitive to US incursions into Mexican affairs, but I don't know that he is any more angered than the next businessperson," said Herbert, still holding the taxi door.

The driver motioned to Harry and started to get out of his taxi to see if this passenger needed assistance.

"What's his name, Herbert?"

"Jorge Blanco. I'm sure there's plenty on his business and public interest activity on the web."

"Thanks, again. We'll follow up. Ciao."

The driver attempted to engage his passenger in idle conversation, but Harry sat in the back seat and was immediately lost in thought.

***

The next day, after a late breakfast, the three Mortons met again in their hotel conference room. Harry reported on the one new piece of speculative information he'd got from his visit with Herbert Cox. Then Mark and Al summarized the data they had gathered on Mohammed and Wallace; mostly filling in gaps left by the picture shared by the feds.

"So, if I might . . . here's where I think we are." Harry stood before a blank whiteboard. "We still don't have hard motives for why these radicals, with quite distinct constituencies, decided to take on this project. It's clear that they have simmering hatred for the current government leaders—their strategy of targeting the well-being and safety of those leaders' families is clear. But we don't really know how they paid the various operatives they used to carry out bombings, to design the cyberattacks, and to plant the ocean explosives. Plus, we lack any clues, emotional or tactical, as to where they are hiding or headed or what activity they may yet have planned."

"Well, we know that Mohammed may be seeking a former girlfriend who's supposed to be in Nuevo Vallarta, and that this guy Jorge Blanco may, underscore may, be financing at least part of APOCALYPSE 2029," Al said.

"That's true. That's more than we knew a couple of days ago. If we could find this girlfriend and/or talk to this possible money guy, we'd be able to narrow in more," said Mark.

Al fidgeted, Mark looked at his phone, and Harry seemed mesmerized by the light rain falling on the streets below. Silence gripped the room.

"OK," Harry said after a while, "I know Al is eager to get back to Honolulu, and I think we may have done as much as we can. Finding Jorge Blanco, even if he is the financier, isn't likely to give us any real leads. It's highly doubtful that he'd admit involvement. Let's just tuck his existence away for now. We can provide some detail for our report to the feds." He seemed resigned to packing up.

"I have to get back as well. But I do think we need to spend a couple of days looking into Puerto Vallarta. Malcolm did mention it once, and his former girlfriend may be nearby. What can we lose?" Mark said, firmly.

"Fine. It is worth a shot. If nothing solid turns up, we write our report, go back to DC to debrief, and collect our fee. Even if our two suspects aren't in handcuffs, we certainly have dug up some value-add information for the government." Harry was content with this resolution.

"Guys. I'm out. I can help with the report electronically, but I would be useless in Puerto Vallarta. I need to visit the Mexico office of my Chinese law firm before I head home. Turns out the Honolulu office forgot to have me sign a document. I can take care of it down here," Al said.

"Fair enough. Let's get a flight this afternoon, Mark. Al, let us know if anything relevant comes out of your meeting. And, son, I'll see you back on the island, where I'll be Uncle Harry," said Harry with a smile.

"Chill, man. This was a blast, and I promise Sonya and I will come visit soon," said Mark, as the brothers hugged.

***

After calling Zhou & Zhou, and, to his surprise, getting through to the managing partner for Mexico, Margaret Feng, Al set up a meeting for that afternoon. Then he secured a flight to Honolulu via Los Angeles and packed his bags.

"*Buenos tardes, Mr. Liu. Es un placer conocerte*," said Ms. Feng. An attractive Han Chinese woman in her mid-forties, dressed in a simple pink-patterned silk dress, firmly gripped Al's hand.

"*Equalmente, señora.*" Al offered his limited Spanish.

"Would you prefer to speak in English? Whatever makes you the most comfortable," she said, guiding him past the reception desk and down a richly paneled corridor of offices.

Al felt slightly self-conscious in the rumpled blue blazer and khaki trousers he'd packed, just in case. As he followed Margaret Feng into her impressive executive suite, designed to show that hers was a big-time legal firm, he remembered that she knew that he was soon to be a serious multimillionaire. His posture straightened and his stride lengthened as they strolled to a teak coffee table set in an alcove looking out over miles of cosmopolitan Mexico.

"English would be fine. Chinese would be only a little easier than Spanish, I'm afraid," said Al with a slight smile.

"Excellent. So, how can we be of service, Mr. Liu?"

"Well, I received notification from your Honolulu office about a document I needed to sign." Al showed Margaret the message on his phone, and she immediately consulted a computer at a corner desk.

"Ah, yes. It's printing out now, and it will take only a minute to read and sign," she said, ready to move on with her day.

"Also, as I mentioned in setting up this meeting, part of the firm's commitment to me in managing my inheritance is to assist . . ."

"Of course. The cultural recognizance of Chinese-Latin population," interrupted Margaret. "We do have a young attorney who informally collects data on the diaspora in our region. She's not focused on mixed-race particularly, but I'm sure she'll have some interesting observations. I'll have her contact you when she returns from the field. She's with a client in Chile for a few days."

"That would be wonderful. Thank you." Al smiled, but realized the "attaché-like" attorney was an exaggeration. At least in this Z&Z office.

An aide entered the room and handed Margaret a sheaf of papers. Margaret sifted through them, as she walked back to Al at the coffee table. Clearly thinking about several different issues at once, she repeated some stock company marketing pitch in an attempt to reassure him that this was the right firm with whom he should do business.

"We provide major commercial representation and are proud to also represent the Chinese government in several matters attendant to their growing trade with Mexico and the Caribbean," she said.

Exceeding the limit of whatever mental multitasking she was performing, Margaret fumbled and spilled the pile of memos as she tried to give Al his document. Al immediately helped sort the sheets. In shuffling through the scattered documents, he noticed and quickly scanned something related to a request by a Z&Z client, Jorge Blanco. He recognized the name instantly, then glimpsed the words *block extradition to US from Puerto Vallarta*. To avoid attracting attention, Al didn't read any further, just continued rifling through the stack until he found the document from Honolulu.

"Oh, thank you, Mr. Liu. I'm so clumsy. Yes, that's it," said a relieved Margaret.

Al quickly read the one-paragraph addendum to a document he'd seen before, signed it, and watched Margaret sign as witness.

"Great, I'll send it back to Honolulu, and forward you an electronic copy." She extended her hand, ending the meeting.

"Much appreciated. Well, I don't want to take more of your time. You've been very gracious, Ms. Feng." Al exuded some of his inherited charm.

"So glad to meet you, Mr. Liu. We at Zhou & Zhou look forward to a long association with you. By the way, keep us in mind as you market your computer game in Latin America."

She escorted him to the lobby. "I'll leave you here, then. Safe journey," said Margaret, turning back to her office.

While sitting in the gate area for his LA connecting flight, Al allowed himself to relax and analyze what he had seen. It had to be—Jorge Blanco would logically hire Z&Z, given China's rising economic prominence in Mexico. And there was a good chance that the extradition he was concerned about was for the mastermind of his big investment in APOCALYPSE 2029—Malcolm Mohammed. There were other possible interpretations, of course, but this could be a missing piece in locating the fugitive. Even if Al was wrong, the information couldn't hurt Harry and Mark's efforts; if he was right, bingo. His spirits lifted, and he sent a Snapchat message to Mark.

Excellent meeting. By chance, got 80% verification of Harry's guess on dollar source and your hunch on target whereabouts. Aloha.

***

Meanwhile, Mark and Harry had checked into their beachfront suite at the Hotel Emperador near the Alta Vista neighborhood in the heart of the old city of Puerto Vallarta. Harry was out on their seventh-floor balcony looking out to the Gulf when Mark called to him.

"Snap. Al somehow got some confirmation that Jorge Blanco is the finance guy and that Malcolm is likely to be somewhere here in PV."

"That's great. Now we just need to find out where he is," said Harry.

Shedding his shorts and pulling on trunks, Mark said, "Well, I'm going to start by looking on the beach, in the shallows and under those lightly crashing waves."

"Sounds like a winner. Then we can get dinner up on the Malecón. There's the Blue Shrimp, where I've had tremendous meals," said Harry, looking for his trunks.

At dinner, they pulled down the latest photo of Mohammed from the web, so that each could have it on his phone. Then they divided up the major real estate agencies, banks, and moderately priced hotels to visit over the next few days. Finally, they ordered two rental cars to facilitate their search.

"Let's give it four full days. If we don't get any solid leads, we'll pack up, write a report and head to DC. Fair enough?" Harry said over a smooth after-dinner tequila.

"I'm down with that," said Mark, clinking glasses.

The next four days were packed and mentally fatiguing. Mark soon grew tired of hopping in and out of his small Chinese car and trekking up and down side streets to locate exclusive real estate offices. Harry was exhausted. A few people indicated that they might have seen Malcolm, but no credible positive IDs were made. Harry convinced himself that they had done all they could, had made more than a good faith effort to find Malcolm, and could give the feds valuable leads. Mark was relieved when Harry said they should consider wrapping up their investigation. So, during the late afternoon and early evening of the fourth day, they began to type up a rough draft of a report they would file with Homeland Security upon their return.

After a Vietnamese meal at Archie's Wok Restaurant, they decided to catch a jazz set at one of the clubs that they'd passed several times during their search. Saxophonist Joshua Redman had a quartet and pianist Cyrus Chestnut was doing a solo set as part of the late-evening entertainment.

"Now that we've completed our obligation, I'd like to see a couple of things and pick up a gift for Sonya," said Mark.

"Smart man, son. What do you have in mind?" asked Harry.

"I noticed a craft market right after you cross the bridge heading out toward Nuevo Vallarta. It's bound to have jewelry and serapes, something tasteful and regional."

"I'm going to forward our draft to Al tonight, so would you mind if I tagged along with you tomorrow?" Harry asked.

"Delighted. OK. Here's Joshua," said Mark.

The lights dimmed and the club got even darker, as the quartet began to play. About a half hour into the set, Harry lifted a Rémy Martin to his mouth, sipped, and scanned the audience. The room held only about fifty-five people, he estimated, spread between tables, deep chairs and the bar. The crowd was mixed Mexican, Anglo, Afro, and other—a cosmopolitan group respectfully quiet and into the music. The crowd was different from its US counterparts in that folks drank tequila, vaped cannabis, and smoked tobacco.

One couple caught his attention. Seated away from the bandstand at a table toward the back, and at least fifty feet from Mark and Harry, was a handsome twosome. The man, dressed in white shirt and pants, sporting short dreads, was Afro-something. The woman, in a simple yellow shift trimmed in red, was hard to categorize in the dim light. Harry guessed she was at least part Latina, part Anglo, but he really wasn't sure. He was positive, however, that she was gorgeous. They seemed unaware of anything but the band and each other.

Harry turned and whispered to Mark.

"Is that Mohammed over there with that foxy lady?"

"I can't be sure, but, maybe," said Mark. He then turned in his seat to get a better look, but his father grabbed his elbow.

"Don't stare, Mark. He might recognize you," said Harry.

Mark looked a little flushed. He surreptitiously studied the man's mannerisms and his profile. Yes, he was pretty sure that the man was Malcolm Mohammed. All this time, this long chase and the attempts on Mark's life that had slowly built tension. Fear and anxiety rushed up through his body and crowded out all other sensations. Mark felt like his head would explode.

"Son, are you OK?" Harry asked in a hushed tone.

"I'll be fine," said Mark, guzzling a glass of water. "It just all came back to me at once. Here we are, after all of this time and effort, and he's less than a hundred feet away. Now what?"

"Well, I need to be sure. You know him, but you don't want to get too close and scare him off." Harry was not feeling as anxious as Mark. Instead, he felt the rush of excitement he'd experienced during some of his international dealmaking days. He felt close to closure, but he knew a wrong move, a physical or mental mistake, could ruin months of progress in an instant. He was wired but not anxious.

Instead of swallowing ice water, Harry sipped a mouthful of Remy.

"Listen, keep an eye on them. Once we're positive it's him, we have to notify DC." Harry took an audible deep breath and forced himself to calm down, slow his pulse. "I want to finish this set. Maybe we can follow them to find out where at least one of them is staying." Harry returned partial attention to the stage. He looked over at the couple only frequently enough to ensure they didn't slip out.

In between the Redmond set and Cyrus Chestnut coming on, Malcolm and his companion finished their drinks and strode arm in arm from the club.

Harry nudged Mark. "Son, can you text and walk in the dark?"

"I guess so, why?" Mark's anxiety rose again, and he turned to see the table Malcolm and guest had vacated.

"Give it a minute, and then we're moving. It's showtime." Harry finished his drink, left some bills and pushed back from the table.

Harry and Mark watched the couple slowly stroll up the hilly cobblestone street from the doorway of the club.

"Dad, that's him. I know his walk; I've seen it too many times. It's Malcolm," Mark affirmed, his courage reinforced by the fresh air.

"OK, I'll keep an eye on them. You should send a quick text." Harry was all business.

Mark texted their DC contact: *Found target here in PV, is with female companion. We will follow from a distance and send address.*

The two sleuths maintained a hundred-foot tail until Malcolm and the woman enter a one-story house on a nearby street. Harry and Mark stood across the street behind a thick eucalyptus trunk. Mark looked up and down the poorly lit street but couldn't find any distinguishing characteristics to help identify it. He noticed a new, green Toyota Prius outside the residence.

"I bet that's their rental car. Japan is still doing some business down here." Mark gave a tension-reducing laugh.

"Can you get that house number? Go ahead and send it to DC, will you?" Harry slid down to the sidewalk and leaned against the tree to rest.

"Dad, you can go back to the hotel, I'll watch," said Mark.

"That's OK."

An hour or more passed, the lights were turned off in the front room of the house, and, waiting outside in the dark, the Mortons began to fade. Then Mark's phone pinged with a text.

"Great. They say not to approach; their men will be here by dawn. We should retreat and not risk scaring the target away." Mark stood and stretched.

"What time is it?" Harry asked, slowly rising.

"It's just after three a.m. Nothing has moved for hours," said Mark.

The street was quiet and Harry's whole being was at rest, meditative and at one with the darkness. Mark, however, was restive. Within reach, across the street was the man who had disrupted his life, almost killed him twice, caused massive turmoil, destruction, and most likely death around the country in order to what? To embarrass national leadership? Could Mark come all this way to just report back to that same odious leadership on the perpetrator's whereabouts?

Mark stood up and angrily punched the air behind the tree. He paced the sidewalk out of sight of the house.

"What's wrong, Mark?" whispered Harry.

"I think we need to take them now. We can't go through this whole odyssey and just phone in his location. The brother has insulted, trashed, and messed with every community he's touched; endangered countless lives and taken some; he's brought our fickle government to its knees, and . . ."

"And, he's gotten the best of Mark Morton on a couple of occasions," Harry calmly noted.

"So, we storm the house, and then what? You know he's got to be heavily armed, right? Even if we do capture him, do we tie him up and call the embassy? You want to get him on a plane and deliver him to Washington? I, for one, believe there are quite a few steps we haven't been asked to execute that are fraught with more danger than we're presently prepared to handle. This brother is not simply going to give up and cooperate. Not with what he's already been through." Harry reasoned, looking up at his frustrated son.

Mark's ears heard his father, but his gut and head boiled in furious opposition to his advice.

More to himself, than to his father, he said, "We need to devise a plan. We've found the needle in the haystack. We can figure out how to take the next step."

"Mark, it sounds like this caper is personal. It's about redress for the anguish Malcolm has caused you. I understand the feeling." Harry paused.

"If you'll consider the experience of an old, stubborn traveler whose made a life's worth of bad personal decisions, don't make it personal. That's when one tends to make bad decisions and costly mistakes. Mohammed and Wallace have demonstrated that they are pros and their impact goes well beyond you, Sonya, DC, the Hill. Yeah, we tracked at least one of them down but recognize that this guy will be a cagy vicious tiger when cornered. We've done the job we were paid to do. Time to turn it over to the government."

"Pops, we've seen how incompetent Washington is," Mark responded, with less energy than earlier.

"The crew that is likely assigned to actually capture this fellow, once they have his coordinates are not political hacks. They will also be pros. I trust they're much better equipped than we are at this point," said Harry.

Emotionally spent and physically exhausted, Mark's body collapsed. He acknowledged to himself that perhaps his ego had gotten out in front of reason. Now, he simply wanted to return to their room and sleep.

"I guess we can go get some sleep. Right?" Harry patted Mark on the shoulder, and they quietly walked back down the hill.

Back at their room, through the open window, the waves from the Sea of Cortez seemed higher and louder than earlier in the evening, but everything else was still.

"You're right. In the morning, let the feds have their report and take it from here," Mark said, putting his feet up on the railing and listening to the surf.

"We have another small problem, though." Harry's expression turned stern. "You can't tell how this news will affect the president. He's surely going to want to take credit for finding this terrorist. That's OK. But if some unseen complication should happen and he needs a scapegoat, we're sitting ducks. We have to make sure our report is with trusted attorneys and columnists, just in case. We can stamp it 'open only under these circumstances' . . ."

"He may not even be president, remember. He decided to take his name off the ballot. Although, come to think of it, his name will still be on the ballot. All he has to do is say he's cleared to serve, raise his hands in a sign of victory, and on November 3, his base will be out in force." Mark was pensive.

"Tomorrow, this morning, I can quickly edit the version of the report forwarded to Al so he can look at it."

"I can give you the name of a couple of secure, high-profile journalists, so Al can send the memo via some secure electronic method," Mark suggested.

"I'll add a couple of law firms and one or two confidential Homeland Security and State Department friends. Lesson, son: never burn bridges you don't need to." Harry placed his hand on Mark's shoulder.

"Dad, I want us at least to deliver the government's original copies personally. That will also give Al plenty of time to get our confidential versions delivered."

"Agreed. See you in the morning, Mark."

Both men flopped onto bed.

CHAPTER 26

"**D**id you notice those two Black dudes in the club, baby?" Malcolm asked Rosalie that night, as they climbed into bed.

"There were all kinds of people there tonight—I didn't notice anyone in particular. Why?"

"I have a strong feeling they followed us home. And I'm pretty sure one of them is a fellow from DC named Mark Morton," Malcolm said, mostly to himself. He walked over to the wide, three-paneled front window, pulled back the side of the curtain and looked out at the street. No sign of human activity.

"Why would somebody want to follow you, Malcolm?" Rosalie sat up, back against the headboard.

Malcolm was silent, trying to decide how much to tell his companion.

"You're not in some trouble?" she asked.

"You know the pigs are never happy with those of us who challenge the status quo." Malcolm was evasive.

"That's up in the States. What about here? I've never had any issues here. So what are you talking about, really?" Rosalie pressed for clarity.

Malcolm decided he had to share some of the truth. "Last time you were up in LA, did you read or hear anything about APOCALYPSE 2029?"

"No . . . wait, is that the group that caused the tsunami in South Carolina?"

"That's the one. Well, a partner and I helped put that together." He carefully watched her reaction.

"Helped? Are you crazy, Malcolm?" Rosalie's face reddened in shock.

"Baby, you and I have always complained about how lame civil rights efforts have been in generating real change. Well, the people behind this finally found vulnerability in the power structure." Malcolm spoke matter-of-factly.

"But, but . . . how involved are you with those activities?" she asked.

"We helped with the planning, but somebody must have snitched, so I think the feds are looking for us."

"Malcolm, why didn't you say something about this before I came? I can't afford to be in some international terrorist thing. Baby, you better not be no head honcho in this. Course that would be like you, not to just be a soldier. Got to be 'the man.' You know this sucks, right?" Rosalie rattled on, in frustration and anxiety. She knew how to be chill around authority, if she had to be, but she wanted to put her active revolutionary days behind her.

"Trust me, baby. Why would I get you involved in something you had nothin' to do with? You know me better than that." Malcolm's indignation was manufactured. Rosalie didn't buy it. But it was late, they both were tired, and at last a weary Rosalie drifted off to sleep, worn out from arguing.

As the small hours of the night ticked by, Malcolm became increasingly convinced that he had to leave. He knew Rosalie was likely to continue to press for more details, information that could endanger her.

He slipped out of bed and checked the street again. He thought he saw shadows across the street. Had they been followed? If so, it had to be Mark Morton. But he was supposed to be dead. So what was he doing in Puerto Vallarta? Mark and the other man must be here looking for him.

Malcolm began packing essentials in a knapsack. He would have Jorge's Chinese connections deliver on their promise to help him relocate. Three questions remained, as he sat at his dining-room table: *Do I try to take Rosalie with me? If she stays behind, is she a risk to me? Do I complete the final task that Duke and I planned?* He'd had no word from Duke yet, and didn't know how on point the Congress was.

If I leave her here, she'll have no idea of where I went, nor does she know any details that the feds don't already have. Once I'm safe, I can communicate with her—although they'll be watching her closely for a while. She's not had time to decide how much she's committed to a life with me, anyway. I have to slip away. Malcolm took a deep breath and arrived at a decision. *I'll set up my passage out of here, and then do the embassy job Duke and I planned.*

He slung the knapsack over one shoulder, the gun case carrying the Russian T-5000 long range rifle over the other, and slipped out of the bedroom. He left a note on the kitchen table.

Sorry, but I'll have to contact you later, M.

He looked at the wall clock: Three forty-five a.m. He checked the streets again and saw no shadows this time. Then he left the house and got into his rental car. At that time, the streets out of town and on the highway were barren; he made excellent time to Mexico City.

Jorge Blanco had worked his magic with the Chinese, so that the only question Malcolm had to answer for the attaché was where he wanted to fly.

"I think Trinidad. It's quieted down from Venezuelan refugees, and I can fit in nicely there," said Malcolm.

The attaché assured him that they'd have a ticket for him at the airport in a couple of days, in the name of Marty Martin, using "Marty's" passport information.

Malcolm found an airport hotel room and opened up the paper with the plans he and Duke had made in case they needed one final APOCALYPSE surprise. With minimal research in local papers, he confirmed that US Vice President Richard Nickle was in town to represent the White House at the Mexico vs. US "friendly" football game, as the long prologue to the next World Cup crawled along. Friendly soccer, even though the countries were anything but friendly these days. Malcolm further confirmed that the VP would be attending meetings at the US Embassy the following afternoon and the next morning, hours before Malcolm was hoping to be on a flight to Trinidad.

Later in the afternoon, Malcolm hired a taxi to drive him to a shopping mall, Galerias Plaza de Las Estrellas. On the first floor, at a music store he had researched online, Malcolm purchased a bassoon carrying case that he could swap out for the rifle case. The rifle was untraceable, having been purchased through a cartel intermediary a few days earlier. He then casually searched for the elevator in an adjacent office tower, and took it to the penthouse. It was a sunny afternoon, so the view from the roof was spectacular. Malcolm was less interested in the scenic vista than the fact that with his rifle scope, he could easily make out the windows of the US Embassy. He reasoned that with the long-range scope on the T-5000, he'd have no problem targeting people in the conference room. He and Duke had gotten floor plans months earlier, from the dark web, via Omar.

After trashing the gun case and hiding the bassoon case with the weapon between two cooling towers on the roof, he took another taxi into the center of the business district and wandered around, looking for a restaurant in which to have a leisurely dinner.

***

"Well, you gentleman have been busy on behalf of the nation, it seems," said Sheila Baxter.

Mark and Harry merely smiled, as they followed her into Secretary Travis Roy's office. Before meeting with Homeland Security, they had checked with Al to be sure that their confidential information had been sent to their legal and journalistic contacts as insurance.

Coming from behind his desk and pointing to his two colleagues, Roy said, "Harry and Mark Morton, I believe you know National Security Advisor Rachel Jones and the president's chief of staff, Ronald Barker."

All parties shook hands and took seats on a couch and chairs around a low rectangular coffee table, fitted with small cold bottles of San Pellegrino.

"The president is sorry not to receive you in the White House, but prescheduled business made it impossible today." Barker delivered a perfunctory apology.

"No problem. We're sure he's busy, particularly now what he's decided to stay on the ballot. I do hope his health has been fully restored. Can we assume that the knowledge of the whereabouts of the terrorist helped improve his health?" Harry asked with a straight expression.

"The information you forwarded has been confirmed, and a team is getting in place to capture the target, as we speak," Roy offered, in a genuinely grateful tone, ignoring Harry's insinuation. "And you should know that we've been informed that the other perpetrator, Duke Wallace, died in an unfortunate accident in Johannesburg."

"An accident or a choreographed accident?" Mark couldn't resist asking.

The cabinet members either stared without expression or smiled slightly.

Travis Roy then placed a brown envelope on the table.

"I think you'll find the receipt for balance due you in order. The actual funds have been transferred to the account we used for your other payments. There's also a nondisclosure agreement for you to sign. I'm sure you can understand that while investigating such a major national security threat, you have been operating as agents of the government, and, as such, your involvement will not be made public." Ronald Barker was clearly hoping that would conclude any business portion of the meeting.

"Many thanks to the president and to each of you for giving us this opportunity to serve. We'll have our lawyers review the agreement, but certainly you understand that we also reserve the right to release our report should there be some accidental leak that in any way misrepresents our engagement in this affair." It was Harry's turn to smile.

"Actually, we would like you to sign the NDA before you leave today," said Rachel Jones, nervously.

"I'm sure you would. That, however, is not possible. No worry, you'll find that I have always honored my federal contract obligations over the years. I have no interest in drawing down the funds before the terms are completed. However, just so we are all clear about the consequences of inadvertent leaks, several trusted sources have full and accurate written accounts of our engagement." Harry looked each fed in the eye.

"I'm not sure that's really legal . . ." Roy stammered.

"Trust me. It is. Congress hasn't yet changed all of the rights of the citizenry. And, given the unfortunate track record on certain normally high-security activities over the last four years, such a precaution is prudent. So my lawyers tell me. Isn't that right, Mark?"

His son nodded.

No one challenged Harry Morton as he extended his six-foot-plus frame, stood erect, and physically dominated the room.

"Gentlemen, madam, you have jobs protecting our country. My son has clients to get back to, and I have a few students waiting to hear about the more boring and nonclassified approaches to foreign policy. It's been an honor. Best to President Spade." Harry and Mark left swiftly.

Later, taking his father to Dulles airport, Mark turned slightly away from the wheel. "That was some shit, Dad. We disrupt our lives, almost get killed, find the needle in an intercontinental haystack, pursue activists who, by the way, have some legitimate beefs, help out an administration that doesn't give a hoot about foundational American values, and we are summarily dismissed. Sent off as though we were bothering them," Mark fumed.

"Son, your expectations may be a bit too high. It's not unusual to encounter distasteful, negative qualities in very skilled, tough, and successful politicians," Harry cautioned.

"You can still be decent," said Mark.

"I agree that one should be able to be, yes. But the admonition 'Nice guys finish last' probably came from politics, not football." Harry tried to redirect the conversation. "So how are you feeling, in general? Eager to get back to work?"

"A bit overwhelmed. I'm glad to get back to a job I love and am good at. But having you back and getting Al in my life is great—beyond great. Still, I think it will take a while to fully process it. Even though I'm ten years his senior, given all that he's recently experienced, Al seems to have matured more than me in the few weeks I've known him." Mark gripped the wheel more tightly. "And this APOCALYPSE 2029 caper has presented me with the first major failure I've had to deal with."

"Failure? How so?"

"Well, the statehood project is a shambles, and I quit. I almost got us killed on Oahu. Malcolm Mohammed may still be at large. That's for starters."

"Look, I know that personal goals and aspirations are important to type As, like us. But don't confuse individual achievements with those requiring the collaboration of others, particularly those in power. If group goals are achieved, great, but there will be lots of misses. Don't let your self-worth be dependent on those aims," Harry counseled.

"But you teach, preach, and celebrate collaboration," Mark countered.

"I do. But I think I've learned that there are few comprehensive, total victories. You end up recalibrating all the time: not giving up on a goal, but reassessing the timetable, or need for partners, or degree of satisfactory outcome."

"That sounds like copping out. I mean we bent over backward to help a bunch of incompetent, arrogant, narrow-minded—" Mark's agitation grew.

"Yes, and we may have saved a lot of innocent lives. Who knows what else Wallace and Mohammed had planned? And this government is not free and clear. Remember, there's an election in a couple of weeks. The APOCALYPSE September destruction, the administration's failures in responding, and the obvious self-serving proclamations won't play too well outside the diehard red states." Harry seemed to be convincing himself as well as his son.

"Dad, I'm not a doomsayer, but I see failure. Failure of our system of government to deliver." Mark remained a cynic.

"I'm not trying to pull the age card on you—" Harry said.

"But," Mark interrupted.

"Yeah, but what I see in the experience you're having is an opportunity for reflection and learning. It's not a test where you can memorize and get right or wrong answers. It's real-time, complex situations where you may have to satisfice—find pleasure in trying, recognize the temporary satisfaction of a glass half full." Harry looked over at his son and added, "I'm so proud of the person you've become, Mark, without, sorry to say, much help from me. With your values and talent, I see a great future for you."

"OK, Dad. Let's not go overboard."

"Why not? I've got a family again. And I can stop pretending to myself that I'm capable of physically demanding, globetrotting problem-solving. I can be satisfied—even happy—teaching." Harry reached for the handle as the car pulled up to the curb of the departure lounge.

"Yes, but what about Malcolm Mohammed, or Robert Spade?" Mark asked, smiling.

"Time will tell, son. Hey, why don't you and Sonya come out for the holidays?" Harry said as he walked to the trunk to retrieve his luggage.

They embraced and Mark said, "I'll think on it, Dad."

***

Back at the newly appointed offices of Homeland Security, on a campus high above the Anacostia River, the president's team was processing their final meeting with the Mortons. After a minute of exchanging wide-eyed glances, Ronald Barker broke the silence with his fellow cabinet members.

"I don't think the president needs to know about the NDA and Morton's security blanket. At least not right now. I'll just tell the attorney general, and let's sit on it for now. Hopefully, with the focus on the reelection and getting started again in January, it won't even come up," he said.

"It would be nice to know that the capture had been completed before briefing the president," cautioned the national security advisor.

"He's aware of this meeting and knows the order was given to proceed in Puerto Vallarta, so he'll want to know what happened here with Morton," said Travis Roy.

"I agree. The three of us should go over to the White House. Travis, have your person try to get the president's son and the attorney general to join us. Let's close the loop now. Maybe we'll get a report from Mexico while we're over at Pennsylvania Avenue," ordered Chief of Staff Barker.

As the president's team prepared to meet with him, thousands of miles to the south three Navy Seals burst into Rosalie Artiste's condo in Nuevo Vallarta, having found that Malcolm's rental unit in Puerto Vallarta had been vacated.

"What do you want? What's the meaning of this?" she asked in a practiced indignant tone.

"Ma'am, you'll have to come with us. We think you have been harboring a fugitive," said one of the Seals.

Thinking quickly, Rosalie pulled out her Mexican passport from a bag. "I don't think you've got jurisdiction here. You'll have to leave, now. Find your way back to whatever hole you crawled out of."

As the Seals looked about her living room, looked at each other, and continued to point their rifles at Rosalie, she texted a Mexican National Police advisor with whom her mother had a connection.

"OK," said the leader. "Maybe you can just tell us what you know about Malcolm Mohammed."

"Well, I'm not sure I know such a person," she said, stalling.

The leader motioned to the other two men, who stepped forward and grabbed her arms.

"Might you be referring to Max Major?" she asked, attempting to disguise Malcolm's traveling identity.

They stepped back for a second.

"OK. Yeah, Max Major. Let's not play games."

"Well, if you'll permit me to go to the bathroom, then I can find a note he left me before he split."

"You can go to the bathroom at the consulate," an annoyed leader said.

"Oh, so you don't want the note?" Rosalie stood her ground.

Stares and silence.

"Ok, George, check out the bathroom and stand at the door," the leader instructed one of his colleagues.

Rosalie was able to stall for another few minutes before she produced the note signed "M." The leader almost tore it up when he realized that there was no useful intelligence on the paper.

The Seals yanked her to the door just as the Mexican police entered the condo.

"There must be some mistake, soldiers. Please, release Ms. Artiste now. And I suggest you get back to your embassy before we arrest you on kidnapping charges," said the captain in perfect Texas English.

Without resistance, the Seals withdrew.

***

In Washington, Prince Spade and Hardy Stennis were already in the Oval Office when Barker, Jones, and Roy entered. The president's son whispered to Barker, "I haven't seen him so genuinely happy in months. This is fabulous news."

"Let's make sure the operation is complete before we drop the curtain," Barker whispered back.

"Killjoy!" Prince laughed.

But when Barker mentioned "the consultants" who had helped locate the fugitive, the president's mood changed. "That Black guy? He should get some financial bonus to his contract, but nothing public. This investigation and successful elimination of a national threat is on *my* watch. We shouldn't let on either that it was the Brits who found the other guy in South Africa. It's the Spade administration that was threatened and the Spade administration that responded appropriately," the president insisted.

"Good marketing. Good timing. And totally appropriate to keep the confidential contract confidential," added Travis Roy. "As always."

"Sir, do you want to hold off the press conference about your clean 'bill of health' allowing you to remain at the top of the 2029 ticket until we hear from Mexico?" asked Ronald Barker.

"Hell, no; we go ahead. If it's not done, I'll just say that we are closing in. The focus will be on the doctor's clearance. I feel rejuvenated! OK, we're done, I need a few minutes with Prince."

As his advisors began to file out, Rachel Jones held up her right hand, while finishing a call with her left.

"Bad news, sir. The Seals discovered that the rental unit had been abandoned and only found Mohammed's girlfriend at her condo. And she doesn't seem to know where he went."

"Well, did they interrogate her?" the president roared.

"Yes, sir. And they found a note he left her that corroborates her story. He's gone. Unfortunately, she's a well-placed Mexican citizen, and the Mexican government is demanding an explanation for the raid."

"Screw them. We'd have had him a long time ago, if they had cooperated," he fumed.

"Shall we cancel the press conference, Dad?" Prince asked.

"Hell, no. Just like I said, "We're closing in, 'Dreadlocks' is desperate and on the run. Can't be long now.' We look strong, in spite of resistance from those incompetent Mexican authorities. Plus, we know his nutty Navy partner was eliminated in South Africa, and we may have one of the guys who set off the explosion starting the tidal wave. That's a good story, right?" The president beamed.

A couple of hours later, the president of the United States made only minor mention of the failed raid, but emphasized that the tidal wave diver was in captivity, one terrorist had been eliminated, and the other was on the run. He embellished his report by adding that his national security team was sure that all other plans for terror activities by APOCALYPSE 2029 had been quashed. Advisors on the dais behind the president squirmed visibly at his inventive claims.

He then proudly held up a one-paragraph "medical report" from his personal physician, indicating that he was now in tremendous physical and mental health. He claimed that he was renewing his position at the top of the Republican ticket. He added that he had "considered" withdrawing when he had exhibited signs of temporary paralysis. Now, he was stronger than ever. He accepted no questions from reporters and exited the briefing room.

CHAPTER 27

Vice President Nickle, in Mexico City, had taken the on-again, off-again news of his position at the top of the ticket in stride. Disappointed that his time to become the free world's top political leader had not yet arrived, he rededicated himself to serving his president, trying to appear loyal, calm, and competent. With the unexpected loss of the House of Representatives in 2024 and the growing anti-Spade national sentiment, he was sure it was only a matter of time before he would be the party standard-bearer.

He was confident that he could play his role, going through the motions of trying to improve relations with the Mexican government. He first had to get thoroughly briefed on trade and border activities from embassy staff. Though Nickle was dismayed to hear that the at-large terrorist had escaped, he was convinced that he would soon be captured or killed. The meetings at the embassy were educational, but what he was really looking forward to was the afternoon soccer game at the historic Azteca Stadium.

Malcolm Mohammed adjusted the scope on his long-range rifle. Through the embassy window, the vice president was in clear and unobstructed view. Mohammed had calculated that the embassy was a little under a mile from his perch, thus a bullet could take less than five seconds to reach its target. The sky was slightly cloudy, but there was no wind that he could detect. He pushed the eyepiece against his eye, placed his index finger over the trigger, released the safety lock and rested his elbow on a box he had positioned below his arm.

Mohammed tried to clear his mind of every thought but the kill, as he had done in the Middle East. But now, his mind didn't cooperate. He wondered whether he was putting Jorge Blanco in a perilous position, should it be discovered that he had financed APOCALYPSE 2029. Would the Chinese revoke their assistance, if they discovered that he had assassinated the VP? Would Rosalie be caught and harassed, or even tortured? Could an assassination backfire and generate sympathetic support for the flagging mess of a presidential administration?

Mohammed and Wallace had thought through these issues months before, when they dreamed up this last terror push to get their demands met or amplify anxiety and fear in the minds of the US political leadership. But now, with the death of an administration official seconds away, the weight of the unknown and unknowable consequences forced Mohammed to relax his grip. He lowered the rifle and tried to breathe more regularly.

The only reason I haven't heard from Duke has to be that they got him, killed him, somehow. Shit, we both went to war, gave up normal lives, and killed for this motha. They sit up there and feather their nests, their sons safe from conscription. Their fortunes grow. They have health care. And these turkeys are probably laughing their asses off at the game they're running on folks, blaming all the ills they have caused on former presidents, immigrants, Muslims, brothers . . . Malcolm thought, his blood pressure rising and his resolve hardening.

He picked up the rifle and resumed his attack position. The vice president had moved from view and the window was blocked by the vice presidential security detail. Malcolm stole a look at his watch. There was still about a half hour before the VP's party would be leaving for the soccer game.

Stay calm. Stay focused, he told himself.

Malcolm tried deep breathing to remain calm and focused, while waiting for the vice president to come back into view. He went over his plan to dispose of the rifle after the shot, his route to the airport. Fifteen minutes passed.

Finally, Richard Nickle came back into view. He was shaking the hands of embassy staff and clearly preparing to leave the room again. Mohammed waited, waited, and finally had a clear shot. The explosion was muffled by a silencer, and the target was far enough away that Malcolm was only able to view the silent movie of reaction. The vice president released the grip of a final staffer and turned to leave the room, when a beautiful pottery vase exploded—blew into thousands of colorful bits. It had been perched on a pedestal against the wall ten feet behind where the vice president's head had been an instant ago.

Malcolm cursed, but recognized that he had had his one last opportunity. No time to reflect on the consequences, on whether he had scared the vice president sufficiently to achieve their objective. No. That had been his attempt. *Follow the plan.*

Malcolm Mohammed wiped and dismantled the weapon, added components from a saxophone and clarinet that he had purchased earlier at a pawn shop, collected the spent shell, and packed it all in the canvas musician's bag. He took the elevator to the shopping center, calmly exited and hailed a taxi. He was dropped at the airport's FedEx depot, where he prepared the shipping label indicating the contents as "musical instruments" and addressed the box to the vice president's chief of staff.

He pinned a carefully handwritten note on the bag inside the box:

To Mr. Nickle—Until next time!!!

Yours Truly,

APOCALYPSE 2029.

Malcolm knew that White House security would intercept the delivery, but its message, he hoped, would reach his intended audience.

The vice president's delegation excused itself from its soccer obligations and rushed to the same airport to take an official plane back to Washington. The public didn't see a severely shaken vice president with bandages over minor facial cuts. The weapon was discovered and delivered to the US Embassy the next morning. Washington was notified and the weapon was subsequently sent on to Langley, Virginia, for inspection.

***

Though it failed to kill the vice president, the attack did have an effect. Mexican press got the jump on the assassination attempt and portrayed it as yet another incident in the strange terror phenomenon, APOCALYPSE 2029, gripping the northern neighbor. US media copied the basic reporting on the shooting and began peppering the White House with questions about its ability to track down and end the reign of terror. The accumulated result of APOCALYPSE's series of terror attacks was to confound the administration and media, and to engulf much of the American voting public in a form of collective posttraumatic stress syndrome. With the mounting pressure of a potentially tight election, the White House catapulted into apoplectic chaos, and state-level right-wing campaign strategists were forced to recalibrate their final campaign messages.

Before the Mexico City incident, the president and congressional leadership's campaign strategy had been one of touting the responsiveness of leaders to protect the nation. While temporary, emergency legislation would be introduced to address some of APOCALYPSE's demands, the party signaled to its base in campaign rallies, and assured NRA and corporate energy supporters in private that no policy changes would last once APOCALYPSE was captured and silenced. Meanwhile, maximum intelligence-service resources would be deployed to find Malcolm Mohammed.

Strategists assumed that this would not only soothe the mass paranoia about the nation's safety and keep the party's base in check, but it would also win over more moderate voters.

Senate Majority Leader Ditch and House Minority Leader Trane introduced emergency legislation to ban assault weapons and the use of new "printed" weapons, and to provide for more liberal immigration reform. Provisions to protect Social Security, Medicare, Medicaid, and the Affordable Care Act were tightened as well. All pipeline construction in sensitive lands was halted; thousands of acres of National Park previously made available for sale or for hunting were reclaimed by the National Park Service. The administration ate crow and began renegotiating its entrance into the international environmental agreements it had previously walked away from and doubled down on its vehicle and industrial emission standards. Congressional debate reflected bipartisan support, but, with the election in November, final votes couldn't be scheduled until late December or early January.

Reaction from the president's political base was swift and severe. The NRA demanded a one-on-one meeting at which it threatened to publicly withdraw all support. But, for once, the president held firm. Coal, oil, and auto executives were less belligerent but insisted on submitting new legislation to replace the emergency bills in 2030. Conservative media gave no quarter on immigration reform, and, after numerous calls and meetings, they published and aired editorials chiding the president for backsliding on his tough stance. These reactions triggered more extreme attacks from previously supportive social media enthusiasts. In its final two weeks, the president's campaign received only tepid social media and cable support, unsettling his strategists.

In the final week before the election, the president focused on visits to formerly safe, "base" locations; he ignored marginal areas where he might encounter dismissive or hostile crowds. But during this period, no crowd was predictable. Supporters noted that the president seemed worn down and more easily distracted while stumping this time. They also saw that his wife refused to accompany him on any campaign stops. His strategy failed to give him the bump in the polls his team hoped for. As coverage of his stops increased, supporters began to openly question his "real agenda," given the pending new emergency congressional legislation. Independents and moderates simply didn't believe the radical shift would either quell APOCALYPSE or ever be implemented. Support began to wane in the polls, with more presidential voters deciding to stay home or to vote for the other party.

The trend worsened, as several administrative actions that might not have been consequential in normal times also began to alienate the president's national base. The national media ran several stories about public funds that were given to three DC-area private schools to bolster their security; extra dollars added to the transportation department specifically for long-needed maintenance of DC-area Metro rail facilities; and substantial increases in the Secret Service details of certain congressional leaders. None of these allocations were illegal, but given APOCALYPSE-induced paranoia around the country, reports painted a vivid picture of self-centered and self-concerned leadership in the face of national crisis. Although right-wing mainstream media tried to dispel the image of a self-absorbed leadership in Washington, the picture gained traction in the national psyche.

Ryan Trane went home to campaign in western Michigan, long a safe conservative district. At dinner in a large banquet hall the day before the huge Ohio State-Michigan football game, he was smiling as he answered questions about his predictions for the game and for the fall elections. Then he called on a young man in a checkered hunting jacket.

"Sir, do you really support the assault weapon ban? I mean, we're a hunting state here, and I don't get this reversal." The young man's questions drew cheers from around the hall.

"Well, I share your concern. I hunt too. But this is a limited ban to satisfy the terrorist that quite frankly have us by the you-know-what's."

Trane's response drew stares and follow-up questions. Then a middle-aged White man raised his hand. "Why did you support the immigration package when the auto jobs continue to dry up here, despite the initial bump from the president's early support? We don't have jobs ourselves." He looked around and got vociferous approval from the predominantly White audience.

Trane fumbled through several more answers and then followed staff whisking him to the exit.

Later in the weekend, a stressed Senate Majority Leader Ken Ditch was holding forth at a large Dallas cookout and fielding softball questions, when a supporter took a microphone and said, "We respect what you've done up there in Washington and how you've gotten a real conservative Supreme Court and all. But, frankly, this APOCALYPSE thang and how y'all responded, has got some of us confused."

"Well, you know these terrorists got our feet to the fire right now," Ditch began.

"C'mon, now, Ken," said a long-time city council friend of Ditch's. "Just us chickens and hens here. How you gonna go with that gun control legislation? And ain't no way in hell we can let more Mexicans in, lessen they got approval ahead. I don't blame 'em for fleeing the gangs, but it ain't my problem." The crowd roared in approval.

Ditch tried to tell them not to worry about the temporary legislation but was interrupted again.

"Senator, how 'bout this? You know the Houston area is still recovering from two hurricanes, right? Well, looks like South Carolina, around the president's golf club, got fixed up right quick. And, not that I blame you, but I hear your granddaughter's private school got public money for security after the APOCALYPSE thing. That don't seem right," complained a middle-aged African American business supporter.

None of the senator's soft-spoken straight-up answers seemed to satisfy the group, and by the time he was able to escape, Ken Ditch looked ten years older.

The president was in Pennsylvania that weekend, so Attorney General Hardy Stennis, a South Carolina native, and Vice President Richard Nickle attended events on his behalf in the South Carolina and Georgia districts hit by the tsunami.

"It sure is good to be back home," Stennis began. "The president was here a couple of weeks ago, but I jumped at the chance to get back among longtime friends."

The crowd applauded the popular favorite son.

"And I'm here with a national hero, fresh back from Mexico, where he bravely carried our banner, Vice President Richard Nickle."

The crowd applauded and hollered even more enthusiastically.

Stennis threw out red-meat policy statements, thanked the disaster relief agencies and local volunteers, and only briefly mentioned that the administration was confident that the temporary legislation would end the terror. After acknowledging the applause, Nickle followed with an embellished revisionist story about how he had narrowly escaped the terrorist bullet. He laced his remarks with religious references to overcoming adversity. Those few in the crowd who knew Nickle wondered about his affect. He looked frightened and continued to scan the audience, as if anticipating a shooter. His words described courage and boldness, but his eyes and muscles revealed fear and tension. Nickle's aides worried that although the assassin's bullet had missed, the attempt and the subsequent package had caused irrevocable damage.

"Mr. Vice President, thank God you are safe and thank you for your service. I also am a devout Christian," a tanned young lady addressed the podium. "I love what y'all are doing on the court, and I understand the short-term need to pass these emergency laws. I mean, it's obvious that we are traumatized here on the coast. But I've got two questions. Even though the tidal wave that hit us was caused by a man-made explosion, it still seems like there's way more bad weather than used to be. I think the scientists might be onto something about man's effect on the climate."

In a disengaged monotone, Nickle responded, "Well, I believe in both the Lord and science, but we don't have scientific proof yet, seems to me." Nickle drew a stern stare from the attorney general.

"But my main concern, though, as a Christian woman, is about how the president treats and talks about women. Seems to me, we got all upset when President Clinton went wild in the White House, but nobody minds President Spade's foul mouth. Don't get me wrong, but it don't seem right," she said with pious sincerity.

Nickle turned scarlet, Stennis looked away, and the audience was silent.

The tension was relieved when an elderly man stood and told Stennis to thank the president for the fast and abundant help most of the area had received after the tsunami. Then he asked about the schedule for repairing roads in his part of the county. Stennis and Nickle exhaled in appreciation of the softball question.

In the van headed for the airport, Stennis turned to Nickle and asked, "Can you imagine what it's like in places that weren't top priority relief areas?"

Nickle only stared straight ahead.

"Boy, you need a serious vacation. You're acting like a live PTSD commercial," said Stennis.

"You're right," was Nickle's only reply.

On election eve, even the most far-right media had difficulty manufacturing suspense, let alone good news, as results began to stream in from around the United States.

REUNION IN PARADISE

January 2030

CHAPTER 28

The tiny waves barely altered the blue-green surface along Maracas Beach in Port of Spain, Trinidad, as a slender, muscle-toned Brown man turned from the sea and ambled up to a bar a hundred yards from the beach. He sat at a table, open to the breeze from the sea, and pulled out his iPhone.

"What do you have, my brother?" A deep baritone surprised the patron.

"Just a Coke with lime, please, my man."

"Wild what's happening up in the US, isn't it?" asked the bartender, placing a paper coaster in front of the foreigner.

"What do you mean, man?" asked the patron, looking up from his phone.

"Well, one day, they allow all sorts of weapons in the schools, ban decent immigrants, claim all these storms are natural, nothing wrong with the climate. The next day, they say climate change is man-made, welcome Brown southern immigrants and ban all sorts of guns everywhere." He placed a Coke on the coaster and continued. "One minute, they lovin' dat crazy strong man Spade, the next they voting him and his party out. It's crazy, man."

Clothed in an old maroon dashiki, rolled-up white cotton pants, leather sandals, and a wig of shoulder-length dreads, the patron pushed down his oval sunglasses, set his phone down on the table and agreed.

"Yeah, man. Last year was shocking! Almost like an apocalypse."

***

On an island halfway around the world, a group of friends and family gathered for New Year's at the Kahukus' spread in a valley outside of Honolulu. The gathering included Laila, Kiki, and Mano Kahuku; Donna, Tommy, and Alaka'i Liu; Donna's cousin, Feng Ying, from Shanghai; Peter Hung; Paul and Muriel Tanaka; and Sonya, Mark, and Harry Morton.

On the spacious deck of the compound's central house, a large wooden dinner table was covered in palm-leaf mats, loaded down with plates of yams, green beans, roast pork, shredded coconut and sea bass, and mugs of beer. Diners sported colorful floral-patterned shirts and blouses, shorts, and flip-flops. Each wore a fragrant plumeria lei.

Those under sixty had enjoyed an early afternoon swim in Hanauma Bay, and then everyone had helped prepare the feast. Some walked with arthritic limps, others spoke more slowly than in younger years, while others talked of family yet unborn and of the demanding global challenges they would confront. But goodwill and comradery infused every conversation.

As the setting sun lent a coral-colored tint to the horizon's clouds, and the Pacific offered a background of shimmering surf, glasses were raised. Muriel Tanaka commanded attention, leaning on the table with one bony arm and holding a cocktail glass aloft with the other.

"It's sometimes discouraging to see Hawaii portrayed as this out-of-touch paradise. So, I'm so happy when there is national awareness of something positive about our islands. I am delighted to have heard a rumor, in more than one place, mind you, that three Hawaiians helped end the reign of terror aimed at destabilizing our country. And, in so doing, they indirectly helped end the political nightmare we've endured for the last four years. So, I propose a toast to those three mystery heroes." Muriel carefully sat down, turned a stiff neck slightly, and, with a twinkle in her eye, winked at the Mortons.

"I propose a toast to Hawaiian family—native Hawaiians, Hawaiian-born of all races, immigrant and soon-to-be Hawaiians. It's been a wild ride, between mean-spirited rule-making and then inexplicable terror and pseudo-terrorist activity, but we've survived. *Ke au hou keia*." Patriarch Kiki Kahuku raised his mug to the new era.

"I would add a toast to the next generation of environmentally conscious and humanly righteous technicians, businesspeople, and political activists," Tommy Liu said, sipping a beer.

"Let me add a thanks to *ohana* —the family that Oahu has made possible," offered Harry Morton with a glass half full.

Sonya turned to her husband, her face aglow, and whispered, "Let's get up early tomorrow, go walk on the beach, and watch the sun rise. Let's enjoy paradise."

ABOUT THE AUTHOR

L. W. Harris is a Washington, D.C.-based novelist who is a retired public and private sector executive, business consultant, writer, and lecturer. He has been a manager in a Fortune 50 company, the White House, and several local governments. He has lived in Guatemala and traveled extensively in Latin America, East Africa, Asia, Europe and Hawaii. He has a bachelor's degree from Hamilton College and master's degrees from the University of Pennsylvania and Harvard University. Writing as John H. McKoy, the author has previously published two novels: *Paying to Play in Hong Kong* and *Son of the Maya*.

ABOUT THE PUBLISHER

The Sager Group was founded in 1984. In 2012 it was chartered as a multimedia content brand, with the intent of empowering those who create art—an umbrella beneath which makers can pursue, and profit from, their craft directly, without gatekeepers. TSG publishes books; ministers to artists and provides modest grants; and produces documentary, feature, and commercial films. By harnessing the means of production, The Sager Group helps artists help themselves. For more information, please see www.TheSagerGroup.net.

MORE BOOKS FROM THE SAGER GROUP

The Swamp: Deceit and Corruption in the CIA
An Elizabeth Petrov Thriller (Book 1)
by Jeff Grant

Chains of Nobility: Brotherhood of the Mamluks (Book 1-3)
by Brad Graft

Meeting Mozart: A Novel Drawn from the Secret
Diaries of Lorenzo Da Ponte
by Howard Jay Smith

Death Came Swiftly: A Novel About the Tay Bridge Disaster
of 1879 by Bill Abrams

A Boy and His Dog in Hell: And Other Stories
by Mike Sager

Miss Havilland: A Novel
by Gay Daly

The Orphan's Daughter: A Novel
by Jan Cherubin

Lifeboat No. 8: Surviving the Titanic
by Elizabeth Kaye

Hunting Marlon Brando: A True Story by Mike Sager

See our entire library at TheSagerGroup.net

THE SAGER GROUP

Artifex Te Adiuva

Made in the USA
Middletown, DE
29 July 2022